AGAINST
THEIR
WILL

AGAINST THEIR WILL

Nancy Livingstone

iUniverse LLC
Bloomington

AGAINST THEIR WILL

iUniverse books may be ordered through booksellers or by contacting:

iUniverse
1663 Liberty Drive
Bloomington, IN 47403
www.iuniverse.com
1-800-Authors (1-800-288-4677)

ISBN: 978-1-4917-0882-8 (sc)
ISBN: 978-1-4917-0883-5 (hc)
ISBN: 978-1-4917-0884-2 (e)

Library of Congress Control Number: 2013917555

Printed in the United States of America.

iUniverse rev. date: 02/26/2014

To Alan, JD, and Brian, your insight, suggestions, and encouragement are cherished more than you know. This is for you with all my love.

PROLOGUE

Infernal stoplight. Could it take any longer to change?

Sweat dripped down Max Duncan's back and dotted his brow. It soaked through his formerly pristine shirt and left stains under his arms and on his collar. Cars swept past, slinging stifling, muggy Houston air into his face. He wanted to slap it away. Instead, he shifted from foot to foot.

"I ain't got time for this freakin' …" A string of obscenities slipped out under his breath. He glared at the crowd pressing against him, pushing and nudging him. He bared his teeth as if he were a lion ready to pounce and rip the entire throng to shreds. Then, he thought of all the germs, the stink, and the sweat that would contaminate him, and he pressed his lips together in a solid line, as if they could be a protective barrier from the totally subperfect world bumping against him.

The temperature rose, heat bearing down on him with such intensity that he was certain a giant magnifying glass was over his head, concentrating the sun's rays on his scalp. When the signal finally changed, Max pushed through the crowd so that he led the pack as he raced across the scorching pavement.

On the other side of the street, he stopped in front of the bank's wall of windows. His reflection stared back at him from the tinted glass. With a stubby forefinger, he dabbed at a smudge on his forehead. Lately, it was as if the years were melting away, like a river birch's curling bark peeling away to reveal the pristine white trunk beneath. If it weren't for that hideous tag of skin growing under his jaw, he could be on the next cover of *People's* "Sexiest Men Alive" issue—but that tag. It had only appeared recently. It was just a flap of extra skin, ridged like a gill, but with no color. He shrugged. Youth and energy, they were the two greatest forces in life. They were all that mattered. He had been blessed with a lot of each lately. Although he didn't understand why or how, he didn't care. Max never questioned the generosity of any giver.

He glided through the brass-trimmed doors of the old bank and into the cavernous marble-floored lobby. He sniffed. Despite artificially cooled air, he could smell it—money, old money. It was like slipping into a favorite pair of jeans, comfortable, comforting. Odd, he didn't remember being around it before.

At the teller's window, Max pulled a sheet of paper from his pocket, glanced at it, and then said, "I'm here for Gerald Humminger."

There was a momentary pause as the woman glanced up at Max and narrowed her eyes. After a few seconds, she said very stiffly, "May I tell him who wishes to see him?"

Max patted his tie. "Yeah, you can tell him Max Duncan is here."

Soon, a tall gentleman in the dark, cut-to-perfection uniform of the business world approached and extended his bony hand.

"It's Max now, is it?" Gerald Humminger grinned. "What a pleasant surprise! I certainly didn't expect to see you again, at least not so soon." He gripped Max's elbow and spoke close to his ear. "But, I must say, you're looking better than ever—at least ten years younger. You must tell me about this youth potion you've obviously discovered!"

Max's fat fingers encircled the man's bony ones as they shook hands. His brows knitted into a frown. Who was this guy?

Moments later, seated in a leather chair in Humminger's office, Max studied the man. How could Mr. Humminger be surprised to see him again? He was certain he had never met the lanky banker before.

As the thought traversed the neural pathways in Max's mind, a small chisel started hammering inside his skull. The throbbing was moderate, just enough to make Max grimace. He pushed the heel of his hand against his forehead.

"Are you all right?" Gerald leaned forward and squinted. Max nodded. "Want some ice water, perhaps, something stronger?"

Max shook his head. "No ... thanks."

"Well then, what brings you here today? Last I heard, you were in some federal prison. It seems something was said about an inmate stabbing you." Humminger giggled. "I believe it was with a fork! Even heard you didn't make it. But it looks like you not only resurrected yourself, new name and all, but you shaved a few years off while you were at it. If it wasn't some magic youth potion, then it must've been one incredible plastic surgeon!"

Max stared at Gerald, his expression blank. Who was this man that he even cared what Max looked like? It was none of his business, except Max couldn't deny the slight pleasure he got from the envy the other man held toward him.

Gerald's smile faded. "Look, we're old buddies. I've held your hand through the worst of them. This room is safe. You can tell old Gerald what's really going on."

"Going on? Nothing's going on. I'm fine." Max shifted in his seat. He pulled a handkerchief from his pocket and swiped it across his forehead. Then he glanced at his watch. "Look, I need to make a transfer. I've got to split twenty million between three accounts. One's in the Grand Caymans. The others are in Switzerland."

"Twenty million? You have that much left? I thought our 'I-feel-your-pain' uncle took all your possessions. IRS and all."

All his possessions? He was simply transferring money on behalf of his new employer.

"It's not mine," Max said as he pushed a sealed envelope across the polished desk. "It's my employer's. The authorization's there," he added, pointing at the envelope.

"New employer, huh? You not only flirted with death, cheated, and won; you're also not wasting any time getting new work, are you?" Gerald tore open the envelope and quickly read the single sheet inside.

"Says here this is your money, and you want it split between three accounts opened nearly five years ago." Gerald dropped the sheet and stared at Max. "Want to tell me the real truth? What's going on, Milo?"

"Milo?" Max frowned. "I tell you, nothing's going on. Never in my life have I had money like that!" The chisel in his skull morphed into a jackhammer.

"Milo, Max, whatever. You've never had that little money in your life. You're used to handling many times more than a paltry sum of twenty million. You controlled accounts the world over. The Grand Caymans was just play money. That's why you can't remember!" Gerald grinned as he patted Max's shaking hand. "Sure, it must be hard giving up what you had. Looks like you're on your way back, though. Pull a few wise investments, and in no time, you'll have all you had before, plus some."

Max tried to swallow but couldn't. So much saliva had accumulated it threatened to overflow and dribble down his chin. Without warning, a wave of nausea slammed into him, sending a fresh sweat river down his cheeks. Yet, he managed a smile as he nodded at Gerald.

"Very well." Gerald stood. "You must sign the proper forms and all that. You know the routine." He rounded the desk and started for the door. "Just sit back and relax. I'll get my secretary on it right away." The door shut behind him.

Max started shaking. He felt like a leaf whipping around in a storm, and he couldn't stop himself. Ringing echoed in his ears. A frantic urgency pushed and pulled at his insides. He got up and started pacing in front of the wall of windows. He felt like he would die if he stopped moving. On the street below, traffic and pedestrians flowed. Heat shimmered off the pavement. Max stared at them and wondered why he envied them.

Gerald returned, breezing through the door with a small stack of documents in hand.

Max spun around and hurried back to his seat in front of Gerald's desk. He pointed at the papers. "Where do I sign?"

"Just like every time before, wherever you see yellow highlighting." Gerald pointed at the various blanks. "These forms authorize this bank to move the money you requested to the accounts you specified, and so on and so on. Soon as they're signed, we'll enter the instructions and wait for confirmation. It shouldn't take more than a few minutes."

The signing completed, Max shoved the papers back over to Gerald who then took them to someone waiting outside the door. As suddenly as it had come over him, Max's urgent energy vanished. His muscles, no longer tight and hard, crumpled into a limp mass. Yet, the pounding in his head jumped to double-time. He had to get out of there. He didn't know why; he just had to do it. Right then. Aiming for the door, Max staggered as the room tilted and then straightened.

Gerald gripped his elbow. "What's your hurry?" He bent over so that he could peer into Max's eyes. "Are you all right? You're looking a little pale. Sure I can't get you something?"

Max focused on Gerald for a moment, and he realized suddenly he didn't know why he was there. Max shook his head, unable to answer.

A young woman in a form-fitting suit pushed through the door and smiled. "Mr. Humminger, the confirmation just came back. I'll have the hard copy in just a moment."

"Thanks, Bonnie, dear," Gerald said. His eyes lingered on her shapely form, and she glared at him as she backed from the room and slammed the door.

The pounding, the ringing, the nausea, all of it closed in on Max. He lunged for the door and reeled through it.

"Wait! You don't have your papers!"

"I'll ... get them later." Max rubbed his temple furiously. Without warning, he gagged, but only saliva streamed from his mouth. He managed to push through the door and half ran, half staggered toward the elevator.

Once inside, he leaned against the wall and panted. Swirling images crept across his vision, distorting the light and the area around him. When the doors opened, he nearly fell into the arms of a waiting woman. Instead, he caught himself and stumbled past her, aiming erratically for the outer doors and the bright light beyond. If only he could make it to the light.

The pounding and ringing intensified, shutting out all sound. Desperate to stop the pain, he pushed his palm against his ear and then pulled it away and stared at it. It was warm and sticky, dripping with bright-red blood. Max stumbled forward. He didn't hear the shouts behind him or car horns blaring before him. He just searched for the light. He pushed his feet faster, desperate to find it.

When Max finally found his light, he didn't see the car to his left. He couldn't feel the crunching and cracking of his bones, the scraping and tearing of his flesh. His world wobbled and spun, dragging him with it. By the time he hit the pavement, it was black. The ringing stopped, and the pounding slowed. Thump … thump … thump … thump …

The newscaster's professionally bleached teeth filled the television screen.

"In downtown Houston today, a tragic accident took the life of billionaire, former federal prison inmate, and alleged Mafia kingpin, Milo Dolnia. Eyewitness accounts vary, some saying Dolnia was holding his head, with blood running through his fingers prior to staggering into the path of a speeding car in the one-hundred block of Louisiana Street. Others could not confirm his injury but saw him moving erratically prior to running in front of the oncoming vehicle. Dolnia did not respond to shouts or car horns. No charges have been filed at this time; however, an investigation continues. Dolnia was the focus of a recent controversy after being released from Bastrop Federal Prison after serving only a small fraction of his sentence for tax evasion and fraud. He …"

The petite, flame-haired woman hit the "off" button on the remote and threw it on her desk. Hands on her hips as if she were a steel-plated superhero, she whirled about to face the towering, almost superhuman-looking man entering her office. Despite the white lab jacket covering a starched shirt and silk tie, he looked more like a professional wrestling star than the genius he was, as tested on the Wechsler Scale.

"Did you see that? Did you?" The woman's voice rose. "They just won't leave it alone, will they? They'll do their investigations, prodding and poking until their brains freeze over. Why can't they believe it was an accident and leave it at that?"

"Whatever are you worried about, Cherie?" The tone of his voice was mostly neutral, except for when he pronounced her name. It was drawn out like a long, soft caress. She might have wondered about him, his heritage, if indeed there was some French ancestry there, but she was too preoccupied to consider his bloodline. More important issues related to blood kept her focused.

"Even with an autopsy, all they'll find, besides broken bones and contusions, is a subdural hematoma, a small intracranial hemorrhage. They'll assume that's what caused him to run blindly into the street. Believe me; they will never know the truth."

"I hope you're right, Charles. For all of our sakes, I hope you're right."

"Why do you doubt, Cherie? Do you not believe me when I tell you of our progress, of our achievements? We have attained the unthinkable, things so unbelievable that if one did not witness them personally, one would never believe them possible. Yet, you have seen it all, firsthand."

Cherie's lips curled into a self-satisfied grin as she rubbed her hand along his thick arm. "Oh, I know, Charles! It's just I get scared sometimes. We've worked for so long on this, put so much into it, that to consider any setback now when we're so close ... well, it just curdles my stomach! You're right; we're almost there. I mean, Milo authorized that transfer of twenty million, not even a question asked! Think of the implications!" A low, guttural laugh rose from her throat.

"Implications?" Charles shook his head. "What it means is we still have not solved our problem. We still cannot determine why they succumb at exactly the same point."

"So who cares if they fall over? At least we can get them to do our bidding first." She licked her lips. "Charles, consider the potential. We've stumbled onto something that could be even more productive than your silly little cures. Why not use it?"

"Silly little cures?" His voice clipped the air with a cold, steel edge. "I thought what mattered most was not to make them our puppets but to perfect the miracles, to give them hope. Is that not the goal, what we are all waiting for, hope?"

Cherie rubbed her chin. "I suppose you can have your hope. Pity, though. We've proven the potential. It would be a shame to waste it."

"Waste it?" He backed away from her. The air between them had become charged. "No, it would never be wasted, but we desperately need fresh blood. Somewhere, there is a person holding the right DNA key, the right genetic blueprint to give us what we lack. When we find that, then we have success. We can give them our miracles and keep them alive."

Cherie rubbed a red-painted fingernail slowly across her plump lips. Her eyes narrowed as she studied him. In a low, seductive tone, she said softly, "Charles, you will find your success. I know you will. In the meantime, though, we can have some fun, can't we?" She moved behind him and began to knead his shoulder muscles through the cloth of his lab jacket. As her fingers poked and prodded the tight muscles, she smiled her trademark Cheshire grin.

"Yes, Charles, we'll have our fun, and you'll solve your problems. You'll get what you need, and you'll be happy. I will be too, for you will have given me what I've searched for—no, *longed* for—all these years. I'm banking the reputation of our entire project on your promises, and you know to whom I answer."

Charles spun around so that his gaze met hers. The heat seemed to shimmer like pavement on a hot summer day. He nodded and said quietly, "I am well aware of the power behind you. But I cannot produce your miracles, or your puppets, without help." Not waiting for a response, he spun sharply on his heel and hurried from the office. The door slammed behind him.

Cherie crossed her arms and stared blankly at the door. Slowly, a smile spread across her face. "Good," she said, though there was no one to hear her. "Glad you understand." Plopping into her swivel chair, she kicked her feet out, and with a soft "Whee!" she spun it once before pulling it up to her desk. She picked up the phone and punched in a few numbers as she muttered to herself, "Now, for that little matter of genetic variety."

CHAPTER 1

L ynn McCane yanked the handle of her carry-on bag. It didn't budge. Stupid wheel was stuck again. She swore under her breath as she picked up the soft-sided monster and resigned herself to carrying it rather than having it roll obediently behind her as she pushed through the massive Los Angeles airport crowds. The bag weighed almost as much as she did—almost—and she wondered why she hadn't tossed the wretched thing months ago. If she'd known she'd have to travel as much as she had lately, she'd never have invested in such a fickle and unsatisfactory piece of ... of crap. Okay, okay. She was angry. Exhausted. Overwhelmed. *Release the anger. Breathe in. Breathe out. Slowly, that's right. In and out. Now, focus on getting home.* That was all that mattered. *Get back to Houston, ASAP.*

For the past three months, she had spent almost every waking moment investigating and researching a feature series to be published in the *Houston Chronicle*. Weeks of interviews with doctors and research specialists, most located in the Texas Medical Center, had given her a fantastic, even personal, hope for the future of medicine. But her research had led to more than the latest medical miracles. She'd also found a trail of politics and corruption, a trail her curiosity forbade her from ignoring. Setting out on that trail had led her to evidence so damning it could topple some very powerful political and business leaders.

Her series, when she'd first proposed it, was supposed to give hope. What it had become was a liability. Without asking for it, she'd been given proof of deeds done and still in progress that were incomprehensible to those who believed their government was a protector, a provider, a magnificent entity who truly cared for the best interests of those who paid its way, the taxpayers. As if that weren't enough, her research had also found, of all things, evidence of living relatives. All those years of believing she had no family, that she was the lone, solitary remaining product of her genetic upline, and now there was someone else. Blood-kin, living folks made out of the same flesh and blood as she, and because of them, she was no longer alone.

She was so tired of being alone, so very tired. For years, she'd longed to have again the comfort of family, that sense of belonging that one inherited and didn't have to earn. She craved it, yet it had been denied her. Until then.

"Good afternoon, ma'am." The flight attendant greeted her mechanically and then frowned as Lynn pulled a crumpled wad of paper from her pocket and thrust it at the waiting woman. "Your boarding pass?"

Lynn nodded. With a small grimace, the attendant pried the dirty folds of paper apart and glanced briefly at it. Then, with a sweep of her long arm, she indicated the opposite side of the plane. "Ms. McCane, I see you've been upgraded to first class. Your seat is the eighth row back and by the window." The attendant pointed as her eyes darted to the next passenger.

Too weary to say anything, Lynn nodded and tugged her bag behind her. It took all the energy she possessed to swing the cursed thing up to the overhead compartment. Once it was secure in the bin above her, she collapsed in her seat. After cinching the seat belt, she closed her eyes and let her head droop. Images darted across her mind's eye. Mr. Chips admonishing her for leaving him alone all week with only dry cat food for company was first. Her fingers curled as if clutching some of his soft fur. Then, his face faded, and two others floated toward her. She couldn't distinguish their features. Her kin? What were they like? What would they think of her? Would they understand the shambles of her life? Yawning, thankful to be alone with her thoughts, she was soon asleep.

CHAPTER 2

Matt Grayson darted through the airport crowds as if he were still a running back on his high school football team. His golden hair, long on his neck and curled against his ears, was like a crown. His skin, tanned from many days working outside, added warmth to the nearly constant twinkle in his eyes. Those who noticed the graceful ease he used to squeeze by slow walkers and then sprint toward the gate might have believed that the small bag he carried under his arm and against his chest was a football. Although he was barely six feet tall, what he lacked in height, he made up for in drive and determination. His agent swore that it was that determination that put him where he was that day. His youthful vigor and easy flowing charm would be worthless, however, if he missed his flight. For one, his mother would never forgive him for missing her birthday. Second, he wouldn't forgive himself for losing out on a much-coveted long weekend away from it all.

When he'd hit the snooze alarm for the last time Monday morning, he'd never figured that by Friday his face would be recognized wherever there was a movie audience. In the short span of a few days, he'd gone from obscure actor to star of a critically acclaimed box office hit. His movie had premiered in Los Angeles ten days earlier, and after a week's worth of talk show promotions and personal appearances, the word was out. Matt Grayson was the next Hollywood legend. While some insiders whispered he'd already surpassed the box office appeal of screen greats Gerard Butler and the aging Brad Pitt, Matt had heard other rumors that studio executives thought he was inwardly calculating and plotting his next move while externally appearing to be a casual player who didn't take his work or himself too seriously. Obviously, those people didn't know how he'd relentlessly hounded his director and producer until they'd surrendered and given him the part. It wasn't plotting. It was stubbornness and persistence; that was what spun his world around.

Matt reached the plane's door just as the attendant was preparing to close it. When he grinned, his eyes twinkled. And his charm did its job yet again. The woman stopped and stared at him for a moment. Then, her red lips stretched into a broad smile exposing a set of even white teeth. She glanced briefly at his pass and without a word, led him all the way to his seat.

"Is there anything else I can get you, Mr. Grayson? I'm, umm, we're so glad to have you on our flight today." Her smile grew bigger. "I mean, we're all excited about your movie. It's been too long since Hollywood produced such a charming hunk … uh … leading man."

Matt stared at the woman. "Uh, thank you, thank you very much." He said it softly, hoping he was successful in suppressing his Texas drawl.

In all the years he'd dreamed of acting professionally, he'd never given much consideration as to how the public might respond to him. Acting and doing it well were all that mattered. Having strangers recognize him and offer unsolicited opinions was unsettling. He just wasn't sure what to do with it all.

After swinging his laptop bag into the overhead bin, he sank into his seat and glanced at the young woman beside him. Her head lolled at an angle that must have been uncomfortable. Dark curls hid her eyes. She looked so beat, so worn out. He tried not to touch or jostle her. He thought he had succeeded, but as he clicked his seat belt, the plane jerked as it backed from the gate and he brushed her with his elbow. The woman groaned as she snapped awake and rubbed her eyes.

"Sorry I woke you. Looked like you were really tuckered out," Matt said, the words flowing out in his natural drawl, all thoughts of suppressing it forgotten. His smile warmed his hazel eyes.

The woman muttered, "Guess I fell asleep in LA. Where are we now?"

"LA. Plane's just now getting ready for takeoff."

"Short nap." Her head dropped against the window, and her eyes closed. She snorted softly as her breathing grew deep and even.

Shortly after takeoff, as the plane was still climbing at an angle toward its predestined flight path, the attendant stopped by and asked Matt if he wanted anything. He confirmed his meal order and then reached for his bag and pulled out his MacBook. He opened it, and the screen flickered. In a few seconds, he had an iPages document open. His contract. Two more pictures—that was what they wanted. Was it true, did they really believe he was that good? His agent had told him so repeatedly. After all, it was Jerry's job to put a positive spin on everything. Yet, his gut wasn't convinced because it churned whenever he considered it. The pressure. They not only wanted more, certain the first would be a smash hit, but they were banking some pretty serious money he'd be worth more the second and even the third time around.

The money was nice, but it wasn't everything. Pleasing those he worked for obsessed him. And they hadn't been pleased when he'd begged off a full weekend of PR events in order to return to Houston for his mother's birthday.

"You've got more talk show appearances and interviews to do. We were even hoping to get a little film shot for that HBO special. All that goes with the job you agreed to do." The guilt grew as his stomach acid burned his throat. He'd reached yet again for his bottle of Tums.

"It's just the weekend. I'll be back Monday morning. She'll never forgive—"

"And you think we will?" his producer had said with a straight face. Suddenly, he pushed back in his chair and roared with laughter.

"Okay, go. She must be some special woman. But you'd better be back here first thing Monday like you promised. We're counting on you. Your work now, promoting this film and preparation for the next one will be as important as the work you did in making it. This film goes bust and you can kiss … Well, am I clear?"

"Clearer than high-definition TV."

Matt shuddered when the attendant bent toward him and smiled. "Your dinner, Mr. Grayson." She stood there a moment gazing at him as she held his tray. Matt glanced at her and frowned, and then he saw that she was looking at his laptop.

"Sorry," he muttered as he shut the computer and stuffed it in the seat pocket in front of him.

Once he managed to get his tray table opened and in place, the attendant set his food down and straightened. "Is there anything else I can do for you?" She waited for his answer, hovering like a bumblebee.

"No, thank you."

The woman beside him stirred and rubbed her eyes. As her lids retreated, she peered about as if trying to focus. Her roving gaze stopped and landed on his dinner. She raised her arm and waved at the attendant.

"Uh, is it too late to get dinner?"

"No, we can still get a meal for you. I can't guarantee the entrée, though. Is that a problem?"

"Not at all."

The woman turned and caught him staring at her. Surprising Matt, she blushed. "I haven't eaten since breakfast, and that lone piece of toast and sip of orange juice left my stomach hours ago!" Her blush deepening, she tried to pull up her tray table, but it refused to budge.

"Let me help." The words slid out of his mouth easily as he reached across her lap and jiggled the release button until the tray moved. "These things can be pretty stubborn."

"Tell me about it," she muttered. "Thanks."

"My pleasure. By the way, I'm Matt Grayson." He paused as if waiting for some reaction.

The woman's brows rose. For a moment she was silent, but when she spoke, a hint of the northeast slipped out in her clipped words. "Lynn McCane."

"Nice to meet you." He took her hand and shook it lightly. "Where're you headed?"

"Houston."

"Me too. Home?"

"Now it is."

"Not always?" She shook her head. "No, I didn't think so. I thought I detected a bit of the East in your voice."

Matt felt rather than saw it. It was as if the protective door to her being closed. Her countenance changed, and he felt the coldness of the wall that she erected between herself and the world.

"Didn't mean to intrude. Guess it's just old Texas pride. Kinda makes the heart jump whenever I meet a fellow Texan." He didn't realize his drawl had slithered out, dragging across his tongue.

The woman nodded but didn't say anything. A moment later, she suddenly elaborated. "I'm told I had—uh, *have* relatives there. It was my husband who brought me to Texas."

"You're married?" Matt's voice fell slightly as he glanced at her left hand.

"At one time."

"No more?"

She shook her head, causing her dark hair to fan across her cheek. She pushed it back and stared at her hands.

"Sorry," he said.

"Don't be." Abruptly, she turned to the window and stared into the empty darkness.

After several moments, he spoke. "I ... I didn't mean to offend you. Old habit, I guess. Where I grew up, everyone's always interested in others. Upbringing is sometimes hard to get rid of."

She nodded and offered a brief smile, but just as quickly, it died on her lips. She slumped in her seat and closed her eyes.

What was it that scared her? For sure, he had glimpsed a hint of fear in her expression. He also saw something else, but he wasn't sure what. The startling awareness he'd found in her violet eyes refused to leave his mind, though. They were so dark, so troubled. He let his head fall against the headrest, but he couldn't seem to take his eyes off of the dark-haired woman. She puzzled him, and he loved a good puzzle. He sighed and watched her act as if she was asleep, yet he knew she knew he was watching her.

The attendant returned with the woman's meal. Seeing her closed eyes, she glanced from her to Matt and raised her brows.

"I'll take it." Matt reached for the tray. Just as he did, the woman stirred and yawned. With her eyes focused on the food as if it would vaporize into thin air if she didn't act quickly, she pulled it from his hands. Unfolding her napkin and throwing it in her lap, she dove into the meal like she thought it would be her last.

Matt couldn't keep his eyes off her. Each movement of her hands, mouth, and face fascinated him. She betrayed so much with each action. The desperate, life-sustaining need to be nourished was evident in her urgent hunger. He didn't need an in-flight movie, or even his computer, to keep him occupied. But when she looked up and caught him staring at her, it was his turn to blush. He fumbled for his glasses and pretended to be absorbed by the pages displayed on his computer screen.

"Finished?" The attendant reached across Matt and took her tray. "Is there anything else I can get you?"

The woman shook her head. She pushed the tray back into its slot on the side of the seat and then pulled her purse out.

"Excuse me," she muttered. Her voice was almost inaudible. Matt jumped at the sound. Just as she started to move past his knees, the plane hit some turbulence and she lost her balance. Matt reached to steady her, and she fell against him.

"Sorry!" he said, trying to keep a smile from curling his lips.

"No. My fault. Please, excuse me!"

Matt sat still as the woman slipped past. Once in the aisle, she quickly made her way to the forward lavatory. He continued to stare in her direction even after she shut the door and the "occupied" sign lit up. When he sucked in a deep breath and caught the faint scent of flowers, a prickle of electricity prodded him and his heart pounded a little faster. The sensation was one he knew to be addictive. But how could she affect him so? Too many women enamored by his newfound status were ready to gush and shower superficial attention on him, but this one was different. She didn't seem to care.

Matt refocused on his computer screen. The fine print blurred, and words ran together. He knew he was the artist to whom the conditions referred. But what were those other words? What was an "agreeor" anyway?

"Excuse me." Her soft voice intruded and dashed any minuscule amount of concentration he'd mustered. This time, he stood before she moved toward him, and she slipped by, leaving a soft hint of the scent of flowers in her wake. She clicked her seat belt, and with it, the door to her soul seemed to close as well.

Matt sighed and forced his eyes back to his contract. He read through the lines trying not to think of her sitting next to him, trying to pretend her presence didn't matter. The harder he pretended, the more she intruded.

He didn't need it. He had too much on his agenda for the coming year to even think about any kind of relationship. Yet, that was all that seemed to stick in his mind—images of him and the woman together, horseback riding the back forty at the family farm outside Houston, hiking a trail at a state park, or watching a good play at the local theater. He shook himself. She was a stranger—a complete stranger.

He aimed his gaze at the computer screen. From the corner of his eye, he spied the woman pulling a paperback from her bag. Matt forced his eyes back to his contracts. Minutes passed, and she didn't turn any pages. She simply stared at it. More minutes passed, and she finally flipped a few pages.

Without warning, the plane lurched. Lynn dropped her book, grabbed the armrest, and gasped. Just as quickly, the plane steadied, and she relaxed her grip.

"Not a nervous flyer, are you?" Matt turned to her.

She shook her head. "No, I've flown too many miles lately to give it a second thought." The plane bumped a couple more times, and she gripped the armrest again.

Matt chuckled. "Yeah, me too. Don't give it a second thought until a bump comes along."

Suddenly, the plane swayed violently and then dropped altitude for an eternal second. Conversations ceased, and the sound of the engines seemed deafening. But when the plane settled and the flight smoothed out, the passengers resumed chatting as before.

"Ladies and gentlemen, sorry to disturb you." The captain's voice filtered through the speakers. "Guess you might've imagined we hit a bit of turbulence. It's nothing to be concerned about. Just a weather front up ahead and we're going to have to detour around it. As we fly over the clouds, look for lightning displays below. They are usually quite remarkable from this altitude." Like obedient children, passengers strained to look out their windows toward the ground.

Just as the woman leaned toward her window and glanced out, a forked display of crooked light fanned across the clouds beneath them. She sucked her breath in sharply, and Matt glanced at her before leaning over and staring out the window too. Another forked display, larger than the first, flared out below.

"Fascinating, isn't it?" Matt settled back in his seat. "Don't imagine most people think of lightning as spreading out like that."

The woman nodded but kept her eyes on the window.

"Reminds me of some of the storms we had as a kid." Matt continued talking and ignored her silence. "We'd sit on the front porch and watch the clouds in the distance. They were too far away for us to hear any thunder. Those were my favorite. I always hated the thunder. Sometimes we'd see the forks of light; others, just the cloud would light up, like a flashlight under a sheet. I loved the different colors. Pink, yellow, sometimes a cold white. Never exactly the same twice."

"You lived in the country?"

"Yeah. Not too far from the city, though. We have a ranch out from Houston. I grew up with country living and access to the city whenever, all for the price of an hour's worth of travel." He smiled and closed his eyes.

The woman's soft voice interrupted. "I never had that much variety. As a kid, I lived in town, a row of town homes actually, in the DC area. Storms meant lots of dirt and muck washing down the drains along the street. They seemed to be the only things that cleared the grime from the air, but whatever dirt they erased returned shortly after the sun came back out. I never knew an open space until I married Sam. He didn't either until his company sent him south to Houston and we began to discover some of the hill country."

"Beautiful in the spring, aren't they?" Matt mused. "The flowers, I mean. You know it's said the flowers filling the highway medians are from Lady Bird. They said she loved flowers so much she wanted them everywhere, so she initiated the Texas wildflower programs."

"Yeah, I'd heard that. I think bluebonnets are my favorite."

"The state flower."

"Yes. Ironic too. I'd always hated Texas, especially after … well, after Sam. For some reason, I never left. Guess I'd grown so accustomed to it, I didn't have the courage to go anywhere else."

Matt wondered about Sam. His curiosity was almost stronger than his reason, but he didn't have to be slapped in the face by an Einstein-caliber brain to know she would resent such an intrusion. He didn't know what else to say, so with a mental shrug, he returned his gaze to his computer. The woman pulled her book out again. The pages seemed to be turning rather quickly, and he wondered if she was a speed-reader.

Conversations waned, and reading lights blinked out as the plane seemed glued to its route in the sky. Some closed their eyes and dozed. The woman beside him eventually did the same. Matt continued to gaze at his computer. When he reached the last page, he realized he'd only stared at it. He'd not read a word.

Matt shut down his computer and slipped it into its case. After stowing it in the compartment over his head, he leaned back in his seat and closed his eyes. Images of the woman's face taunted him, and he snapped his eyes open to steal a quick glance at her. Her eyes were closed, and her chest rose and fell in a regular rhythm. He closed his eyes again and tried to erase from his mind her countenance, her scent, her presence.

Suddenly, a loud boom shook the plane. A ball of light exploded across the cabin and then sizzled off the wing. The plane shuddered and fell through the sky. Matt felt his stomach slam against the back of his throat. Then all was quiet, as the plane leveled and the man-made monster resumed its trail across the highway of the gods.

After the first wave of panic passed, Matt glanced at the woman. Her knuckles were frozen in a white grip on the armrest, eyes transfixed on the window as if she were afraid to move her gaze. Matt started to reach for her hand and gently pry it away when the captain's voice interrupted.

"Ladies and gentlemen, not to alarm anyone, but we were just hit by a little lightning. We believe there is no serious damage, but some of our diagnostic systems appear to be malfunctioning. Because of this, we will need to circle the airport a few times prior to landing in Houston. We need everyone to please remain in their seats and be sure all seat belts are fastened. Attendants, please prepare the cabin and passengers."

Flight attendants cruised the aisles grabbing loose cups and cans and instructing passengers to be sure all purses and bags were either under seats or in overhead compartments. After pillows were distributed, they announced they would demonstrate the standard crash position.

"Crash position?" It looked like everyone mouthed it at the same time.

The plane dropped and rose again. Cups that had not already been seized by anxious attendants sloshed the last of their liquid. Anything else not gripped by sweaty palms became weightless for an interminable second.

"We're going to crash, aren't we? Just like that, it'll be all over in one big fiery flame." The woman beside him didn't seem aware she had spoken aloud. She wasn't looking at Matt. Rather, her eyes were fixed on some distant, unseen object. Her face was so white Matt thought she might faint.

"We'll be fine. I think they just need to check a few things out." Without realizing what he was doing, he took her hand in his.

She stared at him as if she'd never seen him before. "Is that so? You can predict the future? You guarantee it will be all right? Because, I'll tell you, this is par for the course for me. Nothing's ever all right. Every time I think it's going to get better, that things will change for the best, boom! Something comes along and takes it all away." A tear slid down her cheek, and with sudden anger, she jerked her hand from Matt's and hit her cheek as she swiped at it, hard enough to leave a red mark where the moisture had been.

"It's not the end." Matt stared at the mark. "I learned early on that to give up is defeat, and nothing good comes from defeat. Only if you fight it, refuse to let it get the best of you, will the blessings bloom."

"The blessings bloom? Come on; are you some kind of preacher?" She slumped in her seat and glared at him.

Matt winced at the edge in her voice. He shook his head and felt his heart thumping harder. He wanted desperately to take her in his arms and just hold her, to squeeze the fear and despair from her heart, to make it better. But he knew she couldn't, wouldn't accept it. He wished he could change that, and that startled him.

The woman pulled a small note pad from her pocket and scribbled on it. "Listen, if I don't make it," she flinched at his quick frown, "if, only if, would you please …" Her voice wavered. "Get in touch with this man. He's someone I work with, a friend, actually. His name's Barry, Barry Swindmore. He's with the *Houston Chronicle*. Tell him I found it. Tell him to be sure and check the mail." She handed the pad to Matt.

"If you don't make it—isn't that a little premature?" He took the pad from her hand.

"I'm sorry. It's been a bad day, getting worse by the second." She managed a small smile. "I'm outta my head right now. But just the same …"

Matt nodded. "Guess most of us are feeling a little kicked at the moment, but what if you make it and I don't?"

She stared at him. "Well, is there … uh … anyone you want me to see?"

Matt chuckled briefly. "No, because that won't happen. We'll be just fine, you and me. You'll see."

The plane took a sudden dive, and once again his stomach hit the back of his throat. Conversations ceased, and most all armrests were gripped by sweaty palms and white knuckles. Seconds later, the plane steadied. But as soon as it leveled out, it plunged and rocked again.

No one spoke. The plane's engines roared louder as it fought forces plotting to push it from the sky. Thunder crackled, and the sky burst into flame. Like a poorly designed roller coaster, the plane bumped, soared, and plunged through the dark air. The dips were so deep no one risked a sentence. Not even the captain spoke over the intercom.

Matt didn't believe the woman beside him could turn any whiter. He stared at his own knuckles. They too, were tightly clenched around the armrest. For the first time, he truly began to wonder if they would survive. He almost laughed.

"Yeah, life does have a funny ending sometimes." He glanced up at the overhead bin. "My computer, full of documents and some scripts … when you get down to it, it's nothing but a bunch of meaningless legalese that won't mean a lot after all is said and done." Matt stopped, surprised by the look on the woman's face.

"It'll matter to your family. What you've done in this life will affect them for the rest of theirs. You will have left an indelible stamp, a permanent impression that will carry through to their end." She glanced at her hands before looking back at him, and her eyes darkened with sincerity. "A family is the best thing one can have in life. It's not something to be taken for granted."

The flight attendant's voice interrupted. "Ladies and gentlemen, all seat belts should be fastened. No loose items should be out, and tray tables should be up. Let me repeat the crash position for you. You take the pillow and ..." She demonstrated the position. Trouble was, no one was watching.

A loud whine pulsed through the cabin. The plane's nose dipped and pushed them against their seat belts. A series of short bumps knocked them, yet they still plummeted. Several passengers let out short, clipped screams.

The woman peered out the window, and Matt strained to see past her. He could see only rain sheeting against the acrylic pane. There were no lights, no telltale signs that anything lived outside the plane's closed environment. Only darkness greeted their anxious stares.

Shudders rippled across the fuselage, and the loud whine drowned out all other sound. Lynn turned to Matt and peered into his eyes. "Thanks, for everything, for being here, for caring." Abruptly, she turned back to the window.

Matt took her hand in his. She didn't turn her head; instead, she leaned against him. Matt encircled her with his arm, and she relaxed slightly under his touch. No words were exchanged. They rode the roller coaster of life and death and waited. Waited for eternity. Waited to see what their sentence would be.

As the angry elements continued their assault, bumping them across the sky, up and down and then sideways, Matt's grip on the woman tightened. It was as if the harder he held on to her, the safer they would be. Suddenly, the floor seemed to fall from beneath them. The whine increased and then abruptly ended. A long series of bumps tossed the plane as if it were riding across the wake of a powerboat. With no warning, there was a loud boom, and then everything shuddered just before a bone-crushing bump threw everyone forward and then just as quickly slammed them back against their seats. The world catapulted and went black.

When Matt opened his eyes, all was silent. There was no angry engine whine, no roaring, and no loud booming. Blackness was everywhere. Something drummed softly against the fuselage. Rain?

Eyes adjusting to the darkness, he discerned the entire cabin was tilted at a steep angle. Without warning, there was a loud thump, and the floor seemed to drop from beneath him. The plane was like a ship wobbling on the sea, and everything swayed.

Stunned passengers were coming to and realizing their peril. They were caught in a wave of panic and shook the unstable craft. Some cried and moaned. Others thrashed and kicked, desperate to free themselves from their prison. The smell of jet fuel was strong, and it sounded as if there was some kind of hissing coming from somewhere beneath them.

As Matt scanned the space about him trying to get his bearings, weird shapes materialized. Desperate to make some sense of the odd scene, he squinted as if it would help him see better in the dark. Then it hit him. The odd shapes were tree limbs protruding through the skin of the plane. He remembered the woman. Like a madman, he clawed blindly at the space around him. Nothing, he found nothing. After struggling with a jammed seat belt for a few moments, he finally freed himself and stood. However, instead of finding a steady, solid surface, he fell through a gaping hole where her seat had been.

Hands flailing, he grabbed at anything to stop his fall. A large limb, jutting from the side of a giant pine tree whacked him. Finally, his slippery fingers grasped a branch, and gingerly, he wiggled around so his feet rested on a lower limb. Once he had gained some sense of balance, he quickly felt his way down the side of the tree.

On the ground, he backed away and glanced up. The deep gray of the sky was only shades lighter than the outline of the plane, but the contrast was enough for him to see the aircraft had been torn apart in three places. Each section dangled precariously, supported at sharp angles by a thick grove of pines.

He screamed, "Ms. McCane! Where are you?" To his right, he heard a moan. "Ms. McCane? Is that you?"

The moaning grew louder. Kicking at thick bramble and brush, Matt pushed forward, seeking the source of the sound.

"Which way?" he shouted. The moaning grew more distinct as he pushed farther into the growth, thorns ripping at his flesh. A root caught his toe, and he tripped and fell, landing on a warm body cradled in a thicket of briers.

"Is that you?"

There was a small "Yes."

"My goodness!" Matt yanked and tugged, frantic to get the thorny branches out of the way. "Where're you hurt?"

"I'm … I'm not sure. My arm may be broken. My head hurts."

It was dangerous to move her, not knowing her injuries, but when the twisted metal of the aircraft moaned and creaked with its own agony, Matt knew there was no choice. Several limbs splintered like shots from a gun. They had to get away from there. Fast.

With no care for his own pain, Matt lifted her as carefully as he could and pushed through the brush. He didn't care which direction he went. All that mattered was getting away from the plane before it completed its journey to earth.

Feet slipping on wet pine needles, he ran for life itself. Rain stung his eyes and quickly soaked him to his skin. He had to get the woman someplace safe and return to help the others.

As he pushed through the thicket, he heard screaming. Turning, he saw orange flames licking the edges of the central fuselage. The battered sections of metal seemed to be swaying as shadows danced past the windows. People trying to climb out were rocking the plane. At least thirty feet in the air, their balance was uncertain. Matt turned and resumed his frantic push through the brush.

The woman stirred, and she gripped his arm weakly and asked, "What's happening?"

"Sssh! You're okay."

She muttered, "I owe you my life," and then closed her eyes and went limp.

Matt pushed forward, not caring what he had to push through. Behind them, more limbs splintered. Then with no other warning, the plane completed its journey. Beginning with the nose section, moving like a wave to the tail section, the broken, defeated monster fell the last thirty feet. The ground shuddered from the collision, and then to a count of three, the plane exploded.

CHAPTER 3

The explosion knocked Matt to his knees. Flames licked the sky, and an orange glow carved a niche in the dark space about them. What stunned Matt the most, however, was the silence. There were no screams, no sirens, no bustle of activity that signaled some type of help rushing to offer salvation. There was nothing but a roaring inferno.

They must be the only survivors, the only ones to walk away and cheat death. Strangely, Matt was not happy about that. Those poor souls in the plane, trapped with no escape, doomed to the inferno's hell. His heart ached, and he wanted to scream. So many families left to mourn those whose potential in life had not been reached, so many cheated of opportunities unfulfilled. The woman groaned. Jerked back to his own reality, he managed to get back on his feet while still clutching her close to his body.

Matt pressed through the brush, blinded by tears and fear. Only orange flames dancing in the bleak night's blackness offered any beacon of direction. Their light was barely enough to outline the shadows of trees comprising a forest that seemed to be endless.

The piney woods of Texas, that had to be where they were. Were they near The Woodlands, or possibly as far north as Conroe? So, where were the rescue vehicles, planes, helicopters, all the things that usually came screaming to the scene of an accident?

Matt forged ahead, only the diminishing crackle of fire and the constant drumming of rain punctuated the silence. He didn't notice the slight weight of the woman in his arms. He was focused. He knew what he had to do. His stubbornness kicked in.

After more than an hour, woods still encircled them. It looked as if they'd made no progress. His only compass mark was the flaming plane, a faint orange glow in the distance. Matt was reasonably sure he'd not gone in circles. Yet, if they'd crashed in the piney woods near Houston's George Bush Intercontinental Airport, they should have encountered civilization by then. Not many places were left undisturbed in the midst of increasing development and expansion. So, where were those subdivisions when one needed them?

The cold rain numbed him. His legs wobbled, and his arms felt like they were on fire. The woman's slight weight seemed to grow by the moment, and his arms burned with exhaustion. No longer able to run, Matt slowed to a trot. He conceded he was exhausted. The surge of adrenaline that had sustained him had finally given out.

Gently, he set the woman on the ground and then searched about for any loose leaves or branches, anything for cover. There seemed to be nothing but wet pine needles carpeting the entire planet. With little else to do, he curled up beside her and tried to shield her from the elements as best he could. He shivered uncontrollably as he prayed for morning light and salvation.

Matt fought sleep. It was vital he stay awake and alert, watching, listening, ready to let anyone who might come along to offer help know where they were. The cold and damp proved more powerful than his determination. His head nodded, and his eyelids drooped. Without realizing it, he dozed.

Matt jumped, his heart hammering his ribs. Something poked him on the shoulder. It was repeatedly tapping and prodding. The vapors of his unconscious stupor faded, and he catapulted to a world of gray dampness. The black night had been replaced by a dark-gray shroud.

Fog swirled about them. Everything was wet, but mercifully, the rain had stopped.

The woman was still lying by his side; one hand was moving—the one that had tapped him. He pushed up to one elbow and gazed down at her. There was a large gash across her forehead, and her other arm was bent at an odd angle. Her skin was gray and cold to the touch. Shock. He knew it. And he had nothing with which to warm her.

Forgetting his own chill, his own shaking limbs, he climbed to his feet, pulled her into his arms, and started running, if one could call it that. The murky light made it even harder to find his way. There was no orange beacon to remind him which way to avoid.

After an eternity, the trees thinned, and they burst upon a massive field that seemed to spread for endless miles in every direction. At one time, it must have grown corn, he thought, seeing the brown stubble of once-vibrant, green stalks scattered along fading rows. He could see nothing else, except on the horizon; he spotted the outline of some type of building. He aimed for it.

Eventually, they reached an old barn. It looked as if it had been forgotten, left behind in time. Missing planks allowed weak light to fall on a muddy floor. He could not see or smell either fresh hay or any animals. In a corner, tucked behind a rusty, ancient plow, Matt found an old horse blanket. Grabbing the rough, tattered cloth, he wrapped it as tightly as possible about the woman. Next, he stumbled outside and searched for some sign—any sign—of life.

The empty landscape was daunting, and his hopes shrank like skin exposed to cold for too long. A windswept, never-ending field wouldn't stop him; he couldn't let it. The prospect of failure was too frightening—completely unacceptable.

He started running. He pushed his feet as fast as they would go, but toward what, he wasn't sure. The bleakness was infinite, but his energy was finite. His legs trembled, and his vision blurred. As his steps seemed to take him nowhere, he began to believe they'd either fallen off the face of the earth or been sucked into some crazy space-time warp. Both possibilities were suddenly quite believable.

A hidden stone caught his toe, and he tripped and fell, knocking the wind out of him. For some uncounted time, he fought and pleaded with his sore, ravaged body to get up and run. But he simply couldn't coerce any more movement from his limbs.

In the eerie stillness, growing in decibels was the wheezing, stuttering cough of an engine. Matt squinted as he strained to hear. Soon, he caught the image of a man bumping along on a loud, hiccupping tractor. The driver spied Matt and waved grandly as if glad to find a long-lost buddy.

Using what little strength he had left, Matt moved his hand back and forth and then fell back to the ground. The chugging tractor continued on its journey and soon stopped beside Matt.

"Gracious alive." Matt heard a deep voice. "What've we got here?" The man, though appearing to be in his seventies, slipped from the seat as easily as a twenty-year-old. A weather-beaten face bent over him.

"We need help …" Matt's voice faltered. "There's a woman. She's in shock. Please …"

"Slow down, son," the man said as he grasped Matt's arms and, with no apparent effort, pulled him to his feet. "Looks like you've had a bit of a time, you have."

Matt took a good look at the man's machine. It must have been at least forty, fifty years old, certainly made long before he'd worked on his own farm. How was it still running? He thought the same of the old man. He was missing all his teeth except for one in the middle of his upper plate. His face was lined by years in the sun. Nearly nonexistent hair ringed the perimeter of his bald globe. Despite time's erosion on the man's features, there was vitality in his smile and eyes. It enveloped Matt, wrapping him in a strange sense of well-being and warmth.

The farmer asked, "Now what's this about a woman?" With a broad, hard hand, he gently touched the dried scab of blood over Matt's left eye. "Looks like you're the one who's been roughed up."

"No. She's over there." Matt pointed at the old barn. "We ran there. It was the first place we could find. We were in a crash."

"Crash? Now what kind of crash would that be?"

"Plane. Last night. A few miles from here. Certainly you heard?"

The man smiled slowly, giving full exposure to his prized tooth. "Naw, don't reckon I did. All was quiet 'round here last evening. No commotion. No nothing." He frowned as he studied Matt. "Sure you're not pulling one on me?"

"No, sir!" Matt shouted. "Please. Would you just drive me over to your barn?"

"My barn?"

Matt thought he'd die of frustration. "Well, whosever it is, that's where this woman is. If we don't get her help soon, she'll die. Please, will you just take me there?"

Without a word, the old man climbed into the tractor's seat. He pointed to the side step. "Stand there, and hold on!" He didn't wait for Matt to reply. As soon as Matt was in place, he jammed the gear, and the old machine sprang to life and chugged eagerly across the bumpy field.

Matt fell from the tractor before it stopped outside the barn but picked himself up and ran inside, not waiting to see if the old man followed. The woman was just as he'd left her, wrapped in the old blanket, unmoving. Matt knelt by her and poked gently. She didn't stir.

"Lynn! Please, Lynn, wake up!" Matt didn't realize he was shaking her until there was a gentle touch on his shoulder.

"Son, not so hard, she'll wake." The farmer knelt beside Matt, reached past him, and lightly touched her forehead. She stirred and then groaned. With surprising ease, the old man lifted the woman and carried her outside. At the tractor, the farmer handed her to Matt while he climbed into his seat. Settled, he extended his arms. Matt handed her back to him and then climbed onto the step and held on to the old man's seat for the ride. To where, he didn't know.

After bumping forever across the never-ending field, they entered a patch of thick pines. It seemed they wound through the trees for miles before they stopped in front of a small farmhouse. Its whitewashed sides were in need of a new coat, and the garden was nothing but brown stubble waiting for renewal in the spring. But the front door flew open as they approached, and a woman, nearly as old as the farmer, ran to greet them. When she saw Matt and Lynn, her broad smile turned to a frown, and she shouted at the old man, "What is it, dear? What have you found?"

"Martha, get some blankets. Start some hot tea, and get a warm bath ready. We've got injured!"

Martha didn't answer. She was already running back into the house. Matt took Lynn in his arms and followed the old man inside just as the murky sky split open and dumped cold, hard rain.

An hour later, rain pounded the tin roof and knocked at the windows. Lynn slept on a small cot by the fireplace. Martha had tried to get some hot soup in her and then, after little success, gently bound her wounds and wrapped her in warm blankets.

Matt had cleaned up and dressed in some old jeans and a flannel shirt supplied by the farmer's wife. He sipped some strange hot beverage and watched the rise and fall of Lynn's chest as Martha finished cleaning and bandaging his wounds. Occasionally, he winced, but he made no sound. After wrapping his left hand, Martha next focused on the gash on his forehead.

"This is awful deep. Don't know if I've got the stuff to fix it right. But I'll do what I can." After dabbing some type of cream on the wound, she pulled a tight bandage across the cut and taped over it with extra tape.

Matt studied the house as she worked. There was no phone, no modern refrigerator, not even an electric stove. Lanterns and oil lamps lined a shelf over the fireplace. An old-time icebox seemed to be the only refrigeration. Running water appeared to consist solely of an old hand pump at the kitchen sink. A wood-stove attached to a flue running up the wall and out on the side served both as a cooktop and source of heat. Water boiled in one pot, and something smelling like his mom's beef stew bubbled in another.

A small box tucked in a dark corner near the kitchen sink caught his eye. It was about four inches square and had one knob in the center. Before he could ask, Martha announced, "There, finished." She studied her work and smiled. "Think that'll keep you for a while. Now, you rest here while I get you something to eat."

She went to a cupboard and stored her things. Then, she pulled out a bowl and filled it with the steaming concoction from the stove. She set it before Matt and then smiled as she waited for his reaction.

After taking a small taste, he swallowed as he put his spoon down. Changing his mind, he grabbed the spoon and dove into the warm broth. He didn't set the spoon down again until his bowl was clean. He glanced up at the farmer's wife.

"We need a doctor."

"You need to eat," Martha insisted, as she took the bowl and refilled it. "You need more inside. It's very important. Your body is hurting. This will heal it."

"I'm really afraid for her." Matt took a small spoonful as he glanced at Lynn. "I don't understand. Why can't we just go get the doctor?"

The farmer gently laid his hand on Matt's knee. "Doc only comes out from town to make his rounds on Tuesdays."

"That's …" Matt started to frown, but it caused the bandage to pull on his skin, "how long from now?"

The farmer's brows rose. "Today is Saturday."

"Well, could I borrow your car? Or would you drive us to town?"

"Son, wish I could drive you into town, but our car … well, it's broke right now. I should have it back by Monday or Tuesday, though."

"We can't just stay here and wait. We have to do something." He glanced at Lynn. Her chest barely moved with each infrequent breath.

The farmer smiled reassuringly. "Martha here, well, she's one fine nurse. She's done all that can be done now. You just need to wait. Be patient."

"I have to go. I have to do something."

The old couple looked at him with odd smiles. Matt ignored the unease in his gut. He had no other choice.

Without a word, Martha went to a beat-up old steamer trunk. The hinges squeaked as she opened the lid and pulled out an old denim jacket. "At least take this." She held it out to Matt. "Even when the rain has stopped, it'll be chilly outside."

A few moments later, Matt walked down the muddy track that posed as a road. It was nearly thirty minutes before he spotted an old Buick. It passed with a honk and a wave. Matt pulled the collar of the jacket up, grateful for its meager warmth. It took three more old cars before a 1940s Oldsmobile pulled over a few yards in front of him.

"Going to town?" A man, maybe fifty, leaned across the front seat and grinned at him.

Matt propped his hands against the door and leaned in the open window. "Yes! I am. By the way, how far is it from here?"

"Oh, it's about five, maybe six miles. Hop in. I'll take you." The man leaned over so he could study his reflection in the mirror. After spitting on his right hand, he rubbed the top of his slicked-back hair. Matt nearly choked. The driver had two thumbs on his right hand. The man turned toward Matt and grinned. "Coming?"

Matt muttered, "Uh, thanks," as he attempted to swallow a mouthful of saliva, which threatened to spew out his lips. He pulled the door open and slipped into the immaculate car. It looked as if it had just left the showroom floor.

"You must've had a rough night." The man nodded at Matt's bandages. "Looks like you got some nasty bumps there."

"Rough wasn't the half of it. The crash, it was, well ..."

"Crash?" The driver scratched his head with the extra thumb. "That's right! You must mean that mess over on the other side, past the woods. Yeah, I heard. Slammed into them, real hard, they said. There wasn't much left. Say ..." He glanced at Matt, and his eyes twinkled with some inner sense of life. "You're one of them, aren't you? I mean, one of the two left alive."

"Yes! Yes, I was and my ... uh, my friend. I need to get her to a doctor. That's where I'm going."

The man's brows rose. "Well, they said ... the two survivors, that is, had already been taken care of. Looks like you're all fixed up. Why are you looking for the doctor now?"

"No. No, that never happened." Matt's face reddened. "Listen, she's going to die if I don't find him. Please, can you hurry?"

The driver grinned as he pushed his foot into the floor. The car leaped from thirty-five miles per hour to a flying forty-five. "She's a beaut, isn't she?" He patted the dashboard. "She's faster than most 'round these parts! Hang on! I'll have you at the hospital in no time."

Matt thought they'd never make it to town. Despite the driver's bragging that they were "going nearly fifty," it looked as if the passing fields were crawling by at less than twenty miles per hour. Matt wiped his forehead repeatedly. Despite the cold outside, the car was hot.

"How much longer?" he asked, fighting to keep his eyes off the driver's functional offshoot.

"Not long. See the hill over there?" The driver used his extra appendage to point to a slight incline in the road. "It's just a couple miles from that."

"Where are those woods you mentioned earlier?" Matt suddenly asked. "The crash, where was it?"

The driver seemed surprised. "You were there. Don't you know?"

Matt shook his head. "No. I don't. I'm ... not from here."

The man smiled. "That's right. Not from these parts, but you know the farming life." The driver glanced at Matt's rough, bandaged hands and well-muscled body. "Tell you what," he said, grinning, "if you have time, I'll take you there. It's not too far that way." He pointed out his window and toward a rise in the field. "That is, after I run my errands."

"Thanks, but if I get hold of the doctor, I've got to get him to my friend. Maybe another time."

"Sure, another time. You are right, you know. You do need to get help to her. But," he said as his smile grew brighter, "she'll be fine. You don't need to worry. We have the best doctors around; we do! I know these things. Some don't, but I do!"

The man turned his focus back to the road. Matt stared at his profile and frowned. Something seemed out of place to him; something was off-kilter. But he had no clue as to just what it was.

They crossed another rise in the land, and in the distance, he saw the outline of some smaller buildings nestled between two ridges of pine trees. Again, he caught himself pressing his foot to the floor, hoping the car would go faster.

After crossing another rise, they pulled into the small town. The hospital, a one-story, cement-block building painted mint green, was surrounded by graceful magnolias and tall pines, giving it an air of peace and restfulness. The man pulled into the visitors' lot across from the emergency entrance, and before he pulled to a stop, Matt had the door open.

"Thanks for the ride!" Matt shouted through the open window. Not waiting for an answer, he turned and trotted toward the emergency room.

At the reception desk, Matt yelled, "I need a doctor, now!"

The nurse behind the partition slowly raised her eyes to meet Matt's. "Just what seems to be the problem?" Without waiting for his answer, she rounded the large desk and grasped his elbow. "Come over here and sit down." She led the way to the small waiting area furnished with a couple rows of plastic chairs. "Someone will be with you shortly."

"But there's no time to wait. She's dying! I need a doctor now!"

A young woman in a white, starched nurse's cap, the kind he'd not seen in years, approached. Her white uniform was crisp and had a full skirt that rustled with each swish of her well-rounded hips.

Matt stood when she stopped in front of him.

"Tell me about it." As if she had all the time in the world, she nudged him back into his chair and sat beside him. Tenderly, she touched the bandage on his forehead and then studied his hands.

"Looks like you've already been treated. Why do you need the doctor again?" A door slammed somewhere, and the nurse jerked her head, causing her hair to swing back and expose a small tag of flesh adjacent to her ear. It looked like a second earlobe.

"I'm not the one who needs help," Matt mumbled as he stared at the extra lobe. "It's my friend. She's going to die if we don't get back to her soon!"

The nurse leaned toward him and peered into his eyes. "Just where is this woman?"

"Back at the farm."

"At the farm, huh?" She studied him for what seemed like an eternity. Suddenly, without a word, she jumped up and ran through a swinging door and out of sight. A moment later, she returned, carrying a large leather bag. A young man in a white lab jacket, carrying a larger bag, followed.

"He will drive us. You can show us where to go." The nurse said it over her shoulder as she trotted out the door to the parking lot.

They were nearly to the farm when the doctor asked, "Tell me, what's this about a crash? You were in it? Last night?"

"Yes. We hit the trees and were thrown, or at least she was. If we hadn't been thrown out, we would've burned when it caught fire and exploded."

"Exploded?" the nurse interjected. "I didn't know. Of course, I wasn't on duty last night."

When they pulled in front of the farmhouse, Matt didn't wait for the others. He was out of the car and through the front door before the doctor could get his bag from the back of the car.

"How is she?" Matt shouted as he slammed through the front door and nearly collided with Martha.

Martha frowned. "You'd best go see. Did you get the doctor?"

Matt nodded but said nothing as he crept over to the side of the woman's bed. The old farmer peered down at her and didn't say anything to Matt.

Matt knelt by the bed. The woman appeared to be sleeping. He pulled her limp hand into his. Then, he bent so his cheek was next to her lips. He couldn't feel the warmth of her breath.

"What's wrong? She's not breathing!" Matt grabbed the farmer's arm and tugged.

"Is this the patient?" The doctor's curt voice interrupted as he pulled things from his bag. The nurse stationed herself opposite him and took the woman's pulse while the doctor listened to her heart or lungs or something.

As Matt watched, his breath seemed to stick in his throat. The doctor finished his exam and looked up. Staring briefly into the nurse's eyes, he nodded slowly. Then, with slow, deliberate care, he pulled the sheet over the woman.

"I'm sorry. We're too late," the doctor said. "I ... uh ... there's nothing more we can do. She's ...""

"Nooooooo!" Matt's voice sounded as if it were crawling up from the bottom of some dark cavern. He jerked from the farmer's grasp and spun into Martha's. "It's not so. It can't be! She's going to make it. Give her CPR, an injection, something! Isn't there anything you can do?"

The doctor looked at the old farmer and shrugged. Matt ran to the nurse and pulled her hand. "Please, don't just stand there. Do something!" He whirled back to the woman and started compressing her chest and then breathing into her mouth. Nothing happened.

Spinning away, he ran to the wall and pounded it, first screaming and then wailing. When the manic rush of energy passed, he turned his tear-streaked face to the group.

"Son, come. Sit down." Martha took Matt's hand and led him to the kitchen table. Unable to comprehend all that was happening, Matt sank into a chair. Martha went to the stove and poured something into a cup. She turned back to Matt and said, "Drink this. It'll help."

The old farmer, the doctor, and the nurse continued to stand over the woman, talking in hushed tones. Matt's eyes scanned the room. He looked at the ceiling, the walls, out the kitchen window, past the woman's bed, at anything but her. He sipped the hot liquid and kept shifting his focus. It seemed he'd jumped from the plane of normalcy to some hideous, surreal nightmare. That had to be it. It was a nightmare. A very real one, one in which the pain of loss was as real as a knife in his back, as real as the torn skin on his palms, as real as the aching gash in his head, as real as the scalding liquid on his tongue. It was a dream so real he was suddenly ready to give his life to end the suffering. A whirlpool of confusion spun around him, growing higher and faster, its vortex opening, inviting him inside. He grew dizzy as the world blurred. He couldn't focus. Everything dimmed. Suddenly, the world was black.

CHAPTER 4

Voices wavered in the distance. Pinpoints of light twirled, swirled, and cut through the fog, pricking him as painfully as cactus needles in flesh. The smell assaulted him first. It was that sterile, antiseptic alcohol smell mixed with other smells so common in hospitals. He wrinkled his nose as he groaned and thrashed trying to fight the invading evil. He flailed harder, groaned louder. All he wanted was to be left alone, to rest in the easy darkness where nothing could touch his soul. Blessed darkness, he wanted it to flood him, to take away the pain the light brought.

"Can you hear me?" The voice was a man's—he didn't know whose. He thrashed at the sound. "Come on, fellow. Don't fight it. You must wake up now."

He felt the pressure of hands holding him still. Something prodded his shoulder. He thought he slapped at it, but his arms didn't move. A motor whirred softly, and he felt himself sliding as his head rose. Someone lifted him by the armpits until he was propped against something soft, pillows perhaps. Giving up, he blinked several times and opened his eyes only to be assaulted by a sterile bright light.

"Where am I?" He hated that question. Every time he'd heard it in a movie, book, or play, he'd grimaced. It was so trivial. How could someone not know where he was? Well, he didn't know where he was, and he was terrified.

He squinted against the bright light as he surveyed his environment. He was in a bed, confined by metal railings and covered by a thin blanket. It was situated in the middle of a small cubicle. Partially drawn drapes hung between him and glass walls, defining his space. Through the glass, he saw what appeared to be a long desk. A group of men and women in scrubs stood chatting behind its high partition. Behind them was a long wall of charts. Faint beeps and buzzes of phones and call buttons punctuated the otherwise hushed quiet. A hospital, he was sure. Was he in intensive care? Most likely. A monitor chirped rhythmically nearby. He saw the IV line attached to his right hand and felt the weight of his bandages. A chill shook him as it raced down his back. Certainly, it was a hospital, but where? Why was he there?

Two young men in starched white jackets stood on either side of his bed. Arms crossed, eyes locked on him, they waited. The one on his right said, "This is Memorial Hermann Hospital at the Texas Medical Center in Houston. Life Flight brought you here early this morning. It seems you were in a plane crash near Intercontinental Airport."

The words burned his ears. A vague sense of heat and fire, of darkness and damp, seemed to float across him. More intense, however, was the vacuum he felt. Nothing made sense.

"Can you tell us your name?" The men leaned over the railing surrounding his bed. They were so close Matt could feel the warmth of their breath as they focused on him. He frowned and tried to shift his weight so that his back didn't hurt.

"There was no identification," the first man continued, "nothing on you to give us a clue."

"I ... I'm ... uh ... I'm ..." He stopped. Nothing came to mind. The swirling blackness began to rise, and the room dimmed. The comforting velvet cloak started to cover him again. With extreme gratitude, he relaxed and tried to sink into its folds.

"Listen, sir, you must think! It's imperative. Who are you?" One man shook him so hard it felt like his teeth rattled.

"I … uh …" Flashes of light, an older lady toughened by the years but smiling, a boy tossing a ball to him, a field full of cattle, towering clouds in the distance, lightning, thunder, a young face, a woman with dark hair, crying. Pain, so much pain. Then, he saw palm trees, smog, bright lights, and people everywhere. There were makeup artists and small trailers, cameras, long meetings, and lots of papers. What did it all mean?

"I'm sorry. I just can't seem to get it. There are flashes, little things that seem familiar, but no name."

The man stepped back from the bed. Briefly, he conferred with the other man. Matt noticed they both wore ID tags identifying them as doctors from the University of Texas Health Science Center. After conferring, the first man turned back to Matt.

"Don't worry, sir. It'll come back. Just rest now. Rest is all it takes." Much more gently than before, he nudged Matt back under the covers and pressed the button to lower the bed. He checked the IV flow rate and then made a few notes in a chart. With a brief nod, they left.

The comforting blackness swelled. Matt wanted to welcome it, but it didn't quite mask the pain. Pain from what, he was not sure. It was not entirely physical. He moaned and thrashed, hoping to escape it, but it was no use. Finally, the blackness grew stronger than he and finished its job.

There was an orange glow, an explosion. He had to get away. The woman, she needed him. He must carry her. His hands were bleeding, raw, her arm, disfigured. Wet, cold—oh, he was so very cold. He shivered. The pine needles, they were itchy. He scratched, but they kept itching. Where should he go? The blackness never ended. He turned in four directions. He didn't know what to do. He began to scream.

"It's all right. You're safe now!" Hands, big and rough, shook him with surprising gentleness. "Here, take a sip of this."

The old farmer handed him a cup of steaming tea before going to the sink and pumping up some water. "Wife says this stuff is guaranteed to fix what ails ya."

Matt sat up from a bed of blankets that had been placed by a crackling fire. He glanced about and was surprised to see he was in the old farmer's kitchen. Bacon sizzled on top of the wood-stove, and his mouth watered at the aroma. Slowly, he took a sip of the hot tea. It was bittersweet. Two more swallows, however, and everything came back with full clarity.

"Where's Lynn? You know, the dark-haired lady with me?" He tried to stand, but his leg gave way, and he reached for the edge of the table to steady himself before sinking into a chair. It was then he noticed the large bandage wrapped around his upper thigh. He didn't remember a bandage on his leg. He stared at the bandages on his hands and with the tip of his forefinger probed the bandage over his eye.

"The woman, where is she?"

"Well now, son, I'm glad you're so worried about my wife, but it's okay. She's just gone into town to do a little marketing. She should be back before noon." He turned back to the sink and started washing some greens.

"No, not her, the woman with me, the one I brought here! She was so ill. Where is she?"

The farmer turned from the sink, and his eyes narrowed as he regarded Matt. He seemed to consider many things to say before choosing one and spoke. "Well, son, I don't rightly know. You saw, there was nothing more you could do. They took her away."

"Where?"

The old farmer shook his head. "That, I can't tell you. They don't tell me these things."

"Surely, someone somewhere knows something!"

The farmer scratched his bald spot and smiled, his lone tooth gleaming from its latest polishing. "Son, I think you've got a fine noggin on your shoulders. You'll find the answer. But ..." His face sobered. "There's not a lot of time; that I know."

Matt didn't fight the light; he welcomed its stark, glaring reality. A new energy pushed him from the blackness. He no longer wanted to remain in its comforting folds. He was stronger. He knew it before he even tried to sit up. However, something tugged at the edge of his memory. Bacon. He wanted some bacon. He pushed the call button just as a nurse breezed in the door carrying a tray with bacon and eggs.

"Here you are." She set the food on his tray table and swung it in front of him. "We don't usually give food like this to patients in your condition, but you've refused all food since coming here. When you showed the hunger, even though I think you were delirious at the time, the doctor said just get the food in you. So, here it is."

"I asked for this?"

"Yes. Insisted, actually."

Matt scratched his head. "Insisted? When?"

"Earlier today, this morning, actually." The nurse helped to situate him and asked, "Is there anything else I can get you, Mr. Grayson?"

"My name? You know my name?"

She seemed surprised. "It's on your charts, your ID." She pointed to the plastic bracelet circling his wrist. He glanced at it. Printed in block letters on the plastic band was the name Matthew Grayson and a patient number, presumably his.

"What else do you know?"

"Nothing you should be concerned about. All you need to know is you must rest and finish recovering." With a frown pinching her eyes into slits, she turned back to the door.

"Nurse!"

She spun around. Hands planted on her hips, she waited.

"How long have I been here, the hospital?"

"A little over a week."

"I ... I can't remember. It's all lost."

The nurse finally smiled. "It's just the drugs. They make some people see, think, even hear crazy things. It's very common to forget too. So, don't give it a second thought. It's all very normal. It'll stop once you get off the pain medicine."

The bacon distracted him. His mouth watered. He was famished. Truly, he didn't know when he'd last eaten. He wanted to dive into the food, but something stopped him. Bacon. What was it about bacon? Before he could take his first bite, he was interrupted.

"Good morning!" An older man with flecks of gray in his brown hair and a thin, strained smile on his face entered and extended his hand. "I'm Dr. Dereck DeBoe. I was called in to assess your situation. Is this correct," he flipped a couple pages on the chart he held, "that you're suffering some memory loss?"

Matt looked at his cooling bacon and then at the man's face. He picked up his fork and took a bite. The food tasted wonderful. It couldn't be from the hospital.

"How much do you remember of the crash?"

"Crash? Is that what happened? Where was it, I-45 or FM1960? Was I speeding?"

The doctor smiled for a second. "No, it was a plane crash, out past Intercontinental. You don't remember?"

Matt shook his head. "Nurse just said the pain medicine did that, causes one to forget." For a moment, the doctor frowned and seemed about to say something, but the moment passed and his smile returned.

"So, what happened, this crash, that is?"

"Don't know a lot." Dr. DeBoe scratched his chin. "Plane coming in from LA hit the woods north of the airport. You really don't remember?"

Matt closed his eyes. He ran his hand through his hair. "No, I don't, least nothing much."

"What do you mean by 'nothing much'? It's very important you tell me everything you can remember."

Matt kept his eyes closed and tried to concentrate. "Only thing that comes to mind are some vague feelings of things like flames, penetrating cold, dampness, but nothing else."

"What about the flight before?"

Matt gulped some orange juice. "I guess it was the usual pass-the-time type of flight. I really don't remember."

The doctor made some notes in his chart as Matt scooped up more eggs and bacon. He was chewing when suddenly her face popped into his mind. She was in the seat next to his. Violet eyes full of sadness. Anger, too. He saw the white-knuckled grip of her hands on the seat as they bounced through the sky. Fear. Holding her. She seemed glad of his arms about her. A loud boom. Everything dark. He reached for her, but she was gone. Matt screamed, but nothing came out.

"Mr. Grayson! Can you hear me?" Matt's breakfast tray had been pushed away, and he was lying flat. Dr. DeBoe was holding his wrist. "You left us for a moment. Tell me, what're you feeling now?"

"I'm ... not sure. I feel weak, washed out."

"Did you remember something?"

"I hope not!" A couple tears dripped from his eyes. "Please tell me it didn't happen."

"What happened?"

"A woman ..."

"A passenger?"

Matt nodded. "She was sitting beside me. I reached for her, but she was gone."

Dr. DeBoe made more notes in his chart. Then he stared at Matt. "How was she gone?"

"I ... I don't know. I don't even know if it happened."

The doctor stroked his chin for several moments. He peered at Matt and seemed to consider what to say. Finally, "Events such as this are traumatic, not just to the body, but to your mind as well. Combined with physical trauma, the type of confusion you're expressing is very understandable." He patted Matt's hand. "The memory is there, and you're beginning to reclaim it."

Taking a small penlight from his pocket, Dr. DeBoe flashed it in each of Matt's eyes. Then, he checked Matt's reflexes. Next, he peeled back the bandage on Matt's forehead. After checking the wound, he replaced the dressing. Finally, he glanced at the IV bags and added more notes to his chart.

"I'm increasing the dosage on some of your meds, and I'm also adding one new medication. It should help speed your recovery." He pointed at Matt's other bandages. "I'll have one of the nurses in shortly to change these." Then, with one hand propping the other, he held his chin as he studied Matt.

"You've been through a lot, and it will take time to heal, not just physically, but mentally as well. Take your time. Let it happen on its own. Don't fight it, even if you want to."

Later, Matt dozed. It was not a pleasant rest. Spasmodically, he tossed and turned. A commotion in the hall finally awakened him from his semiconscious torture.

"I don't care what you say; I'm going in to see him! You can't keep me away! You have no right!"

A trim woman dressed in a powder-blue suit that made her blue eyes look like glacier ice pushed into the room. She had a few specks of gray at her temples, but she stood straight with perfect posture, and Matt instinctively knew she commanded respect wherever she went. Three men in white lab jackets followed her, and judging by their expressions, Matt guessed she had already put them in their place. When her gaze met his, Matt knew instinctively she brought peace and comfort.

"Matt!" She landed on him, wrapping her arms about him and squeezing tightly. "Oh, my baby, you're awake! Why, you're sitting up! You must be doing better!" She ran her fingers over the bandages on his forehead and hands. "Are you still in much pain?"

"Mom?" The word was whispered, unsure.

"Yes, dear?"

"Mom!" He clung to her. "It really is you!"

She pushed back from him and frowned. "My dear, you don't remember?"

"Remember what?"

She ran her forefinger across his frown. "I'm insulted. My own son doesn't even remember his mother!" She grinned, and her eyes twinkled. "How could I not forgive you? You are my firstborn, and look at what you've been through. It's enough to make one forget anything!"

Matt grasped her hand and whispered, "There was, a woman; she—"

His mom glanced at the men standing behind her. She turned back to Matt and frowned. "Woman? What about a woman?"

"She's lost. She needs help. She was in the crash, and she's hurt!"

Katie Grayson shook her head slowly and a flash of pity crossed her face. Finally, she spoke softly. "You're the only one, dear. You're the only one they found."

"We escaped. We got away from the plane." His heart thudded like a jackhammer.

The men behind his mother straightened. Faces alert and watching him, they eased closer to the bed. One of the men took Matt's hand and counted his pulse. Another produced a stethoscope and listened to his heart. While his mom tenderly massaged his brow, those in the room stared at him, their faces fixed on his, eyes narrowed with concern.

Abruptly, Matt sat up. A picture flashed in his mind. There was one doctor, one nurse, an old farmer, and his wife. "Where ... where did they find me?"

"Why, dear, near the plane, I guess. I wasn't told. Why?"

"I need to know!" Matt kicked weakly at his covers and tried to climb from the bed. "Please, just help me get my pants on, and we can get out of here."

The men surrounded him. Muscled arms pinned him down. Matt kicked and squirmed, almost jerking free. "Come on, now! I've got to find her!" He looked at his mother. "Mom, please!"

"You can't go anywhere, just yet." One man spoke quietly. He nodded to his coworker, who produced a long silver needle, dripping the clear fluid the syringe it was attached to contained. Before Matt could protest, the needle was inserted into his IV line. Almost immediately, he felt woozy.

As the world blurred before melting into blackness, he saw the men escort his mom from the cubicle. They gripped her elbows, and their quiet instructions seemed urgent. She turned once and glanced over her shoulder at him. There was fear on her face. He had to know what they said. He must find out. He must find ... He must ... He ...

"Hey, old man! Just because you signed one of them big studio contracts doesn't mean you get to stay in bed lazing the day away, now does it?"

A young man, almost the spitting image of Matt, only a couple years younger, slapped him hard on the back and laughed. Matt jumped and rolled over. He opened his eyes to see his brother grinning at him.

"I see the old man's finally waking. 'Bout time!" His drawl was much slower and more pronounced than Matt's.

"Chad?" The two men embraced, but it was Matt who clung. "Oh, man, it's good to see you!"

"Now don't go getting teary on me. That stuff's for the womenfolk. Besides ..." Chad winked and leaned closer to whisper. "... there's a little nurse out there I got my eye on. Don't want her getting any ideas. Know what I mean?"

Matt tried to punch Chad's shoulder, but his arm dropped like a cement block.

"You'll get your strength back soon. I know it." Chad propped himself on the edge of Matt's bed. "Tell me, how long are they gonna keep you here? I'm getting tired of doing your chores!"

"Since when have you ever done my chores?"

"Chad! Don't go wearing your brother out. Can't you see he's in no shape to wrestle you?"

"Gee, thanks, Mom, for cheering me up!" Matt tried not to smile as his mom breezed into the room."

"Oh, honey." She hugged him tightly. "Well, you're looking much better today. Isn't he, Chad?"

"Chad's been here before?"

"Partner, I've been here lots of times. You were just too rude to wake up and say hi."

"I don't remember."

His mother added, "Every day for the past week."

"How could I forget?"

"The doctors say it's the pain medicine, the trauma. They insisted that it was pretty normal. But ..." She smiled. "... you're making great progress."

Chad interrupted. "Man, you should see all the commotion outside. The world knows you're in here. The press, fans, all of 'em, they're sending flowers and candy and who knows what else. They've even got your picture on today's front page." He threw a copy of the *Houston Chronicle* onto Matt's lap.

Matt picked up the paper, and staring at him was the headline, "Hollywood's Newest Heartthrob and Crash's Only Survivor Recovering in Houston Hospital."

"Jerry thinks this is the best thing that could've happened to your career, other than an Academy Award!" Chad rattled on while Matt stared at the headline.

"And the phone calls!" his mother uttered. "Lord! I have to use my cell phone just to make a call, and you know how bad the signal is out at the ranch. I think your agent set the record, though. Every hour, on the hour. Jerry's worried his prize possession won't be well enough in time to begin shooting in a few weeks. I've given him strict orders, though. He's not to bother you. You're just supposed to rest."

"Mom," Matt asked as he glanced up from the paper, "would you let Chad and me have a moment?"

"Uh, sure, dear. Whatever." She picked up her bag and planted a quick kiss on his cheek. "I'll run along. You two have a good visit."

When Katie Grayson was gone, Matt said, "Something's wrong."

Chad dropped into a chair and pulled it close to the head of the bed. He propped his elbows on his knees and leaned forward. He stared Matt in the eye. "What're you talking about?"

"I'm saying I don't believe they're telling me the truth."

"The truth? What's not to believe? Yeah, you have been babbling some at times. Just the other day, you were going on about some woman not being the only one. Man, you were just out of it, crazy, nothing more!"

Matt gazed into Chad's eyes. "I don't have the energy to pop you for trashing me, man, but I tell you, I wasn't the only one! There was a woman too. I carried her from the plane. Now, no one wants to tell me anything about her. They claim she never existed and that I'm just delusional or something like that." He slapped the paper. "Not even the paper is saying anything about her."

Chad leaned in so that his face was only inches from Matt's. "You've got to quit talking like that." He hissed the words so that they didn't carry beyond the bed. "You want to go home, don't you? Well, if you do, then you better just toe the line, play along with everyone. That'll convince them you're not crazy."

Matt reached for Chad's shoulder and gripped it. "Do you ... do you think I'm crazy?"

Chad peered at Matt for a few moments. He shook his head slowly. "No. But you've got to accept that you were the only one. They searched a large area around the crash site, and no one else was found. All the bodies were identified and accounted for. You've just gotta accept it and move on!"

Matt stared at Chad as if his brother were talking in Greek. He kept shaking his head.

"Look, man, it's just the drugs. They've got you pumped up on those painkillers, and you don't know what's real and what's not. Why, when I had my appendix out, they gave me so many drugs, that I remember every bit of the pain but not a one of those gorgeous young nurses who were taking care of me. What a waste!"

Matt still didn't respond, and Chad grew serious. "Get past it, Matt. Get on with life. Consider yourself blessed you got a second chance. The rest of those poor souls sure didn't."

Matt started to argue but cringed when he spied a tall and beefy nurse strolling into his room like a tsunami. She carried a way-too-large syringe full of amber liquid.

"Not to worry, Mr. Grayson," the woman said. "This goes in the IV. You won't feel a thing." Then to Chad, "He needs his rest now. Next visitation is at eight. Come back then, if you like."

As Matt relaxed and blackness wormed its way over him, he vowed he would find out the truth, even if it was the last thing he did.

"Well, Mr. Grayson, are you ready to greet your public?" The same well-built nurse who seemed to love poking him with needles and who sported enough muscles to take on a gladiator breezed into his room and pulled back the curtain blocking the warm sun.

"Your audience is waiting for you out there." She pointed to the window. "I must tell you, life is not going to be the same once you're gone! No more crazed teen girls pretending to be candy stripers will be slipping past me. No more press sneaking in trying to get to you when we're not watching." She crossed her arms across her ample chest and shook as she laughed. "And, I tell you, there've been some persistent ones. Thought I'd seen it all until the last two came along. Caught them changing into some soiled scrubs in the janitor's closet across the hall." She shivered. "I don't even want to think about what kind of bodily waste they were exposing themselves too. You know, one can't be too careful these days, what with all these blood-borne contagions. But they must've been desperate. Thought they could just breeze right in here, and while pretending to mop your floor, snap a few pictures of you bandaged and bruised. But, no ..." She wagged her finger at him. "I guard my patients better than that! None of them get past me! Yes ..." She sighed as she leaned against the doorjamb and smiled at him. "... it definitely won't be the same!"

Matt pushed himself up in the bed and winced as a spasm of pain shot across his body. "Home, finally." Moving slowly, he dropped his feet over the side of the bed and started to stand. "Guess I need to get dressed."

"Not so fast there!" The nurse stuck her palm out for him to stop. She then opened his locker and pulled a plastic bag out. "This is all you had with you when you arrived. And, sorry to say, it's not fit to wear. Your mom's bringing your clothes."

Matt took the bag. He stared at it briefly before rummaging through its contents. His fingers grasped a tiny wad of paper, what was left of a small pad. The pages were brittle, and the edges were charred as if they'd been held close to a flame. Gingerly, he flipped through the pages and found only one with writing that he could decipher. The words "*Houston Chronicle*" and "Barry" were scribbled there. Did it mean something? He wasn't sure. He dropped it on the bed and crawled back under the covers. "No point in wearing myself out." He grinned at the nurse. "Better rest so I can meet my public!"

An hour later, Matt sat in the front seat of his mother's new Tahoe as she expertly maneuvered through the heavy Houston traffic on the 610 Loop. He was surprised at how warm it was, even for early February. Windows open, the balmy air tangled his now longer curls. Birds sailed across a cloudless sky, and pears and redbuds strained to release their buds from an all-too-short and mild winter. It was hard to believe only three weeks earlier he'd ridden Life Flight to Memorial's Hermann Hospital.

"That was some getaway, Mom." He draped his right arm on the window ledge. The bandages on his hands had been reduced to large Band-Aids, and the one on his forehead was now a butterfly strip. Only the one on his leg remained in any form similar to before. It still throbbed when he walked.

"Guess you'd better get used to it. We've had to hire someone to keep the press and the fans from storming through the front gate. With all the publicity from the crash and of course, your movie being number one, well, it's been nonstop craziness! I had to do some major maneuvering to lose the few determined ones who wanted to follow me today. Why, there've even been people out in the pasture digging up our cows' piles!"

Matt grinned, and a hint of a mischievous twinkle danced in his eyes. "Mom, don't you worry about it. That's not your job. Your job is waiting on me, nursing me back to health!"

Katie stuck her bottom lip out as she pretended to slap him. "No self-respecting mom is going to let a son get away with that kind of disrespect!" A car horn blared, and she swerved back into her lane. "Better pay attention to my driving. By the way," she paused as she turned her focus on moving over two lanes and exiting the freeway. "Jerry sent over a copy of your new script and new contracts for you to sign."

Matt sighed. He could feel his blood pressure shoot up several points. He was too young to worry about blood pressure.

"He just can't let it drop, can he?" Matt muttered. Jerry never let anything rest. Like his late dad used to say, he was always kicking some dead horse somewhere—although the vision of Jerry kicking anything was enough to make him laugh, almost.

Jerry was short and pushing past forty-five, though he insisted he was only thirty-nine. His balding head gave the truth away. He always seemed to have a cigarette in his hand and spit words out like a machine-gun with an accent that screamed "Yankee!" though he claimed to be from the South. What South he was referring to, Matt had no idea. Jerry rarely ate anything healthier than a doughnut and seemed to exist on only an hour or two of sleep a day, usually in the afternoon in his swivel chair. More than once, he'd let it be known that Matt was his paycheck. And that was why Jerry wouldn't let anything fall through any crack.

At the gate to the Grayson farm, fans and media crews from all the networks and news channels waited. Jerry was in front of them all, waving. When the crowd realized their prey had arrived, they started pressing toward the Tahoe, forcing Katie to halt.

Jerry ran up to Matt's window and shouted, "Go on! Give them a little something! It'll make them happy, for a while."

The questions began.

"Mr. Grayson, how're you feeling?"

"Do you remember much of the crash?"

"What is your next film to be about?"

"Can you tell us about your injuries?"

"Are you seeing anyone special?"

"Were you abducted by aliens?"

"What was their ship like?"

He could see the headlines, "Actor Caught in *Ménage à Trois* with Space Alien!" The questions pounded him nonstop. Matt tried to answer each quickly and lightly. The last one, however, caught him off guard.

"Is it true you were the only survivor?"

"That's what I'm told. Frankly …" His hands shook slightly. "I don't remember any of it." It was a lie. Only during the past few minutes had he been able to forget the look on the woman's face as the pain had twisted it into a horrible sight. Nightly dreams had clarified the vision and burned the image into his mind. He'd even remembered her name. Suddenly, his smile disintegrated. He shut the window.

"Let's go!" He locked the doors.

"What's wrong, dear?"

"Nothing. Just go!"

A few days later, the warm February sunshine was only a faded memory. Cold, damp gray painted the morning. Jerry Cain was at the Grayson breakfast table even before Katie Grayson could get there and make the coffee. Their kitchen was usually warm, a casual place to chat over a cup of her signature extra-bold coffee. That morning, when she pushed through the swinging door into the kitchen, her face was dark and the cheer in the kitchen flew out the window. She gasped and slapped her hand across her chest.

"Lord, Jerry, you about stopped my heart!" She plodded across the clay tile floor in her slippers and robe and poured herself a mug of coffee. "Thanks for making the coffee. Glad you feel at home."

Jerry didn't waste time with pleasantries. "Katie, I'm worried about Matt. He refuses to talk about the contracts. Says he'll do it later. Trouble is, we don't have a later."

Katie's cup hit the table with a thud. "Jerry, he's not sleeping. He paces the floor into the early hours. When he finally sleeps, he cries out. And then all those government types keep calling, wanting to pick his brain. See what he knows. He's …" She didn't finish.

Matt stumbled into the kitchen. His formerly soft curls were now greasy strings. Dark smudges defined eyes that were bloodshot. His skin was sallow, and if Jerry hadn't known for sure he was Matt Grayson, he'd have thought he was looking at a ghost.

"Morning, Jerry." Matt slapped Jerry on the back. "Trying to get on Mom's good side, huh? Dead giveaway, that frown of hers." He winked as he poured himself some coffee and slid into a chair beside Jerry.

"No, Matt, I wanted to see if I could get her to help me get you thinking about getting back to LA and work. But ..." Jerry shook his head, and for a moment, he looked sad. "...it looks like you're still not up to it."

Matt gulped some coffee and then spit back into his cup when it burned his tongue. "No, I'm up to it. Just haven't been sleeping well. Need a little more time; that's all."

Jerry shook his head. "Well, time is one thing that's getting short. You don't have much left."

All three fell silent. The morning light filtered through the pale-yellow curtains over the sink, but the rays were weak, almost lifeless. Jerry thought it fitted Matt perfectly—lifeless.

Jerry broke the silence. "Production company's been real good over this. They're being more patient than I've ever seen one be. Of course, all this publicity's not hurting any. Still, they have their limits. They don't understand why you're not on set yet. You're home; the bandages are gone. In their minds, they think you should be ready to work."

Abruptly, Matt stood causing the coffee to slosh from his cup. "Okay, I hear you. You don't need to hammer me." He threw the rest of his coffee into the sink and banged the mug on the counter before slamming the door behind him on his way out. Jerry glanced at Katie. They both shrugged.

Two weeks later, Jerry and Matt rocked on the back porch overlooking one of the endless cattle fields. It had been warm, breaking the string of cold, damp days that had settled on the area.

"Can't tell you how thrilled I am you're finally ready to get back to work. I just wish you'd forget this nonsense about going out to the crash site tomorrow. What more can you tell them? Those government boys have picked your brain till there's nothing left but empty cartilage. They've given you proof that you were the only one."

Matt chewed on the side of a cold cigar and muttered, "Jerry, don't push it. I told you I'd be returning to LA first of next week. You said that was good. So what're you hammering me for now?"

"You're carrying this new project, Matt. I won't kid you; it's going to be grueling, but you can do it. This is your ticket. This will solidify the ground you laid with your last film. You're hot now, but that heat only lasts a short while. No matter who, it eventually burns out, unless you keep the flames stoked." Jerry ground his cigarette in an ashtray on the table in front of them.

Staring vacantly at the last of the purples fading from the sky, Matt ran his finger across his upper lip over and over. Neither man spoke. Then, Jerry reached over and gripped Matt's arm. Matt pushed Jerry's hand away and stood so fast his chair tumbled to the floor. Kicking it away, he raked Jerry with his eyes.

"Just drop it, Jerry!" Without looking back, Matt jumped from the porch and jogged across the gravel driveway and over toward the barn. Jerry ran after him.

"I just don't get why going to the crash site is so important to you," Jerry sputtered as he panted from his short dash.

Matt glared at Jerry. "I need to. I have to … to see that the whole thing was real."

Sighing, Jerry finally said, "Okay, go. Get it settled. Maybe then, you'll start focusing on the life you have now. Maybe then you'll return to the Matt I know, the one who can appreciate what he was spared. Perhaps then you can forget all this horror and move on to what you're meant to do, to—"

"I'll never be that Matt again!" Matt interrupted Jerry with a shout. "No one could who's been through what I have. It's not something I'll ever forget!"

The following morning, Matt tromped behind a small army of government agents, investigators, and unnamed others as they pushed through walls of dense undergrowth on their trek to the crash site. The morning had dawned damp and cold. Matt shivered as the all-too-familiar gray murkiness swallowed him. It was like walking in a dream. He slipped on pine needles, and thorns ripped his clothing sometimes piercing his skin. By the time they reached the crash site, Matt was trembling.

As he glanced about, trying to study the area, he was surprised to find nothing was left. Latex-gloved officials combed the area, searching for minuscule bits of debris, anything related to the crash. When a rare piece that had been overlooked by all the previous searches was found, it was immediately sealed in a plastic bag and labeled. The only telltale signs were those marks stamped on nature: the flattened brush, broken trees, and charred area where the plane had burned.

As Matt watched the activity, it all came back in a blinding flash: the bright-orange glow, the concussion knocking him to the ground, the screaming, the adrenaline pumping through his veins as he'd pushed through the brush. He couldn't breathe. Everything faded, and that familiar darkness covered him as he slumped to the ground.

"He's down! Quick!" A dark-suited man turned just as Matt began to crumple and caught him before he hit the dirt. "Told you this was a mistake!" the man shouted over his shoulder to another dark-suited man. "It's just knocking him out. He's not going to be able to help us any."

"No, we needed to get him here. Even Dixon agreed with that. He knows something, and this place might trigger that memory. It might cause his subconscious to give something away. It's crucial we learn everything he knows."

Another man ran up and waved some smelling salts under Matt's nose. In a moment, Matt began to jerk and flail his arms at the offensive smell.

"Don't worry," the first suit said as Matt opened his eyes. "It's a bit overwhelming at first, all this." He nodded toward the crash site. "Just rest here for a moment. We'll get you out of here soon."

Matt nodded. He let his body slump against the tree as he tried to focus on some steady object that didn't wobble. But, everything, everyone, seemed to blur. If only his memories would do the same.

Matt awoke the following day with a new energy born from a new determination to do what he must. After calling various offices and not getting the answers he sought, with his temper threatening to boil over, he finally decided to call the office of the CEO of Gateway Air.

"Mr. Trushard's office," the secretary's voice was very cool, very proper, and very English.

"I need to speak with him, please," Matt said with barely concealed impatience.

"May I ask who is calling?"

"Matt Grayson."

There was a pause. "Uh, Mr. Grayson. Yes. Uh, Mr. Trushard is not available at this time. He's—"

Matt's temper boiled over. "I don't care where he is; you get him for me! I don't care if he's climbing the Matterhorn or in Tibet meditating with some ancient spirit. It's been nothing but a run-around, and I'm tired of it. I know your airline is hurting, and the publicity from the crash is not good. However, I assure you, I can make it much worse. The press is camping on my doorstep. I'm bombarded with questions about the crash constantly. All I have to say is the airline is refusing to speak with me and—"

"Mr. Grayson!" the woman shouted over Matt's voice. The English accent had flown back to the United Kingdom and a low-country drawl had replaced it. "Mr. Trushard will speak with you now."

Two days later, Matt met with Mr. Trushard at the international headquarters for Gateway Air in Dallas. Mr. Trushard's young, shapely, and decidedly un-English assistant had greeted him and ushered him directly into the top-floor office.

"I don't understand, Mr. Grayson ..." Mr. Trushard twirled a gold pen between his manicured fingers, "... why you are not satisfied. You've visited the site; the rescue crews have assured us there was no one else, and even you told the NTSB you were the only one. We've accounted for every passenger on that plane, either with a body or—"

"I'm having second thoughts."

"Just what is it you want us to do, Mr. Grayson?" His voice was cold, and Matt felt the wall solidify between them.

"I want evidence. I want to see proof of positive identification. I need the passenger manifest. The home addresses, phone, family information, all of that, I need it."

Mr. Trushard shook his head. "That's highly irregular. We do not give that information out. We simply cannot. You should know, Mr. Grayson, security protocols do not allow us to violate passenger privacy unless it is considered a national security threat. I can assure you, however, all families have been notified."

"I'm not sure there is any living family left for this person."

Mr. Trushard straightened and leaned across the expansive mahogany desk toward Matt. "Which passenger are you referring to?"

Something in his expression warned Matt. "Just another passenger I met."

"Mr. Grayson, the manifest will tell us who sat beside you. It won't be hard to deduce to whom you refer." The silence between them further fortified the stone wall the man had erected earlier.

Then, without further explanation, the CEO's face softened. "I know it's hard, and people cope with it differently. I wish—"

Matt's shoulders slumped. Maybe it wasn't worth it. Maybe he was chasing a dream. "Please, just let me see what you have. I'll get out of your hair then."

Mr. Trushard leaned back in his chair, still fiddling with his pen. His eyes were narrowed into tiny slits as he studied Matt. After several long seconds of silence, he dropped the pen on his desk. "Very well."

That evening, as Matt flew back to Houston, his head throbbed. As he read through the documents for a third time, he idly traced the scar on his forehead. He had her phone number and her address.

Mr. Trushard had even given him a copy of the dental records the NTSB had used to identify her. So many had been burned beyond recognition, he'd said.

In his hands, he held it—irrefutable evidence. What more could he ask? Copies of the reports from the rescue crews, every word of the documentation indicating where every victim was found, including him, he'd read it all. He'd been discovered nearly sixty yards from the plane, lying facedown in pine needles, soaked with rain and blood. The flesh on his hand was ripped. A gash oozed on his forehead, and a jagged tear in the skin of his right thigh had leaked more blood. He had been unconscious when they'd taken him away—alone, no one and nothing else nearby. That was all the reports said.

Depression weighed down his shoulders like granite boulders. That hopeless, it's-no-use feeling grew. Finally, he put his head against the seat and dozed. There were no dreams.

The next day, Matt drove to an address of an apartment on the west side of Houston, near the Galleria. It was the address the airline gave him. It was an older building framed by towering magnolias and surrounded on three sides by a thick grove of pines. It didn't take much of a bribe for the aging manager to let him in. Once inside, Matt wasn't sure which shocked him more: the barren apartment or the stench from the dead cat on the floor.

"I don't understand it, mister. I really don't." The old manager scratched his head and held his nose with his other hand. "I don't know of no one who's come this way. She kept pretty much to herself. Don't think she had no family. Except for someone from where she worked, you're the only one who's come 'round since ... it happened."

"Remember any names?"

"No. But they came, let me see, I guess a few days or so after it happened. Said they'd been told to get her stuff out. They flashed some official-looking papers that looked okay to me. I let 'em in. Didn't take them too long. Guess there wasn't much to move." His drooping eyes peered at Matt. "I'll go and take care of the cat." He shuffled out, leaving Matt alone in the large room.

Methodically, as if searching for something he couldn't see but knew was there, Matt combed every inch of the place. There was no trace of dirt or litter anywhere. He checked the closet in the bedroom and the cabinets in the bath and the kitchen. He even pulled out every drawer to see if something had gotten jammed between the runners. He found nothing that would suggest she'd ever graced the place. Only the stink of the poor cat, which looked as if he'd starved to death, kept the apartment from being ready to rent to the next occupant.

Matt didn't wait for the old man to return. There was nothing more he could do there. In his truck, he wound his way back to Westheimer and then over to the West Sam Houston Tollway. How fortunate he was to have people who cared for him, to have someone who'd never let his cat starve, to have people who cherished his memory and would pass it on. It was something that poor girl had never had.

Suddenly, Matt remembered the pad he'd found in what was left of his clothes after the crash. *Houston Chronicle. Barry.* Slamming his brakes, Matt veered to the next exit and reworked his way back through the maze of streets until he found himself downtown and before the main offices of the Houston paper.

At the front desk, he said, "I need to see Barry."

The security guard glanced up as he slowly returned the phone receiver to its place and glared at Matt. "Barry who?"

"I don't know. Just Barry. He works here, or did, with a woman. Lynn. Lynn McCane."

The man's jaw clenched, and his eyes narrowed. "Just what kind of joke are you playing? Lynn McCane died in that plane crash."

"I know. I know." Matt's shoulders slumped. "I was with her."

"Well, lucky for you. Listen; there is one Barry who works here. Barry Swindmore. Maybe that's the person you're seeking. But he's on temporary leave right now. He won't be back for a few weeks."

"Is there anyone else I could talk to about her?"

The man shrugged. "I could put you through to human resources."

Minutes later, Matt stood before the human resources department receptionist waiting for her acknowledgment. The young girl slammed the phone down and muttered at it, "No, we don't have any positions in die-tay." She looked up suddenly and blushed.

"Uh, sorry. What can I—oh, it's you! Matt Grayson! Oh my!" Her blush deepened, and she fumbled for the first piece of paper she could find, an employment application. She thrust it at him and stared, large, white teeth protruding between her lips as she grinned.

Matt glanced at the paper and smiled. "No, I'm not here for a job, yet." His charm seemed to calm her. "I need some information, however."

"Anything, anything at all, Mr. Grayson."

"Can you tell me anything about a Lynn McCane who used to work here?"

The girl blanched. "Uh, she's the one killed in the crash?"

Matt nodded, trying to ignore the growing lump in his throat. "That's right."

A middle-aged woman with dark, luminous skin strolled into the waiting area toward him. She stopped. Like a hen spreading her protective wings over her biddies, she planted her hands on the back of the receptionist's chair and towered over the girl.

"Is there a problem here?" she asked with a smooth voice that hinted at tropical roots. After raking Matt from head to toe with beady eyes, as if evaluating him for a position in the mailroom, she added, "I'm Leticia Lamb, employment manager. What can I do for you?"

"Uh, this man was asking 'bout Lynn McCane," the blushing receptionist interjected.

There was a long pause, and then Leticia folded her wings and, with what Matt could swear was a cluck, said, "Well, come along. Let me see what I can tell you."

Matt followed the woman to her small cubicle of an office, which was hidden behind ancient green curtains beyond the receptionist's desk.

"Lynn McCane, as you know," she said as she perched in her swivel chair behind her desk, "was killed in a plane crash back in January. Of course, I guess you know that. You were there. And that's all we know."

Brilliant, Matt thought. *And this lady worked for a daily newspaper.*

"I know all that." Matt fought to keep his voice level. "What I need to know is what kind of work she did, who she worked with, anything like that."

"She did feature articles, various assignments, worked under the features editor. Unfortunately, she's no longer with us, left shortly before the crash. We're still looking to fill the position." For a moment, she looked hopefully at Matt.

"What about someone named Barry?"

"What about him?"

"Did she work with him?"

"Not directly, no. They both were supervised by the features editor. But he's out of the country on a special leave and won't be back for several weeks."

"Would you know who might have authorized the removal of all Ms. McCane's things from her apartment?"

Leticia was suddenly quiet. Her lips pinched. "Where would you get the idea I'd know something like that?"

"The apartment manager said someone from where Lynn worked came and moved her things. He said they came a few days after the crash."

"I can assure you no one here authorized it. We don't have that kind of authority. It would have to be someone personally involved with her. We don't get that personal with employees."

With a sigh, Matt stood and extended his hand. "Thank you, Ms. Lamb, for your time."

She jumped to her feet and grabbed the first piece of paper she could find, another employment application. "Could I have your autograph?" she said, suddenly grinning.

Two days later, Matt was speeding north on I-45 past The Woodlands. At the area where they'd parked when he'd come with the NTSB, Matt left the road and pushed his truck through the bramble as far as he could. Still, it was at least a couple miles, maybe three more, to the crash site. A path of sorts had been worn, the briars broken and torn, the way much easier. As he pushed his way through the still-dense growth, briars nipped at his flesh and the damp and cold of that night seeped into his bones. An overwhelming urgency to get away overcame him. Chills tickled his neck, even though it was eighty degrees, and his hands were damp and clammy.

Matt found the crash scene. Slowly, he circled the area, head bowed, as his eyes scanned every inch of the earth. Methodically, he made his way toward the area where he thought he'd found her, but there was nothing there. Only the smallest hint of broken brush and crushed briars belied the truth.

Next, he traced what he believed was the path he'd taken through the woods until he came to the place where they told him he'd been found. There was no evidence he'd ever been there. The futility, the senselessness of the tragedy, washed over him. He paced in circles for a while and then suddenly sank to his knees and pressed his face to the ground, crying out, "Oh God, why? Why?"

When his sobbing quieted, he looked about him. Nothing had changed, yet he felt different. She was gone. There was nothing more he could do. Life must go on. It was all he had left. He'd been given a reprieve, bonus time he didn't deserve. The guilt grew. Maybe it would have been better if he'd been lost and the woman spared. Apparently, God had different plans.

At the edge of the clearing, he paused and looked over his shoulder. Tears had dried on his face. He licked his lips and tasted the lingering saltiness. He whispered, "Good-bye." Turning, he strolled slowly back to his truck. The next day, he would fly back to Los Angeles.

CHAPTER 5

The young woman in the metal-railed bed was surrounded by five men in crisp lab jackets. Behind her, monitors beeped, and machines purred. No beat of the heart, no breath, no synaptic flash occurred that was not recorded, either by machine or by the unwavering stares of the men. The air was circulated through multiple electrostatic filtering devices so that not a trace of outside air or any contaminates could possibly skew any lab values or reactions. Still, there was a hint of the sterile smell so common to hospitals and operating rooms. It didn't matter to the woman, however. She was unaware.

The woman was unaware of the bright, chemically enhanced blood flowing through plastic tubing into her arm, unaware another section rushed spent, depleted blood away, unaware she lived. As the men watched, waited, and considered all possible outcomes, she slept, unmoving, uncaring the world outside her sealed, sterile prison progressed as it always did, self-absorbed and unaware.

"Her lack of reaction is puzzling," the first man said, the cadence in his voice suggesting a French background. "Our treatments seem to have no effect."

"It is amazing, Phillippe," the man next to him added; his voice was loud and not smooth like the first man's. "She should've had some response by now."

A tall man with flecks of gray in his brown hair declared, "Well, I think you're relying too much on merit proven solely by tests of previous versions of this compound. Since only two days have passed since this treatment was initiated, we have no way of knowing how fast or whether it will work at all. This version has not been tested on human subjects yet."

Phillippe responded to the tall man, "But, Dereck, we had extreme success with lab animals. Phenomenal, do you not agree? Combine those results with the earlier human trials, and there is no reason, none, to keep from having some great optimism here."

The fifth man, who looked as if he'd spent the better years of his life in a wrestling ring, was, in truth, the man in charge. Charles Benson stared at the woman for several moments before directing his gaze at the others. "Have we gotten any identification yet?"

The men shook their heads. Phillippe said, "I took it upon myself to run the genetic screen. We should have a result from the database anytime now."

The woman groaned, and everyone fell silent and watched. She jerked spasmodically a few times but never opened her eyes. When she calmed and returned to her previous immobile state, the men stepped back from the bed and resumed their quiet discussion.

"I see no change," Charles said. "Looks like the same cycles are repeating. If the result is no better than this by Friday, I'm going to recommend we abort. We've shown nothing on her we haven't been able to show in earlier studies. We cannot afford to continue with this treatment if we get nothing better than a repeat of previous trials."

"Charles, don't you care what happens to her?" Dereck asked. "She will die if we stop treatment. That's a given. Our intervention is the only thing keeping her alive. Is this not the purpose of our work, to preserve life?"

Charles's eyes narrowed. When he spoke, his tone was sharp. "No one can guarantee life. Our work is to enhance life's qualities, to make it better for those who live, preserve it when feasible. Look at her. She's hanging on by a thread, a weak thread we gave her. You call that quality? She's not even aware she's in the world. Now, who wants a life like that? Gentlemen, if we cannot improve her life in some meaningful way, then why should we force her to continue suffering?"

Dereck's scowl deepened, but Charles kept talking, ignoring his colleague's agitation.

"Sometimes, it's a choice we must make. Besides, think of what we'll learn by terminating now. The postmortem knowledge gained could be phenomenal. It would be our first, controlled termination. We will have controlled each moment, each action from beginning to end. There will be no external influences to skew our numbers." Charles gripped Dereck's arm as he peered into his eyes and lowered his voice.

"We'll save others with what we learn from her."

"The sacrifice of one for the good of many, huh?" A red flush crept up Dereck's neck, and he jerked free of Charles's grasp. "What happened to our oath, to do no harm? You took it; you should know it."

Charles glared at Dereck. "Medical costs being what they are today, we can no longer afford the archaic belief of value in the individual life. It was just that belief that collapsed our country's medical system. No, we must work for the good of the collective whole."

Dereck squared his shoulders and stepped toward Charles. Silence filled the room, but an undercurrent of tension hummed. A few beads of perspiration popped out on Charles's face.

Dereck broke the silence. He spoke softly but with a firmness that dug its heels into the growing tension. "I refuse to accept your blinded beliefs. The individual is what made us great. Saving the individual is what has fueled this project. I refuse to deny the individual's value; it is why I work to preserve it."

The silence was false. Underneath its facade were the curling, forked tendrils of anger, distrust, and confusion. A few of those present glared at Charles. The rest stared at Dereck. Finally, Charles spoke.

"Gentlemen, this meeting is finished. As director of this project, I should not have to remind you that each of you, no exceptions, are expected to follow all directives, despite any personal feelings. I will advise you of any developments and changes of future protocol regarding this case."

Charles snapped his folder shut and hurried from the room. The others, puzzled by the unanticipated exchange, turned to the young woman and watched her.

"Her brain waves look good," Phillippe said as he studied a printout. "That's encouraging. She might make it yet."

"Only with help, Phillippe," Dereck answered quietly. "Only with help."

After the group filed from the room, Dereck DeBoe remained. He stood by the sleeping woman's side, stroking his chin and watching. Finally, with a big sigh, he too turned and strolled from the room.

Late that evening, Dereck reappeared by the woman's bed. He checked her vital signs, noting them in a chart he carried, ignoring the one hanging from the end of her bed. Next, he checked all the monitors and the lines running to and from her slight body. After scribbling some notes in his chart, he went to the supply cabinet and pulled out a couple of glass vials. After filling each with samples of her blood and labeling them, he quickly left the room.

Early the following morning, before the others could even think of the day's rounds, Dereck was by the woman's side again. His hair was disheveled, and dark circles ran under eyes that were bloodshot. However, those were the only signs belying his lack of sleep. His movement was sharp and fluid, laced with determination.

After completing his routine check of all readings and vitals, he pulled a small vial from his lab coat pocket. Grabbing a syringe from the supply cabinet, he inserted the needle into the vial and pulled the plunger back until the tube filled with amber liquid. Quickly, he injected the contents into the woman's IV line. Finally, he leaned over and let her breath fan against his cheek. For a long time, he stood motionless, watching and waiting, recording his impressions, both in his eidetic memory and in the chart he held. After a while, a slow smile spread across his face. He scribbled some final notes in his personal chart and hurried from the room.

Late that afternoon, Dereck was back by the woman's side. After completing his exam and updating his notations, he again injected her IV line with the same amber fluid he had injected earlier that morning. Then, he pulled a chair up by the bed, sat down, and watched. For several hours, he sat there, barely moving. The girl moved more than he did. The cycles were regular; she would moan, thrash against the covers, and then stop all movement, only to repeat the cycle again an hour later. Dereck smiled when each cycle ended. He noted the time and made comments in his chart as he continued watching.

For two days, Dereck repeated his secret routine. On the third, after nearly four hours of observation and pleased with the results he was seeing, he decided to leave for a short break. It was then that Phillippe burst in on him.

"What's going on?" Phillippe's dark eyes burned with accusation as he strolled across the chamber to Dereck's side.

"She's improving," Dereck said softly but with a rapid cadence. He glanced at Phillippe, and a new light was shining in his eyes. "There seems to be a trend toward a shortening of the cycles, less time in the catatonic stage, more in the active. I think she's shrugging it off. She's pushing past the barrier."

"You've documented this?" Phillippe said with a hint of the cadence of southern France. His brows rose.

"Of course, it's all here in the chart." Dereck patted the metal cover he held.

"The others, do they know?"

"Not yet. It is a bit soon."

"But this would assure continuation of this course of study. It's the proof we need. It's what Charles is demanding, is it not?"

Dereck sighed. "Yes, but … well, sometimes, I think Charles is her worst enemy. He seems to forget we're using humans to experiment. I can't get past my oath to *do no harm*."

Phillippe snorted. "Yeah, you Americans, you feel so obligated to make sure you don't hurt your patients. It's not how I learned medicine. Some of the smaller, lesser medical schools in Delhi have no qualms about pushing those lines a bit if it helps us to learn something we otherwise could not have achieved. Perhaps Charles would benefit from a little of that training. We could do without him for a bit." Phillippe grinned, making his eyes twinkle.

"Do without? No, it's his research that gave us a foundation for this treatment."

Silence snaked between them. Dereck gripped the cold metal of the bed's railing. For a long while, he studied the woman as Phillippe stood beside him. A small frown flickered across his face. He turned back to Phillippe.

"Ever get any identification on her?"

Phillippe shook his head. "Nothing yet. The genetics group has it now. They said they are still working. I was promised, however, that I'd have a report by Friday."

The woman stirred and groaned. The thrashing began again. Dereck checked the IV flow rate and noted it, along with the time and duration of her movements. Soon, they ceased, but in an even shorter interval, they repeated. He grinned at Phillippe. "She is making progress. You can't deny it." Then he added, "I was just going to take a break. I'll be back in a few minutes. Feel free to watch, if you like."

Phillippe pointed to the metal chart Dereck held. "Mind if I read through that while you're gone?"

Dereck's hesitation was almost invisible. "No …" He handed the chart to Phillippe.

When Dereck returned less than twenty minutes later, Phillippe was rummaging through a black leather bag. He jumped when Dereck tapped him on the shoulder.

"Charles was in here. Demanded to know what I was doing. Then, he wanted to know where you were. I told him I didn't know. He's gone searching for you."

A few beads of sweat popped out on Dereck's forehead. "Did he say what he wanted?"

Phillippe shook his head. "He searched the room looking for something he didn't find. Then he said he'd find you, sooner or later."

Dereck cast a quick glance at the black bag by Phillippe's feet. "Thanks, for covering. I think I'd better get going, you too!"

Before either could leave, the woman mumbled something. Both men froze and stared at her as if all life had suspended while waiting for her next movement. She mumbled again, writhing in the covers as if being poked and prodded.

"Tell Barry! Tell him now!" she screamed.

Before Phillippe could finish checking her heart rate and respiration and Dereck could check the attachments to the monitors, she relaxed and her body went limp. Each man turned to the other and raised his brows.

"Looks like she's making much faster progress than even you planned," Phillippe said.

Dereck nodded and then smiled. "You're right. This is good. Very good. Even Charles cannot deny the treatment is working." Taking the metal chart from Phillippe, he hugged it to his chest as he strolled from the room.

Two weeks later, Phillippe, Charles, and several colleagues not previously associated with the woman's treatment were gathered around her. Only Dereck DeBoe was missing.

The woman sat in the middle of her hospital bed, talking and smiling, even joking with a couple of attendants as they straightened her covers and brought fresh toiletries to her. All life support had been removed. Only one IV line remained attached to the woman's right arm. Except for the IV and the hospital bed, she looked as if she should be outdoors, engaged in some strenuous physical activity. Her skin was a dewy pink, blemish free. Her energy levels appeared to be high, for she wiggled and rocked as if listening to some music only she could hear.

While Phillippe and Charles were excited, even amazed at what they were seeing, the other physicians seemed puzzled, unsure as to what was playing out before them. Charles turned to the group and smiled grandly.

"As you can see, we have a subject here who is the picture of health. Just four weeks ago, she was not expected to live another day. Since our treatment began, she has improved moment by moment to what you see today. We can only conclude that our treatment was responsible." He continued in a softer voice, "Our course of study determined, based on her reactions to our initial treatments, that a variation of our compound used in conjunction with some altered hormones was necessary to achieve the level of success that we seem to have found. This woman was saved only because of our radical treatment administered in a timely manner. Had we waited for the usual approvals and run the standard clinical trials and then waited for the various red-tape offices to affix their stamps of approval, this woman would've been in the grave for years. Given she's recovered so nicely and has shown miraculous progress, we feel our procedure is justified.

"No doubt, we all know the horrendous hassles, the endless streams of red tape, the months, even years of often repetitive and unnecessary testing that are mandated in order to gain approval for anything designed to improve and prolong life. The public feels these time-consuming and irritating procedures are acceptable because they serve to protect individuals. Yet, none of us can argue that they often harm rather than protect. Our colleagues in the world outside these walls, if they knew of our work, might frown on our approach and might even go so far as to demand we stop the miraculous work we've begun simply because we didn't adhere to their protocols. Yet, I don't think even they could argue with our success."

The men facing Charles seemed unsure, uncertain as to how to take his words. Charles increased the wattage on his smile.

"Results compiled from years of study, and from our latest control group, have shown some amazing trends. We found that a variation of the compound originally extracted from pine rosin, administered in addition to some altered hormones, precipitated new, life-generating results. We've proven this combination successful in regenerating the very essence of life on a cellular level. Tissue, previously so diseased as to be considered doomed, regenerated. New, healthy tissue was generated by living organisms treated with our compound. In the process, diseased tissue was literally choked out, almost like a weed chokes out grass, except in this, we get favorable results."

There were a few snickers and grins that quickly disappeared under Charles's stern gaze.

"So," one of the men finally asked, "what's so special? It doesn't sound much different from some of the earliest work here."

Charles smiled and patiently expounded. "Gentlemen, frankly I'm surprised I must explain it to you. But think for a moment. Just what possibilities can the generation, on a cellular level, of new, disease-free tissue mean? This is not just about erasing the outward signs of aging, which we have done in some cases. And it's not about stopping it, which we've also accomplished."

Charles's eyes scanned the group. "Have we, our profession, not searched for years for a cure for cancer? Have we not toiled long hours yearning for some answer to such things as liver disease, diabetes, and kidney disease? What about AIDS? Can you not see it? By controlling cell functions at the molecular level, the potential we can harness is almost limitless. And we're only on the threshold. The door of opportunity is wide open. There are no limits to what we're sitting on here."

Chins were scratched. Eyebrows rose. Heads shook. One smiled. He spoke, "What is the chemical structure? How is it derived?"

Another asked, "What is the duration of effect?"

A short man on the edge of the group, interjected, "What contraindications have you noted?"

"Aaah!" Charles arched his back. "The drawbacks. Yes, there have been a few. There have been setbacks, even some mistakes. However, in this latest trial, we believe we have found an answer to our biggest problem. The chemical reactions associated with the process leave residues, which, when in contact with various forms of the compound we've developed, produce toxic by-products." Charles didn't linger on his words, didn't give pause for thought. He rushed ahead.

"These toxins have been the bane of most all our research. Only one other test subject, one from some of our earliest trials, seemed to have a similar reaction as this woman. And while the majority of those receiving this version, the most potent and promising version of our compound, suffered from various degrees of disrupted, altered, and damaged brain function, we attempted to compensate for these drawbacks. However, we were not successful in the long term. But this woman has reacted differently. Through exhaustive blood chemistry studies and other tests, we realized she possessed a group of genes that produced a substance that, in conjunction with the altered hormones she was given, changed neurotransmitter activity, thereby protecting brain functions.

"This individual ..." He pointed to the woman. "... is the first to regenerate new tissue without any compromise in brain function. Toxic levels have remained low, and we have every reason to believe she will continue in a positive trend. If indeed we are correct, then we will have found the answer to the problem that has prevented complete success with this project.

"We still have to test this theory. To do so, it is necessary to suppress her memory and implant new memory links. By conducting a series of tests, ultimately exposing her to a trial in the world outside this facility, we can determine if indeed we've found our solution."

The group stared at Charles, stunned to silence. Questions moved their lips; concerns flirted with their eyes. But only one asked, "You're saying you have to brainwash the patient in order for her to survive the treatment?"

No one spoke. Charles glared briefly at the man and then smiled. "For others, yes, but not this one. She's the exception to the rule. In the others, it was difficult to produce a new identity. As you know, all who received that version died. However, this woman's reactions are so different that we feel she may hold the key to helping the others overcome their negative physiological reactions. By determining exactly how her body reacts to both the amnesiac portions of the treatment and to nonerasure conditions, we can develop new uses for this compound and this treatment. Come; let's see where we stand at this point."

Charles led the way back to the woman's bed. The others encircled him. Charles leaned toward her and bestowed upon her a broad smile, one so wide it crinkled the skin around his eyes.

"What is your name?"

"Linda McGowan."

"And, Linda, where do you live?"

"Van Nuys, California."

"Have you always lived there?"

"Yes."

"Where do you work?"

"I'm a reporter for the *Los Angeles Times.*"

"Are you married?"

"No."

"Have you ever been married?"

"No."

"Good. Now, can you tell me about your accident?"

"Accident?" She glanced at each of the men and seemed puzzled. Then she exclaimed, "Oh, the accident! Yes, I remember. It was on I-5, near San Diego. I crashed. Was hit head-on, hit-and-run. Broke my right arm, suffered a concussion. I even had to have stitches on my forehead, leg, and upper arm. I was in the hospital for a month. Then, I came here for rehab."

"Very good." Charles backed away from the bed, and the others followed. "As you can see, in our reprogramming, we tried to keep things consistent or as nearly consistent as possible to the original identity. But this being our first field test using the latest regimen, we want to see how well she will stand up in situations similar enough to her former life and still not overcompensate.

"We have a planned period of gradual introduction to stimuli which will determine whether the past has truly been repressed and the new is functioning as primary. We will take routine blood, urine, and other samples to monitor toxicity levels. We also will have in place observation and safeguard controls. This test will be strenuous. We need to see if our subject can endure the rigors of life in a new place without relapsing into the old one. So, if this test is successful, then the work can go either way. You can use this miracle compound to heal and forget or to heal and remember."

"My goodness, I cannot believe you've done this, and so soon!" One of the men couldn't take his eyes off the woman.

Another rubbed his eyebrows repeatedly. "I am interested in how you managed to perfect the transformation."

Another added, "She certainly seems recovered. Everything appears to be in place."

Then one asked. "Wasn't Dereck DeBoe part of this research? Wasn't he the one who initiated the alteration of the molecular structure that produced this response?"

Charles didn't answer but frowned at Phillippe. Suddenly, Phillippe turned back to the woman.

"Do you remember anything about the crash?"

She bit her lip. Words started to form but died away. "No. I can't."

"But something bothers you when you think of it?"

She frowned. "Well, nothing I can see. My head aches a little; that's all."

Phillippe rejoined his colleagues. "Is that acceptable? She still has a physiological reaction to attempted memory of the event."

Charles beckoned the group to move away from the bedside and follow him to the adjacent observation room. He leaned toward them and spoke in a hushed tone.

"The fact she's only got a headache is very good, far as I'm concerned. In a short while, all physical connections to the event should cease." Charles stared pointedly at Phillippe. "That is, if *your* calculations are correct—the ones you said you performed."

A hint of red tinged Phillippe's ears.

Charles continued, "Each of you is fully aware just how important it is that all memory be repressed. If it is not or if it returns, it would, in effect, create a physical domino chain reaction, which would culminate in death. And we still haven't perfected a way of preventing it."

The gravity of the situation settled on each man's shoulders.

However, eagerness to proceed with the groundbreaking, revolutionary, history-making, and potentially lucrative research proved stronger than any reservations on whether the work was ethical or not. Greed won the round. Not even Phillippe was strong enough to resist the certain profit motive.

Charles stepped up to the room's window and watched the woman for a moment. He smiled and returned his gaze to the group behind him.

"Gentlemen, this meeting is over for now. If you would like to continue to monitor this woman's progress, you may log onto our trials website. The trial number is x-one-zero-one-five, and your password is your ID number."

As the men filed quickly from the room, the woman curled beneath her covers in a fetal position. In less than thirty seconds, she was sleeping, a smile curving her lips.

Charles caught Phillippe's arm as the latter tried to scoot from the room. Out of range of the others, he spoke quietly but forcefully. "Explain that comment about this being Dereck's work? Did you not present it to me as your own?"

Phillippe swallowed. "Dereck initiated the research, tried the alternate regimen. I joined him on it and took over for him." He suddenly grasped Charles's arm and stared into his eyes. "No matter whose it is, can you not see she's still suffering? The healing is incomplete. Besides, we don't know how well the memory repression will work in combination with all these other compounds. It's too risky."

"How else can we proceed? We have no other choice, now that we know her background."

"Her background?" Phillippe asked, eyes widening. "What do you mean?"

"You know about the genetic ID, the match we got, but there's more. This girl knows about us. She dug up some information on this facility, went so far as to divulge what she knew to a certain congressman who is *very* interested in this operation's viability. I was told to terminate her immediately. It's only because she's shown such great potential in providing our breakthrough that we've been allowed to proceed. Regardless of her response, she will not ever be allowed to return to her old identity. Really, there's no choice for her. Either we use her to test this new treatment, suppress her memory, and keep her silent, or she's to be eliminated now. Now, which do you prefer? Personally, I'm surprised they're even going along with our continued testing. The risk of testing this, in the real world, is great."

Phillippe nodded slowly, never taking his dark eyes off of Charles. He continued to gaze up at the Nordic-looking and even more intimidating man. Compared to Charles, Phillippe was slender and short with dark hair and a protruding nose. In his part of France on the coast near Cannes, he was a commoner who was not distinct in the masses, but the work he now pursued would change all that. It could make him a hero to his countrymen; more importantly, it would make him rich.

Charles continued, "I understand you want credit for this undertaking, that it was your additional work that is sending us to this new point of progress. You believe this will change the face of medicine. Who wouldn't want to be a part of it? Our lives, all of us, will be changed because of this." He gripped Phillippe's arm. "Do you realize the potential we're sitting on? The possible uses if this trial goes well? Think about it, Phillippe. Really think. It's staggering what we could do. But we can't flinch when it becomes necessary to proceed in a manner that is beyond the normal, accepted limits. We cannot lose sight of our goal."

CHAPTER 6

Balancing a bag of groceries in one hand and holding her key in the other, Linda McGowan pushed open the door to her apartment with her elbow. As she stood on the threshold and stared into the almost-naked room, only a few pieces of furniture randomly scattered about the small space, she froze. An overstuffed sofa, two floor-to-ceiling bookshelf units, and a small kitchen with an eating area greeted her with a chill not entirely physical. The air had been cooled by a functioning air conditioner. *Thank goodness,* she thought, as the humidity was high that day. Her hair hung in damp tendrils about her face. There was no hint of any smell, however. Rather, it seemed sterilized, overly clean. Was it really home?

After dropping her bags on the kitchen counter and locking herself in, Linda wandered about the open space between the kitchen and the small living area. She ran her fingers across the soft fabric of the sofa. At the bookshelves, she pulled an old volume out. As she flipped through its pages, spirals of dust careened into the fading sunbeams, and she sneezed. After wiping her eyes, she strolled to the front window and leaned against its frame. As she gazed at the parking lot below, she realized there was no comfortable familiarity about any of it, no stirring of memories past. Simply, there was no feeling.

In the kitchen, there was a stack of mail on the counter, bills mostly, topped off with a large Post-It. Written in large block letters was the command, "Call me as soon as you get this!" Call who? She wasn't sure. The docs had said it might happen. They said to expect holes in the memory. But was she supposed to feel so blank, so empty?

The shrill ringing of the phone pierced her cloud of isolation.

"Linda?" a woman's voice asked. "Don't hang up, Linda. It's me, Cherie … Remember, Cherie? You work with me at the *Los Angeles Times*. I'm your boss, your editor, your best friend."

Best friend? "I'm sorry. I …"

Cherie's voice was warm. "Don't give it a second thought, dear. We all understand. We're just glad you're back, recovered, and ready to work—I hope!"

Everyone? Linda glanced at the bills on her counter. "Well, if I can get past all the mush posing as my brain."

Cherie chuckled softly. "There was never any mush in your skull, only solid, hard-core, factual details and a nose for news. It's that nose I want you to use now. I'm making my famous chicken cacciatore for dinner, and I won't take no for an answer."

Linda thought about it. "I'm really not too hungry. Could I take a rain check?"

There was a long pause. "Oh, come on, girl. You've got to eat something. May as well be my cooking. I can't say yours was ever all that great." Linda didn't respond. "Come on; I'm just teasing. Besides, I've got to get my star reporter back up and running. Can't have you starving yourself, now can I?"

Linda's gut thawed a little, and she chuckled softly. "Okay. You got me."

"Good."

"Cherie?"

"Yes?"

"Where do you live?"

"Don't worry, honey. I'll bring it over to your place. See you soon!"

Late that evening, after too much cacciatore, wine, and laughter, Linda strolled about her apartment, a contented smile curling her lips.

The evening had wiped away some of the cold emptiness she'd felt on coming home. It was like slipping into a soft, worn sweatshirt and curling up before a warm fire. Cherie had helped her remember life before the accident. It was an affirmation she hadn't grasped the need of until she received it.

"And," Cherie had said as she'd set a steaming cup of Kahlua-laced coffee before Linda, "I think the coming month is going to be big for you. First, we have the previews and premieres of the summer blockbusters. You'll do a piece or two on that for me, I know. Then, I'd like to get some personal interviews for a series the paper wants on new talent hitting the big screen this summer. I thought you'd be interested in doing most of the work on that. Of course, you'll need to do a little digging, find some dirt, and get the backgrounds. I know you usually work from home, but I think for a while, it'd be good for you to come in to the office, get reacquainted with everyone. There're a lot of new faces since you left."

"Reacquainted?" Linda shook her head slowly. "Funny, when I try to think of everyone, I can't bring any faces to mind."

Cherie squeezed Linda's hand. "That's okay. Your doctor said this would happen." She added quickly, "Didn't he?" Cherie dropped Linda's hand and grinned. "Hey, smile a little. It doesn't hurt. Relax and start living again. Besides, I'm so glad to have my friend back. I missed you!"

Later, in the early morning hours, when only sporadic traffic outside her apartment punctuated the silence of the darkness, Linda studied the pictures on her wall. There was a pair of countryside scenes in the collection. One was of a field filled with wildflowers of every hue imaginable. In the other, horses romped across endless meadows. Idly, she ran her finger across the picture of the flowers. An odd feeling churned in her stomach. It must have been the cacciatore acting up.

Pacing the apartment, she stopped in front of her bookshelves. After glancing at the titles, some old, some new, she reached for a dusty tome and flipped through its pages. It was as if she'd never seen it before. The leather binding and heavy paper were strangers. Returning it to its place, she pulled another out. It was an old geography book that looked at least twenty years old. Inside, she found a map of the state of Texas. The next pages featured pictures from around the state. One in particular caught her eye. Bluebonnets, the state flower, filled a rolling meadow. They cast a brilliant-blue blanket across the entire page. It was a peaceful scene, clouds dotting a blue sky, flowers in the foreground. It made her think of springtime in the east. Why would she think of spring anywhere east of California? She'd never lived anywhere else in her life. Still, the lure of the warm sun caressing her shoulders and the heady fragrance of the carpet of flowers—it all seemed so real that she could almost reach out and pluck one.

Linda slammed the book shut and dropped it on the table. She pinched her eyebrows into a frown as she stared unseeing at the wall. She was a journalist—facts only, that was what she dealt in. Nothing fanciful or fictional. Wherever her thoughts were at the moment, she had no clue what they meant. Those flowers in that book were not fictional, but she had no idea how she knew that.

Still lost in thought, she paced around the room several times before she realized the dull pounding at the base of her skull was working its way up to her forehead. Within a minute, she was gripped by a full-blown, muscle-constricting, pressure-throbbing headache that weighed on her like a lead weight. She pushed her feet toward the kitchen and grabbed the first cup she found sitting beside the sink. She filled it with tap water. Holding it to her lips, she felt her hands shake as she spilled the contents into her mouth. Streams ran down each side of her chin. When it was empty, Linda immediately filled it and drained it again. After the third cupful, she stumbled into her bedroom and fell on top of the bed. She didn't bother to undress. She didn't crawl under the covers. Instead, she lay on top of the bed, shaking, swallowing, and fighting the urge to throw up.

When Linda awoke, she was no longer on the bed but curled in a fetal heap on the floor beside it. Her limbs felt like jelly. She wasn't totally confident they would support her weight as she gripped the bedcovers and pulled herself up.

The bottle of pills she'd been given, along with the instructions to take two daily and more if she had a headache or any pain, caught her eye. She reached for it and shook out a couple. She tossed them into her mouth and swallowed them without any liquid. The pills left a bitter taste on her tongue, and she grimaced.

Cherie frowned when she first spied Linda stroll somewhat hesitantly through the door to the fourth floor suite of offices at the *LA Times*. "You look like you spent the night hugging the toilet! Don't tell me my cooking was that bad!"

Linda smiled weakly. "No, it's just a bit of a headache."

"You did take your pills, didn't you?" Linda stared blankly at Cherie. "I mean, they did give you something for pain, didn't they?"

Linda nodded. "Yeah, they helped, after a while."

Cherie smiled, and the edges of her eyes narrowed as she gazed at Linda. "Very good. Look, here are the first things I want you to go over." She tossed a folder in front of her. "I'll get back with you later, and we'll discuss what you plan on this." Before Linda could respond, Cherie was gone.

As Linda settled in at her desk, she glanced about. She was inside the heartbeat of the *LA Times* organization. People swept past her, each intent on his or her mission. Some carried papers, others chatted on phones while walking. None seemed to notice her. She didn't recognize any of them, despite the fact it was her home, the culmination of her ambition in life. So why did she doubt her right to be there? As she gazed about the office, she noticed Cherie had disappeared into her office and shut her door. Linda shrugged and told herself to focus on her work—to concentrate on the challenge and what should be the thrill of searching for and discovering new information. Whatever it was, it worked. Time flew. She spent most of the day at the paper's in-house library. The following three days passed in much the same way—reading, searching, compiling, and summarizing information for her upcoming series of articles.

But in those random moments when her concentration broke and Linda became aware of her surroundings, it didn't feel quite like what she thought she remembered. The newsroom seemed unusually quiet. Very few people actually seemed to be at work; most stood around with coffee cups, glancing in her direction every few moments.

Cherie had insisted Linda join her for lunch the first day and again on the second. Those minutes free from dusty volumes and old papers helped Linda feel a sense of belonging again. As Cherie laughed and joked, her spirit seemed to spill into Linda and infected her with a love of life she hadn't realized she was missing. It wasn't until the third day, when Cherie didn't suggest lunch, that Linda realized how much she craved the lighter side of her work day.

Left on her own, she ventured outside. A nearby street vendor was selling hot dogs and chips. Linda's mouth watered as she followed the aroma of hot dogs and chili to a place in line. A moment later, hot dog in hand, Linda curled under the shade of a nearby willow tree. Back propped against its trunk, she let her mind drift. Warm sun peeked through the leaves, and a gentle breeze flirted with her hair. Life was good. She felt like she had all she needed as she took a bite of her hot dog. As she leaned against the tree trunk, she gazed up and spied the *LA Times* sign atop the building. Was it really true? Did she really work for the organization of her dreams? It didn't seem real. But the sign was there. It must be true.

A black kitty strolled by and, spying her, stopped. Purring loudly, it rubbed against her leg. Its golden eyes stared into hers, and with a purr grunt, it demanded, "Share with me!"

For some reason, the cat's eyes mesmerized her, and Linda tossed the rest of her hot dog to it. The cat grunted its "thanks" and then inhaled its prized morsel in three bites. Finished, it licked its chops and began the face-grooming ritual. Then the cat cranked up the purr volume and rubbed against her leg again.

As if an old habit, Linda's hand found the cat's ears and scratched behind them. The purring grew louder, and the cat gave a soft, contented purr-grunt before flopping onto its back and curling its paws around her hand. As the cat tried to play with her, being nice and keeping its claws in, Linda felt an odd sense of contentment. It seemed so natural to have a cat by her side, yet, she'd never had a cat in her life.

Linda glanced at her watch and gasped. How had she let so much time pass? She was late and suddenly fearful of what Cherie would say. Gently, she extracted her hand from the kitty's paws and gathered her stuff. With one last pat on its head, she said aloud, "Good-bye, kitty. Be a good boy." The cat arched its back and rubbed against her leg and then strolled beside her, tail high in the air. Just as Linda reached her building, the cat spied a bird. His new best friend forgotten, the cat scampered off in pursuit of his next meal.

Watching the cat run, Linda considered her apartment, thought of the emptiness there. *Maybe I should get a cat, something warm to curl up with at night,* she thought. As she pushed the glass doors open and climbed the short flight of stairs, the notion soon became lost in thoughts of work.

The sun hung poised over the horizon when Cherie found Linda buried in the stacks. An old edition of the *Times* was spread out before her. Linda was so absorbed that she jumped and a short scream blew out her lips when Cherie tapped her shoulder.

"My goodness, you scared me!" Linda gasped between breaths.

Cherie gently pried the paper from Linda's hand and folded it. "Come on; put those old rags up! You've got a dinner invitation, and there's not much time to get there."

Linda stretched her arms high over her head. She yawned and rubbed her eyes. "Cherie, it's late. It's been a long day. How about another time?"

"Late? Girl, don't you remember? You don't know the word *late.*" Cherie crossed her arms. "Besides, it's with a friend of mine you need to meet. She's the publicist for a film in production over at GrantStorm. The star is someone you'll be interviewing for the series. We're to meet her over at the lot for a late dinner. She'll go over some preliminary info and bios, even set dates for the interviews." Cherie watched Linda as she massaged her temples. "Personally, I think it's an invite you can't afford to refuse."

Telltale signs of another headache crept up her neck. Going home and curling up into a tight ball on the couch, pushing all thoughts away, all demands on her life, was all Linda could think of. Next thing she knew, however, she was in the front seat of Cherie's new Lexus IS, weaving through six lanes on the 101 freeway.

At the studio, Cherie and Linda were quickly ushered to an office on the ground floor of the first office building next to their parking spot. "Claire, it's great to see you." Cherie pushed into the office as if it were her own. "This is Linda." She pointed at Linda. "Linda McGowan."

"Good to meet you. I'm Claire Fergins. I guess Cherie told you I'm the publicist for *The Bridge Builder*. I understand she's put you in charge of interviews for this project."

Linda nodded as she clasped the woman's hand briefly.

"I've known Cherie for quite a while," Claire said. "I'm sure she's sending in only her best." Claire nodded at the buildings beyond her office. "This group should be a fun bunch. The star's a relative newcomer, hasn't had time to develop The Attitude, and his agent is open to publicity. I think you'll probably get some good material."

Claire dug through some papers on her desk. She pulled a manila envelope that was nearly an inch thick from the stack. "Cherie requested these to get you started. I know it's not much, but it should be enough to lay the groundwork and give you some direction."

As Linda started to glance at the envelope's contents, Claire pulled her bag from a drawer, locked her desk, and announced, "It's late, so let's eat. We'll talk then." She waited for Cherie and then Linda to exit before she shut her door and locked it.

"I thought we'd eat on the lot. The production company has reserved a dining room that we can use. Some of the crew should be in there tonight. They're working late on a long scene today."

As Claire briskly led the way across the courtyard and into another building, Linda fell back behind the two women. Her headache had blossomed into a full bone-crusher. She opened her purse for some pain medicine and realized belatedly, she'd left it in the car. She caught up to Cherie and tugged at her sleeve.

"My head's killing me, and my pills are in your car. Do you mind?"

Cherie shook her head slowly but narrowed her eyes. "Here're the keys." She dropped them in Linda's hand.

"Linda," Claire said, "when you return, go back to the building over there," she pointed to a two-story stucco building nestled between two others across from them. "We'll be on the bottom floor. You can't miss us."

Fifteen minutes later, Linda finally found Cherie and Claire.

"Did you get your medicine?" Cherie asked quickly.

Linda nodded. "Sorry. It took a little longer to find my way back."

"Didn't get lost, did you?" Claire's question was sharp. "The studio doesn't allow visitors to wander around unescorted. Maybe I should've gone with you."

Linda shook her head. "Oh no, no! There was no problem. I'm here!" She thumped her chest and smiled as broadly as she could. Perhaps it was the cramps in her stomach that kept her from admitting she had indeed gotten lost and wandered onto a set where they were busy shooting a scene. Maybe it had been just instinct. Whatever it was, she knew on some level, she could not admit to her blunder.

As they ate, Cherie and Claire chatted animatedly most of the time. Linda watched quietly and prayed the vise constricting her head didn't make it explode. Not paying full attention to what she did, she kept pressing her palm against her temple. The pain levels crept up so that soon, it was all she could focus on. Yet, Cherie and Claire didn't seem to notice. It wasn't until she fumbled her fork and then knocked her water over that Cherie glanced at her.

"Girl, are you doing okay?" She pinched her brows and studied Linda for a moment. Linda nodded. "You sure?" Linda nodded again.

Cherie turned back to Claire. "I was hoping we could get a time on your calendar to interview this project's star. Linda needs to jump back in there and get her feet wet again—the sooner the better."

There was a pause, and Claire sucked some air in between her lips.

"Not sure how fast I can arrange it. I know they're eager to get the publicity going. We just have to work around his agent. The man's positively ornery if things aren't done according to his dictates. But so long as we stick to his rules and he gets advance warning on the time, it shouldn't be a problem."

Cherie responded quickly, "I'm sure Linda's already got an outline of ideas and wouldn't mind shooting some of them over to you right away."

"Certainly," Claire responded as she glanced at Linda. "Just send them over sometime tomorrow." She pulled a pad from her bag and scribbled on it and then handed a sheet to Linda. "Send it all there."

Later, as Cherie drove from the studio, neither woman spoke until they were in Linda's parking lot.

"Get your questions over to Claire ASAP. I don't want anything to delay getting an interview. This will be the focal point of our series, so it's the most important." Cherie's face brightened, and she punched Linda lightly on the arm. "You may get the scoop of the century!"

As Linda walked toward her apartment, Cherie remained in her parking spot, watching. After opening her door, Linda turned, saw Cherie, and waved. Cherie returned the gesture and then backed from her space and sped from the complex.

Throughout the night, Linda tossed and turned. Dark images floated past her subconscious eye, and when she did wake, she wasn't sure if she was alive or dreaming of some place in hell. Cold sweat covered her, and for some reason, her heart was knocking stoutly against her ribs. As she lay there, she strained to hear any sounds. Only the faint din of early risers greeting the freeway drifted through the morning air.

After dragging herself free of damp and tangled sheets, she grabbed a robe and plodded into the kitchen to make some coffee. When the caffeine revived her enough to focus, she pulled open the morning paper and scanned the headlines. Near the end of the first section, her eyes stopped on the headline, "Texas Airline Fighting Accusations from Federal Government Regarding Release of Crash Data." Leaning close to the paper, she read:

> Gateway Air CEO Charles Trushard is embroiled in an investigation pertaining to Gateway Air's ill-fated Flight 832. An unnamed federal agency, in conjunction with the NTSB, is threatening charges against Mr. Trushard and Gateway Air, stating he acted improperly and possibly violated the crash investigation's integrity by disclosing confidential passenger and crash information to an unknown source. Mr. Trushard, when reached for comment, emphatically denied any wrongdoing and refused to admit such actions had even taken place. However, the NTSB and other federal agencies have stated that they plan to continue their investigation into the incident. Flight 832, originating in Los Angeles, crashed on January 14, near Houston's George Bush Intercontinental Airport. Severe weather was blamed for the fatal crash, which killed all but one of the 120 passengers on board.

Not understanding why she did it, Linda cut the article from the paper and stuck it on the refrigerator with a magnet. Two hours later, she called Cherie at the office.

"I think I've got the basics laid out for the interviews. Want me to send them to you before getting it over to Claire?"

"Sure." Cherie paused briefly. "Linda, I hope I haven't pushed you too hard. I'm just glad you're back. But please, take care of you. Okay?"

"Hey, don't worry. I love it when things start falling into place like they have this morning. It's almost like I'm back to my old self. Why, I'm going to blow them away in that interview."

Midafternoon, Claire got back to Linda. "Everything looks great. I'll call you as soon as I get a time." There was a brief pause. "Linda, you didn't mistakenly enter one of the sets last night did you?"

Linda's heart skipped two beats. "Uh … no. Why?"

"It's nothing. Look, I'll get back to you, okay?"

"Sure."

Cherie's concentration was rudely interrupted by the phone's blaring. She pulled her eyes from a large stack of papers and slapped the receiver against her ear.

"Cherie? Claire here."

Claire didn't wait for Cherie's acknowledgment. "We've got trouble. Someone stumbled in on a hot set last night. Distracted the actor and when he went berserk, the entire place disintegrated into chaos. Now, the actor is demanding to know who it was. I've got his agent on my back, the director too. The producer just hung up. He's insinuating I let some rogue press in just to get some publicity. It's an outright manhunt." There was a long pause. "Cherie. It's your man, Matt Grayson. It was his set."

Cherie swallowed and gripped the handset with a deadly vise. "You think it was Linda?"

Claire didn't answer right away. "I'm not saying anything, but it struck me as possible. If it is, then I could lose my job. I'm not supposed to let anyone go anywhere unsupervised. If it was her …" Claire's voice faded.

Cherie chewed the edge of a fingernail. "You're right. This isn't good." For a moment, she looked like a thunderstorm ready to erupt. Seconds later, she smiled and the edge in her voice melted.

"Actually, Claire, I don't think there's anything to be concerned about. But if it was her, I'll take care of it. You don't need to sweat it."

Slowly, Cherie replaced the receiver. When she leaned back in her chair and stretched her arms over her head, she was grinning.

The morning was fresh with promise. Early summer warmth spread over the land as easterly breezes pushed the metallic smog out to sea.

The resultant clear air exposed nearly forgotten mountains to the east and gave the valley's inhabitants a hint of what fresh air might be like. Being such a rarity for an early summer day in Southern California, it was nearly cause for celebration.

Carrying a bulging briefcase, Linda burst out of her apartment. It seemed her feet barely touched the ground as she trotted lightly to her car. Pausing, she leaned against the door and turned to receive the sun's kiss. A large smile curled her lips, and her shoulders rose and fell several times as she took deep breaths. Moments later, radio blasting and dark glasses covering her eyes, she sped from the complex, a smile still curling her lips. It lingered for as long as Potter was able to keep her in his sight.

"Potter, subject has entered my sector, heading south on Timberlyne. Most likely, she will enter the freeway at the southbound entrance ramp off of Van Nuys. You got that?"

"Affirmative," Potter replied in his evenly modulated voice; the nearly invisible microphone attached to the inner part of his shirt collar catching every syllable. "We'll be in position to pick up surveillance again at the intersection of Timberlyne and 134. Advise of any changes. By the way, I need your report from yesterday, ASAP. Boss's on the warpath today. And you know what that's like!"

Potter ended the call and turned to the man beside him. "Hank, I've never heard her so upset before. And I don't know why. From all I've heard, things couldn't be going better, all according to plan."

"Beats me," Hank mumbled. "Go figure those government types. Everything's a life-and-death crisis. They've spent so many years squeezed into those tight-fitting, butt-crunching black suits that they don't know how to let it hang out anymore!"

Both men chuckled, but Potter added solemnly, "The only reason any of them exist—power and money. Whoever gives the most, that's where their allegiance flows."

His cell phone interrupted. Potter shouted, "Potter here!"

"Status report!" It was not a request.

"Team A has current visual. We should pick up in less than a minute."

"Don't lose her."

"Don't worry, ma'am. Even if visual is lost, GPS tracking has the subject. The subject's location will be known at all times. My best teams are on this."

"I still want visual. Knowing where the car is isn't good enough! I want every second documented. It's imperative."

"Understood."

"And I'm still waiting for reports for the past twenty-four hours. Have them on my desk no later than five, today!"

Static replaced her voice. Hank looked at Potter. "With all that red hair and hot temper, should've named her Fireball. Cherie's much too tame."

The men laughed just as the subject's car crossed their line of vision. Potter accelerated and pulled behind it as it entered the southbound lanes of the freeway. He glanced at Hank. "Let's see if we can figure out why our fireball wanted the best men I've got following this one woman."

Hank stared through his binoculars and grinned. "I'm not complaining. It could be worse, much worse!"

Cherie threw the folder on her desk and then grabbed it as she flew from the borrowed office. Outside the door, one of the secretaries from the floater pool waited.

"Brenda, go ahead and set up the conference call. I'll take it in Room B. And, Brenda ..." Cherie smiled briefly at the older woman. "... I need top-level security on that line."

Confident her instructions would be carried out to the letter, Cherie strolled down the windowless hallway. Far from her office at the *Los Angeles Times*, her destination was deep in the bowels of what appeared externally as nothing more than an ordinary office building. It was a tower filled with businesses, all innocuous, all intent on keeping the profit margin high and expenses low, all unaware of their landlord's true purpose and function. She smiled. Oh, what they didn't know.

Cherie pushed open the door to Room B. In its center was a small, round table surrounded by six chairs. Gracing the table was a fifty-inch flat-panel LED television screen connected to what appeared to be a simple desktop computer. However, the system was far from simple. It included state-of-the-art high-definition cameras and voice-recognition software that was updated almost hourly. The secure channels the connections utilized had been developed by the best of the best of computer security experts. The quality of the projection was not even on the same planet as Skype and Facetime. Satellite uplinks were dedicated and carried by government and military orbiters. Even though all who used the system were required to have the appropriate level of security clearance, each person was required to undergo a retinal scan and thumbprint scan before being allowed to enter the virtual chat room.

Cherie locked the room's door and then sat down in front of the screen. She punched some numbers on the keyboard and waited for confirmation of a secure connection. Moments later, she faced a group of four men.

The projected image was split in two. One side showed three men seated side by side, each wearing the starched white uniform of the world of laboratories and medicine. Projected on the other half was a lone man who wore a custom-tailored navy suit with a subdued red tie. As he sat alone, seemingly staring into Cherie's eyes as if he literally sat across the table from her, he tugged at the cuffs of his shirt and grinned. The other men, who were a half coast away tucked back in an isolated research facility in Texas, were not aware of his presence or involvement. They believed they were the only ones to have an audience with Cherie.

"I am pleased to report our field test is progressing within all stated parameters and projections. It would appear your predictions and calculations are correct." She reached for a glass of water and took a small sip. "Because things are proceeding pretty much according to plan, I feel comfortable in moving the time table up, as requested earlier."

One man scribbled on his pad; the others frowned. However, the lone individual set apart on the screen pinched his chin with slender, manicured fingers. Diamond-studded cuff links peeked from the hem of his jacket sleeves. Perfectly groomed hair crowned a distinguished face, making a picture that could move almost anyone who gazed upon him. It already had, more than once. He looked directly into the camera lens and smiled. Cherie did not acknowledge him. She continued to focus on the others.

The man in the middle of the lab-jacketed group spoke. "What about the reports? We've only received two—certainly not enough to make a conclusive recommendation to speed up the time table."

"Charles." Cherie crossed her arms and smiled casually. "The reports are being compiled as we speak. You should start receiving the latest by early this evening."

Another interrupted. "You said, 'pretty much according to plan.' What do you mean by that? Have things not gone perfectly? Isn't that what was expected? The initial trials certainly indicated that would be the case."

The other added, "Should we assume there have been problems?"

Cherie dropped her arms and her smile. "Certainly, not everything is perfect. Yes, a few minor things have occurred."

"Such as?" Charles asked quickly.

"A few minor headaches, some questions about the past. It's nothing to be concerned about, however. She's enthusiastic about her work and seems to have no mental impairment regarding vocation."

The men at the lab glanced at each other; some were biting lips, others furrowing their brows.

"Gentlemen, I assure you, should there be a need, I will halt the entire process. I will not let it get out of hand. Twenty-four-hour surveillance remains in place. No moment is left to fate. Full data is being compiled and will continue to be forwarded to you. Trust me."

Cherie switched her focus to the center man. "Charles, I need to know about the current trials in phase two. How's progress?"

"The final regimen of the trial was initiated a week ago. Similar protocols as our field trial. Only difference, your girl was deliberately repressed; this group was not. They all have suffered the same impairment of memory function. We feel, however, our altered treatment will allow us to use that impairment, as attempted before, to produce positive results. So far, we've seen no destabilization, no compensation. We feel confident all should continue as planned."

"Very good," Cherie said, and her Cheshire grin bloomed. "That is very good indeed. I expect daily reports on your progress. As you know, there are those besides myself who are quite anxious to hear of favorable results. Our next project will be based on their requests. It's vital your work progresses expeditiously and successfully." She punched a button, and the three men in Texas vaporized into the now-dark screen. The other man remained in clear focus.

"You are confident, aren't you? You have no concerns about moving ahead and igniting a potentially volatile situation?"

Cherie nodded, but her eyes darkened. "Certainly. But don't ask me; ask your physicians. They are the ones with the research and the data. They're the ones who have devised this latest regimen. If you don't trust me, then trust them; after all, they were handpicked by you. But you heard them. Everything is going well. They don't expect a repeat of earlier failures, nor do I. We've come so much further than just extending life beyond its normal boundaries, enhancing it in subtle ways. The subjects are staying viable much longer. I believe them when they say this field trial is going to prove that we have finally achieved the point of obtaining permanent results. I have no qualms about proceeding with our next objective."

The man seemed to peer straight into Cherie's eyes. "I hope you're right. Our scientists and physicians must stay focused on the science at hand and not get distracted with moral or ethical issues. You know the stakes involved. I hold you responsible for keeping them focused. If you don't, we could lose all that we've worked so long and hard for." There was a long pause as each stared at the other. "Should any new developments occur, you will keep me informed?"

"Of course, Mr. Congressman. Don't I always?"

He smiled. However, even near-space airwaves could not hide the threat beneath his famous charm. Cherie terminated the connection and slumped in her chair.

Panting as sweat ran in rivers down his back, with his lab jacket billowing out behind him, Phillippe ran through the lab's maze of hallways frantic to reach Charles's office.

"I got here as soon as I could. What's up?"

Charles didn't stand. He pointed to the chair across from his desk. Phillippe hesitated before sitting down.

"I just received some disturbing news. Some of the patients from the trial that was just initiated last week have died, quite suddenly and quite unexpectedly."

Phillippe paled. "How many?"

"Six total. Three in the past four hours. There could be more."

"Any preconditions noted?"

"Only one, debilitating headaches. The frequency seemed to escalate until each person's transplanted memory evaporated. Not only did repression fail and original memory links resurface, but physiological reactions were accelerated. Internal development proceeded exponentially. Organs leaped past natural age in a matter of hours. At that point, they started falling over."

"Weren't they given an extract of the new DNA strain we developed from our star pupil?"

Charles nodded.

Phillippe relaxed his shoulders and sighed. A small smile curled the edges of his mouth.

"Then, what're we worried about? Our star pupil was not given the physiological repression series. There's your difference. You heard the report. Everything's going well in the field."

Charles frowned. "It doesn't matter that she didn't get that little extra in way of suppression. She still received the same regimen, the same drugs."

"Things have gone well so far. I'm sure this case will be different."

"I hope so," Charles said as Phillippe stood. "Our boss has informed me that we're not to let up on our work. If anything, she's expecting more hours. She said nothing short of success is acceptable."

"Charles, do I not always do my best?"

Charles gazed at some point past Phillippe. With a shrug, Phillippe turned and strolled from the office, not hearing his superior's last comment, "Do you?"

Charles rubbed his chin as he considered all that had happened so quickly that day. When his phone buzzed, he jumped and his heart raced. He grabbed the receiver with a cold hand.

"You're sure?" Charles spoke quietly when the voice on the other end stopped long enough to breathe. "Okay. Okay, I'll alert the rest now." Charles slammed the receiver in place.

"Number seven," he muttered as he ran from the room.

Cherie stuffed the folder in her leather Versace bag and grabbed her car keys. She stole a quick glance at her cell phone. There were only twenty minutes until Linda's interview with that Grayson character. No way she'd make it, not with the usual 101 traffic. The earlier conference call had taken longer than she'd anticipated.

Outside her office, she stopped suddenly at the shrill ringing of her phone. Indecision passed quickly, and she turned around. Before answering, she shouted to her secretary, "Brenda, call Claire! Tell her I'm running late."

Cherie held the receiver to her ear and announced, "Cherie Pittstorm here."

"Cherie?" The voice on the other end was so loud, she could hear it clearly as she held the receiver away from her ear. However, the words shouted at her caused her to push it against her ear.

"You're kidding, Charles. Please tell me you're kidding!"

"No, I'm not. What's more, our girl was given the same regimen. I need to know exactly how many headaches has she had and how severe?" Charles shouted.

Cherie swallowed. The memory of Linda pressing her forehead with the palm of her hand became a bright image. "A few, two or three. I think they've all been mild and passed fairly quickly. She's been working hard, seems eager to get the job done. She has taken some of her pain medicine but not that often—"

Charles interrupted. "I thought you had total surveillance in place. I need to know exactly how much medication has been taken, when, and for what symptoms. Do you not have that info for me?"

Cherie swallowed. "I have some. The latest reports, as you know, are still incomplete. Last count of her medication indicated she's taken ten pills to date. I was with her on two of the incidences of the headaches. Video of her apartment indicates at least one other mild episode. That's all I know right now." Forcing some brightness into her words, she added, "Look, she's done well so far. I have every reason to believe she'll continue to be just fine."

"I'd feel much better if we pulled her in, did a thorough reevaluation, and checked her chemistries and implantation protocols."

"I can't do that now. She's in the middle of our first major test." Cherie glanced again at her cell phone's time. "In fifteen minutes, she's set to meet our first subject. Charles, if she passes this one, then I'm confident we don't have anything to worry about."

"I don't like it, not at all."

"Charles, start feeling good," Cherie hissed through bared teeth, "because it's going to be just fine. Remember, this isn't Dolnia. We've come a long way since then. What you need to focus on is why your test group failed. Those are the answers we need now!"

Cherie slammed the phone on her desk. As she ran from the office, she could not, *would not*, admit cold slivers of ice were poking the tender, ulcerated lining of her stomach. Moments later, she sat pounding her steering wheel and fuming. Traffic was at a dead stop, and she was trapped in the center lane. Fingers of one hand drumming on the wheel, she picked up her cell phone with the other. She'd already missed Linda's interview.

Linda accelerated through the traffic faster than normal. Speeding usually scared her but not that day. She hummed softly while tapping her fingers on the wheel, keeping with the beat from the radio. It felt like a long-lost shot of adrenaline coursed through her veins as the realization hit her that she was pumped, excited about the meeting ahead. Certainly, she had conducted such interviews many times prior to the accident, but she just couldn't remember them. So why did it bother her that Cherie had insisted on sitting in on the meeting?

"Oh, I know you'll do fine," Cherie had said when calling to confirm the location of the meeting. "It's just, well, it's your first big one since coming back. I want to be there. Look, I'm in a bit of a hurry now, but I'll meet you at the studio and we'll talk before."

Speeding smoothly up the freeway, Linda smiled as she mentally reviewed her outline for the upcoming meeting. Art Garfunkel singing, "I Only Have Eyes for You," surrounded her in ten-speaker Bose sound. Transported suddenly to a balmy spring evening, magnolia and honeysuckle perfume filling the air, she felt, rather than heard, the sensual strains of the song. She could almost feel strong arms holding her. Her exit suddenly popped up, and lost in her unidentifiable vision, she nearly missed it. When an opening between cars widened, she zipped through the gap, leaving a few digits pointed in her direction and one car frantically trying to zip through the same opening.

"Sorry." She said it to no one in particular and grinned.

At the studio, Linda was escorted immediately to Claire's office. "Cherie's not here?" Linda asked as she glanced about the small office that had file cabinets running from floor to ceiling in each corner. In the middle, Claire stood behind her desk and pointed at a chair across from her.

"Don't worry. She called a little while ago. Said she was running late," Claire said brightly.

The phone interrupted. Claire put it to her ear but said nothing as she listened. A frown spread across her face, and she started shaking her head. Finally, "Yeah, I can take care of everything. No worries here." Claire stuffed the phone in her pocket and turned back to Linda.

"That was Cherie. She said she's stuck in traffic and probably won't make it here in time. She was worried that you wouldn't be okay with that."

"Worried? No way! This is my thing, my specialty. I'm ready for this as I never have been for any other project. I don't need Cherie holding my hand!"

Claire raised her brows as if somewhat stunned by Linda's sentiment. She shrugged. "I guess we may as well go on over to the conference room, then. Mr. Grayson's agent will want to meet with you first."

With Claire leading the way across the open courtyard, bougainvillea casting shade on the sidewalk from its intricate lattice-filled frames and oleander bushes waving in the soft breeze, they all made their way toward another building in the studio complex. Linda asked, "Tell me about Mr. Grayson's other work, his first film."

"His first? You mean, *Cheap Shot*?" Linda nodded. "It was only a supporting role, but it, along with a screen test, was enough to get the attention needed to cast him in the lead in *Killing Times*, which will be his second starring role, after *The Bridge Builder*."

Linda couldn't understand why she drew a blank when she tried to remember the film. She pulled a notebook from her bag and scribbled a couple notes. "Just so I get this straight, what was the release date of *Killing Times*?"

Claire stopped and turned to look at her. "I thought I included that in my packet. But it was this past December, just before New Year's weekend. It was number one at the box office for quite a few weeks, perhaps because of the plane crash. Who knows? Whatever, it blew critics out of the water. Some even felt he should get an Oscar, though you know how finicky the Academy is. They like to stick with the tried and true, or whatever is currently considered PC. Really splits filmmakers up. They can't decide whether to market to the masses or the Academy. They're never sure which will bring in the most dollars. And it is dollars that dominate, can't deny it."

Outside the conference room door, Claire stopped. Facing Linda, she said, "I'm sure Mr. Grayson's agent will warn you, but stick to questions about the movie. Personal stuff makes this guy go bonkers."

"Like anything concerning his plane crash?"

Claire stared at her. "Yes, stay away from that!" She pulled the door open and waited for Linda to pass. "Have a seat. I'll be right back."

The room was surprisingly small and sparsely furnished. The only item besides a long oval table decked by eight, deep-cushioned swivel chairs, was a small wet bar nestled in the back wall of the room. A coffeepot full of coffee was steaming on a hot plate, and beside it a Keurig single-cup coffee dispenser offered a few additional choices. The smell of the brewed coffee, however, caused a small wave of nausea to roll over Linda. After settling in a chair on the left side of the table, opposite the doorway, she concentrated on arranging her things instead of the increasingly nasty smell of coffee. Just as she pulled her iPad from her tote along with a small voice recorder and a folder of clippings concerning the actor, she jumped when the door blew open. Claire breezed into the room followed by an older man.

"Linda, this is Jerry Cain, Mr. Grayson's agent." Linda extended her hand, and Jerry grasped it lightly.

"Guess you know I have to look out for Matt's interests in all matters. So, if you'll just go over some of what you have planned for today," he said after pouring a cup of the offensive coffee and dumping at least five packets of sugar in it. With his cup sloshing almost to overflowing, Jerry plopped into the chair beside Linda. He looked tired, inner weary, as if he were trying to put on a pretense of all being well when it really wasn't. Despite the slump of his shoulders, his eyes warmed when he glanced at her, and his smile was comforting.

"Tell me," he began, "how did you get the honor of doing this series?"

Claire cleared her throat suddenly, and Linda stared first at her and then at Jerry. "I … uh … guess because it's my job. I'm not sure what you're implying," she said.

"I'm just curious about you, your experience, your background—those kinds of things." His eyes twinkled.

"Mr. Cain, my experience and background are more than adequate to conduct and write up these interviews. I've been with the *LA Times* for …" Her mind drifted. "For …well, it seems like forever. I've written all kinds of stories, covered all types of events and people. I guess my work speaks for itself."

"That is certainly interesting since I haven't found any references anywhere to a Linda McGowan in the journalism business, of any kind."

Linda smiled. "You've done your homework, Mr. Cain. That would be because I used a pen name for most of my work. It gives one more options."

A hint of red crept up Jerry's neck into his cheeks, but he grinned broadly. "By the way, it's Jerry." He pushed up from his chair. "I'll go get our man. Be back shortly."

He exited the room, leaving Linda and Claire alone. In less than a minute, Jerry returned. Following him was a tall, broad-shouldered, athletic-looking man somewhere in his late twenties or possibly early thirties. His light-gold, tousled hair curled at the nape of his neck, and startling hazel eyes swept across the room like a light saber. The man seemed bigger than life, solid and strong. But it was his eyes that caught Linda off guard. There was intensity in them, compassion as well. Despite the few people in the small space, it was as if he commanded the hush of a crowded auditorium. Everyone focused on him, yet he seemed unaware of the attention. The moment his eyes found Linda, however, a palpable tension started to simmer.

Linda's heart bounced against her ribs. When his eyes met hers, she saw something there, a question, a shot of pain or of anger. She wasn't sure. He stared at her forever, it seemed. His lips moved as if he wanted to say something. An emotion flickered across his eyes, and then he shook his head as if to clear it. The pregnant silence ended when he sighed and settled into a chair opposite hers. He folded his hands in his lap and waited for her to speak.

"Uh, Mr. Grayson, let's begin ..." Some dissonant chord resonated inside Linda. She stared at Matt Grayson, uncertain as to what was wrong. He was so familiar. Of course, she'd seen his picture. That was it. But the feeling he evoked was more alive than just memories of a photograph. It was tangible, something she could reach out and touch. For the first time in weeks, Linda's scars began to throb. She wished she'd remembered to bring her pain medicine.

"Matt. It's Matt, please." His voice was tinged with a slight hint of a drawl, so familiar, but why? He leaned toward her and, with a focused stare, spoke again. "We don't need to be so formal."

Linda tried to meet his eyes but couldn't. A small scar on his forehead held her attention. Even so, she felt the heat of his stare searing through her skin to her soul. She wanted to hide. All coherent thought vanished. She felt incompetent. These people believed her to be professional, unaffected by celebrity. She pressed her hand to her forehead to try to stop the pounding.

"I ... uh ... I'm sorry; I've got a bit of a headache." She shuffled her papers and then stared at the top sheet as if she'd never seen it before. Large beads of sweat popped out across her upper lip, and she paled.

Jerry reached toward her and grasped her arm lightly. "Are you all right, Ms. McGowan? Would you like some coffee? Some ..."

Linda shouted, "No!" She shook her head.

"Ice water?" Jerry nodded toward Claire, who reached for a pitcher. She poured some into a glass and set it in front of Linda. Linda didn't see it.

Eyes still focused on her papers, she suddenly muttered to herself, "I can't do this." Then louder to the group, "I'm not prepared at this time, uh, Mr. Grayson, for this interview." Matt frowned, as did Jerry and Claire. "I'm ... I'm sorry I've put you to this trouble. I'll be in touch later to set up another meeting."

She stood so fast, her papers flew to the floor. She knelt to retrieve them, but her fingers refused to cooperate. She couldn't seem to grasp anything. As Linda managed to stuff her iPad and recorder into her tote, Jerry interrupted.

"Here," he said. "Let me get those. I'm a professional. Push papers and people for a living."

Linda slowly stood and waited while Jerry finished collecting the papers. He handed the stack to her and said easily, "Just give me a call when you want to reschedule." Then he leaned toward her and with a teasing smile and a wink whispered, "He's been known to have this effect on women. It's perfectly normal, nothing to worry about!"

Even though her hands and arms were shaking and cold sweat was dotting her forehead, Linda thrust her hand at Jerry, thanked him, and pushed past him for the door. She forgot Matt and Claire as she ran from the building.

As she exited to the parking lot, she began a full-blown panic attack. She'd screwed up, badly. Claire wouldn't schedule any more interviews. Cherie would fire her. She wouldn't blame any of them. Her head hurt so badly, however, she didn't care. She had to run away somewhere, anywhere. She only wanted the pain to stop.

"Cherie, Claire here."

"Yes?" Cherie's stomach stopped churning and froze at the sound of the other woman's voice over her phone.

"The interview went sour. She didn't get the first question out before she made some excuse about not being prepared. She ran from the room."

Cherie wanted to believe anything, anything at all, except for what she'd heard.

"Where is she now, Claire?"

"Don't know. She just flew out. Maybe she's on her way home, or possibly to your office."

"How was she acting before she left?"

"Kept pressing her hand to her head; sweat broke out on her face, and she got really pale. Looked dazed, confused, disoriented."

"How long ago did she leave?"

"A couple minutes ago."

"Get out there, now! Cherie shouted. "Get someone, and flag her down! Get her back. This is critical!"

Cherie threw her phone down and cursed. Her worst fears were coming true.

CHAPTER 7

It was not easy, returning to the dazzling life he'd only begun to live prior to the crash. While he was cocooning and healing, the world had flowed on, caught in life's constancy and change. Life's river pushed and pulled those caught in its currents as those about him either accepted or rammed against the constant ebb and flow, intent on grasping their own rafts, concerned only with their ability to stay afloat. Matt was comforted by their self-centered existence. He wanted neither intrusions nor questions. He wanted no prying eyes or sympathy. He wanted only the forgetfulness found in work.

The day following his return to the glittery left coast, Matt arrived on set. A full schedule awaited him along with expectations from the director as well as the executive producer that he would be ready to dive into his work, giving perfect performances with each take. Ironically, his greatest challenge was acting, not before the cameras, but away. To convince those around him all was well took skill beyond any he'd called upon before. And while he was successful by day, at night, he couldn't escape the void.

Throughout his waking hours, the demands and pressures covered the aching hole hidden in his heart, making a forgetfulness that was only temporary. But when he sought the oblivion of sleep, the dark, empty pit opened and demanded to be filled. Instead of pleasant rest, nightmares crept inside his soul. They left him dripping in cold sweat, her name on his lips. Release came only at daylight's beckoning.

By mid-June, nearly six months after the crash, Matt's work on the production was almost complete. Filming had been a long string of fourteen-hour days, each grueling and exhausting. However, as he contemplated the completion of his second major film role and the space of time before the next began, he dreaded the coming enemy of long, unstructured days free from the confines and demands of his work. He feared the demons of his nights would forsake the darkness and seek the empty space of his wakefulness. Even as he worked feverishly, desperate to shield himself from thought and conjecture, a flash of memory, a reminder in someone else's mannerism would intrude between the seams of conscious thought. The demons' strength grew. They refused his efforts to push them into the dark corners of his night. Instead, their boldness expanded until one day they overcame him and threatened to end all he'd worked so hard to achieve.

The day had been long, crawling past twelve hours. Most of it had been spent shooting and reshooting a single scene in which he was required to give a detailed and emotional monologue. Everyone, cast and crew, himself included, was on edge, irritable, tired. Finally, that evening, when everything was in place and people were in position one more time, the cameras rolled, and they attempted one last take. As he had so many times that day, Matt started from the beginning. At first, the words were forced from his lips, spoken by rote memory. When he neared the monologue's midpoint, however, a sudden energy rose from within. It was that welcome surge of character overcoming the human, taking full possession of him. A new spirit burned in his eyes. He transformed into the symbol of what he portrayed. Passion spilled from him. Lines flowed from his heart, wrapped tightly with a surging, growing, consuming emotion. As the intensity gripped him, Matt knew his soul had connected. It was right. He had captured the essence of what they'd striven for all day. Tears trickled down his cheek. His chin quivered. The agony of the character was his agony.

The crew watched; no one moved, and all eyes were on Matt. The director held his breath, and the producer beamed. This was the take, the one they'd known was possible but had eluded them that entire day of shooting. One could almost hear the pop of champagne corks and the fizz of celebration.

Three lines short of completion, it happened. Behind the line of bright light, in the twilight darkness beyond the cameras, her face popped up. No one else seemed to notice for no one in the crew reacted. Maybe it was a dream, just a vision. He was weary, and the day had been long. His brain was tricking him. But as he stared at the woman, she disappeared into the darkness beyond the cameras. A heavy, black door slammed shut across the spillway of his heart, and without warning, Matt started screaming. He crumpled to his knees and held his chest.

"What is it?" the director shouted as he ran to him. "Are you having chest pains? Oh my God! Someone call an ambulance. He's having a heart attack!"

Matt shook his head. Gasping, he struggled to his feet and ran from the set. Crew members looked at each other and shrugged. The producer threw his notebook down and stomped away.

In the confined space of his small trailer, the world spun about Matt. The vision clouded his eyes, and he was lost. For unknown minutes, he sat on the edge of his sofa, holding himself and rocking, hearing nothing, seeing nothing but her face exactly as he remembered it. An hour later, when Jerry stormed through his door, Matt was still rocking and muttering, "It wasn't her. It wasn't her."

"What's gotten into you, man? They think you've gone crazy, done yourself in." Jerry knelt and gripped Matt's arms.

"Sorry," Matt said softly. "Don't know. Exhaustion, I guess."

"I think it's going to take a better excuse than exhaustion to fly past the director and producer. Right now, they're pretty upset. You know, it doesn't take much to get a bad rep in this business. These guys are questioning whether you were right for the part, saying that maybe your success in the first movie was a fluke. They're thinking maybe you're damaged goods."

Matt didn't respond. Jerry shrugged, went to the cooler, and pulled a couple cans of Pepsi out. After handing one to Matt, he pulled the top on his and took a long swig.

"How's that shrink working out, anyway? Doing any good?" Jerry asked between gulps.

"I'm supposed to tell myself it's over. There's nothing more I can do. Life has moved on. Repeat it over and over. I thought it was working. Haven't had any dreams lately, no more visions haunting me—that was, until tonight. No warning, there she was. Her face, just as I remembered. I … I didn't know what to do."

"You sure there was someone back there?"

"She looked real enough to me. You tell me."

Jerry let out a big sigh. He rubbed his forefinger across his upper lip. "Matt, I can't. I can't tell you anything. I know that girl from the plane is dead. You saw the proof. Even if someone did make it on the set, it wasn't her. Matt, you've got to get over this. You've got to forget it and get on with your life." Jerry clapped Matt on the back and eased toward the door. "If it'll make you feel any better, I'll talk with the crew, see if anyone saw anything. Meanwhile, try not to completely convince them you're loony. Let them see they really did get the best of the best for the job!"

Two mornings later, Matt strolled into one of the studio's coffee parlors. The aroma of fresh-brewed coffee greeted him, and for a moment, the darkness that hovered, threatening to suffocate him, dissipated and he thought of his mom's kitchen—the warmth, the sunlight filtering through the window overlooking the back stable, and the sound of his mother shouting at his brother to stop doing whatever it was that would cause the certain end of the world.

Matt stopped in front of the main counter and eyed the selection of sweet buns, oversized cookies, and muffins as well as an assortment of biscotti. He sighed and settled for a large, dark-roast coffee, hoping the hot brew would jolt him into a state of being alive. Moments later, he carried the steaming cup and slipped into a high-backed booth. His shoulders slumped as he stirred his coffee and waited for Jerry. It wasn't long before Jerry pushed into the booth as he strained to keep the table from pinching his gut.

"No luck?" Matt asked, seeing in Jerry's eyes the answer he didn't want.

Jerry shook his head. He set his coffee down, and it sloshed out onto the table. Jerry slapped down a napkin to mop up the liquid. He then pulled a plate in front of him, which was covered with a large, gooey white-capped cinnamon bun. To the side was an equally large bear claw.

Glancing at Jerry's stomach pinched against the table's edge, Matt said, "What did you find out?"

"Nothing. No one saw anything or anyone. The set was closed; you know that."

"But not locked."

"Of course not. But there shouldn't have been anyone wandering around in there anyway, not at that time of day. Only crew assigned to the scene were present and anywhere near you."

"You're sure?"

"I'm sure!"

Jerry tore open at least five packets of sugar and dumped each in his coffee. He stirred it quickly and said, "You know, they think you've lost your grip, and I'm still negotiating your next deal with Spielberg's group. Do I need to remind you how important that is, of how many would kill to be able to even dream about what you've got before you? You told me you wanted a serious film career. You said you were willing to do what it takes, that nothing could stop you if you put your mind to something. Well, I tell you, this is where you need to pull that old resolve out of your closet and put it on. It's going to take every ounce of it, if you want to finalize this contract and move on to an even higher level of professional acceptance. Word of the other night's little episode could kill your chances if anyone gets convinced you're out of control. Clear enough?"

Matt nodded slowly, but his eyes were downcast.

"Good." Jerry cut his bun into little pieces before taking a bite. Matt sipped at his coffee. Both were silent.

After a while, Matt spoke. "Do you think I'm crazy? I mean, really crazy?"

Jerry almost choked on his bun. "What're you talking about?"

"You know. Have I lost it? Has all this finally pushed me past the edge?"

"That's a question for your shrink, Matt." Jerry wiped his mouth and then took a couple more gulps of coffee. He studied Matt.

"No, you're not crazy. Maybe what's happening is just normal, considering all you've been through. I'm no head doc or anything, but I do know that you're courting an obsession, and obsessions do make for craziness."

Matt watched Jerry finish the last bite of bun. "Okay. You want me to drop it. It's dropped. I've been called stubborn before, I will be again." He scooted across the vinyl and stood. "Gotta go work on some lines. Check you later."

Before Matt could escape the small café, Claire Fergins pushed through the door. She caught Matt by the arm and led him back to Jerry.

"I know this is short notice, but I wondered if you could make some time for an interview this afternoon."

Jerry answered. "You know my rules."

"Oh, you and your stupid rules, Jerry."

Jerry glanced at Matt, and Matt answered, "It's fine with me."

Jerry nodded but narrowed his eyes as he stared at Claire.

"Okay, Jerry. If you must know, it's for the *LA Times*. They're doing a series on new talent. And ..." She handed him some photocopied sheets. "... here's the summary of what's planned."

Jerry scratched his head as he perused the material. "No personal stuff, strictly movie related. You know my hard, fast rule."

"How much time are we talking about?" Matt glanced first at Jerry and then Claire.

She shrugged. "It shouldn't take more than an hour. This will be a preliminary meeting. There might be another later."

Jerry focused on Claire. "Of course, you know the rest of my rules. I approve of the questions beforehand. Any problem with that?" Claire shook her head. "Good. By the way, do you have any news as to who may have walked onto the set the other night?"

Claire's face lost some color. "Uh, no, Jerry, none at all."

That afternoon, Claire escorted Jerry to one of several conference rooms set aside for such purposes as their meeting. A young woman was seated there, waiting. "This is Linda McGowan," Claire said. "Linda, Jerry Cain, Mr. Grayson's agent."

Jerry sucked in a long breath as a big grin spread across his face. He leaned forward to grasp her small hand in his and said, "I don't usually agree to such meetings so hastily, but I'm glad I made the exception."

Linda tilted her face to gaze at Jerry, and her own smile was warm. "Thank you, Mr. Cain, for agreeing to meet. Now, if we could—"

"It's Jerry."

She looked at him and hesitated. "Okay … uh … Jerry."

Jerry settled into a chair beside Linda. As she outlined her plans for the interview and the series, he observed her—violet eyes and dark curling hair cut short; thin but perky. Only a small scar over one eye marred an otherwise glorious image. Her mystique intrigued him so much so, that he considered breaking one more of his rules and asking her out. He never got the chance.

It fell apart the moment Matt entered the room. Linda went pale. Her eyes dilated, and she seemed to have difficulty focusing. Repeatedly, she pressed her hand to her forehead as if in pain. Her papers slipped from her shaking hands and scattered across the floor. After Jerry gathered and handed them to her, she abruptly ended the meeting, saying she'd call later to reschedule.

When she was gone, Jerry looked first at Claire and then Matt. "Just what did you do that scared the poor girl?" He started to laugh.

The expression on Matt's face stopped him. "What's wrong? What did I say?"

"Well, I don't have time for such nonsense," Claire said as she pulled the conference room door open. "Let me know when she wants to get back together, but try not to delay the meeting for too long! Now, I've got to make a phone call!" She slammed the door behind her.

"Okay, sport." Jerry gripped Matt's shoulder as he started to leave. "What gives?"

Matt shrugged. "You tell me. Flaky woman, I guess." He wiggled free of Jerry's grasp. "I've got something to take care of. I'll see you later."

Left alone, mouth hanging slack, Jerry scratched his head and turned slowly. With a shrug, he muttered to himself. "May as well get some coffee; maybe one of those cinnamon buns." He licked his lips as he made his way to the only place on the set that he truly enjoyed.

Matt's stomach was blazing. His pulse knocked so hard against his skull he was afraid it would crack. Forcing some outward calmness on the inner frenzy in his chest, he made some lame excuse to Jerry and slipped away from the confines of the small meeting room as fast as he could. As soon as he stumbled out into the parking lot, he spotted her. She stumbled and fell against a car but immediately straightened and resumed running.

Adrenaline pushed Matt's legs to a feverish pace. When he finally got close enough to grasp her elbow, he couldn't get any words out. All he could do was stare and pant. When his breathing slowed a little, he managed to ask, "Are you all right?"

She nodded slowly, but her eyes avoided his. "I'm fine, thank you. I'm sorry I wasted your time. It was inexcusable and won't happen again, I promise."

Matt considered the vision before him. It was uncanny. Except for shorter hair, she was the same, thinner perhaps. He saw the scar on her forehead, knew it without touching it. All logic screamed it was not true, that he merely wished and dreamed for something that it was not possible to have. Yet, before him was the very picture of what he dreamed about nightly. Living and breathing. Talking and frowning. Only the name was different. How could he be so calm when he was caught in a surreal existence?

"Tell me, why did you run out of there?"

Two dark violet eyes peered into his. "I ... I don't know. This sudden spinning, my head started to constrict like a vise was gripping it. I thought I was going to faint."

"Any better now?"

She nodded. "The fresh air helps, if one can call this smog fresh." Her brief smile left a small glow in her eyes. It was the most refreshing thing Matt had seen in months.

"I've met you before."

"I'm sorry. Did you say we've met? I don't remember it. I know I would remember if we had."

"You were on the lot a couple days ago. Peeked in on my set, didn't you?" Matt said it lightly, with a smile.

She paled again. Her gaze hit the ground. "Well ... yes, I was here. I met with your publicist. I didn't tour any sets." She intertwined her fingers several times and shifted her weight from foot to foot. Suddenly, her eyes met his, and her dark look vanished. She smiled as she returned his stare.

"That's it! I know now why you look so familiar. I did see you ... the other night." She ran her fingers through her short curls. "I must confess I did stumble onto a set. Saw someone performing a monologue. It must've been you!" She blushed and grinned. "I'm sorry," she said. "I didn't mean to disturb you. I hope you can forgive me."

"You've not seen me before?"

She stammered. "Why ... yes, of course. Your press photos, but ... I've never met you. That I know."

Linda unlocked her car and pulled the door open. Just as she was about to slip behind the wheel, Matt laid his hand lightly on her shoulder.

"Would you like to get some coffee, or something? I'd really like to talk."

Indecision wrinkled her nose. "I ought to get back to the office, see if I can salvage my job."

"Please." It was all Matt said. His eyes reached out with a force of their own and begged. Somewhere, on some level, they connected, and Matt felt her respond even before she did. Her nod was minimal, barely discernible.

"Let's take my truck. It's just around the corner."

He took her elbow as if she might vaporize into thin air if he didn't hold on to her. But at his truck, she hesitated. Matt grinned and said, "I'm not some mad rapist or thief or kidnapper or masher or …"

Her face registered no emotion as she interrupted. "No, it's my car."

"It'll be okay. Probably safer here than outside those gates!" He was drunk with excitement. "I promise I won't keep you long. You can go back to your boss, brag how you got the interview after all, and everything will be just fine."

Her shoulders seemed to let go of some weight, and she smiled. "I suppose you're right. Uh, sure. Let's go."

Just as Matt pulled open the truck's door, he heard footsteps pounding the pavement from behind him. Glancing over his shoulder, he wasn't all that surprised to see Jerry, red faced and panting, running toward them. What surprised him, however, were the other three with Jerry. Claire and two unknown men in dark suits looked equally eager to catch them. Somehow, he knew that whatever they wanted, it was sure to interfere with his own precious but precarious plans.

Slamming the door, he backed out with a squeal and a couple black marks. The truck jerked as he stomped on the gas, and the engine roared. For a fleeting moment, he saw Jerry frantically waving, shouting at him. With a quick smile and nod, Matt raced from the parking lot.

"Is there some reason we're in such a hurry?" Linda asked without taking her eyes off the road.

Matt didn't answer. He concentrated on the traffic as he considered what to say.

"Sorry," he finally said. "Look. There's a quiet place not too far from here where we can get some coffee, something to eat, if you like."

"Whatever," she responded with her eyes still fixed on the road.

Soon, they were settled in a booth at the back of Max's Coffeery, two steaming cups of Max's finest Colombian in front of them. As he sipped his coffee, Matt silently studied Linda and waited for her to speak. But instead of pulling paper and pens out for notes, she played with the spoon in her mug.

Matt couldn't stand it any longer. "When I said I knew you, I didn't mean the other night when you stumbled onto the set." He watched for some hint of a reaction. There was none. "We've met before, on a flight from LA to Houston." He continued to watch her closely, still no hint his words stirred any feeling.

"I'm sorry," she finally looked at him, her eyes round and full of innocence. "You must have me confused with someone else. I've not been on any flights to Houston, not lately. Not ever."

Matt rubbed the creases between his eyes. "That's strange, because there was a woman who could've been your twin. She was flying back to Houston from LA. She worked for the *Houston Chronicle*; she ..." Matt suddenly grabbed her hand. "Are you okay? You turned a little gray."

Linda nodded but rubbed her temple. "Head's starting to hurt; that's all." She sipped her coffee and then reached into her purse and pulled out a small prescription bottle of pills. She opened it and tossed two into her mouth. After gulping the rest of her coffee, she looked Matt in the eye. "Thanks for your time and all that. But I think I'd better go. This interview will have to wait. My head is pounding too hard to concentrate right now. Could we just do this another time?"

Matt pinched his lips, pretending to consider her offer, as if he had any other choices. "Okay, give me your number. I'll call, and we'll set it up for later."

Her smile was only a brief flash of white teeth. "That's not how it works. I'm the one who's supposed to call your agent, set it up through him, all professional, you know."

Matt pulled a small scrap of paper from his pocket and thrust it toward her. "Please."

She looked at him and then the paper. After some hesitation, she scribbled a number on it and folded the paper. Before she could pass it to Matt, two men, one extremely tall and thin, the other stocky and short, and both in almost identical dark suits with sunglasses hiding their eyes, approached the table.

"May we join you?" The giant of the two spoke.

"We were just leaving," Matt answered. "The lady here isn't feeling well."

The tall man frowned but bent his lanky frame and pushed lightly against Linda, effectively forcing her to move, opening a space on the seat. The second man said nothing but stared at Matt with his arms crossed. With a sigh, Matt slipped across the booth, and the man sat beside him. Two official-looking badges were rapidly flashed, and Matt thought he saw the letters "FBI," but he couldn't swear to it.

The tall man took his glasses off and introduced himself as Agent Sculler. The stocky man was Agent Maderm. Both were intense in their unwavering focus on Matt and Linda. For several long seconds, nothing was said. Veiled eyes met wide eyes, and the challenge was nonverbal, but no less determined. Finally, Agent Sculler spoke. His focus excluded Matt as he concentrated solely on Linda.

"What can you tell us about your recent accident?"

She frowned as she looked from agent to agent. "My accident? Why on earth would that ever interest you?" Matt saw a hint of tremor in her jaw. He glanced at the two agents.

"Just what is it you need from us?" Matt's voice was terse.

"Mr. uh ..." The second agent started to speak. Matt finished for him.

"Grayson."

"That's right!" The agent's smile seemed less than genuine. "Thought so."

Anger hardened Matt's voice. "We are US citizens, and we do have rights, so you'd better tell us just what it is you want, and you'd better have some good explanation for busting in on us and intruding on our privacy." He glanced at Linda, who seemed surprised.

Agent Maderm ignored Matt and smiled at Linda. "This accident you were in required a hospital stay, did it not?"

Linda's face blanched. "How do you know these things?"

"We make it our business to know," Agent Sculler interjected. "There are some individuals we're very interested in. We believe you have been in contact with them. Perhaps you can give us some insight."

"I don't follow you." Linda glanced from agent to agent, and her eyes narrowed. "Yes, I was in the hospital for a while after a car wreck. I guess I was out of it. Don't remember anything except the day I went home."

Both agents frowned. "You're quite sure of this?" Sculler asked.

Maderm added, "You said *car* accident?"

Linda nodded. "Yes."

"Which hospital were you in?" Agent Sculler glanced at some notes in front of him as he waited for her answer.

Linda's voice dripped with sarcasm. "You're the snoops; why don't you tell me?"

"Ms. McCane, avoiding our questions will only prolong the time it takes to resolve all this. It will just ..."

Linda slapped the table with her hand. "Wait!" She glanced quickly at Matt, and her eyes widened. "He called me Ms. McCane." She turned back to the agent. "My name's McGowan."

"McCane, McGowan, it's all the same. Doesn't matter to me which one I call you," Agent Sculler said firmly.

"But it does matter! I tell you, my name's not McCane!" Her voice rose, and a few patrons turned in their seats, straining to see what scandalous moment was in the making.

Agent Sculler gripped Linda's wrist, and she flinched. "Ms. Whatever-you-want-to-call-yourself, go by any name you want; what hospital were you in?"

"Why do I have to answer that?" Linda retorted as she jerked her hand away and massaged it. "I'm not the person you're looking for, so why do you need to know what hospital I was in, or anything else for that matter."

"Do you want to have Uncle Sam breathing down your back for a while? I can assure you that we can arrange that. It will not be pleasant, not at all."

Linda slumped against the seat, and almost imperceptibly, her head bowed. Her voice was soft. "I ... I was in University Hospital."

Agent Maderm scribbled on his pad. "University, you mean, USC's University Hospital?"

Linda nodded as Agent Sculler flipped back several pages in his file folder. "Says here you were treated at Memorial Hermann Hospital."

"I'm sorry; I can't help you. I've never heard of a Hermann Hospital. Don't even know where it is." Her voice was firm, no room left for argument. "You must have me confused with someone who looks like me, but isn't. That's all I can figure, because I'm telling you, I've never been to this Hermann place and my name isn't McCane."

Matt had to force himself to be calm, to keep still, but he couldn't control the loss of blood from his face, the cold chill running up and down his back, and the sweat on his palms.

Agent Sculler shook his head slowly. "I don't believe it to be so, ma'am." He stared at Linda straight in the eye. "But I guess it's always a possibility. However, I would like to know where I can reach you, should we need to talk with you further." He pushed a pen and some paper toward her.

After staring at it for several moments, but making no move to write anything on it, Linda suddenly shoved the paper and pen back to the agent. "You already seem to know too much about me, or at least who you think I am. I'm sure you already know where I live, what my numbers are, and all that. If you don't, then call the NSA. I'm certain they have them! I'm certain it won't be too hard."

She glanced at Matt and then pushed against Agent Sculler. "I really don't think I can help you any further. Now, if you'll excuse us. We were just leaving."

Sculler moved reluctantly from the booth. Maderm copied him. Linda, once free of the table, headed straight for the front of the shop. With two giant steps, Agent Sculler grabbed Linda's elbow and thrust a business card at her. "Call if you do remember anything." He grinned. "Never know; it might just be the most important part of your life."

Linda didn't answer. She shoved the card inside her pocket and continued toward the exit. As Matt grasped the handle to one of the glass doors, several bright flashes of light blinded them. When he was able to see again, he noticed two young men scampering around the side of the building and headed in the direction of his truck.

Matt muttered, "Paparazzi. Let's get out of here."

Harry watched his partner, Tim, as he spit on his hands and then ran them across his hair. It would've worked had there been some hair to plaster down. Instead, the few remaining strands insisted on standing at attention on top a head ravaged by a premature balding spree.

"Stop it, man," Harry finally said, disgusted. "No one cares what you look like."

Tim shrugged as Harry checked the focus on his camera and made sure the flash was charged. Finished, he peered through the glass door of Max's Coffeery again.

"Hey, Tim, someone's with them. Like dark suits and all. Very officious."

Tim pressed his nose against the door and tried to focus on the figures in the dark corner in the back. All he saw were two dark suits talking to their prey. "No telling, man. I don't know what's going on."

"Me either, but I've got a hunch." Harry pulled an extra SD card out of his bag and stuffed the clear, plastic container holding it in his shirt pocket. He wanted to be ready, just in case. Just in case this shoot turned from a routine, let's-follow-the-latest-hunk-of-the-day to something bigger, more important.

A millisecond before the door opened, Harry spied their prey. Instinct pushed his finger down on the shutter release. The flash popped in rapid succession, and the pictures were recorded instantly. Satisfied with the initial assault, Harry led the way and ran toward Matt's truck.

"That's it, his truck, the green one." Tim pointed. "Get over there, and shoot them climbing in. It should be a good angle for you. Play up the girl. You never know; it might make a couple thousand extra. I'll bring the car up. Be ready to hop in when I honk."

Harry did as Tim directed and planted himself between the cars, ready to spring up and shoot as soon as the hunted scooted past. They would be running; they always ran. Once aware of being tracked by those of his profession, they ran, tossing rapid glances of hate at him. It really didn't bother him. It was his job. He made money entertaining people just as his prey did. Both benefited from the pictures they created. They were just different kinds; that's all.

Harry quickly readjusted the lens opening, set the exposure, and made sure the auto advance was set to fire once he pressed the shutter release button. He couldn't waste a shot. This guy was hot, might be even hotter. And the hotter they got, the more Harry's wallet filled out.

Matt and the woman ran around the corner, just as he knew they would. His timing honed perfectly through picture after picture, exposure after exposure; he knew just when to jump up.

Pop, pop, pop went his flash. The startled looks, hands flying to cover eyes, it was all the same, but his skill was such that he managed to get in several excellent exposures before they sped away.

Tim pulled up, and with no hesitation, Harry jumped in the passenger's side. Tim slammed the gear in first and asked, "How'd you do?"

"Think I got some good ones." Harry pulled the SD card from the camera and replaced it with the fresh one from his shirt pocket.

"Good. We may even be able to get something while we're following. Never know what we may run into."

Camera loaded and readied again for action, Harry sealed the small SD card in a protective bag. He then stuffed it in a small, specially protected box, which kept anything harmful from compromising the digital images stored on the card. He pushed the box under his seat with his feet as he gripped the camera sides and waited for the next big shot.

Just as Tim hit the accelerator, a black, generic sedan pulled in front of them and stopped. Tim slammed the brakes, throwing them dangerously close to the windshield. Two men in dark suits emerged and covered each side of the car. One hit Tim's window with a fist, and official-looking badges were flashed. Tim and Harry reluctantly opened their windows.

"FBI. May I see the camera there?" A tall man in dark glasses leaned through the window and jerked the camera from Harry's grip. As if an expert with photographic equipment, the agent ripped open the camera back and ejected the SD card. "Thank you, gentlemen," he said as he handed the camera back to Harry. "I trust there will be no more pictures, for now." The two men turned and were gone before Tim could sputter.

"That was a new card, wasn't it?"

Harry nodded, mouth open, eyes fixed on the spot where the agents had been. He pointed at the box by his feet. "In there, man. The good stuff, it's all in there."

Neither Matt nor Linda spoke as they sped from the coffee house and the flash of the cameras. Matt was reeling, off center, flashing "TILT" in bright, red letters. There were just too many oddities, too many coincidences. Everything was fuzzy and unclear.

"Just what do you think was going on there?" he finally asked.

"Beats me," Linda answered lightly. She stared at the small bruise Agent Sculler's rough grip had left on her hand. "Funny though, why would they think I was someone else? I mean, if their intelligence gathering is so good, how could they make such an error?"

Matt flipped on the turn signal, as he cut a sharp corner. "Good question." But the truth gnawed at him like starved rats tearing at sore flesh. He glanced at Linda and said, "There's something maybe you should know. Something I kept back in there."

Linda's eyes narrowed as she stared at him.

"They said Hermann Hospital."

"Yeah, what about it? I told them the truth. I've never heard of it, never been there."

"Maybe you haven't, but I have. I was taken there after the crash."

"Crash?" Her face was blank. Suddenly, her eyes widened. "The crash! You were in that plane crash, near Houston, back in January. I read about it!"

Matt nodded. "Yes. And I was treated at Memorial Hermann Hospital."

Neither spoke as silence, born of shock, tugged at the threads of reality. When Linda finally spoke, her words chilled them both. "My God, it's you they want!"

"Wait a minute! They had nothing to say to me, remember? It was all about you."

"But that doesn't make sense. I just look like the person they think I am. But how they've connected me to all this is beyond me."

As Matt drove, any logic or explanation he could concoct for the craziness failed him. Suddenly, he asked, "Are you feeling any better? Your color's back. We really didn't get a chance to talk much. Think you could handle it now?"

Linda stared out the window so long Matt thought she'd forgotten the question. Keeping her eyes focused outside the car, she muttered softly, "I have something to show you. It's at my place."

"What?"

"My place. It's not that far away. I have something there you should see." She pointed. "Take the next street on your right, and it's only a couple blocks over."

He followed her instructions, and they were soon in front of her apartment. "Park around back, if you don't mind. There's lots of shade there. Your car won't get so hot."

They climbed the steps to the first-floor breezeway and soon were around on the front side of the building. They stood at her front door. Matt wasn't sure exactly what he expected, but the neat, uncluttered residence somehow didn't surprise him.

As he waited for Linda to get whatever it was she wanted him to see, Matt strolled about the living room and stared at the few pictures on her wall. Then, perching on the edge of her sofa, he glanced at a book opened to a picture of bluebonnets lining a highway in the hill country of Texas. Bluebonnets, hadn't she said they were her favorite flower?

"Would you like something to drink, something cold, maybe?" He jumped at the sound of her voice when she caught him flipping through the open book. He shook his head, so she joined him on the edge of the couch. She gently took the book from the table and ran her fingers lightly over the page.

"Don't know what it is, but I love those pictures. When I get restless, I stare at them and drift away. Somehow, that calms me. Weird, I've never been there, but something's so familiar about it."

Matt faced her. "Why are you so sure you've never been there?" The challenge hung between them. He instantly regretted it. Her face grayed, and she leaned away.

"I don't understand. Why don't you believe me when I say I haven't been there? Am I not who I say I am?"

"I don't know. Are you?"

Leaning back into the deep cushions of her couch, she curled into a ball, bare feet tucked under her, arms over her knees. "All I know, all I remember is this here." She swept her arm about her. "This is my life, my home."

"But what about before the accident, what do you remember?"

Linda stared at the floor as she massaged her temples. "It's strange," she finally said, as if each word needed to be flashed in front of her before speaking it. "I have no feeling for anything before. It's like I know this was my life, but there are no feelings about it." She contemplated him. "I guess the amnesia is still there."

"Amnesia?"

"Yeah, amnesia. They said it would take a while for all my memory to return and not to force it. So, I haven't."

Turning so he faced her, he said, "So, all this time, you haven't been able to remember your past? You just accepted what they told you; no questions asked?"

"No. That's not it at all. I remember things. There're just holes, like Swiss cheese. Bits, pieces, gaps, but they're coming back."

Matt's eyes narrowed. He focused on the scar just above her eyes. "Why is it you are the carbon copy of a woman I sat beside on that fatal flight? Why is it these people think you were at a hospital that I was treated at?"

Linda didn't look at him. Instead, she picked at her fingers. With a big sigh, she finally said, "Tell me about her, about this woman you seem to think I am."

Despite the clammy grip of the surreal afternoon, it took Matt only a moment to organize his thoughts. He recounted his vivid memories of the flight, of what she'd told him about her husband, her childhood, and her current life. As his words flowed, bubbling from the deep well of denied turmoil, she kept her eyes on her hands. When he paused, she looked up and spoke softly.

"I read about the crash." She pulled a newspaper clipping from her pocket and handed it to Matt. "This is what I wanted to show you. I cut it from the paper."

He took the article from her and shifted uncomfortably. "Everyone says I was the only survivor, but I never believed it. When the plane hit ..." Tears streamed down his cheeks.

Linda put her hand over his. "I'm so sorry," she whispered. "I think I can understand now why you're so haunted by this woman."

Matt pushed away. Through eyes glazed by tears, he said, "I'm not haunted by her! Not anymore. She's alive, breathing and sitting here."

Linda jumped up. "Stop it! I'm not her. Yeah, there might be some similarity, but you're talking about someone else. Face it; that woman's dead! Gone. I can't replace her because I'm not her!"

"It's not true! I searched for her, for you. I flew to Dallas, met with the airline's chief executive officer. I even went to your Houston apartment, found your dead cat. I ..."

"Dead cat?"

He nodded. "In your apartment. And this Gateway Air chief, Trushard, he even gave me a copy of your dental records. All this to prove you were dead."

Linda gasped abruptly. "It's you!" Matt's heart stopped, and hope rose. Then she dashed it. "You're the one in the article, the unnamed source this Trushard got in trouble for releasing information to."

Remembering the scrap of paper in his hand, Matt walked to the window where the light was bright and read the article.

The words burned in his mind. Matt dropped the paper and stared out the window. The parking lot was filling as people returned from work. Small economy cars and a few sportier ones competed for parking spaces that made the lone black Mercedes look even more out of place. He whirled around to Linda.

"Your dental records ... I'd nearly forgotten! Trushard gave me copies. We can prove this now. Compare yours with the ones I have. Come on. Who's your dentist? Give him a call. See how quickly we can get them."

Linda didn't move. She didn't speak. She just stared at him, face blank. Then, without a word, she went into her bedroom. A moment later, Matt heard her rummaging through drawers. He heard paper crumpling and being tossed into a trash can. At her door, he leaned against the frame and crossed his arms.

"What's the matter?"

She looked up. "I'm trying to find my dentist. Surely, I have a record here somewhere of my dentist."

"You don't remember?"

She snapped. "No, I don't! Okay? I guess it's just one of those little details I forgot."

"Okay. It's okay." Matt's voice was gentle as he laid his hand lightly on her shoulder. "We can do this later."

Linda glanced at her watch. "It's late. And my car! I forgot!"

Before Matt could answer, there was pounding at the door. Linda shrugged and went to answer the summons. Before she could pull back the chain and open it, a voice shouted, "Ms. McGowan? Open up, please! It's very important we speak to you."

Whoever waited outside didn't give her time for an answer. Something large boomed against the steel-plated door, ramming it so hard, it almost fell free of its hinges. Another ram shook the room, and a voice shouted, "Will you hurry? We've got to get her now!"

Matt pulled Linda from the door and whispered against her ear, "These are no friends of yours. Is there a back way out of here?"

Linda grabbed Matt's hand and pulled as she dashed quietly to the kitchen. She pushed the window over the sink open and pointed outside to the metal skeleton of a fire escape. The stairs dropped down to an enclosed courtyard, cut off from the exterior entrances to the apartment. Matt followed Linda through the window and down the metal steps. When they reached the pavement, Linda pointed to her right at a door between the fire escape and the next adjacent building.

"That way," she said quietly. She ran ahead of Matt and pushed through the one-way door into the parking lot where Matt's truck was parked. They dashed for the truck, and as Matt slammed the gear in drive and Linda pulled her door shut, a couple of the black-suited men rounded the corner and shouted, waving at them to stop. Matt ignored their shouts and slammed his foot on the gas.

As they raced from the complex, Linda finally asked, "What on earth was that back there?"

Matt didn't hear her. His gaze was fixed on the rearview mirror. Two cars were following them. Both black. Both Mercedes. Both exact duplicates of the one he'd seen earlier in Linda's lot. Each lane change he made, they copied; each acceleration, they imitated. They were obvious, too obvious.

"Lynn—uh, Linda, why would someone be so interested in you that they show up and interrogate you at a coffee shop, then try to bust into your apartment, and now are on our tail?"

She seemed genuinely surprised. "You're sure?"

Matt nodded. "Not one, but two cars."

"Could it be those men from the coffee place? But why?"

"Can't tell, but there're definitely more than two men in each car. Either they got help, or someone else has developed some crazy kind of curiosity about you."

"Why did you automatically suppose it's me they're after? Why not some crazy fans of yours?" She gasped as she glanced at her side-view mirror.

"Something wrong?"

"I saw a car just like the ones behind us near my apartment the other morning. I didn't think anything about it, except I wondered who in my complex would have such an expensive car." Glancing at Matt, she added, "You saw it there today, didn't you, this afternoon?"

Matt nodded. As he gave his full concentration to the road, he drove erratically and fast, much faster than even he felt comfortable with. The black cars were good. They stayed on him like bubblegum on a flip-flop. But his Silverado hugged the pavement and gripped the road so that he was able to stay ahead.

A southbound entrance to the Golden State freeway came up. Speeding up the on-ramp, Matt headed for the far left lane. The cars stayed behind him, almost as if they knew in advance any move he might make.

"I wonder what's so important that they're going to such trouble to get to you. It must be more than just the details of a hospital stay, which you never told me about."

"You really believe this, don't you?"

"Well, it was you they wanted to ask all the questions."

"This is absurd. The world doesn't care about me. They care about you. You're the one they're fascinated with. They want to know if you sleep, eat, drink just like them, and if not, then how do you do it. It's you those photographers were aiming their cameras at!"

One of the cars pulled up beside them on the left. Its speed matched their own. Simultaneously, the other car moved into position on the right. Hemmed in on both sides and stuck behind a tractor-trailer, Matt wished he had a Tums to douse the blaze in his stomach.

Suddenly, Linda shrieked and pointed at the left window. The black car's windows were open, and a man in the front was pointing a badge *and* a gun at them. Matt sucked his breath in sharply when he realized the car on the right was doing the same. They were waving and pointing for him to pull off to the right.

Matt nodded. He turned the wheel to the right, but as the black car on the right moved toward the shoulder, opening the space beside him, Matt slammed his brakes. The car on the left jumped ahead, and the cars behind Matt stood on their noses. Matt jerked the truck to his right and slammed the accelerator hard. Then, without warning, he shifted lanes, first to the left, then to the right, and then back to the left again. By the time he reached the far left lane, the black car from the left had recovered and was gaining on them.

"Matt, they've got more guns!" Linda's scream startled him. He glanced in his rearview. Indeed, more than one muzzle was pointed in their direction. Swallowing, Matt prayed for an opening. When it presented itself, he zipped across all four lanes, hoping an exit would be waiting. But the cars stayed with him. Matt cursed. He pushed the accelerator down, zipping and weaving back and forth across the lanes, almost as if stitching a line of rickrack, all the while keeping his eyes on the rearview. Linda's scream jerked his eyes back to the road ahead.

"Stop now!"

Matt slammed the brakes, and his wheels screamed in protest. Before them was a wall of unmoving traffic, completely stopped by who knew what.

Matt pushed Linda. "Come on! We'll get out and run for it."

Before he could open his door, and with a mind of its own, traffic suddenly sputtered to life and began to race forward. The right lane moved first, and Matt pushed into the line of cars. In a moment, the right lane was flowing while the others remained stopped. Matt bolted ahead. A quick glance behind confirmed the black cars were still trapped in the jam. The hole that had opened for him had closed again.

Just like the parting of the Red Sea, it had swallowed up the enemy. The distance widened until the others were finally no longer in view.

With a big sigh, Matt risked a glance at Linda. "We've lost them for now. Let's get off and go somewhere and talk. Figure this out."

She stared at him. "What's to figure?"

His smile was apologetic. "Oh, there's a lot to figure. Why we're being followed is just the beginning."

"Mrs. Grayson, I'm Dr. Dereck DeBoe." There was a slight tremor in the man's voice. "We've never met, but I was part of a team that attended your son while he was in the hospital following the crash. I like to follow up with cases like your son's several months after discharge. I realize he is probably not there right now, but I wanted to get an indication from you as to how you feel his recovery has been."

Katie Grayson frowned. She switched the phone to her left ear and thought for a bit before responding.

"Mrs. Grayson?"

"Yes. I really don't know how to answer your question."

"Have you been in touch with your son recently?"

"Oh, he calls, usually every week or so. He's so busy, what with his moviemaking and all. He's doing quite well, you know, starring in a new picture."

"Yes, I've heard. Tell me, Mrs. Grayson, has he complained of any headaches, nausea, or disorientation in any of his calls?"

Katie thought for a moment. "No," she answered slowly. "I don't remember him saying anything about any of that. Is there something wrong? Should I be concerned?"

"No, uh, no. But if he should bring up any such symptoms, would you please get in touch? You can always have me paged through Memorial Hermann Hospital. It's Dereck DeBoe. Or you may call me at my office." Without waiting for her agreement, he spouted out a series of numbers. "If possible, when he comes back for a visit, I'd like to see him. Just give me a call. I'll set it all up."

"Mom, who was that?" Chad strolled into the kitchen and rubbed his hand lightly across Katie's back. "Not another babe trying to weasel out the old man's Hollywood number again?"

Katie smiled at her younger son. "No, just one of Matt's doctors doing a little follow-up."

Chad dropped his arm from her shoulder and frowned. "Follow-up. Now? I thought the old man was pronounced healed months ago. Why would a doc be calling now?"

Katie shrugged. "Who knows?" She turned so that Chad stood in front of her, and she stared him in the eye. "Be honest, Chad. Is Matt all right? He tells you things he conveniently forgets to tell me. Is there something I should know about?"

"Mom, he's fine. I think you worry too much."

Katie sighed. "You'd tell me if you thought differently?"

"Yeah, Mom. Sure."

Hands cold and sweating, heart thumping out of control, Matt zipped down the exit ramp. As he wound across less-busy surface streets, he was tempted to stop just so he could catch his breath and figure out what was happening. But something unseen kept his foot on the pedal and their tires racing over the pavement. Soon, an entrance to the San Bernardino Freeway, the I-10 heading east, came up. Matt sped up the onramp and jumped into multiple lanes of traffic all fleeing Los Angeles to unknown eastern destinations.

Matt considered the familiar interstate sign. I-10 was an escape, a back door to normalcy. No matter how bad things got, no matter how big the cow pile he stepped in was, he knew he could keep driving. It was a straight line that would take him home to Texas. The temptation was great. But Linda's words shook the vision of his mom's dinner table from his mind.

"They're gone, aren't they?"

"I hope." He cast yet another glance at the rearview mirror.

"Since they're gone, would you please take me back to my car? Then, I'll be on my way, and we can forget this day ever happened."

"You're not serious, are you? You really think it's all over now just because we don't see them? Have you forgotten what they did to your place this afternoon?"

Linda shook her head. "No. But ..."

"Think about it. First, the FBI comes to you; they know who you are and that you've been in the hospital. Now, they had to do a little digging to get that tidbit. But why do you suppose they made the effort? Next, we're chased on the freeway. They didn't get us, so what makes you think they'll stop now?"

"So, you think it's the FBI chasing us?"

Matt considered it briefly. "Who else could it be?"

"Good question. Those cars sure looked official." She scratched her head. "Wait a minute! I don't know my cars that well, but those weren't your standard-issue government sedans. Those were ..."

"Mercedes."

Their eyes met. "Then who?" she whispered as he shrugged.

Matt had always hated drivers who were too lazy or inconsiderate to use their signals. When the Vineyard Avenue–Ontario Airport exit came up, he broke his own rule. He swooped across two lanes and veered onto the exit without so much as flipping on his turn blinker once. "Just in case," he muttered, praying there was no one to care which way he went.

Vineyard Avenue south of I-10 was mostly commercial, a strip of restaurants and various motels catering to travelers. It ended at the Ontario International Airport. What better place to get lost than at the airport, even a smaller one like Ontario. While it wasn't the heaving megalopolis of swarming masses of humanity pushing and pulling to get to their destinations that LAX was, it did offer escape. Flights left regularly to other cities.

Matt swung his truck into a short-term parking area. In a few minutes, they were inside the main terminal. Most business travelers had already departed for the day. Few commercial flights were left on the boards listed as departing. For an airport, it was quiet, only a few passengers milled about. Matt ran to the first ticket counter he saw.

Slapping his Visa card in front of the agent, he spoke softly, "I need two tickets for your next flight."

"To where, sir?"

"Wherever it's going."

The man's eyes narrowed. He seemed about to say something. Instead, he typed in a command and waited for the answer to appear on his screen. "Looks like the next flight we have is to Denver with a continuation on to Kansas City."

"Good. Two tickets please."

"Names?"

"Mr. and Mrs. Jim Smith." Matt checked his watch and glanced over his shoulder.

"The name on the card is not Jim Smith. Do you have some other form of identification?"

Yeah, Matt thought, his license which further verified he wasn't Jim Smith. He leaned toward the man.

"Listen. You know and I know I'm not Jim Smith. I can give you my license and prove to you who I really am. Right now, I don't need for anyone to know who I really am." Matt showed the man his license. The agent studied it closely and then peered into Matt's face.

"It *is* you. Thought so! I saw *Killing Times.* You look just like you did in the picture. Tremendous movie! Certainly, Mr. Grayson, I'll honor your request, but ..." The agent leaned toward Matt and whispered, "I could get in trouble. Airlines have cracked down on the accuracy of passenger manifests, ever since Nine-Eleven and even more so since that crash near Houston. Big stink rose about some names and bodies not matching. We can't let just anyone on a plane without being certain of their identity, and that's before they're allowed to go through security. We've been given the riot act. Can't screw up now; it'd mean my job."

"Really?" Matt swiped at a little bead of perspiration that hung precariously over his eyebrow. He slipped a couple hundreds onto the counter and used the most desperate expression he could muster from his acting experience. "Please?"

For several moments, there was silence between them. The agent glanced to his left and right. Then with a shrug, he smiled and nodded as he slipped the bill off the countertop and onto his desk where a few seconds later, it disappeared.

"No problem, Mr. Smith," he said brightly, as his fingers typed furiously on his keyboard. Seconds later, a printer beside him spit out a couple sheets of paper and two boarding passes. The ticket agent quickly pulled the sheets from the tray, folded them, and inserted them into a ticket jacket.

"You and the missus, have a pleasant flight now." He winked as he handed the two ticket packets to Matt.

Matt jumped at the light touch on his arm. He turned to find Linda by his side. Her face was a death-white pale, and words formed on her lips, but she made no sound.

"What?" He gripped her shoulder and leaned toward her, straining to hear what she tried to say.

"I can't." The words finally reached his ears. "I can't get on that plane!"

Matt pulled her from the ticket counter toward a small alcove filled with plastic chairs. Gently, he pushed her into one.

"What do you mean you can't get on that plane?"

"I … just can't." Her pallor deepened, and she looked as if she were about to faint.

"You're afraid to fly?"

Linda wrinkled her nose. "No. It's just something about a plane. When I think about it, it's like I can't breathe. I guess I must have some kind of phobia or something."

"Linda, unless you want to meet those people who're after you, we've got to get out of here."

"You know, it could be you too." A bit of color returned to her face.

"Maybe, you're right," he said. "Maybe it's not just you. But we'll never figure this out unless we get to a place where we feel safe enough to stop running and make some sense of it all."

"Fine then. Sit down. Talk to your heart's content. But do we have to get on a plane? Why not go over to the coffee shop over there?" She pointed to a small cluster of tables and chairs across the terminal from them. "I mean, you did lose them back there. They don't know we're here."

As she spoke, a commotion erupted behind them. A wave of dark-suited men spilled through the main entrance. Passengers and airline employees alike were pushed out of the way. Screams erupted and mixed with loud curses. The swarm of suits converged in the center of the terminal, apparently awaiting their orders.

Matt glanced up, and the blood left his face. "Oh no, Linda. I think we've been found." Grabbing her arm, Matt pulled her up, and they raced away from the central terminal down toward the security section for their flight. As he ran, Matt frantically scanned every inch, looking for some way to escape. Then he saw it, a door marked Private Employees Only was slowly closing. He jerked Linda's hand and pulled her with him as he raced toward the escape. Matt grabbed the handle just before it clicked shut.

They ducked through the door, and as it shut behind him, Matt realized they were in a dead end, a janitor's closet. Gently, he gripped Linda's hand and whispered, "Just give me a moment to think this through. Okay?" She didn't answer, but he could feel her movement as if she was nodding.

Moments later, Matt peeked through a small opening of the door. What looked to be like twenty or thirty men, all dressed in dark suits, guns holstered on their belts and communication gear attached to their jackets near their throats, stood still as their boss or commander—or whatever the heck he was—talked. They were about thirty or so feet away. In midsentence, the leader's radio squawked, and he stopped and put it up to his ear. A moment later, his face red, he started shouting. The words "Kansas City" "Smith" and "planes" floated through the air to Matt.

"We're not going on any plane right now," Matt whispered over his shoulder to Linda.

As the leader shouted more orders to the assembled men, Matt gently pushed the door open wider. He gripped Linda's hand in his and dashed out and straight toward the closest exit.

"There, at the door; get them!"

A thundering herd pounded toward them as Matt frantically tugged and pulled on the door. Palms sweaty and swearing, he couldn't get the door to budge.

"Come on!" He jerked away, aiming toward another door. Linda wasn't as quick and tripped. Matt pulled her, not waiting for her to get her balance back.

They ran around the security gate into the passengers'-only area. Even more voices joined in the shouts for them to stop. As they raced toward the next door marked "Exit," a gate opened its door to an arriving flight, and passengers looking tired and weary from traveling flooded the area, pushing against anyone or anything that got in their way. Just as Matt reached the next door, the herd of dark suits collided with the mass of passengers. People screamed and fell. The men in black cursed and shoved. In the chaos, Matt and Linda slipped through the door and ran toward their freedom.

Back on I-10, Matt sped up the ramp for the westbound lanes toward Los Angeles. Once merged with the fast-flowing traffic, he finally asked himself what he was doing. Was he insane? Were those people so monstrous they warranted the fear pushing his foot down on the accelerator? He had no answers. Only the speed of his truck and the distance he put between them made any sense at the moment.

Linda stared out the window, just as she had on the fateful plane ride, and it stirred too many frightening memories. Why had he gone to such lengths to find out about her? What was it that drove him? Was it worth abandoning his final days on a critical film role and risking a lawsuit for breach of contract, no doubt jeopardizing his future just to escape those who chased them? He glanced at Linda. She was a stranger; why was he so willing to give up all he had to find the answers to her?

Grateful to be able to cruise above the speed limit—no traffic jams to slow things down—Matt pulled his phone out, punched some numbers, and hit the send button. Jerry's voice was on the other end before he passed the next mile marker.

"Matt, what on earth is going on? Where are you?" Jerry sounded frantic.

"It's not that easy to answer. I think I may be in some trouble."

"Well, that's news." Matt grimaced at his agent's sarcasm. "Do you know what kind of firestorm you've created? The studio's like a bomb exploded. The producer had chest pains when he heard what you'd done. The director almost overdosed on his Zanex. They're convinced you're over the edge."

"Why? All I did was drive off without saying good-bye."

"Really? Well, that's not the story here. Rumors are flying that you ran off the lot after kidnapping that reporter. The producer is muttering contract violations, and Spielberg's office has called twice."

Matt interrupted. "Whoa, Jerry, are you saying all this erupted just because I skipped out this afternoon for a while? I had no scenes scheduled. I thought I was free for the rest of the day."

"You were, but you know how they are. It doesn't take much of a rumor to fuel major panic."

"Jerry, stars do it all the time. They're known for their temperamental little acts."

"You're not there yet. Your place in this town isn't sealed. And even when you hit the big-time, as I know you will, remember that even the big ones fall. Do I need to name names?"

Matt sighed. "Man, I need some help here. I need some time. Stall them. See what you can do."

"What for, Matt? Is it that reporter? Has she cast some spell over you?"

Matt didn't answer, so Jerry continued, "Okay, I'll try to put them off, think of something that'll appease them. But I don't know how long it'll work. Matt …" He heard Jerry suck on his cigarette before he continued, "this is what you wanted more than anything else, isn't it? To act, to work with the best? Well, you're poised on that doorstep, ready to cross over to real fame, real respect. Are you willing to toss it, just like that?"

Matt couldn't think about it. If he did, he was afraid he'd lose all courage and become unwilling to pay the cost of what he planned.

"Jerry, don't blow this all out of proportion. I've just had a little family emergency of some sort. I've got to make a quick trip back home. I'll be back on the set in a couple days. You can buy me that much time, can't you? It really is an emergency; it's just I can't tell you about it right now. I *will* be back, though. Don't worry about that."

Jerry didn't answer right away. When he did, his voice was flat. "All right. If that's what you say. By the way, where can I reach you?"

After a moment of silence, Matt said, "Just leave messages on my voice mail. I'll get back to you." He ended the call.

Aimed at the bowels of Los Angeles, Matt pushed the accelerator as much as he dared. The City of Angels. He wished for an angel then, one to watch over them, one to show him what to do.

Jerry took a long drag from his cigarette. One day, he would quit. Today wasn't that day. Glancing at the muted TV, Jerry saw a news bulletin flashing across the screen. Fumbling with the remote, he punched up the volume.

"This breaking news just in. KTLA, in an exclusive, has discovered that one of Hollywood's newest film sensations, Matt Grayson, is missing. He was last seen in the Studio City area with Los Angeles Times *reporter Linda McGowan. Authorities will not comment on what may have happened. However, they are asking anyone with any information concerning these individuals to contact their local police department immediately."*

A picture of Linda and Matt flashed on the screen. Jerry blanched as he rubbed his forehead. He saw his career skydiving toward earth, his parachute in flames. Things were not good, not good at all.

CHAPTER 8

Crimson and orange curtains blazed across an unencumbered sky as the sun slipped below the Pacific horizon. The burning light was a bitter reminder. Everything in flames, hope lost. Matt tried to stretch his shoulders while keeping his hands on the wheel. He glanced at Linda. Still sleeping. Amazing how she'd conked out after their little adventure at the airport. And all that time, driving alone, he'd thought about their situation. Still, there were no answers.

He'd taken I-10 to the coast, its end. There he'd turned north on the Pacific Coast Highway and continued his journey, to what and where, he wasn't sure. For miles, he'd seen no evidence of anyone following. The whole afternoon didn't make sense; none of it did. Linda stretched gracefully and yawned.

"Nice nap?"

"Yeah. I can't believe I slept. Hey, where are we? Anywhere close to my car?" She glanced out the window at the rapidly darkening world.

"No. Hungry?"

"I'm famished. What about you?" She yawned again.

"Yes. Starving."

The turn for Topanga Canyon Boulevard came up suddenly, and Matt's wheels squealed as he cut sharply to the right. "We'll go up toward Ventura and Thousand Oaks. Should be less of a chance of us being spotted on this road. If you can hang in there, we'll find some food on the other end."

The road wasted no time in gaining altitude. Sharp twists and hairpin turns pulled them upward over land that rose nearly straight up from the ocean. As they climbed, they were rewarded with an increasingly breathtaking view. Even though the sun was below the horizon, its lingering flames danced across the heavens, leaving them dripping in oranges, reds, and purples. The beauty demanded a pause, a time of reflection on life's goodness and grandeur. It demanded awe, hushed and still, and all breath held, as it overwhelmed all beholders with the majesty of creation.

Matt wanted desperately to stop and savor the moment, to celebrate life found and the miracle sitting beside him, but fear and urgency were two strong opponents. He gave in to their demands.

He stomped on the gas pedal, and the truck's wheels screamed as they careened around each increasingly steep and narrow curve that seemed to traverse the ridge of the mountains. Miles later, they were rewarded, however. The road eventually straightened and became a true boulevard. By the time they crossed Ventura Boulevard, Matt decided to head back toward Los Angeles. Night had become a black cloak offering some semblance of cover for them.

Shortly, the Sherman Oaks Galleria mall complex came into view. Without consulting Linda, Matt swung into the first parking entrance he found.

"The mall?" she asked as he backed into a slot.

"Yeah, the mall. Think about it. It's Friday night. There'll be people everywhere. Makes it easy for us to get lost. I don't think the police or whatever will come shooting after us if we're in the middle of a bunch of teens."

"If you say so."

As Matt predicted, the mall was crowded. Teens hung out, some at the arcade, others loping along in small groups, either bored or awe-inspired by the merchandise begging for their attention. Young couples strolled leisurely, some with dreams in their eyes, holding hands. Others pushed children in carriages and tried to comfort squealing babies with pacifiers or bottles. Older couples, backs bent from years of gravity, moved more slowly, some with the help of walkers and canes, others with an energy the youth might have envied had they taken the time to notice.

As Matt held Linda's hand lightly and pushed through the masses, he wished they were there for pleasure. He envied those who had nothing better to do than stroll about and waste precious time on nothing more important than gazing in shops and buying useless trinkets.

"Like German?" He stopped at the edge of a large food court. "Over there." He pointed to a dark alcove in a corner, stuffed in between a pizzeria and a taco palace.

Linda wrinkled her nose. "I was never too fond of kraut. How about some pizza or a chicken sandwich or something?"

A few minutes later, Matt carried a tray with two slices of steaming pepperoni pizza and a paper plate full of cheese-covered breadsticks. Linda held two large cups of Pepsi. They settled at a corner table where they could watch most all the food court's activity, yet not stand out themselves.

Linda dove into her pizza, and Matt couldn't take his eyes off her. Her mouth formed such a beautiful line as it curved about each bite. The satisfaction of her hunger showed in her enjoyment, and it thrilled him.

"Not hungry?" She looked up suddenly as she wiped her chin.

"Uh, yes. I … I was just thirsty." Belatedly, he took a long, loud slurp of Pepsi.

"You know, pizza's always been my downfall. Ever since I was a kid, I never could get enough." She laughed, and her eyes twinkled. "You know, I haven't given it a thought in months! How weird. I remember it so vividly. Saturdays, Mom always made it for us." She stopped suddenly, and her smile vanished. "Mom. She's gone now. So is Dad, everyone." She looked up, and with a sudden flush on her cheeks, she put her hands in her lap and looked away. "I'm sorry. I really didn't mean to go on like that," she said quietly.

Matt reached across the table and touched her arm lightly. "No, please, go on. You seem amazed to be thinking of them."

She rubbed the creases in her forehead. "I guess. Maybe it's the amnesia." She stared for a while at some unknown object across from them. Then, she shook her head slightly and returned her gaze to meet his.

"I really hadn't given it much thought. In fact, I can't remember the last time I thought about my parents, or anything else from the past."

Matt leaned toward her and was silent as he contemplated what to say. "What about your husband?"

"Husband? I'm not married."

"But you were."

Her voice rose. "No! I've never been married."

"But you told me you were married at one time. You told me not to be sorry."

Her eyes widened, and she paled as she shrank from him. She looked like a bird ready to fly from its perch.

"I don't know what you're talking about. I've never been married, ever." She wiped her hands, threw down the napkin, and stood. "I'm finished. If you don't mind, I'd like to go. My head hurts. I'm tired. It's been a long day." She tugged at her purse strap, jerking it from the chair back. At that instant, it chose to break, and all its contents spilled onto the floor.

Linda dropped to her knees and started gathering lipsticks, nail files, loose change, tissues, and some business cards, as each with a mind of its own, scattered in twenty different directions. Matt sank down beside her and calmly, methodically, gathered all the items and handed them to her.

Jamming them into her purse with a mad, random motion, she muttered, "I just want to go home." Flinging the bag under her arm, she stomped toward an exit sign. Before she got to the door, she abruptly stopped. Jaw slack, she stared at one of the many television monitors hanging throughout the mall. Matt glanced in the same direction. The news was on, and both her face and his filled the screen. A title frame with bold letters said, "Missing. If seen, please contact local police department."

Matt gulped. Linda blanched.

Across from them, a group of teenage girls giggled and pointed. An Asian couple glanced hesitantly at him and then quickly averted their eyes.

Two elderly women shuffled by, one leaning heavily on her cane, the other robust and full of vigor. Robust one punched cane lady's arm. "Look, Edith. It's him, that new movie hunk. The one they say is missing!"

"What's that?" Edith stopped and tugged at her hearing aid. "I can't hear you, Elsie. Speak up!"

"I said," Elsie shouted, "there's that new movie hunk all the girls are talking about. He's right there!" She pointed a gnarled finger at Matt. "Want to meet him?"

"Do I want some meat?" Elsie screamed back.

"No! *Meet him.* Do you want to meet that movie star? You know the one the girls at the bingo table have been talking about for the past month."

"What meat have the girls been talking about, red meat? You know, I can't eat red meat. It gives me gas!"

"Oh, never mind." Edith glanced at Matt, winked, and then tugged at Elsie's arm, urging her along.

Matt pulled at Linda, forcing her to look at him. "It's time we get out of here."

Matt started toward a set of glass doors leading toward the parking area. He held on to Linda's hand as if she might flee from him. They never made it through the doors. A thirty-something man, dressed in custom-tailored slacks and Italian leather shoes and decorated with gold jewelry on his hands and neck, blocked their way. His wide smile was full of professionally whitened teeth. Hair, glued in place so that no strand could ever possibly be errant, not even in hurricane-force winds, stood at attention.

"Excuse me, but you look so familiar. Don't I know you?"

Linda shrugged, as Matt's eyes fixed on the man. Black poppy seeds, obviously left from dinner, were planted along the man's gum line.

"Don't think so," Matt said as he pushed past, trying not to see the man's gums. But, the man's grin grew, and he grabbed Matt's arm.

"No, wait. You're such a sharp-looking couple, I was sure I'd met you before. But never mind about that." He thrust a business card at Matt's hand. Linda dug her fingers into Matt's arm and shook her head almost imperceptibly. Matt glanced at the card. It said, "Jim Gamble, Private Business Development."

Matt handed the card back to the man. "I don't think—"

The man ignored him. "My business is expanding so fast, I just can't keep up with the demand. I was wondering if you could give me a minute. I'm looking for six people who would like to make up to six figures working not more than twenty hours a week." He warmed to his subject, and his smile broadened.

"Now this isn't some start-up, fly-by-night company, but an established, proven business with growing profits every year. Why, in fact, I'll show you how you can buy her ..." He nodded at Linda. "... freedom in six months to a year. Wouldn't it be nice to have your wife at home, taking care of business there while raising the little ones ... Uh, you do have plans for them, don't you?" He didn't stop at Matt's frown. "I mean, having her free to go with you wherever you go, wouldn't that be ideal?"

Matt didn't know whether to laugh or scream. "Sorry. I haven't got time now." He dropped the card in the man's hand and pushed past.

The man didn't give up. "Time is all you've got. Can't waste it. That's what this business is all about. Time. Gaining control. Getting more of it." He glanced at the rejected card and shouted at their backs as they ran away. "I tell you, you're passing up an opportunity of a lifetime! It's a proven thing. All you need is six other people who're interested in earning extra income." The man stopped. His smile vanished.

"Wait a minute! Hold it all. I know you!" The man's voice rose. "You're him, that guy, the one on TV, the one who's got a reward on his head!" He pointed at the television screens. Another news bulletin was on the tube, and this time flashing beneath Matt and Linda's faces was a staggering sum, a reward for information leading to their return.

"Wait just a minute!" The man sprinted after them. "I'm not letting you get away so fast!" He waved his arms and shouted. "Police! Here, Police! I've found them. That couple on TV, the one with a reward on them!"

Like an ocean wave gathering height, ready to spill and crash against the sand, the crowd swelled, and people started screaming and pointing. The wave amplified into a full stampede. Young and old, shoppers and those there merely out for an evening stroll, they all gathered, ready to chase the bounty.

As Matt and Linda ran, two over-sized security officers joined the melee. Panting from the unaccustomed exertion, their feeble shouts to stop were lost in the growing roar of voices. Frantically, the business freedom man pointed at Matt and Linda and shouted, "There! Over that way!"

Footsteps pounded as the wave crashed, and the crowd gained inches by the second as Matt and Linda's feet pounded the polished tile floor. When they rounded a corner, a large department store greeted them.

Matt pulled Linda through the entrance and swerved immediately to his right toward a rack of men's clothing. Behind them, the man, the two out-of-breath security officers, and most of the gawkers followed. Metal display racks toppled. Clothing was trampled. For a brief second after they had darted through the men's suits and were running on to casual wear, it was quiet. Matt actually hoped they'd lost their tail. His hopes died when he heard the shout, "There. Over there!"

Matt plowed through rows of shirts, then slacks and jackets. He flew faster, no longer careful to keep from knocking things over. Linda followed in the path he cleared. Fortunately, there were few shoppers in the store, but those present stopped, stared, and pointed. One shouted, "That's him! Matt Grayson. Come on! Let's get him!"

The store's departments were linked together in an octagonal design. As Matt and Linda fled the men's department, the thundering herd burst into view. The security officers shouted on radios, no doubt calling for reinforcements.

"Where's an exit when you need one?" Matt muttered.

Suddenly, the racks of clothing changed from slacks to dresses. A big sale was in progress in the women's department. Temporary racks of clothing lined the aisle, blocking from view the larger shopping area beyond. Matt pushed through one as Linda followed. Too late, he realized they'd entered a dead end. There was no exit except back through the dresses. The footsteps were louder, closer.

Matt grabbed two garments off the rack and yanked Linda's hand before busting through the swinging doors into the ladies' dressing room. A young clerk with ten earrings in one ear and a nose ring smacked gum while holding a paperback in one hand and fingering the seventh earring with the other hand. Looking bored, she glanced up at them.

"She wants my opinion." Matt nodded at the two size 3x robes he held.

The woman's jaw slackened, and a wad of gum covered her front teeth. She shrugged. "Whatever." She popped the gum, and at least three of her earrings tinkled as she stuck her nose back in the paperback.

Matt opened and slammed each dressing room door, causing the thin walls to shake. Just as he'd given up hope of escaping, the last door opened to a dark hall.

"Like, are you guys all right in there?" The clerk shouted through her gum. "Don't get anything on those robes, now." There was no answer. Matt and Lynn were gone.

They were running down a musty, dark passageway, the only light a single bare bulb several yards away. They finally came to a door. It wasn't locked. After pulling it open, Matt glanced up and down a brightly lit, well-maintained service hallway. No one appeared to be around, so he motioned for Linda to follow. Across from them were some restrooms and a water fountain.

Matt pointed at the men's room. "Wait for me," he whispered.

When Matt emerged moments later, he didn't see Linda. For a moment, his heart stopped. Then, the ladies' room door opened, and she strolled out. Stopping for a quick drink, she linked her arm in his and asked, as if she knew someone was watching, "Feel better, dear?"

They strolled casually down the hall until they stood on the opposite side of the food court from where they'd departed. The crowd had either dispersed, or was in hot pursuit elsewhere in the mall. Trying to look like any casual shoppers, Matt and Linda ambled past empty tables, overturned chairs, and a few bored diners who were clueless to the earlier melee and headed toward the first exit sign they saw.

Tim slurped the last of his Coke and then burped loudly.

Harry grimaced. "Where'd you learn table manners?" he asked.

"Manners? Who needs those? Like, they died with the Cleavers."

Harry shrugged as Tim hockered into his napkin, threw it on his tray, and glanced up at him.

"Good enough for you?" Harry frowned. "Okay then. How 'bout we call it a day? It's been a long one."

"Sure." Harry stretched and looked about. He'd never gotten a clue as to what had caused the earlier commotion. A bunch of people had gathered at the far end of the court amidst lots of shouting. Frankly, he didn't care. Since the crowd had thinned, he was glad. They wouldn't have to push through a wall of people just to get out.

After tossing his trash, Harry glanced at one of the many monitors hanging from the ceiling. Sucking in his breath sharply, he saw Matt Grayson's face on the screen. The woman's face was inserted next to his. Harry jumped on a chair and stretched a long arm toward the volume control.

"... Missing since early afternoon. It is urgent they be located. If seen, please contact ..."

Harry shouted at Tim, "Get a load of this, man!" He pointed at the screen. A reward sum flashed across the bottom edge.

Harry's eyes met Tim's. "Thinking what I'm thinking?" he asked.

"Yeah, dinner's over, and our pictures just got worth a lot more money!"

Harry jumped from the chair and waited as Tim scooped greasy papers, dirty napkins, and his empty cup onto his tray. Just as Tim dumped his trash in the can, Harry grabbed his arm and pointed.

"Look!"

Tim jerked around in time to see a man identical to Matt Grayson shoot by, a dark-haired woman grasping his hand. Tim's tray hit the floor with a loud clatter.

"Harry," Tim shouted over his shoulder as he sprinted in their direction, "got your camera?"

"You bet I do."

Matt made the mistake of pausing at the exit and glancing briefly over his shoulder. For a nanosecond, he felt relief. None of the earlier crowd was visible. A bright flash blinded him. He grabbed Linda's hand and pulled her as a new burst of energy rushed through his veins.

"We've been found!" he shouted as he dashed through the door.

Matt zipped through a maze of cars, weaving and tugging on Linda's arm with each move. Abruptly, he ducked, pulling her with him. Almost instantly, two sets of feet flew past and stopped. After an eternity of hearing nothing but his heartbeat, Matt risked peeking around the front of the car and immediately sucked in his breath. The same two photographers, the ones who'd caught them earlier that day, were waiting barely five feet away.

Silently, he edged back and put a finger over his lips. Linda nodded. Together, they waited for another eternity and were finally rewarded when the footsteps slowly moved away from them.

Again, Matt risked a peek. The men were gone. Turning to Linda, he pointed beyond her and then crept quietly toward the back of the next car. He stopped, and at his quick nod, they scooted across the open space and into Matt's truck.

Wheels squealed, and the engine roared as they sped from the parking deck and into the open air of the surface roads circling the mall. As the slow realization crept into Matt's consciousness that no one followed, his shoulders slumped with relief. Yet, he pushed the gas pedal as far as he dared. The urgency driving him was just as strong as when they'd raced from the Ontario airport.

After several blocks and it appeared no one followed them, Matt started looking for a branch of his bank. When he found one, he quickly turned in and pulled up to the ATM. He inserted his card and waited. The machine beeped several times and then flashed a message on the screen. "Card invalid. Card invalid."

As if the plastic in its grip was foul tasting, the ATM spit the card out. But before Matt could grab it, the machine changed its mind and whirred, sucking the plastic back into its innards. A new message flashed. "Police have been notified."

Matt slammed the gear in drive. The truck responded swiftly, keeping a firm grip on the pavement while leaning wildly.

Linda finally asked, "Anything the matter?"

"Yeah, just a little. Machine swallowed my card. Said police have been notified." He glanced at her between watching the rearview mirror and oncoming traffic. "Ever have that happen to you? I've had my card swallowed before. Several times before I figured out I couldn't carry my wallet next to my cell phone. But I've never had it confiscated and then get informed the police were notified." He flipped the turn signal on, and without easing his foot from the accelerator, he careened around the corner.

When his breathing finally slowed, he said, "Those people are behind this for sure. Who knows what else they've manipulated in our lives. But whatever they've done and plan to do, I'm afraid there's no doubt we can't go to either of our places tonight."

"Uh ... just what does that leave us with?" Linda asked with a voice barely over a whisper. Her shoulders were slumped, and it looked as if all her fight had evaporated.

Before Matt could respond, his phone beeped. He flipped it open and shouted into the mouthpiece, "Yeah?"

No one answered. Matt checked the display to see if he'd lost the connection, but it showed the call was active. He listened again. There was a faint groan.

"Who is this?" he shouted.

The groan grew louder before the static claimed the airspace, and the phone indicated there was no active call.

Matt slammed the phone shut and tossed it to Linda. "Check the display. Read me the number of that last call."

She read the number to him.

Matt's voice was terse. "We're going to Jerry's."

In less than an hour, they were in front of Jerry's house in Pasadena. The older neighborhood was framed by thick-trunked trees and dotted with bougainvillea climbing porch columns and small trellises. Streetlamps cast sporadic pools of light on the sidewalk and asphalt. Jerry's house was dark. Matt didn't see his car in the drive either.

"Something's happened. I'm certain that was Jerry groaning on the phone. He was home tonight. He never misses the Royals when they're on TV."

Matt drove past the dark house to the end of the block. He scanned the neighborhood searching for a clue, anything that might give a hint that something was out of the ordinary. Nothing seemed wrong, however. Circling around, they made their way back to Jerry's house and pulled in the drive as far behind the house as possible.

After they shut their doors quietly, Matt slipped inside Jerry's garage. His car was there. He felt the hood. It was cold. Outside, he trotted quietly up the back steps to the back door. Repeatedly, he pushed the bell. Its hollow chime sounded clearly, yet there was no answer. Matt pounded on the door frame and called Jerry's name softly. Still no answer.

The gnawing feeling in his stomach intensified. Matt groped around the door frame, under the mat, and all around the entrance area, praying for a hidden key. As he searched, Linda stepped past him and pushed against the door. It swung open.

"What?" Matt muttered as Linda strolled in like she belonged. "Jerry would never leave his door open like that. Unless ..." He grabbed her arm and pulled her back.

With Linda behind him, Matt tiptoed forward, running his hand along the wall, feeling his way through the kitchen and into the front living area. He stepped through the doorway and tripped over something. It moved and groaned.

Matt groped around until he found a light switch and flipped it on. Light flooded the room, and at his feet, he saw a bound mass. Matt knelt and rolled the heap over. Jerry's eyes stared up at him. A big blue spot grew under his right eye, and duct tape sealed his mouth. Although his hands were bound, he'd managed to roll to the phone, knock the handset free, and hit the speed dial.

"Jerry? What on earth happened?" Matt's fingers flew as he worked to untie the cords after ripping the tape from his mouth. Jerry licked his lips and rubbed his wrists as Matt finished untying the knots.

Books, torn and ripped, covered the floor. The couch was turned on its side, the bottom ripped, stuffing spilling from its insides. Lamps were broken and shades smashed. Curtains were torn from their hooks. It was as if a swarm of locusts had flown through, devouring everything in its path.

Jerry's hands trembled as he continued to rub the circulation back into them. "It was the Royals. Had a fat lead when suddenly ... suddenly the front door blew open. These men burst in. Faces in black ski masks, black clothes, everything black. They carried some impressive-looking weapons. In a matter of seconds, they breezed through, knocked everything around, tore it apart, and even ran through the attic. Then, they threw me down, tied me up, and left. It was like one of those five-point-five quakes we have. It was over before I realized what had happened." Jerry's hands shook even more as he rummaged through the mound of papers where his end table used to be.

"See my cigarettes anywhere?" He kept digging. When he spied the white sticks on the floor, he lunged at them. Seconds later, he puffed hungrily. "Keep saying I'm going to quit. Stuff keeps happening that makes me hang on tighter than ever." He sucked some more of the calming nicotine into his lungs, and when the shaking of his hands lessened, his eyes brightened. A broad grin broke out on his face as he looked at Matt.

"Man, oh man, is it good to see your face!" He clasped Matt in a tight but brief bear hug. Matt pushed away from Jerry and kicked debris out of his way. After setting the couch upright, he urged Jerry to sit down.

"Do you have any idea who those people were? Police? FBI? CIA? DEA? Did they say anything?"

"Professional," Jerry managed between puffs as he lit another cigarette. "Some type of professional, that's all I know." He inhaled deeply and blew the smoke out slowly. "Can't imagine what they wanted with me. Maybe after they got in here, they realized it was a mistake and that's why they left so fast."

"Maybe, but I don't think so. Those types don't make mistakes. Obviously, you didn't have what they were looking for. Or … they found it quickly and left with it. Whatever the case, I'll bet big money, it has something to do with me … and her." Matt pointed to the kitchen where Linda hovered by the door.

Jerry's eyes widened as he stared. "So, you two fugitives are still together. You've seen the TV, haven't you?"

Matt nodded. "Yes, even the latest about some reward."

"After you left today, I got a phone call from some woman. Wouldn't give me her name or who she worked for, but she implied it was something government related. Quizzed me pretty hard about you, the things you do, she even asked about your life since the crash. Seemed frantic to find out where you were. You know, I don't normally give out information about my clients, but she hinted at bad things if I didn't cooperate. Implied she could send the IRS my way. She …"

"Jerry! What did you tell her?"

"Will you just chill? I didn't have a clue as to what was going on. So, I said our relationship was strictly business, and I didn't get into the personal side of your life." Jerry sucked on his cigarette and blew out with a whistle as he crushed the stub in an empty soda can.

Matt pointed at Linda. "They tried to break down the door to her apartment while we were there today. We slipped out, and on the freeway, they tried to run us down. At the airport, a whole swarm of them went running through the place, looking for us. We were chased from the mall after our pictures were flashed on the monitors in the food court. We had nowhere else to go! You're the only one left."

"Gee, you certainly know how to make a man feel wanted." Jerry grinned. "No matter, looks like you've got some serious trouble. This probably is the best place for you, at least for now. Maybe those buzzards won't think to come looking again." He dropped his head against the cushioned back of the couch. "Guess you don't have a clue as to why all this is happening."

"No. But I'm willing to bet my Spielberg contract, it has something to do with the plane crash."

"What're you talking about?"

Matt's eyes bored into Jerry. "Jerry, this is her." He nodded toward Linda. "The woman."

"The who?"

"Her. You know, *the* woman."

Recognition finally widened his eyes. "Matt, you can't be serious. It's not possible."

"But it is. I just have to convince her; that's all."

"Convince me of what?" Linda asked.

"That you're not really Linda McGowan."

Sculler and Maderm stopped at a deserted intersection in east LA. No cars were passing through the light, yet the signal was determined to run its full cycle. Exhaustion showed on both their faces. The trail was cold. There were no more leads. They'd spent the afternoon checking facts, digging for information. But it didn't seem to exist despite earlier evidence to the contrary. Maderm didn't understand how things could dry out so fast. Their sources were not compromised, he was sure of it. So what had happened?

"It's beyond me," Sculler said with a sharp edge to his voice. "Personally, I think we need to go back to Houston. Retrace our steps. Talk to our doc again."

Maderm grunted.

Sculler continued, "We need to grill Hampton. He was the one who arranged to send us on this little adventure." The sarcasm was thicker than hot molasses. "Something's not right, and it starts with him. I mean, being the special agent in charge of the Houston field office, he should've gotten his facts straight before sending us out on some crazy goose hunt. The director's not going to like this waste of resources. There's too much scrutiny on everything we do as it is."

Maderm scratched his chin. "But if we're successful, then a few tax dollars spent following some lame leads won't put a dent in their pockets, because they'll be so full from the graft we hauled in, they'll never know the difference."

The light changed, and Sculler hit the gas. The car jumped forward. Maderm turned on the radio. Clay Walker's "What's It to You" was playing. When the song finished, the announcer interrupted the commercial for a breaking news flash.

"A massive manhunt continues for missing persons, Matt Grayson and Linda McGowan. Citizen reports indicate they were spotted earlier this evening at Sherman Oaks Galleria. However, local police were unable to confirm those reports. Police are requesting the assistance of anyone who has knowledge of the location of these two individuals. A reward is being offered for information leading to their recovery. There is extreme, I repeat, extreme concern for their safety. It is believed they are in a tan, late-model Chevy Silverado. Please call your local police department with any information you may have."

Sculler glanced at Maderm, who raised his brows. "What do you suppose is going on?"

"Good question, my friend, good indeed."

"What do you know about Grayson, other than what we've been told and the obvious?"

Sculler shook his head. "Nothing but the obvious. I am curious as to his involvement."

"Suppose this is some kind of smoke screen?"

Sculler suddenly slammed the brakes. "That's it. A screen. They know we're on to them. They're in a panic." He whipped the car around in a sharp U-turn and raced toward the freeway. "Something doesn't add up. And we're gonna find out why."

Matt and Linda stood in the kitchen and watched as Jerry fixed a pot of coffee. Soon, the warm, mouth-watering aroma filled the room as the brew dripped. When the coffeemaker finished its cycle, Jerry pulled three mugs out of a cluttered cabinet and filled each with the strong black drink.

"Sugar? Cream anyone?" Matt and Linda both shook their heads. "Fine. I like a lot of both." After setting the mugs in front of his guests, he dumped a couple heaping spoonfuls of sugar into his cup and then two more of instant creamer. After stirring, he settled into his chair and leaned on the table with his elbows.

"So, we know someone is spreading the word you're missing and it's so important you be found that they've put a bounty on your head. Now, one could either deduce they think there's foul play involved and someone has kidnapped you, or they're hoping to entice the greedy public to come tattling forth with info on your whereabouts in return for some nice play money." Jerry took a long swig of the hot coffee. "Me, I think it's door number two. But the real question is, who's doing this? Is it the FBI or someone else?"

"More importantly, why?" Linda asked.

Matt shrugged. "Just as we were leaving Max's Coffeery, two

supposed FBI agents showed up and asked some pretty strange questions. But they were all aimed at Linda." Matt glanced briefly at her, but she was staring at her cup. "We left and went to her place. We weren't there very long before some men tried to break her door down. Someone has been on us ever since. Tell me, why are we so interesting all of a sudden?"

"It is weird." Jerry said, leaning back in his chair. "It makes no sense at all."

As Matt and Jerry talked, Linda sat quietly, staring at her coffee, sometimes stirring it, sometimes just gazing into the dark pool of liquid. The men continued chatting while she said nothing. When she finally spoke, her voice was quiet and barely audible.

"You haven't answered my question. Remember, you were going to prove I'm not Linda McGowan. Did you finally decide to believe me?"

Matt paled as he gulped his coffee. "Uh no. But there are some things I need to tell you, some things about the crash." Matt ran a hand through his rumpled hair. "After the plane crashed, when I first came to, the cabin was dark. There was a hole in the fuselage where your seat had been. I climbed out and down to the ground. You were in some bushes a few yards from the plane. I carried you from there just as what was left of the plane fell the rest of the way to the ground. It burned. No one else got out alive. We slept in the woods that night. It was rainy and cold. The—"

Linda stopped him again. "You told me this, remember? Besides, it was that other woman you carried out. Not me!" She stopped and stared at Matt. His face was white, and he was perspiring heavily.

"Please, just hear me out. The next day, when I awoke, you were by my side, but you were in bad shape. Your skin was gray, and you didn't make a lot of sense when you talked. I carried you through the woods until we came to a massive field.

"For a while, I really thought we'd fallen off the face of the earth. There was no one or anything there, just us in the middle of a massive open field. I kept walking, carrying you. After a while, I found an old barn. Inside, there was nothing but an old blanket. I covered you and ran for help. An old farmer came on his tractor and took us to his house.

"Funny, they didn't have running water, just an old pump at the sink. And no phone either. But, they took us in, covered our wounds, and watched you while I hitched a ride to find a doctor." Matt rubbed his forefinger slowly across his forehead. "You know, it was really weird; everything seemed so old. Old cars, old clothes, no modern conveniences. Strange little hospital in town, nurses still wearing caps and those bouncy skirts from the fifties. Anyway, I found a doctor. Along with a nurse, we drove back to the farmer's house. But ..."

"But what?"

"We didn't make it ... in time. There was nothing the doctor could do."

"Wait! You're trying to tell me this crash was near Houston's airport and there were no ambulances, fire trucks, rescue workers, nothing, and no one out there to take care of us? You're saying we went through this field to this old farm out of the past and we stayed there until, until ..." Her voice trailed off.

"Until a doctor from town came out to take care of you. Except ..." The picture of her still form lying on the bed was fresh, painful. "It was ... too late."

"What do you mean 'too late'?" She took his hand in hers and squeezed with surprising strength.

"I mean, that when we got there, the doctor, the nurse, they all tried to revive you. But there was nothing they could do."

Linda dropped Matt's hand, pushed her chair back, and slapped the table. She grinned.

"Well, that solves your problem right there. Obviously, it's not me. I'm not dead! I can't be the same woman. She's dead. I'm not!"

"But have you forgotten something? No matter what you believe about what I've just told you, people out there want you, and they're willing to pay a large sum. That alone should grab your curiosity. Certainly does mine."

"Okay, so you think I'm that girl. Why? Except for my looks, there's nothing to suggest I'm her. Nothing. Except for those two men thinking I'd been in some hospital I'm certain I've never been to, there's nothing unusual about my life. So, other than this scar ..." She pointed at her arm. "... why do you think I'm her?"

"You are." Matt gently pushed up the sleeve of her shirt. With his forefinger, he lightly traced the scar. "Where did you get this? The woman I carried through the woods, the woman I left at the farmer's house, had a big gash in her arm, exactly where this scar is."

"In the accident, when I wrecked my car." Her voice was petulant. "Do we have to keep going over and over this?"

"You told those men you were in University Hospital. Do you really believe that?"

She didn't answer. Her brows rose up and down as if she were running a database search of the computer in her mind. "I have no reason to believe otherwise. I have my discharge papers; they all say University Hospital."

"Anyone could concoct papers. Is there someone who would know for sure? Someone who can absolutely verify you were there—friends, visitors, maybe your boss?"

Linda ran a finger along her lip. "Yeah, Cherie would. She seems to know most everything else about me."

Jerry interrupted. "This is all cozy and the like, but it's late and I'm bushed. You are too. I think we should sleep on this. Regroup in the morning. But first, we'd better try to hide your truck, Matt. Who knows, those goons, or someone worse might come looking."

Matt's eyes locked with Linda's. "Please, hang in here a little longer. I know this is rough on you—me too. Please, will you give me some time?"

Her eyes lit with a twinkle when she smiled. "Don't worry. We've got other problems now. Who you think I am can wait." She took the coffee cups to the sink and rinsed them out. "Go. Take care of your truck."

After moving Matt's truck to his garage and parking his car by the back door, Jerry said, "Tomorrow, you take my car. Throw those bloodhounds off the chase for a while, maybe."

"Thanks." Matt clapped Jerry on the back and then frowned. "Look, I may need another favor. I tried to use an ATM tonight. Machine ate my card. Flashed some nonsense about the police being notified."

Jerry rubbed his chin. "That's not good. These people who're screwing with you have some big resources if they can get to your bank so fast."

"I've got to get some cash. Mind if I write you a check and you deposit it to your account and get cash in turn for me?"

"No problem. I'll run over first thing in the morning."

Matt said, "One other favor. Don't call the police just yet … about tonight, that is. Somehow, I don't think it will help anything."

"Don't worry. A little mess has never bothered me. I can live with it a while. But I have to sometime. Insurance and all, you know."

Jerry led the way back to the house and stopped at the bottom step. He peered at Matt. The darkness about them was broken only by the faint light from the streetlamp out front. He said, "She is special, isn't she? I knew it when she first walked into the room this afternoon. Whether she's the woman from the plane or not doesn't really matter, does it?" When Matt didn't respond, Jerry shrugged and climbed the steps into his house.

Sometime during the dark, early morning hours, Matt tossed and turned. He flailed against the bedclothes that bound him. He heard the crackling of flames, felt the heat. An orange glow flickered across the ceiling. There were cries for help. He tried to call out, but the words wouldn't leave his lips. He tossed harder, kicking out and flinging his arms about him.

"Easy now, son. Easy. It's all right. You're just having a bad dream." The old farmer helped him sit up.

Matt was by the fire, its flames crackling loudly. The fresh scent of cedar filled the air as logs sizzled in the fireplace. Their light was the only light in the room.

"Where ..." The question died on his lips.

"Why, you're here with us." The old farmer spoke as if it were absurd for him to be elsewhere. "And it's a good thing too. Looks like you're still not out of the woods." The farmer squinted as he studied Matt. "But I think you're getting close. Yep, very close. Don't give up, son. That's not an option."

"Martha?"

"Yes, son. What about her?"

"She's ..."

"She's asleep. Most everyone is asleep now, except for you and those who're mighty interested in you. They never sleep."

"The woman ... the one who came with me?"

The old man's brows rose. "Why do you ask? I thought you knew. She's asleep, too. Has been for a while. You can wake her though. You can indeed."

Matt bolted from his makeshift bed in Jerry's living room. Had he heard a scream? Then, it came again—loud, piercing, and nearby.

"Linda?" Matt fumbled with his covers and stumbled in the dark to her side. She was whimpering like a frightened child. "Linda, wake up!" He pulled her upright and cradled her in his arms. Gently, he rocked back and forth, holding her tightly, afraid to let go. She continued with her soft moaning.

"Linda?" Her voice was barely a whisper. "Who's Linda?"

His lips against her hair, Matt whispered, "Tell me. Who is Linda?"

She pushed against him until she sat up on her own, but Matt kept his arm around her shoulders. She shook her head violently. In the darkness, she grasped Matt's hand. "Where am I?"

"With me," Matt whispered. "At Jerry's house."

"Jerry's house?" She was quiet. "Yes, I remember now." She yawned. Then with sudden energy, she burst out, "I was there, Matt. There was an old farmer. He was bald, had only one tooth. His wife, her name was ... was Martha! He was telling me to listen and to believe."

Matt dropped his arm. "What? What did you say?"

"He was saying I must believe, to trust. He said my life depended on it. Then everything went orange. There was a loud explosion. I screamed. And now ..." She rubbed her eyes as if to clear them. "It was just a really bad dream. I listened to your stories too much."

Matt's heart hammered. His stomach cramped. "Linda, that man you described. That's the farmer I told you about! Don't you see?" His voice rose. "How could you have dreamed it, if you'd never seen him before?"

"You told me about him, remember? I conjured him up from what you told me."

"No, I didn't! I never told you what he looked like, or what his wife's name was." He gripped her shoulders with both hands. "Does it make sense now?"

For a moment, Linda gazed at him. He could see the questions in her eyes. Then she shook her head as a large tear streamed down her face and plopped onto her lap. She closed her eyes and whispered, "I'm scared, Matt. Very scared."

Matt pulled her against him, and for a long time, neither spoke. Then, after brushing her hair from his lips, Matt whispered, "Me too. Me too."

CHAPTER 9

Sun peeked through the curtains with no respect for the boundary they erected. The walls turned orange, then pink, and then just simply bright. In his makeshift nest fashioned out of odd blankets and a few pillows tossed on the floor, Matt awakened and was surprised to see he was curled against Linda. As he bolted up, it all rushed back like a wave, flooding him. He glanced at his watch and then shook Linda.

"It's late. Linda, come on; wake up. We've got so much to do and so little time."

Linda didn't greet the day as readily as Matt. She stretched and yawned. "I'm so tired. I didn't sleep so well!"

Matt pushed to his feet and looked down at her. "I'm sorry you didn't get the sleep you wanted. But we really need to get rolling." He turned from her and stumbled through the obstacle course of debris lying in piles around the room until he found the kitchen. Linda yawned and then managed to get on her feet. She plodded through the maze of mess toward the bathroom.

When she strolled into the kitchen thirty minutes later, she looked much brighter and more alert. "Wonders what a cold shower can do," she muttered. Neither Matt nor Jerry acknowledged her. They were embroiled in a hot discussion on how best to cook bacon while Jerry scrambled eggs and Matt made toast. Linda shrugged and turned away. By the time she returned minutes later, the table was filled with eggs, toast, freshly squeezed orange juice, and bacon—lots of bacon.

"What about coffee?" Linda asked. Both men jumped at her words.

Jerry stuttered, "Uh ... coffee. Yeah, I've got coffee." He pulled some cups from the cupboard and set them on the table. Next, he pulled out a can of coffee and fumbled with the coffeemaker as he measured some of the beans into the grinder. Soon, the aroma of the brewing coffee competed with the mouth-watering smell of the hickory-smoked bacon.

"I can't seem to get enough bacon. I think about it all the time." Matt's mouth watered as he popped a crisp piece between his teeth.

Jerry pointed at a chair. "Linda, here, have a seat." Jerry and Matt sat down opposite her. For a while, no one said anything as they gulped orange juice and sipped coffee between crunching crisp bacon and shoveling piles of fluffy eggs into their mouths. As the food disappeared from their plates, their discussion of possible plans of action grew in proportion.

"First, I'll get to the bank for you," Jerry said around a mouthful of toast. He gulped some coffee and then took his plate to the sink. "But what's next?"

Matt shrugged. "The only sense I can make of all that has happened is that this is somehow related to the crash." Matt turned to Linda. "USC, University Hospital, that's our starting place."

Linda wrinkled her nose. "Why there? What would they know?"

Matt swiped the last bit of egg yolk from his plate onto his toast. He swallowed the combination before answering. "If, indeed, you were a patient there, then they would have your medical history. And from that, we should be able to tell what happened to you. From there, we'll find our next step."

Linda's frown grew deeper. "I still don't understand."

Matt patted Linda's hand. "We've got to retrace the past to find the present, and then we gain a future ... I hope."

Jerry parked in the back of the bank's parking lot, as close to the shade of some magnolia trees as possible. He repeated to himself a reminder to look calm. *Exhale the stress; inhale the peace.* Denying himself his usual don't-stop-for-anything pace, he casually strolled across the pavement and through heavy glass doors to the marble lobby of a branch of the Great Western Bank.

Only a couple customers were in line before him. Jerry shifted from foot to foot while trying to look around without being obvious. Bank cameras covered every inch of the lobby and tellers behind their wall. Every move was watched, but by whom? Just bank officials, or were there eyes that had more specific plans for the info gleaned from their ever-seeing cameras?

When at last it was his turn to greet the teller, he stepped up slowly, grinned broadly, and asked about the weather. *Oh, man,* he thought, *could I be any more obvious?* Jerry swiped at his forehead, slinging droplets of sweat on the check as he pushed it across the counter.

"How would you like this, in hundreds?" The woman made eye contact.

"Uh … yeah. Hundreds and maybe a few twenties as well."

The woman studied him a moment. "Very well. You understand, you have just enough funds in your account to cover this until the check clears."

Jerry frowned. "What do you mean I have just enough funds to cover this check? I'm depositing the same amount."

The woman sighed as if disgusted. "It means, sir, the funds from the check you're depositing today will be frozen for a period of up to five days."

"Five days? It actually takes that long in this age of instant, electronic communications for this bank to communicate to the other bank and so on?"

The woman nodded. "Oh, I've already verified the funds are in the account, but to actually complete the transaction, it can take up to five days, depends on the routing. That's why we hold the funds, in case of error."

Jerry crossed his arms and clenched his teeth. "You've verified the funds, so why freeze them? I'll bet you're earning interest on it." He stopped when he saw the woman's expression harden into a deep frown. But she wasn't looking at him; she was looking at her computer.

"Uh, there seems to be a problem here." She tapped the monitor. "While the funds are in the account, there's a flag on it. Government seizure, it says." She looked at Jerry. "I'm sorry, but for all practical purposes, this check is no good."

Jerry choked and coughed. The woman then asked, "Do you still want this cash from your account?"

When Jerry finished coughing, he answered. "Just give me half, in hundreds." As he watched her count, efficient fingers rapidly flipping the bills, he didn't know whether to be angry or scared.

When she finished, she banded it into a couple of groups and then put the whole in a small zippered pouch. "Here you are, sir, twenty-five hundred dollars. Is there anything else today?"

Jerry snatched the money and shook his head. "No. Thanks." With a quick nod, he turned and fled the building.

"Yeah, I'm sure it's the same truck, a Silverado. No doubt about it. It's the same one that was parked in the drive last night." Tim sounded defensive as he answered Harry's demand.

"Then, go figure why there's no trace of them in the parking lot or bank." Harry's blood was boiling over the fact they had not found their prey that morning. He was even angrier that it meant a delay in receiving the promised reward. The voice on the phone, when he'd called, had transferred him through several different exchanges until he'd ended up speaking with some angry, cold female.

"We cannot disburse the reward money until they are in our care. And we must have current, to-the-moment information that will enable us to acquire them within the hour. Only when they are safely with us can we determine you to be the recipient of the reward money. Then, we'll need all the usual: Social Security number, tax ID, if applicable. You know the routine."

No, Harry didn't know it. He wasn't accustomed to Judas-kissing those he pursued for pictures.

The woman continued, "Call the number I'm about to give you when you have the current, correct information. Be sure to have the exact location, street names, building numbers, time, etc. Once they are apprehended, someone will be in touch to initiate the paperwork regarding the reward money." Harry threw down his phone as he muttered an explicative.

Tim looked at him and shrugged. "So, what did you expect? It's the government. They never do anything straight. Always go from point A to D before jumping back to B and then over to C. They couldn't justify enough jobs if they did it any other way."

Suddenly, Harry pointed and shouted, "Go, man! Over there, it's the truck. Don't let it get out of sight! Did you see who got in it?"

Tim slammed the car into drive and raced forward. "No."

"Well, no matter. Keep following the truck. That's all we focus on, the truck."

Matt was half in and half out of Jerry's open trunk, stowing a few supplies for the unpredictable future they faced. Pillows, blankets, snacks, sodas—he'd grabbed anything and everything. Trouble was he had no clue what he was preparing for.

After carrying out most all Jerry's pantry had to offer, Matt slammed the trunk shut. When he turned, he gasped. His heart double-timed its beat when he spied Linda standing behind him, a strange look on her face.

"What is it?" Matt asked. "You look ... well ... frightened or something."

She shook her head. "I guess it's just hitting me. I mean, I've always taken home for granted. Always known I could go there at the end of a hard day. Now, we're on the run, like fugitives. I can no longer go home. We're innocent. We haven't done anything wrong. But they're hunting us like we're murderers. I never thought I'd be homesick for my sorry little apartment, but right now, I'd give anything to go back and sit on my couch and stare at my four walls."

Jerry pulled the Silverado up to the garage.

"Did you see anyone?" Matt asked. "Anyone interested in you?"

"I didn't notice anyone, but then again, don't take my word. These guys could probably get past any of us." Jerry jerked his head toward the street as a car drove slowly past. Matt and Linda sank into the shadows.

Jerry turned back to them. "It's okay. It's just another car taking its time, nothing to worry about. It did have tinted windows though. Can't tell who or how many were in there. But it kept going. That's the important thing."

Jerry pulled Matt away from Linda. He spoke quietly. "You've got more trouble, though."

Matt's stomach was suddenly cold. "What?"

"Your bank account is frozen. Teller said it was government seizure. She wouldn't give me any money from it; said your check was no good."

Matt slammed his fist against the wall. "You're kidding!"

"Wish I were."

"Guess I'm not surprised, especially after last night. So, what do we do now?"

Jerry pulled the pouch from his jacket pocket. "Here. I couldn't clean my account entirely, so this is half of what you wanted. It should help a little." Matt took the pouch and looked briefly at its contents before stuffing it in his jacket. He put his arm around Jerry's shoulders and squeezed, and then he clapped him on the back.

"Thanks, man. I *will* make this up to you."

Jerry glanced first at Linda and then Matt. His smile wavered. "You can repay me by coming back to work. Finish your project. Start work on the next. Remember the future you still have."

Matt nodded as he slipped behind the wheel of Jerry's Buick. As they backed down the drive, easing past the Silverado, Jerry called out. "Take good care of my girl!"

"What?"

"The car!"

It didn't take long to find USC's University Hospital. "So, we're at the hospital," Linda said as Matt parked at the edge of the visitor's parking area. "What now?"

He sighed. "Wish I had a plan. But for now, I guess we head for medical records and get yours. Do you remember any of your doctors' names?"

Linda pursed her lips. "I don't remember much of anything except for the day I came home. But I do remember someone named Charles."

"I guess that's better than nothing. After all, just how many Charleses can there be on staff?"

Thirty-three. Thirty-three doctors affiliated with USC University hospital had the name Charles somewhere in their lineup. As Linda read over the list, Matt noted the name of the medical records department manager—Alma Nettle—and initiated a battle over information she was in charge of managing.

"It doesn't matter what your procedure or policy is. We need a copy of her medical records. We have a right to know. Don't force me to get the law in here."

Ms. Nettle sniffed loudly. Matt swore she stomped her foot behind the counter. "All right," she said briskly. "Follow me."

She came from behind the counter and quickly led them to a library of records. Computer terminals were interspersed between rows upon rows of files. She must have noticed Matt's puzzled expression for she added, "Despite this modern age of electronic medical records for everything, we maintain a backup of all records in a secure server. Even though the government mandated years ago that all records had to be electronic and all forms standardized, occasionally, we still get some paper addenda for patients. When that happens, we just scan it in and add it to their file. We don't just toss the papers though, although I've been getting some very strong encouragement to do so. No, we keep a paper copy of everything for at least ten years, and then before destroying it, we back it up to microfiche. Oh yes, many laugh at my old-fashioned system, but it works. Last quake we had around here and power was out, the doctors were still able to access their records. You too, can access the record you seek via one of these computer terminals." She swept her arm about her.

"But do they contain the complete information of the paper record?"

She nodded.

"How are the paper records cataloged?"

"Mostly by the medical record number generated when a patient is first admitted. Older records used a person's Social Security number. Now, with identity theft threats and revised laws, we can no longer require a patient to give their number to us, so we started generating a unique number for each patient that utilizes a combination of birth date, last name, and county of birth."

"Thanks," Matt said. He pulled a second chair up to the terminal the manager had indicated. Linda settled by his side as he began to work the keyboard.

"I need your number," he said to her.

"What number?"

"Social Security. That seems to be the easiest way to start our search."

Linda frowned. "Didn't you hear the woman? She said they no longer require it."

Matt gazed at her, puzzled. "So, no Social Security number. How about your medical record number?" Linda shook her head. Matt jumped to his feet and ran back to the front desk. He called for the manager. When she appeared from behind the partition, her voice was as chilly as her face. "Yes?"

"We don't have her Social Security number. Can you help us get her records with the other number you mentioned?"

The woman's beady eyes fixed on Matt. "Does she have her medical record number from an invoice or something from the hospital?"

Matt turned back to Linda, and she shook her head.

"She doesn't have it with her."

"I guess we could ..."

"Could what?"

"We could get it from the master computer. It's indexed by name as well as number. It would be easiest, however, if you could just give me her birth date, county of birth, and the first five letters of her last name. With that, we can then set you up to access her records from a local terminal."

"Well, can't you just use the name to find her records and then set it up so we can access it from a terminal?"

"I need to see some additional identification."

"Like what? You've already seen her license."

The woman glared at Matt, and a fiery challenge burned in her eyes. "Yes, I have. I want to see it again."

Matt motioned for Linda. In front of the woman, she rummaged through her bag and gave the license to her.

"Very well," the manager finally said. "Wait a minute." She disappeared behind the door of her office. A moment later, she returned with a number.

"Thank you. Thank you very much," Linda said as she stuck her hand out in front of Matt's and grasped the card with the information printed on it.

At the terminal again, Matt typed in the number. In seconds, Linda's record flashed before them. He scanned through the pages of listings of medications, procedures, and records of vital signs, looking for admission dates and the names of those who attended her. From all he could gather, it looked as if she'd only been a patient at University for less than a week—three days to be exact. Her admission date was listed as April 2. Her discharge was April 5.

Matt frowned as he reread the notes. The dates made no sense if what he believed was true. The notes said only she was admitted for injuries sustained in an auto accident. No details of the event were noted. The best Matt could tell, she'd been treated for a complete break of the humerus of her left arm; a concussion; abrasions on the face, arms, legs, and back; a couple of contusions; and some loss of blood. No other maladies were listed, other than a note stating the patient suffered from memory lapses. It wasn't until he reached the end of the record that Matt found what he was looking for. A physician's signature was at the bottom of the medical history and admitting form. Trouble was the name was Sonjali Singh, MD. No Charles was mentioned anywhere. Matt quickly flipped back through the previous electronic pages, scanning for the name. It only appeared in the one place.

"Look on your list of doctors. See if there's a Dr. Singh anywhere."

Linda scanned each of the printed pages she held in her hand. After searching them all, she looked at Matt. He was struck again by the clear depth of her eyes—the purity, the energy they held.

"Yes, there's one Sonjali Singh."

Matt jerked the sheets from her and scanned them for himself.

"Don't believe me?"

He grinned at her. "Should I?"

She grinned, and her eyes briefly twinkled. "You tell me."

Matt stood suddenly. "Come on." He trotted back to the main reception counter and called out to Ms. Nettle.

"Do you know a Sonjali Singh? Is he on staff here?"

The manager frowned. "Now, I know most all the doctors here, most on a first-name basis. I don't recall a Singh." She turned her back to them and went to her terminal. After several keystrokes, she looked up and frowned. "Yes, there's one Singh listed, but he's not on regular staff. Record indicates his admitting privileges are probationary and must be authorized by another physician with regular admitting privileges. Which I must say is somewhat unusual. I can't remember anyone in recent years being restricted like this. It certainly is strange."

"Would you pull up Linda's record? Look on the last page. That's where his name is. It's the only doctor's name I can find in her chart."

Alma Nettle did as Matt requested. "You're right," she finally agreed. "His name is the only one listed on the admission form." The manager tapped the monitor screen with her forefinger. "It would appear he was the one responsible for coordinating her daily care, yet this goes against his admitting privileges. There should be at least mention of some other doctor, or at the very least, someone on staff who was supervising his work."

"Could there be records from her prior hospital, something that would show her prior care?"

The manager frowned. "Prior hospital? According to this ..." She pointed at the terminal. "There was no prior care. This is the only hospital your friend was in." The woman continued to frown but said nothing as she hit the keyboard several more times and squinted at the screen. After a while, she came from behind the counter. "Let's go find the paper records."

With an efficient pace surely developed by years of utilizing every second given to her, Ms. Nettle led them straight to the location of Linda's paper record. She pulled it from the shelf and opened it. The first few pages were identical to those scanned into the computer. However, the last page was missing, as were a couple others.

"Hummm," the manager muttered as she flipped the pages. "Strange." She pointed to one of the pages. "Normally, all medications are noted, along with doses and any reactions or allergies. But that's not the case. Instead, there's a note for all nursing personnel to contact Dr. Singh personally prior to administering any meds, even those ordered and noted on the chart. This even includes such things as acetaminophen or ibuprofen. This is very odd indeed."

Ms. Nettle shut the record and gazed for several moments at Matt and Linda. She ran her finger across her upper lip and frowned. "I strongly suggest you find this Dr. Singh and have a talk with him. If anything, he holds the key to what you're seeking. Meanwhile, I've got to find out who's been tampering with my records."

Linda extended her hand to the woman, and a smile lit her eyes as she spoke softly. "Thank you for your help." The manager nodded hurriedly and returned to her computer terminal. Before

Matt and Linda reached the elevator, she was engrossed in her pursuit of answers. As the elevator doors opened, however, they heard her scream.

Matt turned and darted back to Ms. Nettle's desk. Linda was on his heels. As they stopped by the hysterical manager's side, Matt gulped when he realized what was happening. Medical records flashed across the screen briefly before dissolving into a myriad of colors and disappearing. He was just in time to see Linda's name melt and flow into the mass of colors on the monitor.

"A virus! Someone's put a virus in here!" The manager was frantically hitting every button on her keyboard. Nothing stopped the savagery of the computer bug. It ate through everything, carving a path of total destruction. The poor woman collapsed in her chair, head in her hands, tears dropping on papers covering her desk.

"Go! Just go!" she said gruffly, head still in her hands. "There's nothing you can do."

Matt grabbed Linda's hand, and they ran back to the elevator. The doors on the left opened, and they jumped inside. Just as they began to lift, the elevator on the right arrived. Five men in dark suits, carrying displayed badges and hidden guns, spilled into the medical records receiving area and ran straight for the weary manager. When she raised her tear-swollen eyes and saw them, she crumpled in her chair and moaned. "What now?"

The elevator doors opened to the hospital's main lobby. Pink marble floors framed by granite columns defined the two-story, open area. Some people rushed by; others walked slowly, as if in another world they didn't comprehend. Worry and exhaustion was so obvious on the faces passing by that Matt sighed as he realized they had a perfect cover to slip out the front entrance of the hospital. Soon, they were in Jerry's Buick, speeding from the parking lot.

Matt pushed the gas pedal and sped out the parking lot and past the front entrance just as a group of men burst through the doors and onto the sidewalk. Observing the red faces, raised voices, and tense gestures directed at them, Matt knew they had been found.

"There they go! Get them!" The words cut through the metallic smog and filtered into the interior of the Buick.

"Can't we go any faster?" Linda screamed as she stared at the mob of black suits.

Matt shook his head. "Traffic's moving too slow. I can't."

"Why not hit the curb, drive around those cars? They do it in the movies all the time! You *are* familiar with the movies, aren't you?"

Matt wished he could appreciate the humor.

"They're gaining on us," Linda declared, glancing behind them. "You've gotta do something now!"

Two black cars had pulled from the curb, inching closer despite the thick traffic. Just before they reached the Buick's bumper, a third smaller car careened around the corner and inserted itself between the black cars and Matt and Linda.

Horns blared, and angry faces glared, but the two young men in the third car didn't hesitate as traffic began to move again. As the group approached the intersection, the stoplight god chose to bless Matt. The light changed from yellow to red just as he passed underneath. The two black cars had no choice but to halt as the errant car with the young men inside squealed to a stop. But as suddenly as it had stopped, it sped up again and jumped across the intersection, causing two oncoming cars to slam into each other. Left behind, the men in black slammed their fists on dashboards, doors, and heads. For once, they weren't able to rise above the law to pursue their own agendas.

"That's them!" Tim shouted as he spied the Buick corner roughly and speed into the street across from the hospital. "Good hunch, Harry, following the truck back to the house, catching them as they left in the Buick. Anyone else would've let them slip by. Not us, the never-defeated Eyes of Spies!"

"You gonna have that put on a business card, now?" Harry's voice was curt.

Tim shot him a hurt look. "No. But—"

Harry gripped Tim's arm. "Whoa! The light's red."

Tim hit the brakes as the cars behind them stood on their headlights. He paused only briefly, however. Glancing both ways, he slammed the accelerator to the floor. Their car flew through the intersection, swerving to avoid two oncoming cars, which, in turn, slammed into each other.

"Bitchin', dude!" Tim shouted as he slapped Harry's arm playfully. "What's the matter, old man? Not going soft and getting scared, are you?"

"You're gonna kill us someday."

"But I didn't today," Tim said as he pointed. "I didn't lose them either! There they are!" He pushed the accelerator harder and dodged some pedestrians nervy enough to try to cross in a crosswalk in front of them. "See, all's not lost! We'll turn them in and still get that reward money." He popped his gum and grinned.

Harry massaged his temples. They throbbed and not just from a tension headache. Something tugged at the edge of his memory, but he couldn't quite grasp it.

"That girl, she remind you of anyone?"

Tim shrugged, keeping his eyes on the road. "Naw, they all start to look alike after a while. She's just another pretty face, tagging along with some star, hoping his fame will drag her into the limelight too."

Harry stared blankly at the cars before them. Suddenly, he shouted, "I knew it! I have seen her face. She's a reporter, works for the *Houston Chronicle*." Tim said nothing, and Harry continued to muse aloud, "Thing is, if she's with the *Chronicle*, wonder what story she's working on now?"

Tim glanced quickly at Harry and then back at the road. "Sure it's the *Chronicle*? Scuttle I have says she's with the *LA Times*."

Harry scratched his head. "No, that can't be right. I know every female on staff there. I tell you, she's not one of them. She's with the *Chronicle.* I ran into her back in January when I was following that congressman, Thom Jordan. She was talking about an upcoming interview with him." Harry stared out the window, lost in his thoughts.

Suddenly, Tim shouted, "Oh no. I'll bet she's out to get the story on this Grayson guy. She's trying to beat us at our game!"

Harry shook his head. "Man, wake up! She's a reporter, not a photographer. Besides, her face is plastered on TV too. I don't think you need to worry."

"Well, no woman's gonna beat us at what we do best." Tim cut dangerously close in front of another car to decrease their distance from the Buick. "We'll prove them wrong!"

Harry shrugged. "Whatever. Just keep up with them, okay?"

Matt approached the Ventura Freeway and turned onto the eastbound ramp. "When we get to Altadena, I'll stop and call Dr. Singh. If these guys can get inside my bank account, then it's child's play to monitor my cell phone."

In a short while, they were cruising along Altadena Drive searching for a pay phone that still worked. After finding one tucked on the side of a convenience store experiencing an extremely slow afternoon, Matt stopped and called the number from the list. He expected to have to wade through a voice-mail maze, or at the very least, an answering machine, so he was surprised when a human actually answered.

"Yes, this is Dr. Singh." His accent was thick. "And you're ..."

"I'm an attorney representing one of your patients, a Linda McGowan. She's involved in some litigation regarding an accident she was involved in earlier this year. We need to review her medical history, but unfortunately, a computer virus destroyed the medical records at the hospital, and we were unable to get some basic questions answered. I was wondering if we could talk with you briefly."

Dr. Singh was hesitant. *Rightly so,* Matt thought. With lawsuits so rampant, he could be an easy target.

"I did nothing wrong. You'll have to speak with my attorney."

"No, Dr. Singh. I didn't mean to imply you did. This is not a malpractice lawsuit. It's over the other driver's negligence. We simply need to reconstruct the facts so we can put our case together."

The good doctor hesitated. Matt prayed to God the man wasn't completely indoctrinated into American culture. If he was, then Matt knew he would never believe his story.

"All right," Dr. Singh finally answered. "My office is closed this afternoon, but I'll meet you there in thirty minutes." He gave Matt the street address. It was only a few blocks away. "I have a golf game at four. We must be finished by then."

Golf game? Matt was wrong. The man had been assimilated.

Exactly one hour later, Matt pulled into the nearly empty parking lot belonging to the small row of office condos. Dr. Singh's office was at the end, near a grove of magnolia trees.

The doctor greeted them as soon as they entered the cramped waiting room. Three chairs were circled around a cheap glass-top table covered with old issues of *People* and *Entertainment Weekly*. An older issue of *People* peeked from midway in the stack. Partially exposed was a picture of Matt from his film, *Killing Times*. He cringed. The impulse to grab the book or cover it nearly overtook him. Instead, he grinned broadly at Dr. Singh.

"Thank you for agreeing to see us on such short notice. We're under some pressure to get this case ready for court, and ..."

Dr. Singh stared at them but didn't smile. He was already in his golfing clothes; his skin was tanned, most likely from many afternoons spent on the golf course. He was a small man, with long thin fingers that were cold as he grasped Matt's and then Linda's hands.

"Tell me again, just what is it you want?" he said over his shoulder as he led the way down a dark hall past a couple of examining rooms and a nurse's station to a small study at the back of the condo. In his study, Dr. Singh stood behind a small desk covered with files, charts, and journals and pointed at two folding chairs across from him.

"We need to reconstruct Linda's medical records from her recent hospital stay at USC University Hospital. The only doctor's name we could find was yours. Unfortunately ...” Matt glanced quickly at Linda before returning his eyes to Dr. Singh. “... Linda's suffering from some amnesia and doesn't remember anything about her stay there.”

Linda's current medical condition seemed to be of no concern to the doctor. “And this is for some litigation over the accident?” Dr. Singh twitched his fingers nervously but stopped when Matt assured him he was not being sued and therefore would not be in jeopardy of losing any patients.

“Yes, we need to settle with the driver's insurance company, but we must be fully informed of all medical issues first.”

A hint of a smile nipped at the edges of Dr. Singh's lips. “Very well. Let me see what I have in my files here. The last name is ...?”

“McGowan,” Linda answered softly. “Linda McGowan.”

Dr. Singh went to a back room, presumably to search for the file. They heard the opening and closing of file drawers and paper shuffling. After a few minutes, he returned, a small folder in his hand. After sitting down in his chair, he flipped it open.

“Says here you were admitted to University on the second of April and I discharged you on the fifth. Does that sound right to you?”

Linda nodded.

The doctor read further down the page and then frowned. He clamped his fingers together, but they twitched. When he spoke, he kept his eyes on the paper.

“It was a while back that you were in my care. With so many patients, it is often hard to remember the details of everyone. And ...” He finally looked at Linda. “I really do not practice much at University. It's a little far to drive since most of my work is at the local community clinic.”

Linda grasped the edge of his desk and leaned toward him. “Do you know anything about a doctor named Charles, first or last?”

Dr. Singh shook his head rapidly. A few drops of perspiration flew from his forehead. “No.”

He flipped some more pages to the end of the chart. Then he smiled, his small mouth opening partially, exposing a full complement of large, white teeth. "Yes, very much, now, I see you were admitted with injuries incurred from an auto accident." He shut the folder and tapped it as his grin grew broader. "That's it, a simple admission for injuries in an auto accident, nothing else."

"Is there anything in there about my residence, my address, phone, anything?"

Dr. Singh reopened the chart and squinted at the print. "Yes, there is. Custom Hills Apartments, Timberlyne Drive, Van Nuys."

"That's where I live now. Is there anything else?"

Dr. Singh slowly shook his head. "No, nothing else." But it seemed something caught his eye, for Dr. Singh frowned as he scanned the rest of the last page. When he got to the bottom, he tapped it with his forefinger. He looked up at them and shut the folder. "That's it. There's nothing else."

"What?" Matt and Linda said in unison. Matt reached for the folder. "May I?" he asked after it was already in his hand.

Dr. Singh sighed and slumped in his seat as if resigned to some terrible fate.

Matt flipped to the last page, and attached to the upper clip was a copy of admission orders and requests sent from a Dr. Charles Benson. Matt fell against his chair back and shook his head slowly. He turned to Linda.

"Look," he said as he pointed to the print.

Linda studied the page for a long while. She finally looked at Matt and whispered, "I was right, but why?"

Matt asked Dr. Singh, "Got a magnifying glass?"

The doctor wrinkled his nose and started to speak. Then he shrugged and pulled his desk drawer open. Digging through its contents, he eventually produced a small magnifying lens. Matt snatched it and, with Linda leaning over his shoulder found what he was looking for.

"Most emails and old faxes come with a transmission ID. The ID on this sheet gives a number and then lists Memorial Hermann Hospital."

Matt dropped the sheet on the desk. Dr. Singh peered at the point

Matt touched and fell back into his seat, closing his eyes. The doctor looked as if he'd just been given the death penalty.

Linda's face was blank. Suddenly, all color drained from her cheeks and her eyes widened. "Memorial Hermann Hospital?"

Matt nodded. "Hermann, in Houston."

CHAPTER 10

Phillippe, Dereck, and Charles were seated around a small round conference table in a windowless, soundproofed room nestled in the interior of the Nowonizwyser Lab, the central hub of the Piney Woods Project's facilities. Sweat dripped off Charles's forehead. Phillippe fidgeted as if he couldn't get some biting spider out of his pants. Only Dereck seemed calm, relatively so, as he leaned forward, elbows on his knees, and stared at the screen before them. He soaked in every word spewing from the recessed speakers aligned with the screen's video link.

"Gentlemen, our latest test has gotten, shall we say, somewhat out of hand." Phillippe glanced at Charles, an I-told-you-so glare shooting from his eyes. "It would appear our subject's treatment was insufficient and could not overcome the strength of the stimuli encountered. However, a different dilemma faces us. Wheels in motion, wheels which cannot be stopped, have made it imperative the questions as to what went wrong be answered immediately. It must be determined what caused the chemical breakdown and its exact nature. We expect to have the two subjects back to your facility within twenty-four hours. Prior to their arrival, review your data, reconsider all possible scenarios, and prepare for unceasing work until the mystery is solved."

Charles, Dereck, and Phillippe glanced at one another. The voice on the screen continued, "These will be long days and even longer nights. Make any necessary arrangements now so that you will be free for round-the-clock presence on-site. You will not stop work until definitive answers are found."

Phillippe interrupted the caller. "You are aware of the problems we've encountered here? Of the increasing numbers of subjects lost?"

The speaker answered, "Yes, we are." There was a slight pause. "However, it is vital this girl be salvaged, for she alone holds the key to the correction of your problems. This subject can be responsible for the success or failure of all we've worked for."

"You say the girl is vital, but isn't the man being brought in too? What about him?" Dereck asked.

There was a long pause as the speaker rubbed her eyes and frowned. "The man is inconsequential. There is little benefit to be derived from him. However, he cannot be allowed to go free. He is a witness."

Dereck stared at the screen, mouth open. Charles and Phillippe nodded in agreement. The speaker continued her instructions, "You know, as do we, this case is special. Precedence will be determined by its outcome. Gentlemen ..." The caller paused for emphasis, "... need I remind you of the scrutiny you're receiving, even now? The highest level, the most powerful of our country are watching your work closely. Your work is a matter of national security. You must, and I mean *must*, reclaim this operation. Complete the success. Is that clear?"

The three men answered in unison. "Yes, ma'am."

"Very well. You will be alerted when the subject is en route." The connection went dead. Static replaced the voice, snow the picture.

Phillippe turned to Charles. "I hope you're not surprised at the news. I must say, I'm not. I could've told you this would happen. She just wasn't ready. Putting her to such a test was nothing more than courting disaster." He leaned back in his seat and crossed his arms over his chest. A self-satisfied grin curled his lips.

Dereck didn't look as pleased or as relaxed. "This should never have been allowed to happen. Where has our sense of decency gone?" He glared at Phillippe and then Charles. "These people ..." The sweep of his arm included more than those presently discussed. "… never asked for this. They're innocent. They don't deserve what's been done to them against their will—"

Charles interrupted, "But can you honestly argue that what has been accomplished is not of benefit, even to them? Do you not agree that life as we know it has and will continue to change for the better just because of the work we've been a part of?"

Dereck shook his head. "Maybe it has, but does that make it right? Do the ends justify the means? For heaven's sake, lives have been altered, irrevocably changed, held in a state no one can understand. The very essence of their souls has been washed away, all in the name of science."

"Yes, and look what we have. If we complete this successfully, we'll have an infallible cure for cancer! The most dreaded disease of humankind and we can wipe it out!"

"But at what cost? Was the price worth the countless lives given?" Dereck's face flushed, and he stood. Leaning over Charles, he continued, "Yes, we can erase cancer from someone now; we can even replace the damaged tissue that was lost to the disease. We've shown we can generate the very essence of life on the cellular level, and we have developed more than one application for it. However, consider the price paid. Either they lose their life or their soul. There are no winners, for we haven't shared this marvelous secret with the world. No one knows of the miracles we're producing."

"For the very reason you stated earlier, we cannot let the world know because of all the mistakes, all the deaths. If it were known, we'd never be able to continue our work. We must keep it a secret, at all costs, at least until we can produce and replicate our results consistently without any loss."

Charles pushed his chair away and gathered his papers. "Dereck, have you checked your bank accounts lately? Have you enjoyed the deep cushion they provide? You like the car you drive, the house you live in, the ability to buy most anything you want?"

Dereck shrugged but glared at Charles, who continued, "This

project is not just about benefiting the sick and the weak; it's also made you a very rich man. It can make you even richer. You'll never have to worry about ever paying a bill again. No more bill collectors. No more harassing phone calls. You hated that, I know, so much so you evaded the whole sorry lot and changed your name, even your Social Security number."

Dereck's face lost its color. He sputtered, but no words got past his lips.

Charles laughed. "Don't look so surprised. You'd be amazed at the information I have access to. Besides, you owe me, if you want to get down to it. If it weren't for me, you'd still be groveling your way around that insipid hospital of yours, praying for some measly grant to pay for another year of useless research. Be thankful for things as they are, because they're pretty good right now!"

"How dare you?" Dereck finally managed, his voice falling to a growl. "How dare you invade my privacy!"

Charles grasped his sides as he laughed heartily. "Invade your privacy? Do you believe in double standards or something?" His laughter ended abruptly, and his eyes grew cold.

"I for one don't have time for all this ethical nonsense. Gentlemen, we have a task and our orders to carry it out. No less than our mighty government demands our full and highest attention to the problems at hand. We owe it to all who've gone before us and to those who follow to complete this task, this project, in our best and most complete professional manner. As project manager, I demand it and will accept nothing less." He shut his folder, stuffed it with his laptop into his leather carrying case, and strode quickly from the room.

Dereck pulled his papers together and stuffed them into a folder as Phillippe did the same. The silence grew. Finally, Phillippe clapped Dereck on the back.

"Don't sweat it, man. Charles just likes to throw his weight around!" Phillippe chuckled. "You're the key part of this program. He knows he can't get along without you. There's one thing I can say for sure, Charles will never let you go."

Phillippe turned his back to Dereck, and pulling his shoulders back and thrusting his chest forward, he strode from the room as if he were the most powerful man on earth. Just before the door shut behind him, Dereck heard him mutter, "Me, I don't have any problem with money."

Matt pressed the gas pedal to the floor as they sped westward on the Foothill Freeway. After leaving Dr. Singh's office, they had stopped at a pay phone and made calls to the DMV, the insurance company, and the state highway patrol. Linda had said little since. Her face was pale and her eyes red-rimmed. She clasped and unclasped her hands repeatedly.

As Matt sped along the freeway, an exit ramp caught his eye. Without warning, he swerved and raced down the ramp. Pulling the car onto the shoulder, he stopped and turned to her.

"Listen," he said quietly, almost afraid to intrude into the shell that had grown across her face. Only the pain in her eyes gave away the fact she was still alive and feeling something other than numbness. "The key to all this is in Houston. We've got to find out who this Dr. Benson is. We've got to go to Houston now."

She gazed at him and began to blink repeatedly, as if she couldn't focus. "Why do we need to go there? Can't we make some more calls? Do it from here?"

Matt frowned, shaking his head slightly. "If you were in a car wreck in California, then why do you have records saying you were in a hospital in Houston? Think about it! You have a driver's license, but when we called the driver's license administration for California, they'd never heard of you. Why is it you got a statement from your insurance company in the mail, but our phone call to them only confirmed no claim has been made? Why could we find no records of a wreck involving you on the night of January 14? For every call we made, we only got more questions. Can you not see that maybe what you believe is not necessarily the truth?" He took her hand in his and gently rubbed his forefinger across her knuckles. "Please. Please stay with me on this."

She bit her lip, and it wasn't until blood dribbled down her chin that he realized she was unaware she'd bitten it.

"I ... don't know ... I don't know if I can do it."

"Do what?"

She rubbed her temples and then clasped her hands tightly. "I can't get on a plane."

Matt's jaw dropped and then closed just as quickly. "You're afraid of flying, really afraid?"

She nodded.

"Believe me; I don't much like it either, anymore. But ..." He leaned toward her, and his eyes pleaded for her attention. "... this is more important than any fear either you or I have. We must find out what is happening and why. We've got to do whatever it takes to get our lives back, even if it means risking them."

She seemed puzzled. "It's just that when I think about it, my pulse starts to race, my head aches, and I feel like I'm going to pass out."

Matt pulled her into him. She didn't resist. He curled his arms about her. She let her small frame slip against his, and the tension of her muscles seemed to evaporate. Matt continued to hold her, wishing for some miracle, some great insight that would direct him. When she turned to face him, his lips were only centimeters from hers. He wanted to kiss her, kiss her hard. They were so ripe, so ready for his touch.

Abruptly, she pushed away from him. "Okay, I'll do it. Whatever it takes to get you convinced I can live a life of my own, on my own. Just do it okay? I'm tired of this, and I just want to go home and sleep for a very long time. Ouch!" She pressed her palm into her temple and pushed as she shut her eyes and grimaced. "Oh, that hurts." Another stab of pain kicked her, and she moaned.

"Linda, what's wrong?"

She only managed a moan as she fell against the seat and started panting. Then, just as suddenly as she had started showing signs of pain, she dropped her hands and fell against the seat. She sighed and glanced at Matt.

"I don't understand. What's happened to me?"

"I don't know what's happened to either of us, but it's someone else's doing, not ours. We're innocent. We've got to believe that, keep on believing that. Because as they continue to chase us and make us out to be fugitives, it'll be easier to forget the truth."

Matt pulled back onto the exit ramp and stopped at the light. Waiting for it to change, he asked, "What is it, Linda? What is it about you that someone would go to such trouble to keep you silent, keep you from knowing the truth?"

Linda didn't answer. Silence grew between them as they drove toward the Burbank-Glendale airport.

At the airport, Matt didn't bother arguing with the ticket agent. After reserving two seats on a flight to Houston that left in an hour, he threw some cash on the counter, way more than the five-hundred-dollars-per-person round-trip fare the agent claimed was the best he could do on such short notice. When the agent demanded Matt's identification, he merely shrugged and threw his driver's license on the counter.

"Uh, sir, we require passengers have a passport for identification."

Matt stared at the man for several seconds. "Look, I don't have mine with me. This isn't an international flight, so my license should be good enough." Matt waved at Linda to give hers to the agent as well. The man glanced briefly at both and didn't seem to be affected by either name he saw. As he stuffed the tickets into an envelope and handed them to Matt, he said, "You're cutting it close on security. It's a good thing you're not checking any bags. Can't guarantee they would make the flight, it's so late."

Yeah, late, so that's the excuse, Matt wanted to shout. How many times had he been charged a hundred dollars or more for his bags and they still hadn't shown up when he landed, even when he'd gotten to the airport much earlier for the flight.

He turned from the counter and took Linda's hand, and they sprinted through the crowd toward the gate. Once in the plane, seated side by side in nearly the same section as they had been on that fateful flight months earlier, their destination even the same,

George Bush Intercontinental Airport, it hit Matt just how much life had changed.

The flight attendants sealed the plane's doors, and the pressure caused Matt's ears to pop. Preflight announcements began as the plane backed from the gate. Suddenly, the plane stopped moving. The attendant stopped midsentence and apologized. "Sorry for the delay, ladies and gentlemen. We'll be off the ground shortly."

Hair stood at attention on Matt's neck. Cold bumps broke out on his arms, and he strained to see what was happening. The cabin pressure changed, and the whoosh from the passenger door opening was more felt than heard. A man in a dark suit and two young guys in T-shirts and ripped jeans slipped in. As they passed Matt and Linda, the man seemed uninterested in anything but getting his briefcase in the upper compartment and settling down with a drink and the latest edition of the paper on his Kindle. The two guys, however, looked at Matt and grinned briefly as they loped toward the back of the plane. The pressure changed again as the door was sealed and the attendant resumed her speech.

"Sorry for the delay, ladies and gentlemen. We'll be on our way now."

Matt's shoulders slumped, and he let out a big sigh. The hair on his neck drooped. They were on the plane, and no one had bothered him. He must relax. Soon, they were sailing effortlessly through the sky, gliding across supportive currents of air. Matt's muscles released some of their tension, yet he squirmed in his seat, unable to find a comfortable position. More often than not, his eyes rested on Linda. It was as if he were watching a ghost. Déjà-vu hit him. Same seats. Same kind of plane, even the same destination. The only thing different was her name.

Linda stirred, catching him staring. "I just don't know what's wrong. I feel so tired." She rubbed her eyes and temples. "My head feels like it's ready to split in two."

"It's worse?"

She nodded. "You know, my head didn't start hurting like this until I met you." Matt winced. "Fact is life has become decidedly painful since your intrusion!"

Matt had never intended to cause her pain. Now it appeared as if she credited him as being nothing more than just that, pain. "I'm sorry," he muttered quietly.

She managed a small, lopsided grin. "Hey, it's okay. I'm just kidding. You didn't cause it, at least not completely."

"Well, that's some consolation. Glad you think of me as being only a partial source of all the problems in your life."

Her smile was weak as she vigorously rubbed her temples. Outside, stars were dotting the twilight sky. A wall of clouds seemed to be creeping toward them. Matt didn't believe in premonitions, usually. But something cold and clammy gripped his stomach and twisted it. His palms grew wet, and he wiped them on his pants.

Turbulence bounced the plane without warning. Matt grabbed the armrest. Linda did the same.

"Old habit," Matt said with a small grin. Linda only nodded, releasing her grip and putting her hands in her lap. Matt saw them shaking.

"Do you think we're safe, really safe here?" She locked her gaze on his eyes.

"Certainly, the odds of this plane crashing are too small to consider."

"No, I mean safe … from them?"

Matt shrugged. "I don't know. I don't think anyone followed us onto the plane. But I can't guarantee no one knows we're here." He glanced casually about. He leaned close to Linda and whispered, "I'll go use the facilities; see what I can see. Okay?"

Linda let out a loud giggle and then clapped her hand over her mouth. "Facilities? That's what you call them?" She giggled again, softly.

"Just because I'm from Texas doesn't mean we don't have indoor plumbing. Would you rather I call it a john? I was trying to be polite."

Linda shook her head. "The Southern gentleman, aren't you?"

Matt didn't respond as he stood and stretched. He wobbled, as the plane hit more turbulence. Slowly making his way to the back toilets, he studied each face he passed. Some passengers dozed while others read magazines. A few glanced at him and smiled. One woman seemed surprised, and she grinned and winked at him. Even so, none showed any evidence of suspicious interest.

Back in his seat, Matt felt only slightly better. After clicking his seat belt, he said, "Looks okay. I didn't see anyone that worries me."

Linda's shoulders slumped, and her head fell back against the seat. "Good." Suddenly, she squeezed her eyes shut and grimaced. Vigorously, she massaged her temples while biting her lip. The pain must have been intense, for when she spoke, it seemed like her words had a hard time getting off her tongue.

"No. I've … never … been to … Houston. I've … never … been … to … Houston." She repeated it over and over like a chant, each repetition increasing in intensity. Matt tapped her shoulder, and then gripped her hand. Nothing broke her concentration.

"What're you trying to say? I don't understand, Linda."

"I am not … Lynn. My name is Linda. My name is Linda …"

"Linda, you're frightening me!" Matt squeezed her hand as hard as he could. She closed her eyes and grew pale.

As she continued squirming and grimacing, dots of perspiration broke out on her forehead, and she began to pant. Suddenly, she gripped her side and doubled over, groaning.

Panicked at what he saw, Matt punched the call button for the attendant.

"Yes, what can I get you?"

He nodded toward Linda. "She's ill. Could you get us some ice, a cold cloth maybe?"

The woman nodded and left. She returned a moment later with the ice and a washcloth. The woman stared at Linda and then asked Matt, "Do you want me to see if there's a doctor on board?"

Matt started to shake his head and then rethought the question. "Yes. Yes, I think so."

The attendant started her search while Matt wrapped the ice in the cloth. Gently, he pressed it against Linda's temple. "Does that help?"

She didn't open her eyes but groaned again and clamped her hands around his wrist as he held the ice in place. For a while, she was still, only the grip of her hands belying the pain she felt. Then, she began to shake violently. Even Matt, who knew so little about things medical, recognized a convulsion.

"Come on, Linda! Stay with me! Linda, please!" Matt whispered as he gripped her hands at the wrists and tightened his arm muscles. Stubborn will kept them clasped as Linda thrashed and pushed against him with surprising strength. Her eyes remained closed, and he knew she didn't know what she was doing. He clung to her as if she were a drowning person, determined not to let go.

Potter hated flying. When life dealt cards that demanded he fly, he usually insisted on first class. It wasn't a matter of deserving it, which he did. It wasn't a matter of status, although he had earned that as well. It was space, merely a small consolation for the claustrophobia that terrorized him whenever he flew. That day was not his lucky day. As he squirmed in his aisle seat in the middle of the economy section, he hit his neighbor in the ribs with his elbow, and when a large but stately woman squeezed past in the aisle, she bumped his shoulder. Cheap airlines. He wondered how that woman managed to get between the narrow protrusions pretending to be armrests. She wasn't all that big. Any large-size person would have trouble with the airline's allotted space per person. He sighed. There had been no choice. He was lucky to have made the flight. An angry contingent of standby passengers threatened a riot when he had been moved to the front of the line.

After readjusting his position for the tenth time, Potter decided it was futile to hope his legs might arrive in Houston still possessing good circulation. He tried to massage his left calf but could only touch the tip of his knee without hitting his head on the seat in front of him. He finally decided he might as well get up and stroll to the restrooms.

It would be the only way he could restart the blood pumping to his ankles. One was already so puffy it drooped over the side of his shoe. Before he could stand, there was an announcement over the intercom.

"Ladies and gentlemen, is there a doctor on board?"

A cold chill sprouted goose bumps on Potter's arms. Without really telling his arm to do so, with some intuition that moved it on its own, he raised his hand and the woman acknowledged him.

"Sir? You are, sir?"

Acting solely on gut instinct, Potter nodded. "Possibly I can help. What seems to be the problem?"

The attendant's brows were pinched as she answered, "I'm not sure. Looks like some sort of convulsion."

Potter swallowed over the knot forming in his esophagus. "Take me to him."

"Uh, it's a her. A woman."

Potter's eyes warmed. "Uh, her, then."

He followed the attendant to the first-class section and immediately saw the commotion the emergency had created. It looked as if every passenger in the forward section was huddled around two people seated near the front. He could see the tip of her head cradled in the man's lap. Potter pushed through the crowd.

"Please move. Doctor here. Please move over. Thank you. Yes, thank you for moving." With confidence that was a complete act, he made his way to the front of the group and leaned over the couple. They were surprisingly handsome, despite the terror on the man's face and the unconscious stupor on the woman's. They appeared so innocent. He wondered why it was the agency wanted them so very badly.

He looked the man in the eye and introduced himself. "I'm Dr. Potter. What seems to be the problem?"

While Matt described what had happened, Potter nodded as if it all made sense. Gently, he pulled each of Linda's eyelids open, quickly studying each eye. He had no clue as to what he was looking at. Next, he felt her neck for her pulse. It was rapid but weak. None of it meant anything to him. It was all he could think of, his only training years of watching medical dramas on TV where the solution to 99 percent of problems in the ER could be resolved by inserting a chest tube.

"She's about over it now, I think," he said to Matt as he watched Linda's jerking movements slowly subside. "There's not much more we can do now except watch her." How could he spew all this doctor crap like it was something he did daily? He almost grinned but caught himself in time.

"I think we should get her checked out, however, when we get to Houston." He caught himself. "You are going to Houston, aren't you? Not on to Birmingham?"

Matt shook his head. "No, we're getting off in Houston."

"Good. I'll call and have an ambulance waiting for you."

Matt felt the blood drain from his face. "Ambulance? Why couldn't we just drive her to your office or to the hospital or something?"

Potter shook his head with authority. "It's standard after such an episode. She needs to be checked out in a state-of-the-art facility, top to bottom. Without tests, we won't know if this was just a simple seizure or something more. Does she have a history of such episodes?" Man, he was good with the lingo!

Matt shrugged. "I don't know. She's been complaining of headaches recently, though."

Potter scratched his chin as he studied Linda. "We'll get those tests run, see what we can come up with."

Matt nodded. "Right now ..." He glanced at Linda, who appeared to be sleeping in his arms, "I just want to make sure she's okay."

Potter swallowed and hoped Matt didn't see the perspiration on his brow. "In that case, I'll leave you now and see about getting that ambulance."

Potter patted him quickly on the shoulder and made his way back to his seat. Most of the crowd had returned to theirs. He couldn't believe his good luck. They actually believed him, accepted him! He slipped into his seat and picked up the plane's version of a cell phone. Glancing at his seatmate, he noticed the man's eyes were closed and his earphones were blaring some hard music. Good, he couldn't eavesdrop. Quickly, Potter dialed in the appropriate numbers. Soon, her voice was on the other end.

"Potter here. Situation is in hand. Completely." He explained what he'd done and what he needed. In a moment, he ended the call and settled back in his seat. He couldn't stop the grin that split his thin face.

Agent Maderm saw it first. "There, to the right! That's the unit number, the one for Grayson's place, isn't it?"

"The one we were given, yes." Sculler pulled their car into a small space between a dumpster and one of the buildings in the condo complex. The men climbed out and, moving slowly and methodically, surveyed their surroundings.

"Odd," Maderm mused. "You see that white panel van? Wonder who would have one of those here?"

He jogged toward it. "I think we should check it out."

The agents never made it to the van. Just as they ran into the open parking lot, two muscular men, dressed in black turtlenecks and black pants, trotted from the same building as the one housing Grayson's condo. Sculler and Maderm jumped behind a bush and each held their breath as they stared.

The two men were each carrying a couple of boxes. At the panel van, they pulled open the rear doors revealing a bank of electronic equipment, equipment the two FBI agents were very familiar with, as they had spent a great deal of time using it in the past.

"They're one of us!" Sculler could barely contain his voice. "But why weren't we notified? Obviously, someone else is onto this Grayson kid and didn't tell us."

After stowing the boxes, the two men returned to the building.

"Could be," Maderm answered Sculler. "Let's just watch right now."

Shortly, the two men returned carrying more boxes. As Sculler and Maderm observed them, the routine was repeated three more times.

After loading their boxes from the third trip, the two men climbed in the front of the van, and its engine roared to life.

Sculler and Maderm raced back to their car, and Maderm took the driver's seat. They followed the van up to the freeway and for a while, drove uneventfully.

"Why don't you run those plates?" Maderm said while keeping his eyes on the road. "They're not government, but I'll bet we find something interesting if we do get the registration."

"We know they're some of ours."

"Possibly, but not for sure. They may just look like us and use the same equipment we do."

Sculler suddenly sucked in his breath. "You don't suppose they're undercutting us? Could they have given up on our investigation and sent someone else in?"

Maderm laughed. "Get real, Sculler, and stop jumping to conclusions! It's probably tied to some investigation not even related to ours." He gazed out the window for a moment and then continued, his voice soft but determined, "We'll check it out to be sure."

Sculler punched in a number on his phone and waited. Soon, he was relaying the license numbers and requests for information. Shortly, he snapped his phone shut. Turning to Maderm, he said, "No one seems to know what they're up to. Plates came up no owner, counterfeit."

"Man!" Maderm spit. "You think we're getting the run-around?"

"Hard to tell, but I think Dixon's behind this. He's been pushing a little too hard lately."

Sculler shouted suddenly, "Right! The van turned right!"

Maderm slammed his brakes, as did a number of cars behind him. He swerved over two lanes to his right and just managed to escape being slammed in the rear by a tractor-trailer rig. The van sped down an exit ramp, and Maderm followed. When he saw the sign, he was surprised. They were headed for the cargo area adjacent to the Burbank-Glendale airport.

"Give the boys over at Justice a call. Hampton, I think he might be able to dig up some answers. I mean, it looks fairly definite the Grayson boy's a lead. Why else would these guys have been there with all their surveillance equipment?"

Maderm swung their car behind a large shipping container and parked. Sculler got on the phone again, and moments later, he was told Hampton would get back to him. When he did, Sculler was surprised at his words.

"Those people you're following are not part of our group or our investigation. In fact, no one seems to know exactly who they work for. All I can say is they are connected to the government and apparently have some very high clearance. Unfortunately, the director chewed a good chunk off my rear for asking the few questions I did. And while I think investigating these people further might prove interesting, doing so is risky, and I cannot officially condone it."

"Wait," Sculler sputtered. "You're saying you think we should investigate, but if we get caught, you will claim no knowledge of our activities?"

There was a long pause. "I would suggest caution, extreme. Let me remind you this is not officially authorized. If this should turn out to be a legitimate operation and you interfere or compromise it in some way, then I think you already know what will happen. How does a stint in the Salt Flats of Utah grab you?"

Sculler swallowed. "Understood."

"Good. Now go fast and keep me posted! I'll do what I can on this end to cover you." Hampton ended the connection before Sculler could hit the "end" button on his phone.

"Hampton?" Maderm asked.

"Yeah. He said no one knows who these people are. Also, said it might be prudent to investigate, but that it's not officially authorized."

Maderm laughed. "Translated, he's covering his butt and not ours."

"More or less."

Climbing quickly from their car, Sculler led the way as Maderm backed him up. The panel van had parked near a loading dock adjacent to a hangar used to house private aircraft. The two men were unloading the boxes and their equipment and hauling it into the hangar.

Quietly, Maderm and Sculler raced across the pavement, their soft-soled shoes quietly plodding the hard surface. Both of them released the safeties on their pistols, their fingers coiled and itching to pull triggers.

CHAPTER 11

The landing gear doors thumped just a little too loudly as they opened. The flaps on the wings whirred with a piercing whine as they angled into position. Matt's heart skipped a beat. A few more bumps, and the nose dipped lower. He felt himself straining against the restraint of his seat belt. Another loud thump was followed by a squeal as rubber hit cement. For a few seconds, they were held only by the webbing of their seat belts as g-forces strained to throw them against the front of the plane. Then they slowed and coasted to a gentle stop.

"Sir?" Matt turned as the flight attendant spoke. There was a worried look on her face. "Are you all right?" He nodded slowly. "Good. Just wanted to let you know the ambulance is in place, and you will be the first to leave the plane. May I assist you with your things?"

"Thanks. We … uh … we didn't bring much."

The woman nodded. "Very well. Soon as we're at the gate, we'll assist you in leaving the plane."

After the plane was tethered to the Jetway, the other passengers waited patiently as Matt maneuvered up the narrow aisle cradling Linda in his arms. Dr. Potter followed like a mother hen chattering with each step he took.

"You've made the right decision, Mr. Smith. It was Smith you said?" the doctor asked Matt. Matt nodded, and the doctor kept talking. "Incidences such as the one your friend experienced can be dangerous. It is imperative that proper specialists determine just what happened."

Matt didn't answer. The mixture of jet fuel and engine exhaust seeped through the thin walls of the Jetway and mingled with the stagnant air, causing him to have to fight for breath. An airline employee waited with a wheelchair and assisted Matt as he gently settled Linda in the seat. Soon, they were outside on the tarmac hurrying to a waiting ambulance, its lights flashing and back doors open.

Dr. Potter jogged past Matt and Linda to one of the attendants standing by the truck. After rapidly discussing something with the man, he motioned for Matt to roll Linda to the ambulance.

One of the attendants took control of Linda's chair from Matt. The other attendant joined the first, and together, they lifted her onto a waiting stretcher. As they were strapping her down, she squirmed and stretched her hand to Matt. They pushed her into the vehicle.

Dr. Potter turned to Matt and pointed at the truck. "Go on; get in with her. You should be with her now." His eyes didn't warm with his smile.

Matt nodded and quickly climbed the steps to find a seat beside Linda's stretcher. An attendant pointed at the seat belt and motioned for Matt to strap himself in. Matt glanced out the open doors, expecting Dr. Potter to join them. He caught Matt's stare and nodded. The double doors slammed shut.

With the sirens screaming and lights flashing, Matt and Linda left the light and security of George Bush Intercontinental Airport. As they merged onto the freeway, it didn't take Matt long to realize they were heading away from downtown Houston and the Texas Medical Center. A wave of alarm hit him. They were going away from the city, away from anyplace remotely related to medical care. They were heading north toward the piney woods of Texas.

Potter watched the ambulance speed away. He flipped open his phone and punched in a number. When there was an answer, he said, "Confirming. Our two packages are en route as we speak. They should arrive within the hour."

After listening briefly, he ended the connection and slipped the phone into his pocket. He wondered, just for a moment, what that young couple was feeling, to know they had not outsmarted those who sought them. He shrugged and strolled casually toward his waiting car.

Tim scratched his head while Harry dropped another SD card full of pictures into its protective pouch. No x-ray machine, no magnetic force could erase his card while encased in its special, protective material. As Tim maneuvered their rental car from the parking lot, Harry still couldn't make sense of what had happened.

They had been fortunate to catch the flight to Houston. Three seats had opened, and they, along with an older man, had grabbed them. They knew their prey was on the plane, for they'd followed them all day, relentlessly. It was the only reason they had headed to Houston.

During the flight, Harry had become aware of a commotion in first class. Several times, he'd tried to sneak a peek, but all he could see was a crowd of people bending over one of the forward seats, frowns and concern on each of their faces. Discreetly, he asked a few passengers if they knew anything. No one admitted knowing anything of use, so he returned to his seat and called the attendant.

"Sir, you need not worry. A passenger just had a moment of airsickness. She is in good hands. We have a doctor who was able to care for her. There's no need to be concerned."

When they landed, Harry and Tim pushed past other passengers, uncaring there were angry stares at their backsides. They were the first to scramble out the door, but they were too late. Grayson and the woman had already deplaned.

Inside the terminal, they strained to peer through the thick glass window overlooking the tarmac. Their only reward was the sight of an ambulance speeding away and lights flashing.

Harry grabbed Tim's arm. "Hospitals. We call them all."

Sirens screamed as they fled the city for the bowels of the piney woods. Each mile they traveled caused Matt's fear to escalate. Linda was quiet but awake on her stretcher. Matt gazed at her and prayed she didn't see the fear in his eyes. He forced a smile when she squeezed his hand lightly.

Just then, the attendant pulled a syringe out and filled it with some fluid. Matt tapped his arm.

"What's that for?"

The burly man shrugged and continued filling the syringe. Matt asked again.

"It's none of your business," the attendant finally muttered.

With a grace Matt would never have expected from someone who looked as if he were a world heavyweight champion, the attendant inserted the needle into Linda's IV. Then with surprising swiftness, he swung his beefy arm toward Matt, knocking him against the side of the ambulance. The blow only dazed him, but it was more than enough to erase any further doubt about what was happening. Before he could clear his head and gain sufficient position to defend himself, the attendant was on him again. His blows were placed like strategic weapons in a surgical strike. The man seemed to know just where to hit. As the attendant came after him with blow after blow and Matt felt himself sinking into a dark oblivion, he cursed himself for walking into their trap.

Jerry threw the phone on his desk. Grabbing a heavy volume of cross-referenced movie titles, he threw it with strength an Olympic discus thrower would envy. A hole in his wall framed by spreading cracks of plaster was the only reward for his effort, however. If he'd been a cartoon character, smoke would have billowed from his ears and sweat would've boiled on his cheeks. But it wasn't Matt's absence that had Jerry steamed. Despite not hearing from him since he and the girl had taken his car on a quest for truth, Jerry was angry over something bigger than the price of a rental car.

Production company weasels, trying to slither through some fabricated, legal loophole, were claiming Matt was in breach of contract. They were demanding he be on the set no later than six the following morning. It was a laughable threat. But when a warning of legal action had been added, Jerry's smile had faded. Matt's actions were not being taken as the idle whim of a spoiled star. Rather, he was close to being blacklisted. It didn't take much in that town to do one in. Start the right rumor and it could be over in a day.

Jerry paced behind his desk. Why could they not believe he truly didn't know where Matt was? Had they not seen the news? What did they think Matt's disappearance was—some silly publicity stunt he'd concocted?

Earlier that day, the local reports had confirmed:

"Matt Grayson and LA Times *reporter Linda McGowan were rushed last evening from George Bush Intercontinental Airport via ambulance to some undisclosed Houston area hospital. No details were available at air time as to why or what condition necessitated the urgency in getting medical care."*

The picture, the words, still burned in Jerry's mind. The most compelling scene, however, was a brief shot at the end of the story. While the camera zoomed over a mob of reporters, paparazzi, and television crews all outside a Houston hospital, all firing rapid questions at the hospital's spokesperson, the reporter had continued.

"While all hospitals have been contacted, it seems no one can verify just where Matt Grayson and Linda McGowan are. None of the local

hospitals claim to have them under their care. Herein lies the mystery: exactly where did that ambulance take these two people yesterday just after arriving at Houston's Intercontinental Airport?"

As the cameraman panned the crowd, two faces jumped out at Jerry: Tim and Harry. They were two paparazzi noted for getting the picture, and the story, even when others shied away. Those two rascals were pushing to the front of the mob. Jerry sighed as he sank into his chair. How many times had he cursed those two? They had to be the most doggedly determined, irritating, and infuriating pair of newshound photographers he'd ever encountered. Yet, he had to admit, if Tim and Harry couldn't find answers to the mystery of Matt and Linda, then no one could.

The phone rang. With a lightning jerk, he grabbed the receiver and shouted, "Hello!"

"Jerry, it's Katie Grayson." He was surprised to hear her voice and even more surprised at her next words. "Jerry, I saw the news last night. It was the biggest story around here, Matt taken from the airport in an ambulance. I didn't even know Matt was in Houston." She stopped.

Jerry could feel her heartache in the silence. He sucked on his pen, fighting the urge to light another cigarette. "Katie, sit tight. I'm going to hop the next plane to Houston."

He heard a soft intake of breath. "Would you?"

"You know I'd do anything for the boy. Anything for his family," he muttered, as he flushed over her gratitude.

CHAPTER 12

Congressman Thom Jordan's district claimed only a small chunk of the vast geography in the heart of Southern California, yet the influence he wielded blanketed the entire country. Although the geographic size of his district was minuscule compared to those of some of his comrades, his constituents provided the power. What made his district special was money, lots of it. Liberal money. Movers and shakers, they all resided within his boundaries.

His constituents agreed with him on one thing, spending. They were wholly committed to it, and the more the better. Their only requirement, it must be government money, never their own. Oh, but they were quick to ante up when it came election time. They were never slow to support those who believed in their priorities. So, Congressman Jordan found his task quite easy, compliance with their requests never a burden. The occasional hate letters he received and the threats of putting him out of office were met with hearty laughter. So long as his more prominent constituents kept his campaign coffers filled, he'd never worry about those errant discontents. As chairman of the House Ways and Means Committee, spending the taxpayers' money was the thing he did best.

For the fifth time that day, the congressman pulled a stack of papers nearly two inches thick across his desk. As he glanced over the first few paragraphs for probably the hundredth time, a chill raced along his spine. The mere thought of the potential unfolding at that very moment filled him with a delicious expectation that was so tangible he nearly drooled.

The papers he studied appeared to be just another trite piece of legislation. Actually, they held, hidden in their volumes of words, provisions for the continued funding of a top-secret project conceived and initiated nearly sixty years prior. The program was not anything Congress would specifically vote on, but by passing the bill, Congress would agree to continue funding and thereby endorse the existence of this program that was so near and dear to his heart.

He smiled. He thought of the many self-righteous and pompous old fools casting their votes to spend money on a project none knew the first fact about. By voting, they sanctioned it, stamped the blessing of the United States Government on activities so unconventional and controversial that even his most liberal colleagues might shudder if they knew the truth. Just promise a little pork-barrel spending in their district, toss in a little influence, mix in some girls, and cover it with a hushed mouth. It was always the same. It was a crime, really, it was so easy. They were always sold.

A small beep came from the intercom integrated with his phone. "Sir, they're waiting for you in the conference room."

"Thank you, Bess. I'm ready now."

Congressman Jordan picked up his papers, stuffed them in a leather briefcase, and after donning his suit jacket and adjusting his cuffs so that his cuff links twinkled at the prescribed distance beyond the hem of his jacket sleeves, he locked his desk and strolled confidently toward the outer office. Stopping by the desk of his young executive assistant, he didn't bother to hide his long glance at the exceptional cleavage peeping from her open blouse.

"No calls, please, Bess. I don't want anyone to know where I am or what I'm doing. Just say I stepped out for a stroll or something."

Bess returned his smile and gripped his hand briefly. Warmth flowed from her finely manicured fingertips to his skin. "Everything is taken care of. Have a good meeting. I'll see you later?"

Representative Jordan nodded and added a wink. "And if my wife calls, tell her I'll be working late, very late tonight!"

Using a private side door, he slipped from the office to avoid the waiting room where it seemed there was always some needy constituent ready to bend his ear or some pushy reporter scooping the latest legislation he sponsored. Ever since January, he'd been wary of them, reporters especially. One had gotten too close, had learned too much. Although he was told the situation had been taken care of, he'd become careful, paranoid almost.

His arrival at the conference room was unnoticed. Pausing briefly before the heavy mahogany doors, he sucked in his stomach and took a deep breath. Yes, that day would become a landmark day in history, a turning point to new frontiers, and he was leading the way.

Patting his lapel, he entered the room. Facing him was a circular table, surrounded by seven individuals. Chest thrust forward, shoulders pulled back, he set his briefcase on the table in front of his chair. Still standing, he said, "Good afternoon, ma'am, gentlemen," and then pointedly to the man on his left, "and Mr. President." Congressman Jordan smiled warmly at all seven faces and settled into his seat. "Shall we get started?"

The president of the United States was young, at least by presidential standards. However, he felt old. The pain in his side persisted despite discreet and highly confidential consideration by the best doctors the world had to offer. Nothing helped. Too much fun during his college years, that was what they blamed. The excess of youth, they whispered. For most, the excesses were handled and disposed of by the body, but his was defective. His liver had gone against its inherent genetic programming and decided to live, and die, a life of its own. He, the most powerful man in the world, was stuck with a defective piece of biology and could do nothing about it. He still didn't understand why a transplant was out, why the doctors wouldn't even discuss it with him. None of it made sense. It just wasn't fair.

Well, he blamed them: the doctors, the pharmaceutical companies, the research fellows, all of them. They should have developed a better treatment years ago. Never mind that he'd endorsed and signed into law legislation that effectively wiped away any incentives for companies to fund research or for doctors to work with those companies in the quest for knowledge. He'd listened to the cries of the ignorant, blind, bleeding hearts to spend more on social programs and cut tax incentives for corporations sponsoring research. How he wished he could take it all back.

At the prime of his life, seated as the leader of the free world, he stood a greater than even chance of losing it all. The latest report said he probably had less than a year. In the Oval Office and enjoying immense popularity, he didn't want, simply couldn't afford to accept those words of defeat. He would search until he died for a cure, a solution, something, anything that would take this problem away, even if temporary. It was that important.

Even more important was complete secrecy. Political experience had taught him well. Immense popularity was not enough to ensure security in the office he planned to hold for another term. From the moment of the first twinge of pain deep inside the peritoneal cavity and his confession to his personal physician about how debilitating it was, to the time when he had received the devastating news in response, he'd committed to a mission. He would find a cure.

Third-world countries were being recognized daily for their old folk remedies that had suddenly found popularity in contemporary medicine. But he found no answer in the third world or elsewhere. He reviewed all available information on alternative medicine. Nothing there either. He refused to believe that with the world's vast resources at his fingertips, there couldn't be something somewhere that could help. The frustration grew, as did his despondency.

To the world, he continued to appear robust and healthy. Media orchestrations became the order of the day. Inside, his despair grew. Hope suffocated under a shroud of doom.

Resigning himself to defeat, he prepared a speech of resignation.

Two days before it was to be delivered to the country, an answer had been found. And it was one he would never have imagined, even if he'd tried. It was not in some third-world country. It was not cloaked in superstitious ritual. It was, rather, a miracle, something developed at home, almost under his nose.

Few details of the cure and its availability had been granted him. He'd only learned of it through discreet inquiries. It was from a company, one in which one of his more liberal supporters, a Representative Thom Jordan of California, had connections. He was told research that had been secretly conducted for years held the possibility of a cure. He'd been surprised that activities of such magnitude were held secret, kept from the public. After a few reminders from his advisors, he understood the need for secrecy in such work.

That afternoon, he'd met with Representative Jordan and some of his colleagues. For the first time in months, he'd regained hope. The proposal they'd outlined was nothing less than a miracle. All he had to do was sacrifice a few days for the treatment, and the promise of life regained was assured. He saw no reason to hesitate, had no reservations, despite later urgings from his chief of staff to wait, to reconsider, to allow time for final testing of the product. He didn't have the time. He must proceed with treatment immediately. He needed his cure yesterday.

When Cherie stepped from her limo in front of the main building of the compound housing the Piney Woods Project, she was greeted by stars twinkling above and soft breezes flirting with her skirt. She sucked in several deep breaths of fresh air. There was no LA smog to leave a metallic aftertaste on her tongue, no grit of exhaust to itch her eyes, nothing but the dewy, wet sweetness of a balmy Texas night.

Katydids, crickets, tree frogs, and other chirping creatures were joined in one loud song. Rows of oleander framed the edge of manicured lawns that surrounded the massive, glass-walled building, the headquarters, central hub, the heartbeat of their project. Beyond the wall of flowers were miles of uninhabited woods, empty fields, and barren land. It was true isolation. It was perfect.

Cherie sucked in another deep breath of air spiced with pine rosin. She straightened her shoulders and began her slow march toward the glass-doored entrance. A big smile curled her lips. Oh, the sweet smell of pine rosin. Would she ever get tired of it? Even if she did, she would never be without it. None of them would. It was the center of their lives, the foundation for all they hoped to accomplish.

The miracle had been discovered many decades earlier, by accident. Men working in the piney woods constantly exposed to pine rosin began to develop interesting traits. An enterprising young scientist and a businessman collaborated to research and develop the potential. Connections in high places brought in money and secrecy. Thus, the project was born. Some sixty years in the making, it now approached its zenith.

Pulling the glass doors open, Cherie glided through, confidence decorating her shoulders like epaulets. She sighed as air-conditioned air fanned her face. She could forget that horrible stint acting as a concerned editor, nursing a sick employee back to health. Finally, she could get back to the place that was the heart of her work, the heart of her.

Cherie possessed the same determination as the founders of the project. She had adopted their vow of no failure. Only her motivation was different. While they claimed they worked for the children and their future, her future held no children, no hope of grandchildren. What she did, she did for herself and herself alone. Nothing would stop her. Nothing.

Across the marble-floored lobby of the project's main building, "the lab," as most called it, was Congressman Jordan. As she approached and extended her hand, the congressman rose.

"Thom. Glad you managed to get here so soon."

"You insisted."

Although the Jordan name no longer graced any official letterhead, payroll listing, or current articles of incorporation, his grandfather's name long replaced with new names all untraceable to the project, he was one of the key people responsible for its continued existence. His critical role came not only from his command of power and respect in high places but also from his history. For with the pioneering insight, determination, and direction of the first group of scientists, his grandfather was the businessman responsible for conceiving and giving birth to the project. And through the years, the Jordan name had become increasingly important to the work.

Though Thom Jordan's current function most importantly ensured the continued funding of the entire operation, he was no less determined to assure the work progressed to its successful completion. His vision of millions of lives changed, miraculously, solely because of the work his family had initiated and become responsible for, was only one goal. The fact the project's success would make him wealthier than even Bill Gate's biggest dream iced his cake.

Cherie smiled and touched his shoulder lightly. "A wise move, coming now. Even you must admit how important the coming days are. Although we've met with him, and he's taken the bait, the deal still won't be a sure bet until we can prove the success of our treatment."

Thom Jordan nodded slowly. "Yes, he's waiting for our report. Anxiously, I might add."

"Excellent." Cherie pointed at the bank of elevators facing them. "Shall we?"

When Matt realized he was awake, déjà-vu was a veil over his eyes. For the second time in less than a year, he didn't know where he was and wasn't entirely sure who he was. Yet, the certainty of its occurrence was more real than the curtain surrounding the sterile cubicle or the IV needle pressing painfully into his flesh.

Stretched across a hospital bed, an IV in his left arm and a thick curtain surrounding him, cutting off vision to the world beyond, he heard no sounds, had no clue what might be happening beyond his range of knowledge. Wiggling, he tried to sit up but was surprised to find his arms bound at the wrists, tethered to the metal rails forming his prison. A clammy chill raced across his back.

Matt tossed and thrashed. The binds on his wrists loosened. He jerked harder. His right arm gained some freedom. His stubbornness kicked in, refusing to concede any semblance of defeat. He kept pulling and tugging. Nothing would get the best of him. He kept working, making minuscule progress at loosening the straps. Exhaustion set in, and just as he was ready to give up, a familiar face peeked through the parted curtain.

"I see you're fightin' it," the farmer said, a wide grin exposing his gleaming tooth. "But don't fight at it so hard." He wandered over to Matt's side. His fingers lightly touched the cord, and it fell away.

"I'm dreaming, aren't I?" Matt said to the vision, not expecting an answer.

"It all depends on your perspective, son. Why, me, I'm as real as any of this gets."

"Why am I here?"

"That's a good question. I'm sure there're many reasons, most of which I don't know. But …" He winked at Matt. "… the most important one is very close to you. And it's that one you need to get out of here for."

"Would you please stop talking in riddles? Why do I need to get out of here?"

The farmer's lips closed over his tooth. The warmth in his eyes chilled. "There are no riddles, but you need answers. I don't have them to give. First, you must take care of her. She needs you, more than ever."

"And just how am I supposed to do that? I don't know where I am, not sure who I am or even what's going on. I don't even know if I'm dreaming or not." Matt felt the pounding of blood behind his ears. He tried to hit the railing with his fist, but it fell limp to his side. "I'm so tired of this!" His shout was a weak whisper.

The farmer was too calm. "We all get frustrated, tired, confused. It's just part of living. You push too hard, don't wait for what you need.

I think I can help you, though. She's nearby, but don't wait too long. Time is precious."

Matt opened his eyes. His head hurt, throbbed actually. Looking about him, he realized he was stretched across the length of a hospital bed. A curtain surrounded him, blocking any view that could possibly give him a clue as to where he was. An IV bag hung from a pole, and a needle was under his skin, but no plastic line was attached.

He saw a face, not in front of him, but in his mind. The farmer was leaning toward him, smiling. He was telling him to take care of her. *Her! Linda!* They had flown to Houston, together. When? That day? Yesterday? Last week? He had no idea. But he had to find her. He felt the evil. It permeated the air, surrounding him, pressing against him as tangible as ice on flesh, cold and penetrating.

He was surprised to find two loose cords wrapped about his wrists. Strange. Matt pushed the covers aside and climbed from the bed. He had no clothes that he could see, only the standard too-short and too-skimpy hospital gown. Forced to be content with his back end bare to the breeze, he peeked through the curtains. He saw nothing but empty beds lining both sides of a long ward. At the far end, a set of doors led to a lighted corridor.

A shadow grew along the wall outside the door, and it stopped briefly before pushing the door open. Matt caught a quick glance of a young man, whose muscular arms strained against the cloth of his white shirt. Matt ducked back behind the curtain and huddled next to the head of the bed, partially obscured from the immediate vision of his unknown adversary. An IV pole, one without a bag attached, was beside him. He jerked its top section free and grasped it like a club.

The curtains parted, and the man peered in. Questions flickered in his eyes when he didn't immediately see Matt, but before he could respond, Matt lunged from his crouching position and slammed the attendant's head with the steel pole. As the man crumpled to the floor, he added two more hard blows.

The attendant's muscles relaxed, and when they did, a syringe filled with some amber liquid slipped from his fingers and rolled a short distance across the floor. Intended for him, Matt was certain. Without thinking, or even considering possible repercussions, Matt jabbed the needle into the attendant's arm and pushed the plunger in. Then, he dragged the man as far into the curtained cubicle as possible. Working as fast as his weak muscles would allow, Matt pulled the shirt and pants off the attendant. Quickly, he donned the stolen clothes. They were at least two sizes too big. Cinching the belt as tight as possible, Matt prayed he didn't look too odd in the oversized pants. Next, he grabbed the man's shoes. Hopelessly big. If he had to run, he'd never make it. Still, he couldn't risk raising suspicions by not having any, so he stuffed them with tissues and slipped them on. Didn't feel the best, but at least they didn't fall off when he walked.

Finally, Matt struggled to wrap the skimpy hospital gown across the bulky man. With the gown barely covering the man's front, Matt pulled and pushed until he managed to get him into the hospital bed. For good measure, he wrapped the cords that had been on his wrists around the attendant's arms and tied them to the bed's metal rails. Last, he moved the IV pole and anything else out of reach of the bed, just in case.

As Matt started to run from the cubicle, something made him stop and glance at the man. He appeared to be sleeping. However, when Matt stuck his hand over the man's nose, he felt no telltale warmth, no rush of breath. Fingers suddenly clumsy, he probed and pushed against soft flesh, searching for a pulse. There was none. The empty syringe, gleaming in the artificial light, caught his eye. Matt felt as if icy water had washed over him. That syringe had been intended for him.

Phillippe, Charles, and Dereck were gathered around a small conference table in the heart of the Pine Woods Facility's lab. Empty coffee cups and crumpled napkins full of sandwich crumbs had been pushed to the edge, forgotten as each man hunched over laptop screens filled with secret contents. Deep lines pinched their foreheads.

"Charles, you didn't hear me," Dereck declared.

"Sorry."

"I said …" Dereck drew the last word into two syllables. "… this latest data isn't conclusive, but I think we've got a link. Look." He hit a button on his keypad, and two transparent films came into view. Dark blotches filled each image in a seemingly random order. He pointed at two of the many spots that covered each image. Only to Dereck, the order and the form of the blotches were far from random, as together, they told a unique story of an individual from the viewpoint of a molecule.

"See this?" The other two nodded slowly. Dereck hit another key, and yet a third image projected onto the screen. "And see this? It's identical to the first two. Since we got her back in here and initiated the treatment, her body is producing the same results regardless of the variation in treatment."

Dereck tapped a few more keys, and more images were displayed on the screen. He briefly perused them before casting his gaze back on the others seated around him.

He pointed at the top image. "This latest data coincides with the data from genetics. From both the first trial of erasure and reimplantation to this latest where the opposite was the case, it seems our girl's genes are making the treatment successful. She has what the others lacked."

"So what now?" Phillippe asked softly, his eyes still fixed on the images.

"It means more testing, of course. We have to isolate the specific code, replicate it, and find an appropriate host to use for insertion."

"A long process," Phillippe added somewhat sourly.

"Certainly not quick," Dereck agreed.

"But there are things we can do to speed it up," Phillippe said, suddenly smiling.

"Like what?" Dereck responded, his eyes narrowed as he peered at Phillippe.

"We could speed up the timetable on her treatments, allow for less rest in between. We could start a new round of testing on a fresh group of subjects. We could search our databases for a genetic match, someone to use as a control. We could—"

"Wait!" Charles slapped the table. "We don't have time for new testing. They're demanding a final report today! They want to know if we can say, conclusively, this treatment will work. Can we treat based on our findings to date?"

"How can we?" Dereck asked. "There's still so much we don't know. Her responses to this latest regimen have put our work in a whole new arena filled with unknowns. The success we've had with her may or may not be replicable. Further, even it is not perfect. You know the problems we've had. Who's to say they won't repeat or be even worse?"

Phillippe interjected. "All we have to do is isolate and replicate. We don't have to worry about the impact. What it does to the girl is of no consequence. Right, Charles?"

Dereck's eyes bored into Charles as the senior physician and lab director blushed. "Are you saying we're to simply use that girl until she expires?"

Charles retorted, "That was not my directive. It was given to me. But, yes, the girl is never to be allowed to leave the facility. Please …" He put his hand out as if to stop Dereck. "… don't go into that ethical quagmire again. My hands are tied. We have a directive, and we'll follow it. We're to test and keep testing until we get an answer. This girl holds that answer, so there is nothing stopping us from using her to her complete potential." He turned to Phillippe. "Go over your latest data again."

Phillippe opened a new file on his computer and scrolled through the pages. "Three treatments have been completed. She was returned to her room within the past hour. She should sleep at least eight hours before rousing. Then, we'll administer treatment number four."

"And her response?"

"Like I said earlier, normal, within predicted parameters. She fought the first dose, became physically violent and verbally abusive. By the second treatment, she was much more docile, less energetic. By the third, she was easily distracted, unable to focus, could not concentrate for more than minimal amounts of time, and seemed unsure of her identity."

"Mental status?"

"After the third treatment, she was unable to give a name, employment, or any evidence of past memory. Current facts seemed to have been erased, yet the implant does not seem to have taken hold."

"Enzyme levels? Organ viability?"

"Levels are somewhat elevated, but nowhere near the levels found in those who were casualties. Organ viability seems good. No problems noted."

"Okay, we move forward as planned. I'll report that we're on schedule and will agree with their requests to proceed as recommended. We will vigorously pursue code isolation and the replication process."

Dereck slammed the cover on his computer and pushed his chair back so hard it slammed into the wall. "I cannot sign off on this. It's not right, and I will not go along with it!"

"You will, and there will be no further discussion—that is, if you cherish your life as it is now!"

Dereck didn't answer. He turned on his heel and stormed from the room, slamming the door behind him. Charles glanced at Phillippe, and the latter shrugged.

"Very well," Charles said, "you know the procedure. Get to work. Let's hope Dereck comes to his senses soon. We need his input on this."

"Do we, Charles? I'm not so sure. I think we've got enough to complete our testing without his data or research."

"Do we now? Can I believe you, Phillippe? After all, you're the one who claimed Dereck's work as your own. Perhaps you've managed to copy *all* his records?"

For a long moment, Phillippe stared unsmiling at Charles. Suddenly his teeth broke the stern exterior of his face as he grinned. Charles grinned too. Soon, the two men were bent double laughing.

"Charles, you are evil!" Phillippe said, still holding his side as he stumbled from the room. "But I like the way you operate. We're two of a kind, just alike. I like working like that!" His laughter followed him down the hall.

Charles's smile faded the moment Phillippe was out of sight. He pulled out his phone and punched in some numbers.

"I believe we have encouraging news." Charles spoke slowly into the mouthpiece, emphasizing the words. "Progress is good. Best of all, it seems the subject is suffering no ill effects and organ functions are well within normal range."

"What about the others?"

"All terminal. She's the only one to survive this latest round."

"So, what's the good news?"

"We believe we've isolated the gene responsible for the girl's viability. After isolation and replication, it's just a matter of finding a suitable host for insertion."

There was sarcasm in Cherie's voice. "But there's something else, isn't there? Like, you're going to ask for more time. Isn't that right?"

Charles swallowed. "To be certain and to perfect what we plan, yes, more time is needed."

"Well, time, you don't have. Our special patient has just arrived. As we speak, he's being settled into his suite, and I don't have to tell you how impatient he is to start. You must focus on completing your preparations for his treatment. You won't let me down, Charles. You won't let the most powerful man in the world down either, will you?"

Cherie's seductive voice flowed over him, and he hated his reaction to it. It was like an addiction he could not control despite the danger he knew was hidden beneath its charm.

"I know I can trust you," she added smoothly, "to manage your group effectively so that you can get maximum performance from them. The incentives are great, and the rewards will be many if you succeed. Do I have to remind you of just how great?"

"No." Charles swallowed. He understood too well. "I'll give you a report on progress soon."

Terror squeezing his lungs, Matt raced from the cubicle. The sight of the attendant, prone and lifeless in the bed where he'd rested his head only moments earlier, was permanently burned onto the picture plates of his mind. Forcing himself to focus instead on the light spilling through the glass doors, on his escape, his freedom, Matt raced across the empty space and surged into a long hall. Empty. No one there, no sound either. There was nothing except for the clap of his feet hitting the tile floor.

Turning right, Matt trotted toward an intersection of hallways. Studying the opposing passageway, he spied a lone stretcher, parked to one side and accompanied by a pole with two IV bags hanging from it. A shock of dark hair spilling from beneath the sheet made Matt gasp. Could it be?

Just as Matt reached the stretcher, two attendants emerged from a set of windowless doors and nearly collided with him.

"I was sent to relieve you," Matt offered first.

One of the attendants leaned over and stared at the ID hanging on Matt's shirt. "Sorry, uh ..." He squinted as he read the name. "John. No one told us we were relieved."

"Guess they didn't have time." Matt smiled broadly. "They said you were needed downstairs."

"Really?" the second man asked and shrugged. "Well, if you say so."

"Yeah, they said you were to take a break. I'm to handle things for the next hour or so."

"Okay, if that's what they want," the first man answered. "I'm sure not gonna miss an extra break!" He grinned and punched his partner. "You know she's to go to 304?"

Matt nodded. "Sure thing."

The two men strolled toward the doors from which they'd come. Matt pushed the stretcher in the opposite direction. He spied the room number, but before he could decide what to do, two other men turned the corner and headed briskly toward him. Trying to act as if he were merely doing his job, Matt pushed the stretcher into the room. The men followed.

"Thank you. That'll be all for now," the first man said to Matt as he stepped up to the bed. The other joined him.

Matt backed from the room, but not before he heard one say, "Vitals look good, but she'll probably be out of it for a while. We might as well check on her later." He started toward the door and Matt.

Caught, Matt jumped backward and pushed into a janitor's closet. He listened as the footsteps faded. Seconds later, he was by her side.

"Who are you?" Her voice was hoarse and raspy.

"It's me. Matt. Don't you remember?"

She jerked the sheet free of the bed and held it under her chin. "No, should I? You're just one of them." She pointed to the ID badge pinned to his "borrowed" shirt.

Matt didn't move. Finally, he asked, "Well, who are you?"

She bit her lip and then frowned. "I'm … well, I'm …" She stared at the ceiling as if it held the answer. "I'm just …"

"You don't know."

"Yes, I do!" Her words were short, hot. "I'm … Linda!"

Matt leaned toward her and gazed into her eyes. "Do you remember coming here?"

She shook her head. For a brief moment, she gazed past him and suddenly squeezed her eyes shut. She whispered, "Yes, I do! We flew to Houston from Los Angeles. You sat beside me and told me about living in Texas."

Matt's mouth dropped slightly. "You remember that?"

She nodded. "Why shouldn't I? I was rather sick, as I remember." She glanced about her. "But this place, I don't remember it. Where are we?"

"I don't know, except I'm sure it has to do with those people who put a bounty on our heads."

"Bounty? Did I miss something?"

Matt smiled. "Not much. Look, someone wants something from us pretty bad. That's why we were brought here. And the sooner we get out of here, the better."

"Just where do we need to go?"

"I don't know. Anywhere."

Matt suddenly realized the obvious. They must be watching, probably through some hidden camera. Searching the ceiling, the walls, all that was visible, he saw nothing suspicious. He scratched his head. Her bed. Checking the call button, he found it, no camera eye, but a small microphone.

Still not satisfied he'd found all there was to find, Matt kept searching. Nestled in the middle of the switch plate beside the door, posing as the screw, was a small camera lens. Standing by the door, hoping he was out of the camera's range, Matt pointed at it and mouthed, "See?"

Linda's eyes widened. She nodded.

Slipping quickly from the room, Matt returned a minute later holding a white bundle. "Put these on!" he whispered as he thrust the clothes toward her. "Not the greatest, but better than what you're wearing!" He grinned as his eyes raked her scantily clad body.

Linda glanced at the thin, grossly skimpy hospital gown covering her. Despite her thin frame, its material was not too generous, and it left a lot exposed. She pulled the IV from her arm. Some blood spattered the white sheets, but she ignored it as she yanked the monitor's electric cord from the wall. It's beeping silenced; she ripped the sensors from her skin. Quickly, she donned Matt's meager offering of scrubs, a lab jacket, and some soft slippers, and then followed him to the door and waited. After checking the hallway and finding it empty, Matt led the way from the room.

Turning right, they moved quietly down the hallway until it ended in front of a fire exit. Pushing the heavy steel door open, Matt realized there was only one choice: down. By the time the door closed quietly behind them, they were at the next level.

Each level curled around in a square. Doors were unmarked, and Matt was unsure how many floors they'd descended when they arrived at the bottom. Trying to slow his breathing and calm his pounding heart, Matt placed his ear against the door. He heard no sounds; apparently, the door was soundproof.

Matt yanked the knob, but the door resisted. He tried again, and then, without warning, it swung back to reveal a long concrete hallway lined with bare bulbs in wire cages. At the opposite end was another steel door. Immediately to its right was another.

Despite shoes so big they flopped and in spite of the fact Linda was still a bit woozy from her latest treatment, they sprinted the short distance of the hall. Faced with the decision of which door to open, Matt opted for the one on the right. When he pulled it open, the last thing he ever expected to see greeted them.

Before them was a long electronic console facing a wall of monitors. The room was dark except for the light flickering from more than a dozen screens. Some showed pictures of people in hospital beds, various tubes and lines connected. Some slept peacefully—or at least they were still. Others thrashed and writhed, obviously in pain. The oddest, however, was that no one was present in the room watching. Just as Matt started to back from the room, Linda pushed past him and ran up to one of the monitors and pointed.

"Look!" she hissed loudly.

Matt glanced at the monitor she indicated. In a bed, propped up with a number of pillows, a Kindle, an iPad, and a Nook on his lap and reading glasses perched on his nose, was a face he was not prepared to see.

"Is that who I think it is?" Linda asked quietly.

Matt stared, his jaw slack. "Yeah, the president. And I don't even want to think about what they've got planned for him!"

Suddenly, alarms started blaring and whooping. Matt pulled Linda's arm. "I think we've been discovered. Come on!"

Back in the hall, Matt pulled the steel door open easily. On the other side, they were faced with yet another door. Matt yanked the knob, and it swung back freely. Sunlight flooded in at them, and without waiting for their eyes to adjust, they flew down a short flight of steps and landed in a massive parking lot overflowing with cars.

Beyond the pavement was a small expanse of manicured lawn hemmed by woods. As they scooted across the lot, aiming for the cover of the trees and bushes, Matt decided that in all his twenty-eight years, sunshine had never looked so good.

CHAPTER 13

Alarms blasted through the thick, humid air. Doors burst open and spewed masses of thundering feet. Shouts could be heard despite the blaring alarms. From the sky, it appeared as if a Texas-sized ant mountain had been stomped by a bare foot and angry, vengeful ants, full of venom were racing out on a solitary mission to inflict as much pain as possible on the one disrupting their highly ordered routine.

Matt gripped Linda's hand as if a vise had glued their flesh together. They sprinted across the parking lot toward the woods, but just before reaching the edge of the pavement, Linda jerked Matt's hand, forcing him to stop. A slender man, impeccably dressed in a dark suit, stood by the trunk of a black S-Class Mercedes sedan. He shifted from foot to foot as he listened to some voice shouting at him from his cell phone.

"What're you doing?" Matt shouted at Linda. She didn't move, so he yanked her arm. "Come on! We've got to get out of here!"

Just as quickly as Linda had frozen to inaction, she thawed and tore past Matt, her hair whipping in multiple directions from the violence of her motions.

More shouts erupted. Footsteps pounded. Cars screeched to a stop, and doors flew open spilling even more hunters. It sounded as if every troop in the state was on their tail, no less priority than if they'd escaped from death row.

Matt jumped after Linda, caught her arm, and pulled her by his side as they plunged into the shade of the trees. Pushing his legs harder, faster, Matt flew, pulling Linda with him.

Ignoring the slap of supple branches and briars ripping their skin, they raced. Adrenaline pumped on high, pushing their human strength to inhuman boundaries. Uneven ground and hidden holes didn't slow their pace. They ran blindly, deafly, deeper into the endless woods. Panic and adrenaline pushed them beyond any normal limits. It was all or nothing, life or death.

It wasn't until Linda fell, clutching her side and groaning, that Matt slowed.

"Where did you … get … so much … energy?" she asked between labored breaths.

"Not energy, fear." Matt dropped beside her and asked, "Tell me, who was that man, the one in the parking lot?"

"I'm not sure. For an instant, I was sure I knew him. Then, the feeling was gone. Why?"

"Looked to me like you were terrified of him."

Linda shrugged. "I don't know. It was just that one moment; for a second I thought I knew him."

Matt stood. "We don't have time to chat about it now. We've got to keep moving."

Linda offered him her hand. Matt grasped it. Together, they plunged deeper into the seemingly endless stand of tall pines. As they raced from enemies, man and nature, time blurred and senses dulled. Yet, Matt couldn't shake the feeling that unseen, deadlier traps awaited them.

They were speeding at least twenty miles over the limit as they raced north on I-45. Maderm's death grip on the steering wheel had turned his knuckles white. Glancing quickly at Sculler, he asked, "Found our spot yet?"

Sculler jabbed the Google map displayed on his iPad and looked up. "You know, I grew up in Houston. Always thought I knew the back roads, but if what those two goons we followed to the airport in LA told us was true, then we're headed for uncharted territory. This map sure doesn't show any of the roads they talked about."

"I hope we've not been duped and taken on some idiot chase for trolls in the woods. It's possible, though. I sure wish Hampton would get back to us. How long does it take for him to run this stuff down?"

Sculler's cell phone beeped, and the man stiffened as he listened to the voice on the other end. When the call ended, he glanced at Maderm.

"Looks like we've gotten a break, but things aren't what we expected."

"What do you mean?"

Sculler turned back to his map. "The good news is Hampton was able to intercept some communications, get a little heads-up for us. Bad news is, looks like they've got a top-notch team working this place."

"You mean at the facility? In Conroe?"

"Yep. Means we're going against forces that have a lot more muscle and bigger pockets of money than the two of us. Hampton said he's going to set up covers for us by the time we arrive, and for us to use our alternate IDs. But ..." Sculler's voice grew quiet. "... the bad news, he fears we may not be recognized by these folks."

"So, who cares if they know us or not?"

Sculler shook his head. "I can't believe you said that. I don't mean 'know us' like that. I mean, as in accepting our credentials, our reason for being there, whatever it is. We have to wait for Hampton to let us know just what it is."

Maderm blew out a long sigh. He glanced over his shoulder before changing lanes and muttered, "Not good. Not good at all." The two agents rode in silence for a while. Maderm broke it.

"Did he say anything else? Like, does he have any clue about this facility? Are we even barking up the right tree?"

"Yeah. Said this might be what we've been searching for all along. He said we couldn't quote him on that, though."

"More of him covering his butt, huh?"

Sculler snickered. "You got that right."

When they exited from I-45, they had to travel over several local FM roads before turning off onto a road identified only as "Government Property—No Trespassing." As their car followed the isolated and curving stretch of pavement, both men were silent, eyes scanning, searching, taking in every detail of the wooded land surrounding them. Neither had a clue what it was they looked for.

They rounded a sharp curve and saw, careening toward them, a canvas-sided truck, one that looked ready to transport troops. After blinking its lights at them, the driver waved for them to pull over. Maderm pulled to the shoulder, and the truck backed up until it was beside them; each driver facing the other. Instead of the other driver getting out, the truck's front passenger walked around the front of the vehicle and planted his beefy forearms on the car's door as he leaned in to peer at Maderm.

"Afternoon, men. Mind if I ask what you're doing here?"

Maderm fumbled in his pocket and produced a government ID. Rapidly, and with years of confidence built into the movement, he flashed it in front of the camouflaged-clad soldier.

"Your ID says government officer, but not what kind. This is a classified area. Only those with special security clearance are allowed on this property."

Maderm seemed to study the man's uniform before looking him in the eye. "Well, I can assure you, we're here on orders. You may call this number and ask for Assistant Director Hampton. He'll give you any information you need regarding our visit." The soldier frowned as Maderm thrust a small card at him.

"This tells me nothing! It only gives a number."

"Sir, as you said, this is a security area. Our business here is also classified, and we're not to divulge it to anyone except with direct orders from this man." Maderm pointed at the card. "We're under executive orders. Orders issued by the president of the United States."

The soldier's brows shot up, and then he narrowed his eyes as he scanned Maderm's face yet another time. Several moments passed, the only sound the cicadas and locusts in the underbrush singing their lazy songs, so common on hot summer days in the South. When he finished his scrutiny, he shrugged and turned to hand the card to the truck's driver.

"Call this number now. We need authorization on these men." He turned back to Maderm and Sculler and said to Sculler, "You got an ID?"

Sculler fished in his pocket and produced an ID that named him as Agent Scofield. He handed it to the soldier. After careful scrutiny, the guard returned it to Sculler.

The soldier leaned in the window toward Maderm. "We've got a classified operation going on. Security's tighter than normal. Once we clear you here, you'll need to check in with the main guard station about three miles up ahead. They must have a record of your orders."

There was a chirping sound inside the truck, and the driver answered it. "Yes, sir! ... Very well, sir ... I will, sir ... Thank you, sir." The driver shouted to the guard. "Let them go. I've got the authorization."

For some reason, the soldier lost his stern demeanor and seemed to relax. "By the way," he said grinning, "last I heard, the president's doing just fine." Turning, he ran back to the truck. No good-bye, no apology, no sorry-to-have-detained-you, not even a generic, "Have a nice day now!" The truck's gears ground, and in seconds, it resumed its lumbering trek down the road.

"Where'd you get that bunch of crap about us being on executive orders?" Sculler asked.

Maderm grinned. "Just a little stretch. We are here to serve, protect, and defend our country, aren't we? Isn't that what our good president would want us to do? Well, then, I'd say that's executive orders."

"What do you suppose that man meant by 'the president is doing just fine'?"

Maderm shrugged but said nothing.

Taking the curves with tire-screeching speed, they soon approached a large, glass-walled building planted in the middle of a broad, lush, tropical landscaped clearing. Trees and forest had been pushed out of the way to make room for the glass on the five-story building to grab all the attention. The front elevation blazed with reflected sun.

Maderm stopped in front of the guard's booth, leaned out the window, and confidently flashed his badge. Before the guard could acknowledge Maderm's outstretched arm, the guardhouse phone rang. Pushing it against his ear, the man leaned toward a row of TV monitors and stared. A deep frown inched across his forehead. Suddenly, the peaceful quiet of the hot summer afternoon shattered. Alarms started blaring.

Maderm slipped from behind the wheel and positioned himself so that he could study the row of monitors that held the guard's attention. The action bouncing across the screens caused his heart to skip a beat. Men ran everywhere, scattering like ants kicked from their hill.

Maderm shouted at Sculler, "Get behind the wheel and drive! Don't wait for me!"

Sculler obeyed his partner's command without even a flicker of his eyes. He scooted over, and the car leaped forward. But in the rearview, he saw Maderm and the guard wrestling in the booth. With a swift movement, Maderm pulled something from his pocket and jabbed his hand against the guard. The man fell to the ground in a puddle of flesh and clothes.

Sculler cut the engine and jumped from the car. Maderm joined him, and they sprinted toward the front entrance.

"You won't believe what I saw!" Maderm shouted as he ran.

"Must've been good, for you to pull what you did. Was it really necessary to use the needle?"

"Absolutely. It was the only way we were going to get in. Something happened, and that guard wasn't going to accept our flawless credentials."

The agents were almost to the main entrance when the doors flew open and men in military garb emptied out of the building, splitting into two groups, one running to the left, the other to the right.

Caught in their tide, Maderm and Sculler ran with them and rounded the building's corner in time to catch a glimpse of two people in ill-fitting hospital garb scooting across the parking lot and fleeing into the woods.

"Sculler!" Maderm shouted over the clamor. "Did you see that? Those two in white running for the woods? Look familiar to you?"

Sculler stopped, and shielding his eyes from the sun, squinted. "Could it be?"

"The girl? That Grayson boy? Yeah, it could."

Their minds as one, born out of years of working together, no words were needed as the agents changed course and took off after the couple.

It seemed like days, when in reality it was less than three hours, since they had broken free of their prison. Countless sticky pine branches had scraped exposed flesh and left pine sap clinging like glue as they'd plunged recklessly through the forest. The flimsy hospital clothing was little protection from briars that grabbed them, gouging and poking at skin already tender. Pine needles turned even the smallest incline into a challenge as they made traction next to impossible to capture. Rest was short and only when absolutely necessary.

Matt stopped and put his hands on his knees. His chest heaved as he strained to suck in enough air to ease the burning in his lungs. Linda did the same. No words were spoken; the effort was too costly.

Trotting again, Matt reached for Linda's hand, but she shrugged him off. She was panting harder than before. They needed to rest longer, get some water, but he was so scared, so filled with urgency he couldn't stop.

"Please, Linda. Try to make it a little further. The more distance we put between them and us, the better."

Linda grunted as she pushed forward and stumbled several times. She flicked her hair from her damp forehead, which was covered in sweat and grime. There was no breeze. The air was as thick and humid as she'd ever remembered a Texas afternoon being. She almost stopped when it hit her. How would she know what a Texas afternoon was? This was her first visit to Texas.

They pushed forward until abruptly, the trees ended. Before them was an endless, barren field. Only spotty weeds dotted the brown dirt. Matt surveyed the terrain, increasingly aware of time's swift passage. The sun was sinking. Little time was left before darkness would completely cover them, and when it did, a whole new set of challenges would arise. Even in the warmth of summer, exposure was a real concern, not from cold, but from living creatures. Texas was famous for them. Come dark, a new jungle would emerge, and they would be surrounded.

"Over there!" Matt pointed to a small shack, more of a lean-to, that was hidden in some brush by the edge of the field. It looked as if kudzu vines had taken it over years ago. Possibly, could it possibly …

"I've got to rest!" Linda fell to her knees. Her panting shook her whole body. Her face was flaming red, and her hands trembled.

"Come on, Linda. Can you make it just little further? Over there?" He pointed to the small shelter. "We need to get out of sight."

Linda stood with Matt's help, and he kept his arm about her as they limped toward the vine-covered retreat. Once inside, Matt situated himself so he could see out the opening and across the barren field.

For a while, neither spoke. As they sat side by side, the sun dipped below the horizon, leaving behind a faint tinge of pink and orange to stain the sky. It looked as washed out and faded as Matt felt.

"It's going to be dark soon." Matt finally spoke, his voice low and flat. "I have no clue where we are. I'm certain they will search for us through the night. No doubt, they have the means."

He climbed to his feet and paced in front of the opening, all the while keeping his eyes on the fading horizon. He saw nothing.

Linda moved to stand beside him. Gently, she tapped him on the shoulder.

"Okay. Tell me what to do. We'll make this like a campout. We can build a fire; we can—"

Matt interrupted. "No! No fire! That will bring them to us like hornets."

"I'm sorry; I wasn't thinking," she said it softly. "I've never done this before, roughed it, stayed out in the wild. I've never even camped. My family was strictly city. So you have to tell me what to do, and I'll do it. I'll—"

She stopped. "Playing in the street, a never-ending row of houses, each touching the other, no yards between them, I remember! The constant sound of cars and trucks roaring by, dirt running down the gutter from thunderstorms in the summer. Sometimes, the fire hydrant sprayed a fountain in the air and all the neighborhood kids crowded beneath its spray. That was what we considered swimming. My parents ... were ... they were ..."

Matt turned slowly to face her. He stared at her, and his mouth opened, but nothing came out.

"You know what?" Linda suddenly shouted. "I didn't live in California all my life! I lived in ... I'm not sure where, but it was a city. We had seasons, not the eternal summer of LA. Snow in winter, and hot, muggy, steamy heat in summer. The only green I ever saw was at the neighborhood park. I'd always thought living like that was normal. I never knew there were wide-open spaces until ..." She stopped.

"Until what? What happened?" Matt asked.

"I'm not sure. I'm not even sure how old I was. I just remember going to a place where there were wide fields filled with flowers, every color you could think of, especially blue. I loved the blue ones."

She took a few steps away from him and gazed through the small opening at the dark sky. "Is it safe for us to stay here in this place? I feel like we need to keep moving, that if we stay here, they'll find us. I just have this awful feeling."

Matt took her hand. "Don't stop; don't stop what you were saying. You're remembering! Things are coming back, things different from what you said was true of your life before. You just said you lived somewhere other than California, yet before we got taken in to that ... that place back there, you swore up and down you'd lived in California all your life." He gripped her hand harder. "What you've just described agrees with things you said when we first met on that flight to Houston. You told me then you grew up in the Washington, DC, area, that you lived in a row house."

"I don't … I don't know what to say." She pulled free of his grip and put her hand on her head. "Everything … it all seems to be swirling."

As her knees buckled, Matt put his arms about her and gently lowered her to the ground. She gripped her head. "It hurts. Oh, it hurts so bad!" She doubled over and groaned.

After a while, Linda's moaning grew quieter. Matt continued to hold her, rocking her gently in his arms. He wished it were for other reasons that he held her. He stopped on the thought, surprised at himself and unwilling to explore it further.

Without realizing what he did, Matt leaned down and kissed her. He couldn't let go. He wanted to keep kissing her. Instead, she jerked away.

"What were you thinking?"

"I'm … uh, I'm sorry. I don't know what I was thinking." He shook himself, physically and mentally. A light flashed on the horizon suddenly, and he pointed. "Look!"

On what must have been the other side of the vast field, possibly a mile or more away, were the moving headlights of a car. The ugly dark bruise of the sky seemed to swallow everything except for the odd-shaped hole cut by the car's faint headlights. They weren't the bright halogen or coronal ones of modern days, certainly not like the rows of minilights that had first become fashionable on the luxury cars from Europe and now were on status symbol cars in the US.

Matt whispered, "Civilization. People!"

Neither said anything further. Matt grabbed Linda's hand and tugged. Soon, as if of one mind, they raced together toward the light as fast as their beaten and ravaged bodies would allow.

"Hold it right there! Stop!"

Maderm and Sculler reluctantly obeyed as strong hands gripped their arms, forcing their compliance.

"Can we see some identification?" the guard holding Maderm's arm demanded.

Slowly, the two agents produced their Muldoon and Scofield cards. The guard glanced at both, pocketed the cards in his fatigues, and then pronounced, "Gentlemen, you need to come with us."

Moments later, Maderm and Sculler found themselves in the deep bowels of the glass building. They were seated in the middle of an office that appeared to be vacant except for an empty desk and a couple of chairs. The guards had handcuffed them to their respective chairs and then had stepped back to wait. For what, neither Maderm nor Sculler was sure.

Time was lost on the two agents. The room was silent; no outside sounds filtered through the windowless walls. Neither man knew just how much time had passed since they had been strapped into their chairs and isolated in the vacant room.

Suddenly, the door flew open with such force that it banged against the wall. Strolling in first was a petite, flame-haired woman. Following her was a lean, tall man with a face that showed the hardness of the years on his skin. He was dressed in a rumpled suit, and his head was covered with light-brown fringe masking as a buzz cut. The man stopped and crossed his arms, and the woman spoke.

"Potter," the red-haired woman said as she smiled seductively at Maderm and focused briefly on Sculler. "Who do we have here?"

"These two claim to be Agents Muldoon and Scofield, but we have already verified their IDs as false. They are refusing to cooperate, so it looks like we'll have to take some, uh, measures to get that information."

The woman rubbed her hands together as she grinned. "Excellent, Potter. I do so love it when you 'take measures'! What fun! For us, not them, of course! Why, you never know what you'll get and the pain ..." She chuckled, and the sound gurgled deeply in her throat. She slowly strolled around Maderm and Sculler, arms crossed across her chest.

"I'm sure once you're finished, they'll be sure to give us all the information we could ever want! Until then …" Her voice trailed off, and she strode easily back to the door. She was reaching to open it when it flew open in her face.

Two tall, muscular young men in dark suits with small hearing pieces in their left ears pushed the woman to the side as they ran into the room. Stopping in front of the agents, the first asked, "What do we have here?"

The second replied, "Looks like there is some 'splaining to be done!" Both men chuckled as one whirled around and grasped the woman's arm before she could slip through the door.

"Not so fast, ma'am! We are going to need to ask you some questions!" The first man gripped the woman's arm and steered her toward the door.

When everyone was gone, and silence reclaimed the room, Maderm spoke quickly, "Did you see that?"

"Yeah!"

"Tell me, why are Secret Service agents here?"

"Presidential detail, that's what!"

The two men stared at each other, jaws slack.

The field seemed to go on forever. It rose and fell in small increments, just enough to make it nearly impossible to run in the dark without falling flat on one's face. Matt was determined not to slow. He pulled Linda along, continually encouraging her. The first car's lights had long ago faded, but maybe, just maybe, another's would shine soon.

Without warning, Matt stumbled. Linda, one second behind him, tripped and fell. They both hit the ground panting.

"This is insane," she said as she crawled off him and sat back, kicking her feet out in front of her, "running like this in the dark, without even a clue as to where we're going."

"Or as to what we're gonna do when we get there!" Matt suddenly burst out laughing. "Know what's even more insane? Imagine what someone's gonna think when they see us, two stragglers, dirty and tired, running out of the woods, one with nothing but a few shreds of a lab jacket and the other in baggy pants and clown shoes!" He chuckled briefly.

Linda said quietly, "So, what are we going to do? Looking like this, no one will ever believe a thing we're saying."

"You're right."

On the horizon, a light flickered and then grew stronger as it moved toward them. "There's another one!" Matt said softly. A fresh jolt of adrenaline pushed them to their feet. Clothes flapping in the breeze, their appearance forgotten, they raced for the light.

Sculler massaged his temple. It still ached from the whacking that surly guard had inflicted on him when he'd pushed them into the small cell built to house one person, not two. Thing was, the guard had given Maderm an even harder whack. His partner was still out of it, snoring, mouth open as he lay sprawled across the narrow cot in the small windowless cubicle they were locked in.

Without warning, their door blew open, and in strolled one of the two Secret Service agents he'd recognized earlier. With him was the guard who'd kicked his head in. The Secret Service agent was shouting at the guard.

"There'd better be a good explanation for this fiasco. Don't you idiots know who's who around here?" The agent swept his arm, indicating Sculler and Maderm. "These two men could have your rear fried and out of here, just like that!" He snapped his fingers. "No excuse, no explanation. You'd just be gone. Forget that pension. Forget that fat bonus you were promised. Vaporized like that."

The guard was silent. Quickly, he undid the locks on the cuffs holding Sculler's hands together in a prayerful pose. Then, he unlocked Maderm's, even though the man didn't stir and continued his obnoxious snoring.

After briefly massaging the circulation back into his ankles, Sculler stood. He didn't smile but stared, mustering as much chill, forcing as much venom as possible into the look he showered on the burly guard. The guard hurried from the small room, slamming the door behind him.

The Secret Service agent extended his hand to Sculler. "Man, I'm so sorry. Had no idea you were on-site until I stumbled in on you at the command center. But you know how it goes. I had to verify everything before doing anything. Executive procedure and all. You know how it goes."

Sculler nodded. "You verified our authorizations from whom?"

"Well, we got the confirmation from your chief, Hampton it was. Wouldn't say just what the nature of your visit was, but did confirm that you had orders. However, I'm to tell you they've changed. You're to return to your district office immediately. Said your work here was finished, whatever that was." He grinned. "Anyway, sorry about the hassle. I had to get those jerks straightened out." He shook his head and grinned. "Sorry bunch, if you ask me. None of them seem to have a clue as to how to run a security detail."

"Mind if I ask," Sculler said, "but just why are *you* here?"

The agent smiled quickly. "You should know I can't tell you that."

Sculler chuckled and said, "You're on presidential detail, aren't you?"

The agent didn't answer.

"Thanks for your help." Sculler clapped the man on his arm as they shook hands.

"Not a problem." The agent shut the door behind him as he left. The sound of the door latch clicking woke Maderm.

"What'd I miss?" Maderm sat up and yawned.

"A lot," Sculler answered. "Right now, you need to get those cobwebs out of your eyes. We've got to get out of here."

"What's the hurry?" Maderm yawned again.

"Hurry?" Sculler shook his head as he studied his partner. "We're only in the middle of the biggest hornet's nest I've ever seen. And it's a miracle we haven't been stung yet."

"Stung?" Maderm squinted at Sculler. "How're we supposed to get stung?"

Sculler shook his head and sighed. "Just go ahead, sleep through it all. Let me take care of everything. The Secret Service, Maderm! You saw them. Now tell me why would they be hanging around here?"

Maderm's eyes widened as he stared at Sculler. "Umm. Umm. Umm. I'm not sure who's going to drop the biggest load over this one, Dixon or Hampton."

Matt clutched his side and doubled over, panting. Linda did the same. Both strained to refill their lungs, desperate for life-sustaining oxygen.

Since spotting the last light, they'd run with more energy than they possessed, with more determination than before, with more hope, but as they'd pushed through the darkness, tripping and stumbling on uneven ground, no more light had broken the dark. Now, as they rested, both of them slumped, weighed down with disappointment and growing fear.

"Are you sure it was this way? Could we have made a wrong turn somewhere?" Linda asked, panic raising her tone.

"No, we didn't make a wrong turn, I don't think. There's no way of knowing now." Matt ventured forward a few steps and suddenly tumbled into a small ditch. Climbing to his feet, he teetered, lost his balance, and fell, hands scraping asphalt.

"Linda! A road! I'm standing in it now!" He jumped on the pavement. "We have to be in the right place." Dropping to all fours, he felt his way across the ditch and scrambled back beside Linda. "I think we can rest now. If a car comes, we'll see it."

Her hand in his, he helped her ease down into the ditch. It was more like a small dip in the land between the field and the road than a true gully capable of draining large amounts of rainfall. As they sat, backs against the rising dirt, Linda, with what seemed to be unconscious habit, leaned against Matt. For the first time he could remember recently, Matt felt some of his tension lift.

"I'm so tired, I could sleep standing up." Linda yawned, and her head drooped on Matt's shoulder. In less than a minute, he heard her soft breathing change to that of a person sleeping. He yawned too. His stomach growled, and in the distance, he heard the faint sound of a cow mooing. How he longed for a large steak, pink in the middle, dripping in juice and some cowboy potatoes like his mom used to make. He licked his lips and spit. They were crusted with dirt. His mouth felt like it was full of cotton. He couldn't remember the last drink he'd had.

Matt kept thinking about water, iced tea, and fresh-squeezed lemonade. Large frosty glasses floated about him. He kept reaching for them, gulping the sweet liquid. But he was still thirsty. Nothing quenched his thirst. He wanted more. "More!"

He jerked, startled, unaware he had dozed. He turned his head, straining to hear. A noise? Movement? Was it getting lighter off in the distance to his right?

Matt closed his eyes, leaned his head against the dirt wall, and listened. What was it? Had he heard something? Rattles. Hissing. First on his left. Then his right. He turned and saw a large snake, coiled, ready to strike. Matt reached for his gun. It wasn't there. His jeans. What had happened to them?

Matt lashed out at the unseen terror, coming fully awake. It was still dark. Linda was by his side. He yawned and wished he knew the time—wished for his watch, his clothes, his car. Anything.

Linda muttered, "What's that?"

In the distance, coming toward them, he saw it. "A car!" He scrambled to his feet and pulled Linda up. They stepped to the edge of the road and waited.

"How do we know it's not *them*?"

"You're right; there's no way to tell."

"So, what do we do?"

"Cross our fingers. Pray."

Headlights flashed over a rise in the ground not a hundred yards away. The car was coming toward them but very slowly. The engine puttered, instead of purring. When it got within a hundred feet, Matt stepped onto the road and started waving. The headlights washed over him, and the car slowed. In a moment, it stopped beside them.

"Mighty early to be hitching a ride," the driver said as he leaned out of the old Plymouth. "Most folks round these parts are still asleep now. Me, well, I've got to go into town and pick up some medicine for my cow. Got a sick one, I do." The driver was about fifty and driving a car older than he was.

Matt frowned. "Sir, we've run into some trouble. It's a long story, but we need some help. Could you give us a ride into town?"

"What kind of trouble?" The man's eyes narrowed as he studied the ragged and dirty pair.

Matt started to explain, but as he considered his words, he realized there was no explanation that could possibly make sense. Finally, "We were kidnapped. They handcuffed us, took us … to some place … we had to get away … we—"

The driver interrupted. "Wait a minute! You look like you came from the hospital. Is that where you're from?"

"Hospital?" Matt whispered the word. "Yes, uh, we had to, uh, get away from there."

The driver interrupted. "Is that a young woman with you? She got dark hair?"

"Yes. Why?"

The driver gripped the steering wheel with his bony fingers. "I heard about you two. They was talking all about you! Said to stay away from you. Let them know if you was seen!"

The car's wheels spun and sprayed gravel over Matt and Linda. In a second, it was speeding down the road faster than it had arrived.

"Now, what do you suppose happened?" Linda asked. Hands planted on hips, she watched as the car disappeared over the next rise in the land.

Matt didn't answer. He didn't even hear her. He was lost. Lost in a world of the past. He couldn't put his finger on it, but something was familiar about it all.

"Matt?" Linda tapped him on the shoulder. "I said, what was that about?"

"I … I don't know." He scratched his head and turned, as if seeing her for the first time. "We'd better get moving. He may come back, bring someone we don't want to see!"

"I don't think I can. I'm too tired, and my feet hurt. I think there're blisters on every inch of them."

Matt took her hand and tugged gently. They walked in the opposite direction from which the car had gone. Running was no longer an option. Dehydration had set in, along with exhaustion and hunger. They had two enemies, humanity and nature. Which was more dangerous, Matt was no longer sure.

The edge of the horizon was thinning into a faint gray when Matt fell beside the road, fully, totally, completely exhausted. For the first time, it was Linda who urged him on.

"You can't quit now! No way, not after all you've drug me through! Come on, soldier! Up and at it!"

Matt groaned softly. "I can't. No more." He curled into a fetal ball in the dust.

Linda pulled on his arm and relentlessly jerked. "Come on; don't leave me now!" Her voice rose. "Matt, please. Don't leave me here!" She fell beside him and leaned over him, her tears wetting his face. Gently, with tenderness unknown to Matt, she rubbed his face, traced the outline of his brows, his lips, his cheeks. She whispered against his ear, "I need you." Matt didn't move. She kept moving her fingers across his face. Her tender touch didn't revive him. Instead, he fell into a deeper sleep.

She sobbed, quietly at first and then desperately, wildly. There was nothing except for the small creatures of the earth, small and seemingly insignificant, to hear her grieving. After a while, Linda collapsed on top of him and slept too.

A red light flashed on the team leader's radio. He motioned for the others in his group to stop. They were deep in a pine forest within the research facility's borders. As the others waited patiently, some shifting from foot to foot, he pushed the side button on the unit while he adjusted his mouth and earpieces.

"Team Leader here," he said quietly.

"What's your position? We tried raising you via the vehicle's responder but no answer."

"Foot pursuit, sector five. Trying to follow their trail through the woods, but it seems to have grown cold."

The voice on the radio sounded tired, irritated. "All this time, and you've only managed to find a cold trail in the woods? You haven't even made it past sector five?"

"Sir …" The team leader sighed. "… it's been a tough night. You know as well as I do the multitude of directions those people could have gone. They had too much of a head start before we got here! We're trying to reconstruct their movements. Even with the night gear, it still takes time. And the helicopters are no good, not with these dense woods. Too many places they could hide. Unless they find the field, we have no choice but to proceed like this. Besides, you told us, there's no way they can leave the property. So, what's the rush? We'll get them, eventually."

Static crackled over the radio before the same voice boomed back. "Well, we have a new sighting. One of the residents has reported seeing our subjects in sector seven, fifth quadrant. They are thought to be heading south-southwest, bearing toward sector eight, sixth quadrant, last seen on road ten. They made the field, and if you don't hurry, they'll be past it and back in the woods again before you get there!"

"Roger that," the team leader responded. "We're correcting our course now. How recent is this information?"

"We received it just now. We believe the sighting occurred within the past hour. I don't think I need to emphasize this again, but we must regain the girl within the day … alive. Unharmed."

"What about the man?"

"Doesn't matter."

"Okay," the leader sounded confident. "You've got the experts. Won't be long now!"

CHAPTER 14

"Son, wake up! Son!" The old man shook him with a teeth-rattling force. Matt cracked one eye open and saw the farmer hovering over him. Even as he spoke, the sun flirted with the horizon, promising to burn the open fields with its glory in a matter of moments.

Matt whimpered and moved his arm over his face as if to shield it from some invisible blow. Without straightening, the farmer stepped over to Linda and peered at her. As he touched her shoulder, she murmured and rolled over.

Gently, the farmer lifted and carried her to the old Buick parked a few yards away. After depositing her in the backseat as carefully as he could, he returned to Matt. Despite his bent frame and weathered body, neither Matt's nor Linda's weight seemed to affect him.

After propping Matt in the front seat, the farmer slid behind the wheel and slammed his foot on the gas. The Buick leapt forward, continuing in the direction Matt and Linda had taken before collapsing with exhaustion.

As they bumped along the uneven road, Matt vaguely realized the farmer kept glancing at him. Each time, the man's frown deepened. Matt ran a finger over his lips and grimaced as he realized they were cracked and oozing. He felt welts covering most of his face and arms. Skimpy clothing, ripped and torn, exposed large areas of skin.

Using most of the energy he had, Matt turned and glanced at Linda in the backseat. Her skin was tinged pink, like sunburn. There were insect bites on her arms and a few on her face, but outwardly, she appeared to be no worse for wear. Her eyes darted about, scanning the scenery as if memorizing it. She looked as if her energy stores were replenishing, not depleting. He, well, he felt as if he'd aged a hundred years.

They crossed a series of small rises in the land, barren fields running along either side of them. After about half an hour, the air grew fresher, full of the fresh scent of pines.

Cutting off the main road, the farmer turned left and plowed through pine saplings and brush, following the barest hint of a trail. As the shade of the forest swallowed them, Matt tried to focus on the scene about them, but his eyes drooped.

After a while, the path smoothed, and by comparison, they seemed to glide across the forest floor until a small, sparkling river crossed their path. Without taking his foot off the gas, the farmer headed straight into the current. Water rose and lapped at the car's doors but never higher. Soon, nearly a quarter of a mile downstream, they crossed onto dry land again.

Matt stared at the sparkling water and tried to lick his lips. He managed one word, "Water."

"Can't stop now. Time's too precious. Soon, though. Very soon."

Shortly, the woods thinned, revealing a meadow hemmed by trees on either side. However, just before entering the field, the farmer made a sharp right turn and drove through a wall of brush and bushes. On the other side was an old, seemingly abandoned cabin. Its boards, aged by years of weather and sun, added to the natural camouflage of the surrounding growth. Slowing for the first time, the farmer eased the car into a hedge of bushes beyond the rustic building.

As the farmer pulled him from the car, Matt tried to hold his head erect, but it rolled freely. His mouth was slack, and he couldn't find the strength to hold on to the farmer's neck when the man wrapped his arms about his shoulders.

Inside the cabin, the farmer helped Matt as he collapsed onto a small cot. He covered him with a blanket and then left only to return moments later with Linda following him. After pumping some cool water from the old hand pump at the sink, the farmer helped Matt hold the glass as he sipped. When it was gone, and before the farmer could return with more, Matt sank into a deep slumber.

The old man knelt before a beat-up trunk. It took several whacks at the rusty lock before it opened. He rummaged through the contents and finally pulled out some jeans, shirts, socks, and work boots. He handed the stack to Linda. With no hesitation, she quickly found items that would fit and handed the rest back to the farmer. He then put what was left on the foot of Matt's cot. Linda slipped behind a small screen to change.

A few moments later, she emerged, dressed in the mismatched clothing that smelled of cedar but was clean and whole, not in shreds like what she'd had on when the farmer found them. Linda sat down at a small table. She was silent as she watched the farmer work in front of a small, wood-burning stove. The clothes the farmer had given her, though faded and far from the latest styles, to her weary and sore body, were as soft as heaven's clouds and just as clean and welcome.

The farmer glanced over his shoulder at her while he continued stirring a steaming pot. "Hungry? I have some stew here. Or maybe you'd like some coffee?" Linda didn't answer right away. The farmer shook his head. "What could I be thinking? You probably want something cold."

Linda smiled and nodded.

At the sink, the farmer pumped more water using the old hand pump. "Straight from a deep spring. Doesn't get any better than this!" He handed a glass to her and grinned.

Linda grabbed it from his outstretched hand, and in two gulps, the water was gone. She thrust it back toward him.

The farmer chuckled. "I know. More." He turned to the pump and filled the glass again. This time, she managed to slow her consumption to five gulps.

"More?" he asked. She shook her head. The farmer smiled briefly. "Can you eat now?"

She nodded. The farmer poured some of the bubbling concoction from the pot into a bowl. He found a spoon and stirred it briefly before handing it to her. As she gobbled the warm stew, the farmer pumped more of the cool water into a small metal bowl and then took a cloth and wet it. After wringing it slightly, he went to Matt. Gently, he dabbed the cool cloth on the unconscious man's lips, wiping away some of the dried blood and caked dirt. After rinsing the cloth and dipping it again in the water, he dabbed around his eyes, forehead, and face, paying particular attention to the welts. Afterward, he returned with a glass of the cool water. Propping Matt up, he forced the edge of the glass between his lips. Some life-sustaining instinct parted them, and a trickle of water slipped past and made it to his tongue. Matt stirred and opened his eyes. He straightened and took the glass from the farmer. Soon, the water was gone. The farmer went to refill the glass, but by the time he returned, Matt had curled on his side, and his eyes were closed. Sighing, the farmer set the glass down and turned to Linda.

"Is he going to be okay?" she asked quietly.

"I hope so."

Matt groaned and rolled onto his other side. The farmer pulled another light blanket from a shelf over the cot. He arranged it, covering Matt from his shoulders to his feet. Then he turned back to Linda. "Only time will tell. All we can do now is let him sleep."

As if obeying some silent command, Matt began to snore softly.

"Thank you," Linda said as she handed her empty bowl back to the old man. "I don't know what that was, but I've never tasted anything better in my life!" The farmer grinned as he took the bowl back to the sink.

"Just say, it's food for life," he said over his shoulder. "More?"

"No. Thanks."

Without further comment, the farmer finished cleaning up the few dishes he'd used in preparing the small meal. When he was through, he settled in a chair in front of Linda. His blue eyes blazed, but the warmth they cast was gentle and comforting. He leaned toward her and gently touched her hand.

"Can you tell me about it?"

Linda studied the man, the room, and the beauty outside the window. When she turned her gaze back to the farmer, she asked, "Where are we? Do you live here?"

The old man chuckled. It was more like a small rumble that grew from his stomach. "Naw. Don't live here. This is just a hunting cabin my granddaddy built. I used to come here with my dad and him when I was just a runt running around. I always felt like such a big guy when we came here." He stopped and shook his head. "But that's not important. Not now. Please, can you tell me what happened that you two were out there, dying on the side of the road?"

She wasn't sure what to say. There were still too many questions and so few answers. She wasn't even sure she believed any of it.

"What can I say? I don't even know you or how you came to rescue us. How do I know you don't work for them?" For a moment, she felt the urge to bolt from the room.

The farmer laid a hand gently on top of hers. "Believe me; I'm not one of them! More than you know, I do understand some of what I think you've been through. But I think it would help for you to talk it out. Tell me what they've done to you!"

Linda stared at the man, even more puzzled by his words. But his eyes cast such a spell of peace on her, she found herself talking, spilling all she could remember.

"I woke up in some strange, hospital-like room and found I was hooked up to a bunch of machines and had needles poking my arms. It was him …" She nodded at Matt. "… who burst into my room and told me what happened. He convinced me to get out of there with him." She took a deep breath and watched the farmer's brows rise, but he said nothing.

"He told me we were taken from the Houston airport. And ..." she stopped, frowning.

"Who are they?"

"I don't know. But ..."

The farmer rubbed his chin. "Go ahead. It's okay."

"I've had memories, some that I think aren't true."

"What do you mean?"

"I mean, I believed them to be true, at one time. You see, I believed I'd lived in California all my life, that I had worked for the *LA Times*. Then he ..." She pointed at Matt. "...comes along and tells me I met him on a plane to Houston and that I told him all this stuff about living in Houston, about having had a husband, and all that." She dabbed at a trickle of perspiration running down her cheek. "I thought he was crazy, still do a little, but as we were running from that ... that place, I started to remember some things; things that didn't agree with what I thought was true."

She walked to the window and stared out at the field. For a long time, she leaned against the sill, lost in thought. When she spoke, her voice was soft, far away. "It's like I have two lives, two people living inside of me. I no longer know what is real, what isn't."

"I'm not surprised at what you're sayin'," the farmer answered. "It makes sense."

She whirled about and stared at him. "Why do you say that?"

"Because I've been there; we all have. Now, most folks around here don't realize it; don't know any differently. But it wasn't the same with me. For some reason, I was different. It didn't change me the way it did the others."

Linda tensed, and her eyes widened. "What do you mean?"

The farmer scratched his head and stared at the floor. When he looked up at her, his blue eyes blazed even brighter.

"See," he started slowly, "it was many years ago. They came into our community. Went to every house, every farm. Said they were from the government. Told us there was some dreadful new disease going around. Told us it might possibly be something the animals were passing along. They warned that it would kill us, if we didn't get the vaccines. Told us we would have to be quarantined for a while. They said too many people might lose their lives if we weren't kept from them." He rubbed his hand over his eyes and then across his bald head. "They said we should come into town weekly to get these vaccines." He stopped and stared at her. "Did you start to say something?"

"Oh no, please, go on. Don't pay me any attention." Linda learned toward him, her eyes fixed on his.

"Well, most folks around here agreed to it. They didn't question it, because after all, it was the government. They all liked the idea of Uncle Sam taking care of us."

"When did all this happen?"

"I don't recall exactly, but I remember it was around the time everyone was talking about the fighting in Europe. Everyone was wondering if we'd get involved. It was all anyone could talk about. But time passed, and somehow, we forgot about it. Never did hear if we got in the fight."

"Forgot about it? You mean, you didn't know about World War II?"

"World War II?" He shook his head. "There was the Great War, but never heard of a second. Are you saying that fighting in Europe, it was a world war also?"

Linda nodded sadly. "Somehow, they kept the war from you. Wonder what else they've hidden?"

The farmer shrugged and continued as if it were not important. "Anyway, Martha and me, well, we joined the others and got those vaccines. Painful as hell, they were." He rubbed his arm as if he'd just gotten another injection. "After a while though, guess we got used to 'em. Didn't seem to make the welts like they did at first. I guess this went on for several years. I never noticed much at first, but after a while, it seemed people were different. Life was different. I can't tell you how; I just knew it. I didn't tell anyone, not even Martha. I was afraid. Don't know why, I just was. So, I did nothing. Kept on with my farming, kept going into town for those vaccines."

"Do you still get your vaccines?"

"Yep, every week, just like I've done all this time. Time just kept passing, and we kept getting them. But you know, the strangest was, it seemed to stop. Days passed, seasons came and went, yet nothing seemed to change. If anything, some folks got to looking better. Their skin didn't look as wrinkled. Hair was thicker." He patted his bald head and chuckled.

"Well, some got thicker hair! Why, old Josh down the road, he started taking his wife to the Saturday-night barn dance. He hadn't left the farm for anything other'n church and those vaccines for years. It was like he, and a few others, got a new lease on life. Now, it was nothing drastic, it's just that some quit getting older, and a few seemed to get a bit younger." The man suddenly frowned. "But there were a few ..." His voice faded.

"A few what?"

The farmer shook his head. "Oh. There were ... well, a few that didn't react like the others."

"How's that?"

"They grew different. Got new parts."

"New parts?"

"It was like their bodies added new things. This one farmer, old Earle, well, he got an extra lobe on his ear. Tim Brock hatched a new thumb. Didn't happen to many, though. It's a shame for the others."

"Why's that?"

"Well, all those that died. They never got that new lease on life so many of the others got."

"Some died?"

"Yeah, at first, a lot. 'Bout half the town got sick and died. They said it was that disease they were vaccinating us from. Said those poor souls didn't get theirs in time. Then, for a while, no one died. Then, it seemed every so often, a bunch would die. It always seemed to happen once a season." He shrugged and smiled, his lone tooth glimmering. "Me, well, I was different from them all."

"How's that?"

"I know things. Don't know why. Don't know how. I just do. I know them before they happen. Some people smell; others hear. Well, I think. It all happens in my head, but I can see it clearly."

"Is that how you found us? You saw it in your head?" He nodded. "But how?"

"Don't know that exactly. It just happens. I get this feeling and know I have to do something."

Linda's mouth was partially open as if she was ready to speak, but nothing came out. Suddenly, she frowned. "When were you born?"

"Eighteen seventy-five."

"And how old are you?"

"Seventy."

She squinted as she let her eyes study every detail of his face. It was true; he did look seventy, not a day older.

"You're telling me this whole thing is about time?"

"No, I'm telling you it's about stopping it. It's like everything's frozen, stranded in some past time 'round these parts. Everywhere you go, it's the same—cars, homes, the town, everything. Now, I know that sounds crazy, and it may not even be true for you, because you've been out *there*. But far as I can tell, around here, it's still the 1940s. I wouldn't know any differently. See, I've never been anywhere else."

"You've lived all this time in this place and never left? Don't you ever go to the city?"

"There's been no need. Everything is here." He rubbed a knobby, wrinkled hand across his mouth. "My only child, my son, I was told he and his family died in a fire. That was right after the vaccines began. We were told we couldn't go to the funeral because of the quarantine. He was the only family I ever had, other than Martha." He scratched his head, and then his eyes found hers. "So, when he was gone, there was no reason to leave here, not that we could've, what with them keeping us in the quarantine and all. In fact, we hadn't seen anyone from the outside until you first came to our house."

"You mean today?"

He shook his head. "No, months ago."

"I've been to your house before?" Linda's voice squeaked.

He nodded. "It was a while back, back during the cold, wet weather. I found you and him …" He nodded toward Matt, "in an abandoned barn out in a field quite a ways from my place. Don't usually go over that way, but for some reason, I took the tractor over there that day. There wasn't a clear picture like sometimes there is; just I felt this big need to go check that barn. The car had been broken down for a while, so I went riding on the tractor. When I found him, he was frantic, screaming for help. Took me inside the old barn, and there you were, lying like you was dead. I knelt over you, and suddenly you awakened. Like a miracle."

Linda's brows arched. "I don't believe it!"

"Well, it's true. We took the tractor back to my house and tried to bandage both of you up. But you weren't doing so good. He …" The farmer nodded at Matt. "… went for a doctor. Had to hitch a ride into town to get one. Trouble was it was too late. You wasn't breathing when he got back. Doc said there was nothing more to do, so they took you back to town. I thought you were … dead."

Linda fought to keep her hands from shaking. Nothing worked. Flashes, pictures swirled in her mind. So many faces, so many things, none of it and all of it made sense. From habit or instinct, she massaged her temples, expecting a horrible headache to come creeping up her neck. But it didn't happen. Only the dizziness of the overwhelming information spun her head. Suddenly, she looked into the farmer's eyes. A tear ran down her cheek.

"I'm not, am I? I'm not dead."

"No, Lynn, you're not. And that's a good question. Why?" The farmer paced across the wooden floor, the ancient boards creaking softly under his feet as he rubbed his bald head. For the time, there was no answer.

Oh, they were so foolish, every one of them. They had the truth, as clear as any truth could be, but they refused to see it. No matter how logical, no matter how irrefutable the evidence, they believed only what

243

they wanted to believe, and their beliefs were based on lies, deceptions, and falsehoods. These people were supposed to be the smartest, the best of the best, the wisest men the nation, the world even, had to offer the field of science. Yet, they behaved just like the gullible masses, who refused to believe a sitting president could lie, even when the evidence was solid and documented. Why were they so blind? Was it stupidity or simply selfish greed that kept them from refusing to acknowledge the validity of his data, of his assertions?

Dereck DeBoe paced in front of his desk. Just hours earlier, he'd completed compilations of all the data his research had produced to date. Despite round-the-clock work and use of every available resource, he could find nothing to justify the belief they could safely proceed with the treatment of this mystery patient everyone was so excited about. All he could forecast with certainty was that they were courting disaster. His conscience refused him rest. So, he'd requested a team meeting.

When Dereck had pushed open the conference room door, he'd nearly dropped his folders. Seated before him were not only Charles, Phillippe, and two others from the science team, but two men in dark suits—two men whom he'd seen in pictures and on television numerous times, two men he'd never met.

"Gentlemen," Dereck said after managing to seat himself without tripping or dropping his papers, "I'm sorry. I wasn't aware of ... What are *you* doing here?"

The president's chief of staff smiled. "I apologize for the shock. You were to have been informed later today. Because of the need for haste, Ms. Pittstorm asked us ..." He nodded to the man by his side, the president's personal physician. "... to come ahead. She'll be here shortly."

Dereck nodded slowly. "I still don't understand. Why is the president's chief of staff and his personal physician ... why would either of you ..." His voice died, and his eyes widened in shock. "No. You don't mean him, the president? That's who the patient is?"

Both men nodded slowly.

"No! No way, he's the picture of health." Then Dereck remembered the medical files, those incomplete files for the mystery patient, the ones containing a diagnosis no person ever wanted to have. "Just what kind of garbage has the media been reporting, anyway?"

The president's personal physician shook his head. "You are not aware of the gravity of the situation. For security purposes, we could not allow you to have total access to his medical records. However ..." He pushed a stack of files to the middle of the table and waited for each man to take one. "... this is the complete file. I'm sure I don't need to remind you this is classified material; this discussion is, too. However, in the interest of the president, I am compelled to enlighten you on some aspects of his condition." He rubbed his forehead. His eyes held no warmth, only darkness from the urgency of the situation.

"The president of the United States is terminally ill. He will die if a cure is not found and administered soon. By soon, I mean within the next two, three weeks tops." The physician slowly met the eyes of each face before him. He did not acknowledge any surprise he saw.

The chief of staff added, "Yes, the president appears healthy. But what you see, at least through the media, is not always what you get. Appearances and shots are choreographed; makeup and special effects enhancement are also utilized. In short, the viewing public is being sold a package of goods that does not necessarily exist. But it is critical that the package truly exist. Glossy shots and glitzy special effects do not rule a country."

The chief of staff continued, "Polls suggest the nation is resistant to the idea of the current vice president stepping into the president's place. The party, of course, does not want to see something like this happen. They've ridden a wave of unprecedented popularity for too long now to give it up. Despite the shortcomings of our president's predecessor, the acceptance is high, and they are unwilling to do anything to jeopardize that. In short, we must save the president. Whatever it takes, it will be done. That is your role, your job, to make this thing work. There is no time for further testing, further delays. It must be done now. Or soon, it will be too late."

"Wait a minute!" Dereck jumped to his feet. "Can't you see the problem here? You just said the president must be saved at all costs, that to lose him is unthinkable. Yet, that is why I called this meeting. I simply cannot bless the treatment. Not with the recent results we've had. Yes, we've had promising success; we even believe we're close to finalizing a comprehensive, successful treatment. But I said close. We're not there yet. To proceed now is to take a grave risk, one that is statistically probable to end in death."

The door of the soundproofed, top-secret conference room burst open. Breasts thrust forward, shoulders back, Cherie Pittstorm strolled in, and nothing was the same after that.

"Good afternoon, gentleman." She extended her hand first to the president's chief of staff and then to his personal physician. "Good to see you. I trust this meeting is nearly over and that all details are finalized for the president's treatment?"

Seven pairs of eyes stared back at her, but no one spoke. Finally, she asked, "Well, is it?"

Dereck sucked in a long breath before addressing her. "No, ma'am, I'm afraid it's not. My data suggests that it is simply too risky to begin the president's treatment at this time. We need further testing and time to compile the data and make corrections. To rush ahead now is homicidal."

Cherie continued to smile, and she clucked gently as she said, "Oh my, Dr. DeBoe, must we be so dramatic? Yes, I think we all know there are inherent dangers in this, as there would be over any new and previously untried procedure. But we have the data, the success of other trials behind us. Is that not right, Charles?" She glared pointedly at Charles.

Cherie continued as she moved her gaze to the eyes of the chief of staff. "We simply need a few days yet to complete some final testing and to fine-tune a few things. I do believe we'll be ready to serve our president sooner, rather than later, and certainly before things get beyond critical."

Dereck glanced from Cherie to the chief of staff and then to

Charles and back to Cherie again. Saliva thickened on his tongue. Words failed him as he silently watched those people plot a series of events that would indubitably change the face of the world.

The president's personal physician summed up his feelings. "Although there are some concerns as to the complete reliability of this regimen of treatment, I feel, after looking at all possible scenarios, that we must proceed. With the data that Ms. Pittstorm has been relaying to me, I feel it is in the best interest of the president to initiate treatment immediately. We cannot afford to waste another moment." After stuffing his notebook into its case, he stood. Smiling briefly at Cherie, he quickly left the room and the chief of staff followed.

The remaining group slowly came to life and gathered their notebooks and memory sticks full of data and reports, before quickly making their way from the room. Dereck was not quick enough. Cherie slipped close to his side. With a sweet smile and a voice husky with crystallized sugar, she spoke against his ear.

"I hope you didn't take things too personally. It's just that this is so important. It's almost as if this project were my own baby." She rubbed a hand over her stomach and studied him from the corner of her eye. "But you know I'd never want anything to happen to you. You're too valuable to our team."

Dereck stared at her, unsmiling. "You mustn't flatter me so. The others could easily pick up where I left off."

"You know as well as I, the only success we've truly had has involved a complete suppression of the subject's memory functions associated with identity. We had to wipe the person's memory clean and implant a false one. Then, even with the success we had with the girl, not everything was perfect. There were cracks, chinks in the new identity. Still, she survived. She gave you the key to what made things different. And though you don't have her here now to further your testing, you have the knowledge that you need to find that answer. Run your genetics search again. See what you find. You may be surprised."

Dereck frowned. "Why? We've already searched the database. Only one hit, a local who was one of the first subjects. And the similar codes were not ones related to this particular phenomenon."

Cherie winked. "Just check. Trust me." Then suddenly pretending to pout, she ran her hand behind Dereck's neck and squeezed the skin between her fingers, kneading and pushing it. "Why, you do trust me, don't you?"

For a moment, a brief moment, Dereck was distracted, tempted. "No!" he said suddenly. "It doesn't matter what you do; I'll not back down from my position."

"Well, honey," Cherie cooed against his ear, "I'd think twice about that. See, life is pretty good right now. You have your lab. You have your funding. You have most anything you want. You've got freedom and autonomy in your work. You come and go as you please. You're free to set up and conduct your trials without some FDA official standing over your shoulder hindering your progress. You're free from the legal bull and red tape that keeps conventional research from making it to the patient in time to help. Oh, I know you work hard, too hard, perhaps. You're here all the time; you never sleep, never go home. Do you want that to stop?" She took a few steps away and stared solemnly at him.

"You never again want to tell a family their loved one has died and there was nothing more you could do. You never want to lose a patient because medical miracles weren't available to save them, do you?"

Dereck slowly shook his head.

"It is why you got into medicine, isn't it? You can't stand the thought of death, of losing patients you wanted to save. Well, you're nearly there. You're part of a team that can regenerate life. You've seen it happen. You wouldn't dare walk away from your work. You can't. You're addicted. You're so close you can smell the victory. Well, don't you think our president deserves the fruit of that victory? But if we don't get this treatment to *our* president, he'll die. Bottom line. I know you don't want that to happen. See, this president is very sympathetic to our cause, our mission. Without his help, we might lose our funding.

We'd have to close up shop, go home, everything we've worked so hard for all these years, wasted. All of it for nothing."

Dereck stared into her burning eyes. A thin film of perspiration covered her forehead. As if she were a tiger, panting to cool off, her tongue flicked across red lips. She smiled.

"So, you can see, can't you, why we mustn't let anything stop us? The president knows what the stakes are. He's willing to take the risk. Are you?"

Dereck pushed her away and ran from the room. Back at his office, he fell into his swivel chair and spun it around and around. Thoughts swirled in his head as his body did the same. For the first time he could remember in a long time, he was scared—scared for his future, his career, and his life.

He considered going to the lab and destroying everything in it. Get rid of the blasted serum and all its components. He saw himself enraged to the point of grabbing the first thing he saw and swinging, swiping, wiping counters and shelves clean. In front of the freezers, he punched in his security code, pulling open the heavy doors, frosty air swirling about him, fingers curling about the tiny vials. He could feel the cold glass between his fingers, see himself throwing them, smashing them, doing whatever to expose the volatile liquid to room temperature.

Suddenly, his eyes opened. He was in front of his desk, leaning on his arms, staring blankly at some papers on his blotter. Then he saw the girl's face. Her name, her real name flashed in his mind. The nagging memory that had eluded him all that time suddenly jerked free. He knew then why they were so desperate to use her and then eliminate her. She had known the truth. Did she still possess it?

Unconsciously, his fingers started tapping computer keys. He hit the "enter" button and leaned back in his chair to wait. Soon, the printer started whirring, and sheets flowed from its bowels. Dereck grabbed the pages and after reading the first one, slapped the papers and grinned. Next, he logged on to the research database and keyed to the genetics section. Out of curiosity, he did as Cherie suggested. He searched the data again and found a new hit, recent, an admission from the day prior. With startling clarity, he knew why the girl's genes were so valuable. They didn't just want to stifle her from exposing the truth. They wanted her because she held the genetic key to the president's successful treatment.

Furiously, his fingers glided over the keyboard as he copied, pasted, and inserted the new information into a new document. Then, he typed in a short report summarizing his latest thoughts, his newest theory. Then, hitting the print command, he waited for the final sheets to spit out of the printer feeder.

When the printing was complete, Dereck then saved all his work as PDF files and copied them to multiple USB sticks. He stuffed all the printed sheets into a manila envelope. His gaze moved to the computer screen. A screen saver danced across the monitor, multiple colors twirling and cavorting, mesmerizing the observer. His computer, it held all his secrets, some even his colleagues were unaware of. His password, could they crack it and access his files? Could they gain entrance and take his secrets?

Suddenly, the term *computer security* became all-important. Every aspect of accessibility became an issue. Vials were forgotten. Freezers were left locked. There were other matters of national importance he must attend to.

Linda's voice was little more than a whisper. "I never knew my grandparents." Tears brimmed in her eyes. "I didn't get to meet them, and I was always so sad. All the other kids talked about their grandparents, but the only ones I ever had were dead. My dad was an orphan. He told me his parents died in a fire when he was less than two. He said that was all he knew. He never knew anything about any other relatives. And my mother was adopted. So, I never had any true relatives.

"I moved to Texas when I married Sam." Her words flowed like water over a cliff. "I remember the flowers, the fields, and the countryside. There was so much space, so much sky. It never ended, and I'd never seen anything like it." She stopped suddenly and covered her mouth with her hand. Her eyes rounded like small saucers, and a flush rose on her cheeks. "I remember! I know!"

The farmer watched her, his eyes wide and bright. "You remember? What had you forgotten?"

Linda didn't hear him. Her eyes widened with terror. "Oh, my God, no!" She hugged herself, her arms tightly clinging to her flesh, and swayed back and forth. "Oh no. Oh no, no, no." She groaned.

The farmer rushed to her side and dropped to his knees. Gently, he grasped her wrist. "What is it? What's wrong, dear?"

She rocked back and forth and moaned. "Things are coming back … so many images. So many facts, or are they facts? I can't tell the difference, I don't know which is real and which isn't. But …"

The farmer scuttled over to the sink, dipped a rag in water, and returned, handing it to her. She pushed his hand away and ran to the window but didn't stay. Back and forth, she paced across the room, manic energy driving her to move constantly, never stay still. The farmer caught her with his big hands and pinned her arms by her side.

"Please, be still. It's all right."

"No, it's not! Oh, you don't know! It's so bad." She wiggled free and resumed pacing. She couldn't stop. Her heart pounded, and sweat soaked her back. Cold chills ran down her spine, and her ears burned. She turned and strode back toward the farmer and then back to the wall. Over and over, she repeated the sequence. "Got to keep moving," she muttered softly. Finally, at the wall opposite Matt, she turned and leaned against it. She hugged herself and stared at the farmer.

"So much is flooding my mind. But if what I'm seeing inside here …" She touched her temple. "… is true, oh … we are in deep trouble."

The farmer took her arm and led her back to the chair. "Sit," he said as he pushed her gently down. He handed her the cool rag.

Silently, she took it from him and dabbed at her face. The coolness against her skin was heaven-sent. She sighed as she tilted her head and let the cloth lie there. The farmer stood by her, patiently, as if he had all the time in the world. When she handed the cloth back to him, she smiled. It was feeble but determined.

"Something's going on here."

The farmer nodded but didn't smile. "I know."

Her voice was low. "There is much I don't understand, but what I do know is that they … those people that had us, they have been working on some secret project. It's a government project, but so secret very few people know the truth about it, and those who do, don't know all there is to know." She got up and started pacing again. The farmer watched. Suddenly, she clapped her hand over her mouth.

"That man!"

"What man?"

"The one I saw at the facility. I know him!"

The farmer shrugged. "That's nice."

"No, I know him. He's involved in this."

The farmer clucked. "Do you know his name, anything about him?"

She didn't move. "Yes and no. Somehow, I'm sure I know a lot about him; maybe more than I should know. I think he knows that. Trouble is I don't remember just what it is, only that he's up to some serious trouble."

At the sink, she pumped some water and splashed it on her neck. When she turned back to the farmer, her eyes were bright.

"Some people plan to profit from this research, this project. They're the ones who're out to get us. It's because I know too much!"

"You know too much?" The farmer's eyes widened. "You lost me a quarter mile back. Can you slow down a bit?"

Linda's eyes warmed as she smiled. "It's all about that man. I'm remembering. I met him a while back. I interviewed him. I just can't get it to come to me. I know I was with a newspaper, but was it the *Times*?"

She clenched her fists, and with every muscle in her body straining against some unseen enemy, she wandered across the floor and then stopped in front of the old man.

"I was working on a story that led me to him. We did an interview and ..." Her voice faded. "Oh, if it would just come back!"

"Relax. Nothing comes to mind when you're tense. Be patient. It will come; I'm sure."

Linda sat down and leaned against the chair back, closing her eyes. Slowly, she breathed in and out, willing the strain to melt and the answers to flood her. After a while, her muscles loosened, and a few more clues slipped past the dissolving barrier in her memory.

"I worked as a reporter on various features. It was a series on medicine and new miracle cures that led me to him. Last winter, I think, I flew to Los Angeles to do some follow-up work. In my research, I'd stumbled on something that led to him."

"Him?" the farmer asked.

"Yes, that man. His name is almost on my tongue. I interviewed him for that series. I don't think I learned anything that day he didn't want me to learn, but I'm sure now that before we even met, I had found out something pretty damning about him. I just wish I could remember what it was."

"Wait a minute!" The farmer pulled a rag from his back pocket and wiped his forehead. "You've lost me again."

Slowly, Linda spelled it out. "I'm a reporter, or was. I thought I worked for the *LA Times*, but now I believe it was the *Houston Chronicle*. I remember doing a feature series on some of the more famous doctors from the Texas Medical Center." She propped her chin with her hand and talked as if she were musing to herself.

"There was one doctor who intrigued me more than the others. He seemed secretive about his work, yet I sensed some pride beneath his smile. So, I befriended him. Took him to lunch several times, tossed on the flattery, convinced him I found him attractive. It worked, like a charm. One evening, we went to a little Mexican restaurant on Westheimer. The margaritas were endless. He began to talk. I had a small recorder."

The farmer nodded, but Linda kept talking into her hand as it propped her chin. "It was then I found out about the project, Project Dust."

"Dust?" The farmer chuckled. It was a deep, resonate sound, which seemed to tickle his entire body.

"I'm serious! That's what he said it was. Dust, as in God took the dust of the ground and created man. And now they think they're playing God. But I don't think that is the official name of it now. I think all their work was consolidated into the Piney Woods Project.

"Anyway, this doctor told me the project began way back before the seeds of World War II had sprouted in Europe. Someone discovered that men working in a logging camp, those who worked with pine wood and were exposed to the rosin in its raw form were different. Their lives were longer, more static. A scientist began to study it and isolated a compound from the pine rosin he felt was responsible. He had some success, enough to attract attention.

"They began crude testing and got results so impressive that they gained the attention of some very influential people. War was rising on the horizon, and suddenly, Uncle Sam became very interested in their work."

She stared at him, a new recognition hitting her. "People—*you*, it was you, all those around you, you were the ones picked to be studied, to be used in the research of the potential of this compound. They needed a controlled setting, a place where they controlled everything, from the land, to the animals, even the people. What better place could they have picked than the piney woods of Texas?

"They cordoned off the area, miles of it, secured it, and isolated it. Then they visited every person living inside their newly built prison and gave them some story, like you told me. Then, they began injecting everyone with various dosages and versions.

"Years passed. Refinements were made. New uses were discovered. They learned early on that in some people it stopped aging, just like in you. In others, it seemed to regenerate growth in things that had stopped growing. It even seemed to heal certain diseases—"

The farmer interrupted. "This doctor, he told you all this?" Linda nodded. "But it's just his word. How can you prove it?"

"You're right. It was his word, and it was given in a drunken stupor. I couldn't prove it. So, I started investigating. I dug up some old land records and tried to trace the history of the land owners north of Houston. I found inconsistencies and dead ends. I even found evidence of altered records and names no one knew anything about. Oh, I wish it would all come back!"

The farmer gently laid his hand on her forehead. "You're so hot! Drink some more water. You need to relax. Things work better that way." He went to the sink and returned with another glass of cool spring water.

"Anyway," she said after emptying the glass and handing it back to him, "the trail led me to Los Angeles and to Congressman Thom Jordan."

Linda blanched suddenly. Her eyes grew wide as the color drained from her face. "That was him!"

"Him who?"

"The man at the facility, that's who I saw. I know now why he scares me." Her eyes met the farmer's. "You see, I'm sure I got the proof I needed. That week I was in Los Angeles, I think I put enough together to blow this whole project apart. And he knows I know the truth about it all."

"Well, where is it?"

Linda frowned. "I can't remember. But I know I had it!"

"So, they're lost, your notes; is that it?"

"Uh, notes? Yeah, I guess. But ..." She shook her head. "No, that's not it. I'm sure I made copies. That's like me to do something like that." She grinned. "Just like me! If I have to, I'll retrace my steps. Rebuild from what I remember."

Matt's snore punctuated her statement. Linda whirled at the sound, surprised she'd forgotten him. Running to his side, she knelt and gently touched the red welts on his face and arms. His skin was very warm, and a yellowish fluid oozed from cracks on his lips. It was shocking, how badly he'd fared. By contrast, she seemed to be in even better shape than before. What had happened to her?

With no warning, her pulse accelerated, and her heart pounded against her ribs. A cold chill rose from the base of her spine and tingled her nerves all the way to her neck. Facing the farmer, she asked softly, "Earlier, you called me Lynn. Why?"

"Why, that's your name." The farmer seemed surprised.

"My name? My name is Linda. Linda Mc ... Gow ... uh ... McCa ... Cane. McCane. Lynn McCane!" She closed her eyes. "It's true," she whispered. "That's my name! I'm not Linda! Everything he said, it's all true!" Suddenly, she frowned. "My cat! My apartment. My things!" She stopped. All her memories ran free, released from their prison. "Sam!" She glanced at Matt. "He doesn't know about Sam!" Lynn covered her mouth and stifled a cry.

Suddenly, the farmer doubled over, and he fought to catch his breath as if he'd been kicked in the gut with a sledgehammer.

Lynn gripped his shoulder. "What's the matter?"

"My stomach, it's gone cold, hard. It's much worse than before." With obvious effort, he straightened and took Lynn's hand.

His words were quiet, but she felt his urgency. "They're close. Those who hunt for you are near. We must get you out of here now!"

Lynn stared at him, not understanding. He added, "Like before, I can see it! And, we're nearly out of time."

CHAPTER 15

Dereck DeBoe's anger needed no fuel. Its flames blazed, consuming him and threatening all things within his reach. He glanced at the adjacent lab, the rows of vials stored in glass-doored coolers. He considered the backup supplies for the formulation of varieties of the original formula kept in secure containers in custom-built thermal controlled units. He shivered, feeling like the items mocked him with some hideous, evil laugh—inanimate objects that were the irony of all his research.

The earlier meeting with the president's men, the discussion of their plans, was unbelievable; if he had not witnessed it personally, he wouldn't believe it. Could they not see the mockery of their stated beliefs in their plans for the president?

Massaging his wrists and wiggling his fingers, Dereck fought the numbness creeping down his arms to his fingertips. Five hours had flown by; he spent them hammering on the keyboard; typing and retyping; checking files, directories, and folders; and creating new folders—all of it, every byte of information he'd gleaned through years of work on the project was reviewed, cataloged, and backed up on various electronic media. He clicked on the "complete" button on the computer screen, and the last of his data scuttled off into cyberspace to be stored at some remote location, presumably safe from hackers and his colleagues. Presumably. He knew in reality there were hackers out there who were good enough to find his trail and trace it. He just prayed he had slowed them down sufficiently so that he could be long gone when it was eventually discovered.

Now, he was finished, really finished. He stuffed the newly burned CDs into a protective Faraday cage pouch. He added five sixteen-terabyte memory sticks full of data and slipped them into the pouch along with the few paper files he'd allowed himself the luxury of taking. He sighed.

It was sad in a way, all his work, ending so abruptly. But it must. He could no longer continue at the facility. Things had gone beyond even what his depraved sense of ethics could tolerate. He could no longer condone the work they were promoting.

Yes, the money had been good, very good. But what good was money when one did not have the luxury of time to use it? He'd worked all day every day for years, barely taking enough time to sleep on any given day. What had it gotten him? A fat bank account, that was all. Just a lot of money sitting there, unused, lacking in any joy.

Dereck began one final task. Assured he had copies of all his work, he initiated a formatting program that would erase his hard drive, as well as any record of intranetwork and Internet activity from his computer. When that was complete, he reinstalled his operating system. The computer booted, and when it did, Dereck took his final precaution. He activated a small program he'd developed years earlier in his graduate days. Research had taught him many things; computer programming was just one of them. Anyone who might try to retrieve the erased data, no matter how remote the possibility, would be assured their efforts would be in vain, for the program would copy stealth files to their destination. And though the thief or thieves might believe they'd achieved success and gotten what was sought, in reality, they would only be transferring a lethal virus to whatever computer they tried to copy the stolen data to.

The greased wheels of his chair moved silently as he pushed from the desk. It was time, but there was one more important task.

Slipping to the lab adjacent to his office, he unlocked a small freezer. From it, he took several amber-colored vials and several bluish ones. Then, finding a small, special packing container, one that would keep the vials at the proper temperature for hours, he stowed his precious cargo and sealed the lid.

Back in his office, he surveyed the space. It had been more of a home to him these past years than his real home. He had no family, no wife—no one cared where he slept. He didn't care, either. After all, his work was what he lived for.

After stuffing a small box with the vials and adding his briefcase to it, he set it down. He went to his file cabinets and opened the top drawer. Withdrawing three DVD disks, he added them to the box. After locking the cabinet—a small deterrent, he knew—he returned to the computer.

He'd done all he could do, taken care of every detail. Everything must now move forward. After locking his desk, he inserted his new code into the computer and rebooted so all the changes he'd made would take effect.

There was no turning back. Taking the box, he stopped in the doorway and looked briefly at his office, one last good-bye. After locking the door, he slipped silently down the hall.

It wasn't until he was roaring down a back road from the facility to a little-used security gate that the magnitude of it all hit him. He would never come back to the facility. He was saddened in a way, but it had come to that point, that predetermined place in time where he could no longer rationalize the extremes, pushing beyond reasonable limits to achieve goals that he felt were no longer in the best interest of mankind. He'd compromised his ideals, his standards. Now, it was time to amend his errors.

The girl's face flashed across his mind. He wondered how she was faring since breaking away from her prison. Despite his growing guilt, he knew she had little chance of survival—really none. Eventually, they would regain her and the man she was with.

It was hard to admit that he'd spent the majority of his professional life with people who were ruthless. It had taken a while for the blinders to drop, but reality had a way of slipping past the cracks. Despite an overpowering urge to deny all of it, especially his role, he couldn't escape the fact that little stopped his colleagues from getting whatever they put their eyes on.

Without even considering the ramifications, he'd trotted along with their plans, rationalized that it would all work out for good. He'd participated as they'd experimented; he'd even added his own course of treatment. Although it was his work that ultimately saved the girl's life, he'd stood by and watched as they pushed beyond that invisible limit and used her in ways no human should ever be used. They'd taken her life, picked it, pried it, mutilated and changed it, all without her consent. They'd taken others, filled them with unknown substances and watched as they'd writhed in pain, uncomprehending of the evil pulsing through their veins, again without consent. Many had died. Others were left to live lives even the devil would cringe over. And he'd helped them do those hideous things.

Approaching the back exit from the compound, he was surprised to find a guard standing in his way. Usually, there was no one there. Normally, he'd key in one of his many false codes and slip through the automated gate. But seeing human flesh, he suddenly felt cold, clammy. Surely, no one had discovered his activities so soon.

As he slowed, obeying the stop sign the guard held out, sweat pooled under his arms and clotted in his shirt collar. Cold, damp hands slipped on the wheel, and his car wobbled as it halted in front of the uniformed officer.

"Evening," Dereck said through his partially open window.

The guard glanced casually in the car and then asked, "Open your trunk, please."

Dereck popped the release, and the trunk opened partially. The guard poked around briefly and then slammed the lid shut. He walked back to the driver's window. "Very well, you may go. Have a good evening." Before Dereck's car was through the gate, the guard was back inside his air-conditioned patrol car.

Slowly, forcing himself to calm, Dereck let out his breath and his pulse returned to normal. Sweat dripped down his cheek, and he swiped the back of his hand across his forehead. Pushing his hands against the wheel, he stretched, releasing tension from his shoulders and upper arms.

He pushed the gas pedal down, and the car roared. He sailed down the lonely road. He'd only gone a couple of miles when he saw it. A lone figure swathed in white floated in the middle of the road. Dereck blinked several times. The illusion only grew bigger. Slamming the brakes, he reminded himself he didn't believe in ghosts, never had. But when he stopped, his beliefs suddenly changed.

Lynn slammed the door of the farmer's car, turned, and leaned back in the window.

"Thank you ... for everything," she said.

The farmer stretched his hand toward hers. "You be careful. Don't let them get you again. I'll be fine, but you, and him, watch out. And don't forget about us."

A tear dropped from Lynn's eye. She squeezed the man's hand and smiled. "Never," she whispered.

The farmer's taillights faded into the growing twilight. As she turned and glanced at Matt, Lynn couldn't remember ever feeling so alone. Taking his arm, she pushed gently at his back. He groaned but limped by her side quietly.

Welts flamed on his pale skin, and his eyes drooped. So little time had passed, yet he'd changed so drastically. Gone was the strong leader who'd held her up while pushing and pulling. Present was someone who leaned on her. She shivered.

Lynn pulled Matt's arm about her neck to help support some of his weight. Their first steps together were awkward, hesitant. After a few more, it grew easier as they synched.

The farmer had driven them to what he believed was one of the outer boundaries of the quarantine area. He'd stopped out past the end of the dirt road and as far in the woods as his car could go before a solid fortress of tall pines squeezed the path such that a car could no longer get past. Pointing in front of him, he'd told her he thought a road was a couple hundred yards ahead.

Lynn prayed the farmer's word was right and that they were not circling back into enemy hands. She saw no evidence of anyone. Yet, she couldn't shake the farmer's gloom.

Lynn paused and listened. In the distance, it sounded like a car engine might be heading their way. She swiveled her head in several directions trying to determine the direction of the sound. The engine roar faded toward her right. She adjusted her direction and aimed for a point she thought would intersect the car's path.

Matt was silent as they walked. He grunted only when they stumbled. The deepening twilight was exacerbated by the dense grove of trees. Night would rob them of the last remaining traces of light at any moment.

Lynn caught the glimmer of an approaching headlight. She pushed forward, pulling Matt with her. Over the next rise, the forest was split in two by an asphalt ribbon. No markings identified the road, nor were there any signs to confirm or deny its identity. Lynn could only hope it was the sought-after escape.

They stopped and crouched behind a bank of bushes overlooking the road. Silently, they watched and waited. It wasn't long before a vehicle passed.

"Couldn't see the driver, could you?" she whispered against Matt's ear.

"Too dark," he muttered softly.

To attempt to flag down any car would be a gamble of great proportions. As each passed, covered by darkness, there was no hint as to the occupant's identity. To step out and flag one down was a bet with less than a 50 percent chance of success. It was a gamble they had to take.

More lights wavered through the trees. Sucking in a large breath and squeezing Matt's hand, Lynn burst through the bushes. Carrying a white sheet, one she'd taken from the cabin to cut and use for bandages if necessary, she stood in the middle of the road, holding her breath, praying and waving. Just as car lights rounded the curve and washed her in their glow, a sudden gust of wind picked up the sheet and whipped it about her legs. She struggled to free herself, as it billowed grandly, puffing itself out as if a proud soldier.

Lynn vaguely heard the car's brakes squealing. Her heart pumped too loudly to hear more. Somehow, she managed to make herself run to the driver's window. "Please, sir, can you help?"

The driver leaned out the window. For an eternity, he stared at her, mouth dropping open. Suddenly, he pushed a button releasing the car's locks. "Of course, get in." Lynn hesitated. "Come on! We don't have all day!"

The driver killed the engine and opened his door. The interior lights kicked on, flooding his face in light. Lynn gasped and jumped back.

"No! Uh, no, thanks. I've got to go." She bundled the sheet in her arms and scampered up the opposite embankment and behind the brush.

The driver shouted, "I'm not your enemy but your friend!"

Lynn heard footsteps crashing through the brush. She crouched low beside Matt and tried to keep her breathing quiet. It wasn't enough. His face peeked through the branches, and he crawled around and dropped beside them. The man held a flashlight, and in its faint light, he studied Lynn.

"You don't need to be afraid of me," he said softly. "I understand ... too much. Things are different now. I can help you."

Lynn stared at him, her body unconsciously inching away, but she said nothing. The man continued to study her.

"Your memory's crumbled, hasn't it? You remember, don't you?"

She nodded slowly. "Yes. You're one of them ... the doctor ... you're the one who ..." She jumped to her feet and tried to pull Matt with her, but he was too heavy. She couldn't do it.

"Yes, I'm Dereck DeBoe. And yes, I know you. I *was* one of them. But please don't be afraid of me now. I mean you no harm. I only want to help, and trust me, you need it."

Lynn scowled at him. The flashlight didn't reach his eyes, and she'd always believed in reading people's eyes. "Why? Why would you be willing to help us? You just want to get us back in that awful place; that's all." She tugged at Matt again, and he tried to stand, but the effort was too much and he slumped back down.

The doctor laughed quietly. "Get you back? Not in there, no."

"Then, what do you want?"

The doctor glanced at Matt, and suddenly, he seemed to be in a hurry. "There is much we need to talk about, but right now, we've got to get out of here!" He reached for Lynn's hand. She flinched and backed away. The doctor continued, "I know you have every reason not to trust me, but you must. Believe me when I say, I can help and you need help, now!" He glanced again at Matt and then at her. "If what I suspect is true, he's got little time left. If I don't get my antidote in him soon, there will be no chance for him!"

As if on cue, headlights twinkled through the trees. "Get down! Hide!" After glancing quickly over his shoulder at Lynn and Matt, he jogged back across the road. He ran to his trunk and fiddled with the lock.

Crouching beside Matt, Lynn peeked through the brush. An odd-looking patrol car stopped beside the doctor's. It wasn't a state trooper's car, nor was it a town police car. It had a green, revolving light and looked as if an odd assortment of gadgets had been planted on its dashboard. A young, muscular man, one with no tolerance written across his hard face, climbed out and strolled toward Dr. DeBoe.

"Problem here?" The revolving green lights swept across them in an eerie arc.

"Just a blown fuse, I think. I noticed my interior light wouldn't come on."

The officer scanned the trunk with his high-powered flashlight. Then silently, he strolled around the car, flashing his light throughout the car's interior, and underneath. After completing his search, he rejoined the doctor by the trunk. "Looks fine to me. Everything else okay?" He stared straight into the doctor's eyes. The doctor didn't flinch.

"Everything's fine."

"Good. I'll be heading on. Have a good evening."

The doctor waited for the man to return to his car before climbing back in his. Soon as the cruiser was gone, the doctor raced back to Lynn and Matt.

Lynn instinctively leaned away from him as he bent down and reached for her hand.

"Please, you've got to trust me. I'm the only hope you have of surviving this!" He didn't wait for a response but gripped her hands and pulled her to her feet. "Now, help me get him up!" He nodded at Matt. Together, he and Lynn pulled Matt to his feet and they all hobbled back to his car.

When they reached his car, the doctor asked, "How long has he been like this?"

"I'm not sure. I've lost track of time. I just know he's getting worse."

Dr. DeBoe didn't say anything as he and Lynn settled Matt in the backseat. When Matt was semiprone, a light blanket covering him, Lynn said, "I don't understand it. He's getting worse while I'm getting better."

The doctor turned sharply and stared at her. "This is all very interesting; believe me. And I want—*need* to know more. First though, we must get out of here. No telling how soon the next patrol will come along. Next time, I won't get off so easily, especially if they find you in here."

They pulled from the side of the road and had only gone a few yards when Matt started groaning and clutching his stomach. "I'm going to be sick!"

The doctor swerved toward the shoulder, and before the car was at a full stop, Matt managed to stumble out and heave on the side of the road. Nothing came up, however.

The doctor said to Lynn, "I know what you want to tell me. Yes, he's getting worse, and until he gets help, it's only going to get worse. Fortunately, I've got some serum with me. Soon as we get to a safe place, I'll administer it, hopefully in time. Right now, we must get moving. I assure you, they are already on our trail!"

Dr. DeBoe helped Lynn to steady Matt as they slowly got him back in the car. He collapsed against the backseat and closed his eyes. Soon, they were flying as fast as possible along the curving road.

"Tell me about you," Dr. DeBoe asked after several moments of silence. "How are you feeling?"

Lynn recounted a summary of how she felt, of what she was remembering.

"That's good, really good. I believe you got away at an opportune time. You were between reprogramming. They had wiped your false memory but had not implanted another. Your repressed memories were then free to surface. That's what's happening. What is curious, however, is your condition. You seem to be in better health than ever. Makes me curious about a lot of things, things I wish I could check out at the lab." He stopped at the sharp intake of her breath. "No, don't worry. You've got to believe I'm not with them anymore. I could no longer condone what they were doing. They had plans for treatments that were manipulative, selfish, and destructive, as if you don't already know that. It's why I left. I'm not going back. I'm washing my hands of them. I couldn't condone their latest experiment, what they wanted to do."

"Treat the president?" Lynn asked softly.

"Yes! How did you know that?"

"We saw him. When we were running from that place, we stumbled into a control room of sorts, saw the president on one of the screens. It didn't take much to figure it out."

"I can assure you, while they claim to have a noble purpose, saving his life, doing so means they must alter his mind. Our past work using those means, well, look at you and all that went wrong. Even with you, although you withstood and physically overcame a lot of the problems, others who received the same treatment didn't. The process still isn't perfected, but they're willing to take that risk, to alter his memory and see what happens. Think about it, having the ability to manipulate and alter the mind of the world's most powerful man. Imagine the ramifications!"

There was a loud groan from the backseat. Lynn twisted around to study Matt. He was bent double, gripping his gut as saliva dripped from the edges of his mouth. He groaned again, louder than before. "Matt, do we need to stop again?"

He didn't look up at her but slowly shook his head. "Keep going," he whispered.

Lynn turned back to Dr. DeBoe. "What about him? What's going on with him?"

Dereck was quiet, and he stared at the road. "I have to be honest; it's not good. Looks like they were in the middle of starting the repression sequence with him, and it was interrupted. I can only guess, as I wasn't part of his treatments. But, honestly, I haven't seen pustules like that since some of our earlier work was initiated. No telling what version of the serum they used on him. Still ..." Lights flashed briefly behind them in the darkness.

The threesome was quiet as Dereck maneuvered through the twists and turns of the nameless, nonexistent road. There were no more signs of lights anywhere, and no other cars passed them. Shortly after Dereck turned onto a county road that would take them to the interstate and ultimately to Houston, three pairs of headlights suddenly appeared behind them.

"I don't like this," Dereck said, glancing at the rearview mirror. "Those lights are gaining on us."

The speedometer edged higher, and the tires squealed as he fought for control while rounding a sharp curve. The lights behind moved as one. There was no hesitation. Their speed increased, and they inched closer.

"I'm going as fast as I can," Dereck said. "I know this road well, every curve, every bump. I've traveled it daily for the past fifteen years. I'm hoping they can't say the same. Soon, we'll be on I-45 heading south. It'll be easier then."

Suddenly, the car behind rammed them. Matt groaned, and Lynn sucked in a large breath. Dereck pushed his car to its limit, but the modest increase in speed was soon matched and they were rammed again.

"We're getting close to the highway now, but …" Dereck's voice faded as he stared at the red light in the intersection ahead. Traffic was so heavy even a new teen driver would've said it was too dangerous to run it. Lynn clasped and unclasped her hands. Dereck held his breath. The light turned green just as he entered the intersection, and they sped through and on to the freeway ramp.

Despite evening traffic that was still heavy, Dereck cut through the lanes, doing anything he could to put distance between them and those other cars. Years of fighting Houston traffic had taught him well, perfecting his considerable skill of swerving at the last moment to cut someone off. It had become a perverse sport of sorts.

Dereck zipped across a lane and back two and then waited until the space between cars dwindled before darting back again. Suddenly, a space opened, and he cut it close, going all the way from the far left lane to the exit ramp.

"Whew!" Dereck wiped his forehead and sighed as he hit the brakes and they began to slow. He glanced at Lynn's white face. "A little close, but we made it!"

Before he could celebrate, however, he glanced in the rearview mirror just in time to see a truck careening out of control in their direction. Dereck cut the wheel to the right, but the car fishtailed and went into a spin.

In slow motion, Lynn watched in horror as the truck skidded, racing toward them sideways like a crab. Dereck's car spun like the Wheel of Fortune, no one knowing just where it would stop. Lynn closed her eyes and waited for the end. There was a surreal quiet about her, but in her subconscious, she heard the brakes squealing, felt the sickening crunch of metal followed by a loud pop. When she opened her eyes, she couldn't believe she was alive.

The truck's nose was inside the car, mangled with the metal of

Dereck's door. Dereck was slumped against the wheel. Lynn checked him for a pulse and found none. Growing frantic, she turned to check on Matt. He was crumpled against his door, eyes closed.

Lynn whiffed the fuel even before her brain could register what it was. Finding her door jammed, she scrambled out her window and yanked on Matt's door. It only moved a fraction of an inch.

"Come on!" she screamed, pulling harder; still there was only minuscule movement. Harder she tugged, using all the strength she'd ever owned. Sweat ran down her cheeks, mixed with her tears. "You're not staying in there," she vowed through clenched teeth. Just as she was about to give up and run for help, the door broke free, and Matt fell out. Not caring how rough she was, she dragged Matt across the pavement and to the opposite embankment.

Leaving Matt lying on the ground, Lynn raced back to the car. The smell of fuel was overpowering, and she had to back out more than once to gasp some fresh air. But finally the box she'd spied in the back was in her hands. She ran back to Matt and set it beside him. Glancing at the growing crowd, she prayed no one would catch her doing what she planned next. She returned to the car once more.

"Miss! There's fuel spilled. This thing could blow any moment!"

Lynn nodded but ignored the warning.

"Miss! Didn't you hear?"

"Yes, but there's something I've got to get!" Two men started in her direction. Hands trembling and fingers fumbling, Lynn frantically searched Dereck's pockets. She hit pay dirt in his breast pocket. A wallet stuffed with hundreds, credit cards, even his license, was waiting for her, as if a parting gift, his recompense for all that had been done to her—to *them*. She stuck the wallet in her jeans and turned to the crowd and screamed, "There's still someone in here! Can someone get him out?"

The crowd swarmed, led by the two men who'd warned her to stay away. Frantically, they began tugging at bent metal and yanking at Dereck's seat belt. In the melee, Lynn slipped away and ran back to Matt. No one tried to stop her; no one even seemed interested.

"Let's get out of here before someone finds us and asks too many questions."

Matt was slumped, holding his head. He groaned. "If we don't move now, someone's going to come along and insist we get in an ambulance. Now tell me you don't remember your last ambulance ride."

"What about those cars that were chasing us?"

"No sign of them. But it doesn't mean there isn't someone around here that is pretty interested in us."

There was a loud explosion. The concussion knocked Lynn on top of Matt. The heat was scorching. The roar of the inferno was deafening. A greedy mountain of flames consumed what was left of Dereck's car and the truck that had rammed it.

Pushing up, Lynn hissed in Matt's ear, "We've got to go now." She pulled until he was able to get his balance. Then, with him leaning on her, they hobbled down the embankment, across a shallow ditch, and up a slight hill to a convenience store. A phone booth on the side actually had a phone book with a few pages intact. Lynn called for a cab. Trouble was she wasn't sure where to tell it to take them.

Cherie spun in her chair, and the daggers in her eyes were as real as the fire in the fireplace.

"You say he's dead and no evidence of them? How can that be?"

"Looks like Dr. DeBoe was burned when his car was crushed by a truck and the two caught fire. No one has found evidence of the others."

"But, Potter, they were with him! He was not alone. I'm sure of it!"

"Ma'am, we cannot confirm that. We suspected he picked them up as he was leaving the facility, and even though our men got close to his car, they were not able to determine if indeed anyone was riding with him. The patrol that stopped him earlier saw no evidence of anyone else."

"And your men lost him on the freeway. So now we'll never know."

"Oh, we'll find those two. The APB is out. Same media campaign as before, pictures everywhere. They can't go far without someone recognizing them. We even cranked up the reward money."

Cherie slumped in her chair. "Keep me posted. Anything, no matter how small, I want to hear about it, yesterday!"

Potter nodded and then strode quickly from her office. The door slammed behind him.

Cherie turned to the other person in her office and smacked her palm on the desk. "We don't need this now, not with us being so close to finalizing the deal with the Department of Defense. We needed Dereck alive. He was the one who perfected the final serum. The others never duplicated it. And now that we've been unable to crack his passwords or access his computer, I don't know what we'll do."

"What makes you think he would've cooperated with you?" Thom Jordan paced in front of Cherie, a cup of steaming coffee in his hand. "Besides, the defense deal is just a little side dressing. We've got what we need for the big one. The president's all set, right?"

"Yeah, but … the girl. Charles keeps saying we've got to have her to be sure."

The phone's shrill ring interrupted. Cherie grabbed the receiver and didn't bother with any pleasantries. She stopped pacing only long enough to absorb what the voice on the other end shouted.

"All the progress you said we'd made is now reversing?"

Charles shouted over the line, "Yes. We need Dereck's notes or the girl to get additional blood samples, preferably both."

Cherie sighed. "Impossible. Impossible requests! Seems I'm the one who gets them all. I don't have the girl, yet. And, no one's been able to crack the security on Dereck's computer. Can't you reconstruct something based on her records?"

"No. We need an actual sample of her blood."

"Well, search the labs again; see if he safeguarded extra samples. Find someone who can crack his computer. Do something!"

Cherie threw the phone down and went to the window. For a long while, neither she nor the Congressman moved. Then quietly, he slipped from the room, leaving the flame-haired vixen to stare at the night outside her world.

Light seeped slowly into his dark world. Muscles, aged before their time, were slow to respond, weak in their strength. Joints screaming and muscles crying, Matt pushed up against the pillows and rubbed his eyes. Sunlight pushed against the boundaries of the heavy drapes covering the windows. Outside the thick walls, birds chirped cheerfully, happy to greet the day.

Glancing about, he realized he was not in a hospital. The comfortable, queen-size bed planted in the middle of a tastefully decorated bedroom must have been in some nice hotel. How had he gotten there?

He felt old, worn out. His back hurt. Sliding against the sheets, he felt the burning and oozing of blisters on his arms, legs, and buttocks. His fingers traced the outline of his face and came away with puss. He frowned at the smell and wiped them on the sheet.

With effort that required huffing and groaning, he managed to fall out of the bed and pad across soft carpet to the bathroom. At the mirror, he leaned toward it and stared. A face, pockmarked and oozing, stared back at him. Red welts were swollen. His skin seemed loose, sagging. Gingerly, he touched a lump and winced. What had happened?

His legs started to wobble, and he felt he would pass out if he stood any longer. He made it to the bed just as wooziness crept over him. He tried to remember, to think. Fuzzy pictures darted in his mind but remained unclear. Soon, the desire for sleep was stronger than he, and he succumbed to its oblivion.

From the darkness, he sensed light at its edges. He tried to see the world about him, but it consisted only of dark, swirling drapes of mist, rising and falling, occasionally allowing a dim shaft of light to penetrate. He wasn't even sure if he was alive as the pain no longer tortured him.

Something slammed. A familiar soft voice muttered somewhere beyond his realm. Still as death, he lay, a thin sheet the only line of defense between him and the world beyond. Palms cold and wet, he waited, eyelids pinched tightly shut.

The aroma of bacon assaulted his nose, coffee too. When had he last eaten? His world rocked as someone moved close to him. He opened his eyes to see her perched on the edge of his bed.

"How are you?" Her voice was soft as her fingertips traced the outline of his forehead. "Feeling any better, like eating something?"

"I think so. But ..."

"But what?"

"What are all these sores?" He lightly touched his forehead.

She frowned. "I'm not sure. Dr. DeBoe said he hadn't seen them in years. Yet, he insisted you needed the serum; that it was the only thing that would keep you alive ..."

"Alive? You're ... you're giving me that stuff from that ... that ... place!"

Linda nodded. "I would've thought they would be better by now. No matter, you need to eat, and I've bought out the local Burger King. You've got your choice, a Croissan'Wich or some of their version of French toast."

"Breakfast? Are you my angel or what?" Matt grinned but the effort made him grimace. For a moment, the trouble they faced was forgotten. He could only stare at the beauty in front of him—Linda, healthy, whole, and well, smiling at him.

As Matt ate, he couldn't pry his eyes away from her.

"Tell me," he said between mouthfuls, "where are we?"

"You don't remember?"

Matt shook his head. "Uh, last night we ..." She recounted their escape.

"This DeBoe died in the accident? Why don't I remember?"

"You were out of it. I had to almost carry you here!"

Matt actually looked horrified. "You didn't!"

"You'd be surprised at what I can do when I have to. Survival often gives one strange abilities. Now, I'm trying to play doc and treat you with this serum, and it's time for another shot!"

"I swear, if I didn't know better, I'd think you enjoyed sticking that needle in me!"

"Moi? Enjoy sticking you with sharp metal objects? What do you think I am? Some kind of kinky sadomasochist?" She giggled. "Trouble is, DeBoe didn't say how much or how often. I'm just hoping that because he had several vials with him, that this is what he meant to use to help you. Still, I'm taking wild guesses here."

"Whoa!" Matt pushed back from her. "You're not seriously giving me drugs made by that crackpot doctor!"

Her eyes darkened. "Matt, you don't have a choice. Dr. DeBoe said you would die if you didn't get his treatment. He—"

"Look, I ... uh, I can't ..." Matt tried to push away from her. She grabbed his arm.

"Matt, come on!" she shouted. "You have to have this!"

"Where is he? He's paying you to do this? That doctor, he's outside, right?" Matt laughed bitterly. "He's watching you do this; getting his jollies from this sadistic little ..."

Linda slapped him across the cheek.

"Sit down, Matt!" she ordered as she pushed him into a chair. "I don't want to hear another word out of you!" She pulled his sleeve up and pushed the needle into his sagging skin.

Matt sat silently as Linda cleaned up the food wrappers and then went to the table and rearranged some of the folders. For a long time, no one said anything. Linda studied the papers, and Matt sat silently, staring at her.

After nearly fifteen minutes of silence, Matt reached for Linda's hand. "I'm sorry. I never should have doubted you."

She frowned and then said softly, "I'm the one who should apologize. I'm the one who doubted you. If only I'd listened earlier."

Matt narrowed his eyes and stared at her. "What do you mean?"

Linda shook her head. "First of all, my name in Lynn. Lynn McCane."

The silence crackled from the unspoken words as their eyes locked.

"Are you ... are you saying you're Lynn? Not Linda?"

Lynn nodded. "Yes. And there is much more you need to hear." She stopped. Matt's eyes were drooping, and just as he started to slump, she roused him and helped him back into bed.

"Sleep, kiddo. We can talk later."

Lynn turned from Matt and picked up the box from Dereck DeBoe. She spread the contents out on the table and began trying to digest his research.

Three hours later, as Matt snored without interruption, Lynn concluded she was in over her head. DeBoe's box had not only contained multiple memory sticks and DVDs; it also had a stack of files. So much of it was foreign, but what made more sense than she'd ever wanted to have was the summary he'd written, apparently just a few hours before they'd met up with him.

As she read the condemning words for yet another time, tears ran down her cheeks. It was just too unbelievable.

> The data is irrefutable, the conclusion impossible to deny. The girl is a definite genetic match. And because of that fact, I now understand the urgent need of my colleagues to find her. Her genetic markers on the key DNA strands are identical to his. This being so, her blood is essential in formulating his treatment regimen. Hence lies the question of ethics. She has already been violated, used against her will; can she be forced to again? And if she is, what is to stop future occurrences of the same? Can anyone anywhere be forced to comply simply because their genes match another's, especially if that other is a figure of international importance and power?
>
> Treating the president of the United States at this time, even if the girl is found, returned, and her body forced to further become science's playground, is unacceptable. My

colleagues say the man must be saved at all costs, yet they are willing to take great risks in treating him. Something doesn't figure.

I do think I know the reason. A successful treatment won't mean just saving his life; it would mean the successful implantation of various mind-control variables. And the possibilities of having control of the mind of the most powerful man on earth—I should have seen it coming.

Patients have been my life, ever since medical school, ever since I saved my first life on an ER table. I knew then I wanted nothing more than to save lives. When the opportunity to work on this project arose, the potential for life-saving, life-enhancing developments was too great to refuse. I knew I could contribute something positive to the world of medicine, and I did. But the price was very steep, and somewhere along the way, it got too high.

I no longer belong to this team. They know it too. That is why I have taken steps to preserve my research, my work. I now run for my life.

Lynn put the sheet aside and opened a folder bearing only a case number on its cover. Inside, however, there was no question who it belonged to. Her name was on every page—her real name, Lynn McCane. She even found the page where it was detailed just what new identity information had been implanted. She stared at the words, not able to take it all in, even though she'd read through the file once before.

The oddest thing, though, was the one sheet attached to several clear transparencies. The transparencies looked like grainy photographs of twine crossed and connected in each pair's center. A label on the bottom said something about DNA strands. In bold orange on each long piece of "twine" were sections that were circled and highlighted. When the transparencies were overlaid, almost all the orange highlighted spots matched up. After comparing again the various sheets, she happened to notice the name of the president on the bottom of two and hers on the other two. There was yet another pair of sheets with the orange markings, but no name. In comparing them all, the only thing she could conclude was that her genes had similarities with two other individuals, one of whom was the president. Other than that, she had no clue.

Unable to sit alone any longer, she went to the bed and deliberately plopped on its side.

"Matt. Wake up, Matt! Come on, Matt! I need to talk to you!"

Matt rolled over and grimaced. Slowly, he pulled his eyes open and squinted at her.

"What's up?"

"I'm not totally sure. But you need to see what I've been reading."

Minutes later, after Lynn had struggled to help Matt take the few steps from the bed to the small table by the window, she blurted, "They used us as guinea pigs!"

"They who?" Matt scratched at his eyes, picking at the crusty globs in the corners. The blisters on his face seemed to be drying somewhat, yet he still looked like he'd been run over by a dump truck.

Lynn continued, "The government doesn't care what happened to us. We're only valuable to them as test mice. Just like the postwar radiation experiments on troops."

"Government?" Matt stared at her. "How do you know it's the government?"

"My research and my work, I discovered it before going to LA and interviewing the congressman."

"Congressman? Whoa!"

Lynn grinned briefly. "After the farmer rescued us and you were sleeping, things started to come back—a lot of things." She nodded at his surprise. "There're still a few gaps, I remember most of what happened. More so, you need to know what I know. It's very important."

Matt memorized again every detail of her face, as he listened to her recount the conversations with the farmer.

"I'm afraid you got caught up in all this mess quite innocently," Lynn said as Matt started to interrupt. "Dr. DeBoe … I knew him before, before the crash."

"And …"

"I met him while researching an article for the *Houston Chronicle*." She then filled him in on all she'd learned.

Matt stared blankly at her as he listened. When she paused, he said, "The man at the complex, the one staring at you, that was Thom Jordan?"

She nodded. "He knows me. My research, my digging led me to him. On that fatal flight from LA to Houston, I was returning from a week of research and from an interview with him."

"So, why was your meeting with him so important?"

"I knew before the meeting that Thom Jordan's grandfather held the original patent issued for the pine rosin compound. His grandfather was the original founder of the corporation that funded the research and development for these experiments. Older articles of incorporation papers show Thom Jordan as a director, but current ones don't. The current papers, however, are even more interesting."

"How so? Lots of people sit on company boards, even ones their granddads founded."

"Matt," she paused while forcing him to connect with her gaze. "This corporation is in existence only on paper. I'd been unable to find any evidence of fiscal activity since the early sixties. Now, why keep a corporation in existence if it isn't functioning?" Lynn reached for Matt's hand and squeezed it.

"I believed, and still believe, Jordan is the one responsible for the funding of this lab complex. What he's managed to do is divert tax dollars to this so-called research, and he's not in it for the good he can do. Believe me; he's not."

Matt's eyes narrowed at the bitterness in her voice. She continued, "See, I also found he's got some bad debts, from way back, some from past campaigns, and some from gambling. No matter the source, he's under pressure to make some big money fast."

"How do you know that?"

"He's bought a lot of people with borrowed money. He feels he's got some powerful friends, people who are in his debt. Although he won't hesitate to call those debts in when it's to his advantage, he's still feeling the pressure."

"That's a pretty big accusation you're making."

"Look ..." Lynn's violet eyes connected with his. "I understand what you're saying, and I know I had the proof before, I just don't remember where. It's bugging me, nagging at me, but I can't get at it. I just know these things are true, and they know I know stuff I shouldn't. That's why we're in the mess we're in.

"When we crashed and you took me to that farmer's house, you unknowingly walked us right into their operation. Now, no one expected us to do that, to go there. It was unplanned, but they saw the opportunity to silence me because I'd learned too much and was going to expose them. So, I guess it was their good fortune we ended up at the farmer's. When it looked as if I was dead, that was when I was taken to the facility and used, used in their experiments as their little lab rat.

"Yeah, they took some unheard of measures to save my life, and no doubt, without them, I would've died. Apparently, I was in such bad shape that even with their new treatments, they thought I wouldn't make it. But Dereck DeBoe proved them wrong. First, without their knowledge, he gave me a new version of the compound that he'd developed. I recovered. When his comrades found out about his work, they insisted on using me to test a different regimen.

"Seems when they stumbled on me, they felt it was the perfect chance to see just how far they could go in reprogramming a person's mind. It didn't matter. I was never to be allowed to remember anything from my past. And when they were through, well, you know the rest.

"The success they had with me at the lab seemed so complete, so perfect, they were sure a real life test would only cement the proof of their assumptions. And when they got the proof they were so sure they'd get, then it was just a matter of how soon they could exploit the potential.

"You know most of the rest. They gave me a phony job, a background, even a reason for feeling weird. They kept an eye on me, and when it seemed I was handling it all very well, they pulled the strings and got you in the picture. But ..." She grinned suddenly. "I don't think they expected your reaction! In a million years, I don't think they ever thought you'd abduct me and go running into the wild blue yonder with their little lab rat!"

Matt didn't share her smile. Staring at her, shaking his head, he muttered, "I can't believe it. You remembered all this, or did the doc tell it to you?"

"Most of it, I remembered. Some, I got from reading these files this morning. And who knows how much more is on those disks? No matter, I think when you see it all, you'll agree, the work at that place must be brought to light. The country deserves an explanation, to know what their trusted government has been doing to their neighbors all these years. We're the ones who can do that. We're the only ones, other than those running the project, who truly know, firsthand, what has gone on and is still happening there."

CHAPTER 16

Tim slammed the gas nozzle back into its slot. He punched the button to print his receipt and waited. And waited. After what seemed like forever, a message flashed on the small screen informing him he must go inside to retrieve his receipt.

He blew out a long, hot breath and felt in his pocket for his wallet. Anger churned as he strolled across the pavement to the inside registers. "Want anything?" he shouted at Harry just before pulling open the store's glass doors.

"No!" Harry didn't look up but kept fiddling with some adjustment on his camera.

Inside, Tim spied his favorite brand of gum. Oh, what the heck. He might as well get some more. No one could guarantee when he'd get another chance. After all, he and Harry were on a stakeout—one that he was certain would end up with big bucks in his pocket.

When Tim returned to their car, Harry was foaming at the mouth and pointing.

"There!" Harry's finger pressed the shutter release, and the camera's shutter fired in rapid succession, capturing image after image of the scene across the street from them.

The stretch limo was nothing unusual—not in their town, what with powerful people and others feeling the need to appear powerful all over the place. But when he spied the man in a dark suit leaning against the limo's door his hand resting on the shoulder of a redheaded woman in a business suit that looked suitable for business anywhere but the boardroom, he frowned.

"So, Harry, what's so special about some man in a suit in a limo? We see them every day."

Before Harry could answer, the man pushed the woman into the limo and turned briefly to face them. When he did, Tim got a full view of his face.

"That's that congressman from California!" Tim shouted as he jumped behind the wheel, gunned the engine, and hit the gas, "Got any more cards for your camera?"

Harry grunted as he pushed a new SD card into his camera. Tim cut between two cars to get behind the limo. As he turned the wheel hard left, Tim said, "Bud, I think we've got ourselves a hot one! For sure there's a once-in-a-lifetime picture outta this one!"

"Yeah, just like that star and the woman," Harry answered sourly.

"Hey, I don't think this is just about a well-heeled, moneyed congressman," Tim replied. "No, it's not just about getting a little behind his wife's back. Gut instinct." Tim patted his stomach. "This one is hot, really hot."

"Well, I hope so. All our other leads sure fizzled out. Nothing came of that star and that woman. They just disappeared into thin air. Suddenly, no one cares about them anymore. We got all those pictures no one wanted to buy; we couldn't even cash in on the reward for locating them. Man, I hope your instinct is on target this time."

Overwhelmed, stiff, and tired, Matt pushed back from the table of files. He paced the room, saying nothing as Lynn continued to peruse the material. Unable to stand the silence any longer, he punched the remote and turned the TV on. The morning news was breaking.

"In a fiery crash last night just north of Houston on I-45 heading

south, there were two fatalities. A tractor trailer, apparently out of control according to reports, slammed into a car as both were on an exit ramp. Police are still investigating and do not believe alcohol was a factor. Both drivers were wearing seat belts, and no cell phones were in use. Of the two fatalities, only one, the truck driver, has been identified. The identity of the driver of the car remains a mystery.

"In other news, Police are asking the public for help in finding two missing people."

Matt's heart jumped as he was assaulted by Lynn's image, followed by his on the TV screen. *"Missing for nearly two days, it is urgent the girl be found as there is a rare medical condition involved. Any information should be relayed to your local police department."*

"Lynn?" Matt tapped her on the shoulder. She grunted. "Lynn, can you stop for a moment? This is important. They've got us on TV again."

"TV?"

"Yeah, said we've been missing for two days. They're encouraging the public to turn us in. They're saying you've got a rare medical condition."

Lynn froze, not moving for a moment. Then, without a word, she started stuffing the files back into the box. "Hurry," she pleaded with Matt. "Get anything out of here that can identify us. We've got to go!"

Matt crossed his arms and stopped in the middle of her frantic path, just like a mule. "And just how are we going to go to wherever it is we don't know where we're going?"

For the first time in a while, Lynn grinned. "I know just where we're going, the perfect place. Don't know why I didn't think of it before! And I've already rented a car to get us there!"

Tim slammed the brakes. Harry lurched forward and just as quickly was jerked back in place, the stubborn nylon of his seat belt refusing to give an inch of its hard-earned "law" status.

"Man, did you have to stop so suddenly?" Harry complained as he rubbed the back of his neck.

"They stopped. Okay? Just like that. I would've hit them if I hadn't hit the brakes."

The limo sped up again and this time didn't slow when it took the exit to Houston's George Bush Intercontinental Airport. Tim followed the car down the exit ramp and onto the feeder road. After entering the greater airport complex and following the maze of roads leading to various terminals and cargo locations, neither man was surprised to find the limo exited to the area housing the private terminals for those privileged enough to enter and depart Houston on their own, or someone else's, private plane.

The limo stopped in front of one of the private passenger terminals, and the driver jumped out and ran to open the back door.

"See?" Tim taunted Harry. "There's our man."

Following the congressman from the limo was the same shapely, red-haired vixen they'd seen earlier. Even her petite frame and well-tailored suit didn't hide the fire in her soul. She literally flew across the pavement, and the congressman had to run to keep up with her.

"Well, don't just sit there! Start shooting!" Harry fumbled with his camera, surprised the notion hadn't come to him first. Soon, the auto advance was clicking away, and he shot one shot after another until his card was full.

"I wonder who they're meeting."

"Well, don't just sit there wondering. Let's go!"

They sprinted across the pavement and slipped inside the terminal, using an "employees only" entrance.

Just as they ran into the passenger lounge, the congressman and the red-haired woman exited on the opposite end onto the tarmac. They stopped and waited, hair flapping in the exhaust of a small jet rolling to a stop nearby. When it stopped and its engines quieted, the rear door opened, and two uniformed guards stepped out and stood at attention by the door.

"Those uniforms, they look familiar," Tim whispered as he punched Harry in the side.

Harry almost dropped his camera, but he couldn't afford to miss a shot. He muttered under his breath, "Stupe! That's US Army. They're ours!"

"Oh!" Tim answered quietly.

However, when Harry saw the next man exit the plane, his hands suddenly got sweaty and the camera nearly slipped from his fingers. He'd never had that kind of reaction before when taking someone's picture. And he'd certainly seen a number of stars. However, this man, in this place, with no publicity, it was bound to be a secret. He lost his cool. The man stopped on the bottom step and waited for the congressman and the red-haired woman to approach.

"Tim!" Harry hissed under his breath. "Do you know who that is?"

"No, who?"

"That's the secretary of defense!"

"You're kidding, right?"

"No, I'm not!"

Tim smiled. "Man, I told you this would be hot. Was I right or not?" He grinned and slapped Harry on the back just as the shutter clicked on Harry's camera. He added in a louder whisper, "And who's that getting off with him?"

Harry only shrugged as he pulled out his full SD card and inserted a new one.

John poked at the fire in the grate and turned to Martha. "I feel a deep chill tonight." He rubbed his arms briskly.

"Why, dear?" Martha came to him. "You've never been cold like this before. Why, it's so hot out. And you with a fire."

"I don't know what it is. I suddenly feel so old, so worn out. As if it's all ending and it's way past due."

Martha touched the back of her hand to his forehead. "Why, you don't feel cold, not hot either, just right." She frowned. "Tell me, John. What really happened that afternoon at the cabin? You've not been the same since."

He shivered. Shoulders bent and back stooped, he limped toward an old cedar chest. The hinge creaked as he opened it and pulled out an old quilt. When he'd wrapped it about his shoulders with Martha's help, he settled in a chair by the fire.

"I told you, dear, all I know. Now I'm afraid. They know. I know they do. Now, I'm waiting for them to come for us." He stopped, breath held in his massive chest, and pointed at the window. "I've had this awful feeling ever since I took that girl and boy to that road. I don't see anything, don't hear anything; I just feel it, and this hasn't happened to me before. Those kids, they're not safe." He shook his head slowly.

"John, this isn't like you. Not like you at all. You of all people have got to stay on their side. Don't give up, John. You can't give up hope!"

John grasped his wife's hand. How did she do it? Even after all those years together, she still turned his heart's crank faster and harder than a good romp wrestling a steer.

"I love you, Martha," he said, a tear slipping down his cheek.

CHAPTER 17

Matt ground his teeth as Lynn careened through heavy traffic on the 610 Loop. "Just how do you know this Barry guy that we're going to see? Is he your boyfriend or maybe your former lover?"

Lynn's soft laughter escalated until tears ran down her cheeks.

"Come on; stay on the road, okay? You're not getting weird again, are you?" His question seemed to only tickle her further.

"I'll be fine." She spit out the words between giggles.

When Lynn finally squelched her laughter, Matt was stunned by her radiance. Sunlight sparkled off drying tear tracks, and she had more color, more life than he could remember. Even more surprising was the fact he wasn't so sure he liked the effect this Barry guy had on her.

"I used to work with Barry," she said as she brushed the final tears away, "at the *Houston Chronicle*. We shared the same boss. I did human-interest features; he frolicked around the bridal and society pages."

"Frolicked?" Matt uttered as she swerved around a slow car in their lane. "That's an odd description." Suddenly, he slammed his fist against his armrest. "Barry, you said?" She nodded. "You mentioned him on that flight from LA. Said something about going to him. I went to the *Chronicle* to find out about him. They said he was out of the country or something."

Lynn's brows rose. "Really? Barry's not much for travel. He always said it messed up his intestines." She started another fit of giggling.

"What is with this Barry?"

Lynn wiped another tear from her cheek and between spasms said, "Just wait till you meet him."

Four hours later, after three DVDs, two pizzas, several six packs of Pepsi, and at least two pots of Barry's espresso, Matt understood Lynn's description. When Barry entered the world, there never had been, nor ever would be, another like him. He was tall and round in the middle with toothpicks for arms and legs. Balding on top, his thickest patch of hair was a dark fringe lining his upper lip. Barry's gravelly voice was surprisingly deep and totally incongruent with the gentle flapping of his hands whenever he warmed to a topic while speaking. At first glance, Matt would never have imagined the man frolicking around anything, but after an hour, he understood Lynn's description perfectly.

When Matt and Lynn first arrived at Barry's older Bel Air home, they waited by his door, knocking and ringing the bell, hoping and praying he had not left for work. When the heavy door finally swung open, Barry's reaction reminded Matt of someone who'd stepped in dog poop and didn't realize it until he'd walked across some woman's freshly cleaned white carpet.

"Oh my gawd! I don't believe it! No!" Barry jumped back and covered his mouth. Then he lunged forward, grabbed Lynn by the neck, hugged her tightly, and yanked her through the opening. The door slammed in Matt's face. Then, it opened again.

"Sorry," he said quietly and pulled Matt inside just as roughly and slammed the door behind him.

"My goodness, girl!" Barry stood back from Lynn, one hand propping the other against his chin. "If I didn't believe in ghosts, I would now." He poked tentatively at her arm. "Yeah, real flesh. I guess there's real blood in there too!"

Lynn's smile covered her whole face. She was positively beaming. Matt turned his gaze to Barry and frowned. Barry, seemingly unaware of Matt's scrutiny, started flooding them with questions.

"Oh, where do I start?" He chuckled and rubbed the fringe on his lip. "But how did you get here? I mean, how *did* you come back from the dead? It must've been tough. And you ..." Barry stared at Matt. "Someone spray you with shotgun pellets? What're all those little holes on your face and arms?"

"Barry, chill!" Lynn stopped him. "It's nothing."

Barry leaned toward Lynn and squinted. "Nothing! I'm supposed to believe that, what with you rising from the dead and bringing Buckshot guy with you? Just who is this guy, anyway? I mean, you don't have to tell me his name. I've read all about him. Begged Darlene to let me do an interview for the society pages when his first film came out, but I mean *who* is he?"

Lynn seemed to understand Barry's intent exactly. "It's nothing, just a friend." She glanced quickly at Matt. "Just someone I met on a plane."

Barry clapped his hand over his mouth. "Oh my gawd!" His voice rasped over the gravel in his throat. "The crash. He's the survivor. You didn't make it. But how—"

"That's what we're going to tell you," Matt interjected through clenched teeth. "But we're in a spot right now, and time's running out. We need your help."

"Why, certainly."

Barry grasped Matt's arm lightly, and in what Matt would soon consider Barry's trademark move, shuffled them into his living room, such as it was. The walls were framed with pictures of various brides in almost every thinkable pose and attire. Plastic figures and various toppings for wedding cakes adorned a bookcase of shelves, and on the other side were brass arches, candle stands, and other accouterments associated with those who produced weddings. One such arch still clung to filmy white gauze woven between its curves, and dead flowers hung from fading ribbons. On the far wall was every shade of the rainbow. Gowns for bridesmaids lined a long rod that traversed half of the room. The more Matt saw, and heard, the more convinced he became that Barry could outproduce even the biggest producer in Hollywood.

Barry caught Matt's stare. "Been busy lately. Haven't had the time to clean that one up. And I still haven't gotten over that big one I produced in Nassau back in April. Seems I don't get through with one before another takes its place."

"One?"

"Weddings. I do weddings." He winked at Matt. "Among other things."

"Barry." Lynn fell into his huge, overstuffed sofa and slumped in its comfort. "We're in some deep trouble."

Barry's grin faded. "You're telling me, girl." He plopped down beside her, placed his hand gently on her knee, and looked her in the eye. "Just what kind of trouble is it, dearie?"

"Some people are after us. Want us pretty badly. And they're—"

Barry sprang to his feet and pointed at her. "You're right! I saw it on the news. He's, uh, you are or *were* wanted. They've got a reward out or something. And there was a girl …" He sucked his breath in loudly. "She's you, isn't she? That was you that was listed with him! But it wasn't your name. I remembered thinking at the time she looked like you, but I never considered, never dreamed in a million years it could be you!"

Lynn nodded and tugged his hand, pulling him back to her side on the couch. "It's very complicated, and we don't have much time." She began, and with Matt's help, filled him in on all that had happened to them since the plane crash. After hearing their story, Barry slumped against the couch cushions and stared silently at them.

"So, you see," Matt finished, "we've got these DVDs and USB sticks from the doctor who helped us get away, and we need to see them, now."

Barry nodded briskly. "Certainly," he said drawing out the word with his slow Texas drawl. He jumped up, suddenly full of life again.

"Let me just run and make us some nice espressos. I've got some divine little Italian cakes to dip with. They're to die for! Why, we can get all comfy here and just have a day of it, watching home movies!" He shuffled toward the kitchen.

"Don't you have to get to the office?" Lynn glanced at the wall clock, which peeked out between two rows of arched candleholders.

Barry stopped at the kitchen entrance and leaned back toward Lynn. "Dearie, if the answer to why you're here now is on those DVDs, there's not a paycheck in the world big enough to drag me away from your side. Darlene's just going to have to believe I'm out sick today!"

Hours later, Matt, Lynn, and Barry sat side by side, mouths gaping, eyes fixed on the TV screen. The television's picture had diminished to static; the last of the DVDs had finished, yet they continued to stare, frozen in place, dumbfounded.

The table in front of them was littered with greasy pizza boxes and empty cans of Pepsi. But the cans and boxes were the only things void of content. Their minds were reeling, full of information no lifetime could've possibly prepared them to grasp and hold on to, much less understand.

Lynn pressed her palms against her temples. Barry was frozen in place, only his eyes swung back and forth as he stared alternately at Lynn and then Matt.

"You guys are in some big heap of ... well, you know," Barry said, breaking their silence, "crap." He grinned at Lynn's frown. "Biggest pile I ever saw."

"Even being there and seeing what I saw, it's still hard to believe," Matt said. "To think, they believe they've found a cure for most cancers and the secret to ageless life. That alone is worth billions. But I guess that's not enough. They want more. They want control. Looks like that is what they have in mind for the president and who knows who else. Even though we saw the president on a monitor at the facility, I don't think I truly believed it, not really. Not till now." Matt's voice faded.

Lynn continued to stare at the blank screen. Through clenched teeth, she finally spoke. "They're getting away with it, too. Murder, fraud, you name it. There's something else," she said without looking at Barry or Matt as she rummaged through Dereck's box.

"What else? What *else?*" Barry asked, his hands fluttering as if ready for takeoff.

Lynn pulled out some papers and waved them in front of Barry's face. "This is why they want me so much. See these? They say I'm related to the president of the United States!"

Barry jumped back and looked down his nose at her. "Get real, girl! You *are* banged in the head! You don't have any relatives. Never had, that I know of. Now you want me to believe they've hooked you up with the president! Well, that is something, if they can create relatives."

"No, not create. But somehow, they determined that some of my genetic code matched his, and that explains partly why they were so desperate to get me in that facility to do more testing. We know they planned to use the same treatment on the president as they used on me. Part of the treatment used on me robbed me of my memory!"

"Whoa! I mean sure, we saw the president chatting with that doc on the videos, but that doesn't prove he got any treatment, does it?"

"Well, I can assure you, that whatever they plan to do to the president, it's not just for his health and well-being." Lynn got up and strolled to the window. She pulled the curtain aside and stared into the early evening twilight. "There's something else, though. Something said on that video. The doctor said something about the president signing a House bill. I wonder what that was about?"

No one said anything. Barry started pacing. He propped his chin with his hand while the other held his elbow in place. With his long fingers, he rubbed the fuzz lining his upper lip. Back and forth, over and over, he paced. For a long time, he said nothing.

Finally, he stopped in front of them and with his flair for the dramatic, announced, "You're sitting on a time bomb. Something so big, that when the world finds out about it, there's no telling what all will hit the fan. Trouble is, how can we corroborate your stories? Those

DVDs could be explained away, even the video of the president talking to that doctor. I mean, enough bought people and you can come up with most any story. No, what we need is something conclusive, something that will open a crack in their armor and expose the rest."

"You're right." Matt jumped up. "All those people in that village, they were used all those years. Remember, you said the farmer mentioned that every so often a group would disappear?" Lynn nodded. "Could they be deliberately growing new organs and then selling them to the highest bidder?"

Lynn's jaw dropped, and she sucked in a sharp breath. "Why not? Or even if not for organs, for research. What's to stop them? They've had complete freedom all these years to do what they wanted with their research. Oh, those poor souls, like the farmer; they all have gone along with it, not even realizing what's been done to them against their will."

Suddenly, Matt paled. "What if they didn't just want you back at that facility to test you more? What if they wanted you back so they could harvest your organs? Maybe because of your genes, they plan to use you as a backup in case the treatment on the president didn't work. Maybe that's the plan—to use you to make sure the president lives. Dereck said in the video they needed something new if the treatment didn't work. Maybe you are the only one who has what they can use!"

Lynn sucked in her breath sharply but pushed Matt away. "No! That can't be right."

Barry interrupted. "But it might be. If indeed all this is true, you can't let it happen. I mean, I like the president and all, despite his penchant for women, but even I wouldn't give up my liver for that man!"

"Wait a minute!" Lynn almost shouted. "What if they've used those people in that place to alter their genes, so that they match whatever person they want to match? Then can you see it? Not only have they got the perfect alibi of developing this miracle potion that can save the world, but which we know in reality doesn't work that great since most everyone dies, or loses their mind, but they can produce and harvest organs on demand. The waiting lists for transplants are unreal, and the market is there." Silence filled the room.

"No!" Matt suddenly shouted. "That's not it. Look at you!" He punched his finger at Lynn's chest. "It's all about you. You've got the secret to success inside. You didn't die from their treatment. You survived their mind control and their experiments. For some reason, you're different. Now, they need you so they can study your genes to see what makes you different from the others. When they figure that out, then failed trials will be no more. In their hurry, they rushed to get the president in there to treat him because he had enough similar gene matches for them to think they could be successful. Question now is why the hurry?"

Barry pinched his lips together as he stroked his chin. Silence weighed heavy on the group, as each looked to the other for answers none had. Finally, Barry stretched his arms over his head and yawned loudly. "It's late, and you two look beyond exhausted. We're all bummed over this. I think we should sleep on it. Start fresh in the morning."

"The sticks!" Lynn jumped up. "I forgot about them! We've got these USB stick drives. Whatever is on them must be important; otherwise, the doc wouldn't have included them in his box." Lynn sucked in a deep breath and expelled it. "My notes!" she shouted. "I forgot about them!" She spun around hugging herself.

"I set up anonymous email accounts prior to leaving LA. After my meeting with the congressman, I realized they would never let me expose what I'd learned. So, I emailed copies of my work to myself. I sent the notes that led me to the congressman, the path to the proof of his involvement, and copies of all I learned that week in LA. With those things and us showing what's taking place now, we have the proof. It wouldn't take a rocket scientist to figure it out. All we have to do is expose the fact that so many people have been used deliberately for gain, and we've got it. Once we crack the door, it's just a matter of time before that crack will bring it all down." She stopped and touched Barry's cheek gently. "I also did something else," she added softly. "I set up a box under your name and copied all the files to it."

Barry's brows jumped nearly to the top of his head, and his eyes stretched wide enough to slip a ship into their dark depths. "No kiddin'? You put all this in a box with my name? You mean I've had access to the story of the century all this time and didn't even know it?"

"Yeah!" Lynn grabbed a piece of paper and scribbled on it. "Here ..." She handed it to him. "The Internet address, the mailbox name, and the password, Genesis. It should all be there."

Barry hugged Lynn and then, on impulse, Matt too. "I hope what you say is true, that this stuff is all there. If it is, and I can break it open at work, then after I accept my Pulitzer ..." He winked at Lynn. "... all we'll have left to figure out is your reunion with the president of the United States. I can see it now, the headlines, byline by Barry Swindmore, of course. But it'll say something like, '*Long-Lost Relative Saves President's Life.*'"

Katie Grayson poured three cups of coffee and set one before Chad and another in front of Jerry. The long day was finally ending, and she'd greeted it with resignation and complete weariness. In her robe and slippers, she inhaled the brisk, steaming aroma. It refreshed her briefly, but after the first sip of the hot brew, she slumped. Head on her hands, she muttered, "I don't know what to do."

Jerry dropped onto the bench beside her, something that seemed so natural to him, especially in that kitchen on her farm. "What can you do? Yeah, you're worried crazy about Matt. But what else can you do but wait? Sooner or later, you'll hear something. You'll know what to do then."

Katie gazed into Jerry's eyes and smiled when he grasped her hand in his. "I wish it were as easy as all that. But I just can't get past this awful, sinking fear that something so bad has happened, he won't ever make it back. I can't even bear to think what he might be going through."

Jerry squeezed her hand. "Don't go thinking like that. It won't do any of us any good. You've got to keep a positive spin on this." It hit him suddenly; he'd forgotten his true role with the Grayson family, acting as a spin doctor for Matt's career. He honestly couldn't remember when he'd stopped worrying about Matt's career and redirected his concern for Matt himself and his family.

There was a loud knock on the kitchen door. Chad jumped up to open it, and looming in the doorway, larger than life, were two rather formidable and intimidating dark-suited men. Flipping open his badge, the one on the left stared at Katie and said, "Please excuse us, but we're Agents Sculler and Maderm with the FBI, and we need to speak with you about your son."

Katie clapped her hand to her mouth and keeled over. Jerry dove to the floor in a vain effort to catch her before she cracked her head on the tiled floor. Instead, he landed on top of her.

"Mom, are you all right?" Chad knelt by her and patted her gently on the forehead. Jerry wrung his hands as he hovered over her. As if on cue, Katie groaned, rolled to her side, and rubbed her eyes. "Where … what …"

"It's all right, Mom. You just fainted. Think you can sit up now?"

Katie allowed Chad to help her to her chair. She gripped the edge of the table with one hand, steadied her swaying body, and then straightened. With her direct, electric-blue gaze, she scoured the faces of the agents.

"Gentlemen, I think you have some explaining to do."

Jerry went to the coffeemaker. "Guess I'd better put on some more coffee. Something tells me we're going to be here a while."

Hours later, they were still around the table. Katie's eyes burned brighter than ever as she swept her gaze from agent to agent to Chad and then back to the agents.

"I don't think I could've dreamed anything more bizarre than what you've just told me, and you say the president's involved?"

"I must emphasize again, this information is confidential, classified, but, yes, ma'am," Sculler answered. "We believe he is. We don't know to what extent at this point. That is what we must find out. Please understand, we're very concerned about your son's welfare, but we're also trapped in an urgent situation to determine the nature of the president's involvement and hence his welfare."

"You want to know his involvement, yet you're not even sure just what this place is?"

"Not necessarily. As we mentioned, we were on-site, briefly, but were ordered to leave by the Secret Service. However, we caught a glimpse of two people running from the property that we believe could be your son and the reporter. Added to this is information we gained from some individuals connected with the operation. Seems your son, uh, Matt, has been inadvertently involved from the time of his crash. A couple of the doctors who treated him at Hermann Hospital appear to be highly placed in this project. I can assure you, we will find every lead, turn over every possible clue, until we get the answers. We have men all over working on it now, and with your help, maybe we can determine just where he might have gone."

"I would hope he would come here, if he could. But other than that, I don't know. I assume you've checked his place in LA."

"Ma'am, we've checked all sources. To our knowledge, he's still missing."

Katie's stoic, steel facade crumbled and floated away in sudden tears. After several uncomfortable moments in which the others watched helplessly as she sobbed, she looked up and said quietly but with every ounce of strength she possessed, "I don't care what you do, or what you find out. I want my son back, now!" She slammed her fist on the table, jostling the coffee from her cup. Standing, she strode from the room, back erect, shoulders pulled back, stomach sucked in. She looked like a general, more determined than ever to win the war.

Barry brought out a blanket and pillow and patted the couch. "Sorry I don't have more space."

"This is fine, thanks. It's really nice of you to do all this, but I still think we're putting you in danger by staying here."

Barry looked Matt in the eye and didn't smile. "Oh, that's a bunch of junk and you know it. See, if they're on to you, then they know I know too. So, if they're going to get you, they'll have to get me too. But I don't think they know yet; otherwise, they'd be storming my door. So, we sit tight." He dropped the blankets and pillows on the couch. "You know where the bathroom is. You just make yourself at home now." His arms fluttered as he spoke."

"And Lynn?" Matt asked.

There was a sudden twinkle in Barry's eyes. "She's on the daybed in the other room. So, night, night. Sleep tight. Don't let the bed bugs …"

Lynn came padding into the living room, wearing one of Barry's oversized T-shirts. "Almost forgot. It's time for another dose of your serum."

"You're kidding."

"No, I'm not. You're getting better. Can't you see? The marks are shrinking, your flesh is firmer."

"This stuff firms flesh?" Barry interrupted pointing at the bottle in her hand. "We've got to get that formula! We could market it! We'd make billions! Say …" He pinched his cheek. "… got any extra for me?"

"Stop it, Barry!" Lynn softened her words with a grin.

"Okay, get it over with." Matt pulled the sleeve up on his arm.

"Doesn't go there." Lynn giggled. "Don't you remember?"

"How do you know just where it goes? No, I think you're just getting a kick outta seeing my naked tush!"

Lynn swung at him, but he ducked out of the way.

"Down with the pants, buster!"

When the humiliation of the medicine was past, Lynn left Barry, arms across his chest, staring at Matt.

"Give her a chance," Barry said quietly. "It'll take some time, but she's worth it."

Matt slumped. He yawned. "What do you mean about giving her a chance?"

Barry peered knowingly at Matt. "She's had it rough."

"We both have."

"No, I mean before all this. Her and Sam. Did she ever tell you about him?"

Matt nodded. "Said that he was gone and not to be sorry."

Barry nodded slowly. "Yeah, she was right there. But she's got to tell you the rest. It shouldn't come from me. It's very hard for her. But she's worth waiting for."

Matt shrugged. "Thanks, I guess."

On the sofa, Matt squirmed and wiggled, shifted and twisted. No matter how much he moved, he couldn't find a comfortable position. Mental pictures kept flashing across his mind's eye. The facility, the attendants, the congressman, and finally, Dereck DeBoe's burning car. Try as he might, he couldn't erase the final image. Instead, more pictures rushed at him, faster and faster, until they blurred and melted into one.

With a start, he jerked and opened his eyes. Sweat dripped down his cheeks, and he felt like he had a fever. The crackling fire in the hearth was putting out too much heat, yet he shivered, suddenly cold. The old farmer appeared in the corner of his vision and came toward him, a concerned smile on his face.

"I see you're awake now. Things must be getting clearer, for you're sitting up and looking about you." He handed a cool rag to Matt. "Wipe this on your brow. It'll help cool you."

Matt did as he was ordered and then handed the rag back to the old man. "Thanks."

"Hungry?" the farmer asked.

A wonderful aroma assaulted Matt's nose, and his mouth watered. "Umm, yes. What is it?"

"Just a little something the missus cooked up. She's worried about you. Said you still don't have your full strength yet. She wants to get you strong again so you can fight them."

"Fight who?"

"Them, you know, those that've done all these things. I think you now know better than I who they are." The farmer sighed. "Even now they're learning more about where you are and what you're doing. It won't be safe much longer. Soon, you'll have to move on. Stay ahead of them. But you must act fast. Be the first. Take the offensive. Surprise, it's your only chance."

Matt felt suddenly dizzy. The room swung about him and then went black. When he next opened his eyes, he heard dishes banging and silverware clanging. The aroma of fresh brewed coffee flirted with his nose.

Arms over his head, he stretched and fell from the couch. When he managed to crawl to his feet, his back kinked and cramped. When he finally straightened, he realized, despite the discomfort of the couch, he felt more refreshed than he could remember in a long while. Yet, something tugged at the dark edges of his mind.

Matt stumbled into the kitchen, lingering drowsiness still blurring his vision. He stopped when he spied Barry, dark suit on, apron tied over it, washing dishes.

"Morning," Barry said, turning. "Hope I didn't wake you. I had to tidy a few things before I left for the office." He took a sponge and quickly wiped the counter while gently closing a cabinet door. He untied his apron and hung it neatly on a peg in the broom closet.

"Now …" He touched Matt's arm lightly. "I want you two to stay here. Sit tight till I get back, even if it's late, which it might be. Absolute orders. Any calls, be sure and check caller ID before picking up the phone. I've written down the numbers I'll be calling from. Any other numbers or if it says something like unknown name or number or private name, etc., well, let the machine get it. Only answer a call if it comes from one of these numbers. Okay?" He stopped suddenly and put his fingers over his mouth.

"You know," Barry added slowly. "If they do know you're here, then they might have my line tapped. I don't think you should even answer the phone. Don't make any calls either. Just wait till I get home."

Matt nodded, but his eyes wandered to the coffee brewing. Barry followed his gaze. "Cups're here." He pointed to the cabinet above the coffeepot. "Help yourself. I'm afraid it's just plain Colombian this morning. I'm out of my favorite. Got to get some beans at the fresh market today."

"Thanks. This'll do just fine." Matt grinned, suddenly ravenous for a big hit of warm caffeine. "Don't know how I'll repay you, though."

Barry grinned. "When this is over, you can give me that interview." Matt didn't smile. Barry dropped his grin and gripped Matt's arm lightly. "Don't worry. This will work out. It's got to; I must have that Pulitzer!" Matt just stared at him. "That's a joke, son," Barry added after dropping his smile. "Have some faith. You've just got to be patient. Today will be the hardest, just sitting and waiting. But you can put it to good use." He winked as he slipped out the back door and locked it.

An hour later, hair ruffled, only a triple-X-size T-shirt of Barry's covering her, Lynn stumbled into the kitchen and found Matt sipping coffee while reading the morning paper.

"What's up?" she said as she slipped into a chair across from him.

Matt pulled his eyes from the paper and was stunned as if he'd never seen her before. Dark hair framed her face, enhancing the violet of her eyes and making her cheekbones more prominent. There was a rosy flush on her cheeks, but it enhanced her smooth skin. The delicate persona she radiated was misleading, for he knew the strength she harbored, hidden deep inside.

Before Matt could even consider that there were much more urgent matters needing their attention, he felt the stirring in his gut just as a flush hit his cheeks. He swallowed a big gulp of coffee and choked. He spit it out, his flesh throbbing from the scalding heat. When he finally calmed, he managed, "Barry's at the office," and told her about Barry's orders.

"Don't you think this is a bit of overkill?"

Matt considered her words, and then he shook his head. "No. After all that's gone on, I think he's right. In fact, we're probably putting him in jeopardy by staying here."

"But how could they possibly know where we are?"

"If those people can steal a whole village, making the residents vanish as far as the rest of the world is concerned, then I don't think finding out where we are is going to be any problem."

"They haven't managed to catch us yet."

"*Yet*. Key word. I think it's only because we've surprised them, done what they didn't expect. I don't think they've realized you would go running to one of your former work buddies. Eventually, they'll figure that out too."

"Then, let's hope we beat them at their game. Let's hope Barry's successful and we get there before they do. He did take the sticks, didn't he?"

Matt nodded. "And yes, he's getting copies as well." They were both silent for a while. Matt stared as she read the paper, everything about her consuming him. He felt a sudden urgency, as his eyes roved over her features, to memorize them, as if he knew his time with her would end soon and abruptly. Even as he drank in every detail of her face, fear grew in his gut, and he resented it.

Lynn waved her hand in front of his eyes. "Anybody home?" He was so lost in his thoughts he didn't realize she no longer held the paper in her hands.

"Sorry," he muttered.

"Don't know about you, but ..." She glanced at her T-shirt. "I sure could use a change of clothes. Maybe a quick trip to the mall, perhaps?" She stretched, pulling the thin knit tight across her breasts. They pointed at Matt.

"A trip to the mall? Who needs clothes ... uh ... new clothes?"

Lynn strolled to the sink, emptied her cup, rinsed it, and then turned and leaned against the counter. She crossed her arms, which hid her pointing breasts, but the action pulled up the hem of her T-shirt and exposed the line of her panties and the hint of a flat belly beneath. Innocently, she asked, "So, what do we do now?"

Matt could only stare. "Want to do, or have to do?"

"Is want even a part of the picture?"

Matt's lips parted in a short grin, and before he could erase the twinkle in his eye, he said, "Want is always a part of the picture."

Lynn turned to Barry's breadbox and pulled a couple slices from a bag. After putting them in the toaster, she pushed the button down.

While the bread turned brown and crispy, she kept her back to Matt and said nothing. When the bread popped up, she turned around to face him.

"You still haven't answered my earlier question: what're we going to do?"

"What're we going to do?" Matt parroted. "We're going to sit and wait. Stick to the plan we concocted last night."

"You're content just to sit and wait? When there's so much at stake?"

Matt shrugged. "Yes, I'm content to wait until we hear from Barry."

Lynn started pacing, her toast forgotten. "I don't like this. I feel like we're sitting ducks, waiting for them to grab us."

"You just said you thought we were safe enough for now. You even wanted to go to the mall."

"Yes, I do! But …" She stabbed her chest with her fingers. "… it's here. I can feel it." She resumed pacing, and her speed increased dramatically, as if she were suddenly afraid of some invisible demon that would eat her if she stood still. "They will find us; I'm sure of that."

"Tell me," Matt asked, "have you remembered anything else?"

She paused. "No, I think I've remembered all of it. I do have this feeling, this burning in my gut, that tells me something's missing. But if Barry can do what he says, maybe remembering the rest won't matter."

The aging tiles lining the long hallway sparkled from their latest polishing. That gleam wouldn't last long. Soon, the throngs would return for the day—harried reporters, bosses running from one desk to the next, each one adding his or her signature scuff mark on the shiny but aged floor. The whole building, especially the newsroom, would throb with anticipation, anxiety, and even excitement as the news once again reigned until the next edition was put to bed.

Barry rounded the hall corner and nearly fell as his feet slid on the smooth surface. He barely noticed. The only thing that mattered was the stack of papers in his hands. He never saw the two young men he shuffled into. The first jumped back and glared. As hot words started to form on the man's lips, the other interrupted.

"Barry?" The young man stared at his face as Barry nodded slowly. "I thought so. It's been a few years! Remember, Lyle Lovett? Julia Roberts?"

Barry suddenly burst into loud laughter. "I'll never forget! Oh my gawd." He gripped the man's arm. "It's you, Harry! It's been that long since I tried to have you arrested for crashing my interview?"

Harry nodded. "Yep, that long!"

"And those sorry pictures you tried to sell me?"

Harry grinned. "Burned, long ago. They only live in your memory!"

"So, who's this with you?"

"This is Tim, my new partner."

After formal introductions were exchanged, Barry asked, "So what drags you guys from the left coast out to our Texas hospitality and humidity? You must be following someone hot!"

Harry didn't answer, but Tim grinned and nodded. "Real hot, man. Harry says this is big stuff. All started with that new star, Grayson, and some reporter."

Barry's back straightened, and his eyes widened. "That so," he said, stroking the fuzz of his lip.

Harry interrupted. "The reporter, someone said her name was McGowan, but I swear, she looked just like a girl I remember seeing here; in fact, I know she was here. Same time I was trying to sell you those pictures. Had eyes a guy could go blind looking at."

Barry nodded and glanced sharply at Tim. "So, how did you get involved with all this?"

"We caught them in LA, and their trail led here. But we got to the airport and they just disappeared. Last report was they were taken to some hospital, but not a single hospital in town could confirm their existence. Not even our best sources could dig anything up."

Barry poked his forefinger in the fringe on his lip. "Is this the same two that were wanted? Had a reward out or something?"

Tim nodded rapidly, but Harry answered, "Yeah, we even called in the reward. People on the phone dodged and avoided giving us a straight answer. Never got any money out of it."

Barry frowned, but Tim ignored it and continued with his story. "Then we stumbled upon that congressman from California." He glanced at Harry. "Who was it again?"

"Jordan," Harry answered grudgingly. "Thom Jordan." The hair stood up on Barry's neck.

Tim continued, "Yeah, that Jordan guy. He's been on the news a lot lately, pushing some new health-care initiative that's supposed to fix all that went wrong with Obamacare. Got people worked up, so I hear. Anyway, he's with this red-haired woman, a real looker, if you ask me." Tim's eyes developed a faraway glaze. Then, he jerked, and his eyes focused on Barry again. "So we decide to see where they might lead us."

"And ..." Barry was leaning so close to Tim, he could feel the other man's breath on his face. "What did you find?"

Harry interrupted and took over. "We followed them to the private terminals at IAH. We got some pics of them meeting a private jet."

"Tell 'em who they met!" Tim interrupted.

Harry cast a scathing glance at his partner. "Be patient, will you?" He turned back to Barry and patted the thick folder in his hand. "Got all these pictures of them greeting the secretary of defense and—"

Tim interrupted. "Tell him who the other man was!"

Harry frowned at him and turned back to Barry. "Trouble is, your editor isn't too interested. Didn't believe these were legit." He patted the envelope again.

Barry's hair, what was left of it, stood at attention. With a will of its own, he found his hand reaching for Harry's envelope. "Mind if I ...?"

Harry's grasp got tighter. "Uh, I'm not so sure here. These are priceless, the only ones in existence."

"Come on, then." Barry forced a smile to hide his tension. "Let's just go someplace private, get us a nice cup of coffee."

Harry and Tim didn't budge. "Oh, come on, guys; I'm not about to steal any of your work and claim credit."

"Well, you do cover the type of people we follow. Who's to say you don't steal from this." Harry patted his envelope.

"Listen," Barry started easily, "you guys want to sell what you got there. Sounds like you need to convince someone that what you have is hot and desirable. If you want a little help getting my editor sold on the idea, well …" Barry winked. "I know what she likes, and maybe I can grease things up a bit." Tim and Harry stared at him, and Barry increased the wattage on his smile. "Come on; we'll get that coffee and see what we can come up with."

The two younger men agreed, and Barry quickly led the way to a conference room where he knew a fresh pot of coffee was always brewing. Not only was this conference room known for its perpetual fresh coffee; it was also known as the quietest, most soundproof room in the building. More interoffice liaisons had taken place there than anywhere else, except for perhaps the janitor's closet. He'd produced at least two weddings that had begun with a hot, steamy fling on the conference room table. Now, he just hoped to produce something that might help his friends regain a life that might become full of such intimacies.

They were silent, each lost in his or her own world of worry and fear, exasperated by the long, tedious growing hours of the day. They had each showered and eaten and then dressed in the worn clothes they'd been given by the farmer. The day had been long and uneventful.

Lynn fell on the couch and drew her knees to her chest. Arms curled tightly about them, she propped her chin on her kneecaps. Matt lowered himself gently beside her. Softly, he asked, "Tell me more about your childhood."

Lynn stared at the wedding arch still clinging to its array of dead flowers. "I told you before," she said softly, staring at the brown petals, "I grew up in DC, in a town home. I have no living relatives. My—"

Matt interrupted. "At least none you're aware of!"

"Yeah, none that I *knew* of." She scratched her chin and glanced at the ceiling as if readying herself to recite a memorized poem.

"My parents died shortly after Sam brought me to Texas." Her eyes darkened. "I think you know all the rest." She abruptly changed the subject. "Tell me, what will you do when all this is over?"

It was something Matt hadn't considered in a while. He rubbed his chin as he gazed out the window. There was silence between them for several moments. When he spoke, it was quiet, as if he were talking to himself.

"I want to work—that is, if anyone will have me. I'm pretty sure I blew my current project. And the next, a film for Spielberg, well, I guess that's been tossed overboard by now. My contract was supposed to have been signed the day after we ran from the studio. I may be back in the ranks of unemployed and have to cry to Mom for a job on the ranch."

He was surprised when Lynn turned to him and taking his hand, looked him in the eye. "I'm sorry." Tears wobbled on the edges of her eyes, and he stared at her for uncounted moments. When Lynn spoke again, it was very quiet, and he had to strain to hear.

"I've caused you so much trouble. What's worse, I doubted you when you tried to tell me what I believed was all wrong. If you hadn't kept after me, I wouldn't be alive today. I owe you!"

Matt tried to ignore the trembling of his lips as he spoke. "Owe me one? My prices are pretty steep. I don't think you can afford it, so we'll just call things even."

"How can you call it even? What have I done for you?" She seemed genuinely worried.

"Besides saving my life and humiliating me by sticking that needle in my rear, what have you done?" Matt shook his head. "You'll never know just how much you've done for me." *If only you know how much I care,* he wanted to scream.

Abruptly, he asked, "What about Sam? Tell me about him."

Lynn lowered her chin and stared at her toes. She wiggled them back and forth but said nothing. Outside Barry's house, it seemed unnaturally quiet. There was no roar of planes, no honking car horns, no televisions blaring—nothing but silence to distract them from the question hanging between them. Finally, she muttered, "What about him?"

"What do you think of when you think of him?"

Lynn slowly tilted her head so that her eyes met Matt's. Moisture pooled at the edges and slipped slowly down her cheeks. "Remember him? How could I ever forget? The hell I went through because of him." A sob slipped past her lips, and she covered her mouth with her hand.

"What is it?" Matt stretched his arm toward her and gently gripped her hand. "What happened that was so bad?"

"I told you," she spat angrily, "he's dead. That's what's so bad … supposed to be, anyway." She pushed his hand away and went to the window. Fingering the curtains, she stared at the gray twilight.

"There's more, isn't there?" Matt said softly as he came up from behind and stood there, his breath teasing her hair.

Lynn continued to stare out the window as if she hadn't heard him. Suddenly, she pushed past him and ran toward the front door. She grabbed the car keys from the foyer table. Stabbing her feet into the old shoes she'd worn from the farmer's, she ran through the door, slamming it behind her.

"Lynn, wait!" Matt shouted as he burst outside after her.

The dull gray of a long day nearly spent cast eerie shadows over the car and the house. Lynn slipped behind the wheel of their rental car and gunned the engine as she slammed the gear into drive. Just as the tires began to churn on the gravel, Matt yanked the passenger's door open and jumped in.

Lynn hit the gas as they left the drive and screamed along the pavement. After making a sharp left, they fled from the aging neighborhood and sped onto the freeway.

An hour later, Lynn stopped the car. As if she were nothing more than a remote-controlled piece of high-tech equipment, operating with no thought or emotion, she slowly climbed from behind the wheel. She said nothing to Matt. She'd said nothing during their entire erratic, crazy, disorienting trip through Houston.

Despite Matt's questions and pleas for a response, she'd ignored him. A few tears trickled down her cheeks, the only sign that indicated she was something more than a machine. He'd said one word, "Sam," and it was like a switch was flipped, turning her into a mindless machine; void of feeling or thought.

When they pulled into the parking lot of Lynn's old apartment, however, Matt wasn't surprised to see the destination she had chosen. Somehow, he knew there were demons chasing her. Her old apartment was perhaps the only place she could exorcise them.

As Lynn quickly climbed the few steps and knocked on the door of her old home, Matt kept several feet behind. There was no answer, so she knocked again. After a moment or two, an older gentleman came stumbling toward them. He looked familiar. It hit him suddenly. It was the same man who'd let him inside that apartment months earlier.

"Ma'am, there's no one there. Place has been vacant for months."

Lynn's stare bore into the old man. "Vacant? That's my place."

The man moved closer and glanced briefly at her before leaning over and staring at the lock as he fumbled with a key. "No one seems interested in this unit. Having one heck of a time getting it rented. Some kind of nasty rumor got started about the former tenant dying in some kind of satanic sacrifice. People hear that, and they run." Keys dangling in his fingers, he looked at Lynn and smiled hopefully. "Say, you interested in renting?"

"I used to live here."

The old man's mouth dropped open, and he stuttered. "No, it can't be. That girl's dead."

"Well, I'm not, am I? It was one big mistake. Now, I don't suppose you have any clue as to where my stuff might be?"

He shook his head. "Sorry, I can't tell you anything. All I know, it was taken a few days after you were reported … uh … gone. I can let you in now, but don't expect to find anything. Those people cleaned everything out."

He unlocked the door and stood aside for Lynn and Matt to pass by. "Stop by the office when you're through, and I'll lock it back up."

Lynn entered the apartment, her eyes slowly taking in the few details the barren room had to offer. Dirty walls desperate for new paint did little to bring light into the dark space. Kitchen cabinet doors hung open, revealing their black emptiness. The hardwood floor was swept clean, no debris or dead cats could be found.

A small tremor of unease ran down Matt's spine. The place was creepy before; now it positively chilled him. As he watched Lynn move slowly around the perimeter of the living room, she seemed unaware of her surroundings, lost in some dark, private hell, from which she refused to flee.

"Come on, Lynn," Matt pleaded again. "Tell me what's going on."

She muttered softly, "Mr. Chips. Where are you?" She whistled softly.

"Lynn, Mr. Chips is gone. He was …" Matt couldn't finish. It didn't seem to matter that he'd found her dead cat months earlier when he'd visited her place. Lynn didn't respond.

As if her feet had memorized each step she took, Lynn walked toward the bedroom and then to the closet. Looking inside, she tugged at the wooden shelf until it came free of its brackets, and she pulled it from the wall. In a small space, crudely carved in the dry wall, were some tightly rolled papers. Quickly, she pulled them out and stared at the crinkled sheets. She started to stuff them into her jeans, but Matt gripped her wrist. With a sigh, she let him take the documents as she pushed the shelf back into place, backed from the closet, and shut the door.

"What are these?" Matt asked.

"Old records of landowners whose land was taken by the Piney Woods Project. I did a search, found no death certificates for any of these people; yet, no one can verify they're currently living."

Matt flipped to another sheet and looked up. She answered, "It's a copy of some articles of incorporation filed by a group of men back in the thirties. Look at the names, Matt."

He did and the last one caused him to gasp. "Jordan! Our congressman?"

"Grandfather. And …" She pointed to the next sheet. "… that's the most recent listing for the board of directors for the group."

Matt nodded. She continued, "Look at the next sheet. A copy of the patent issued to that corporation for their little miracle compound. That's the group who started all this. And their descendants are the ones who plan to profit, at our expense."

Matt stared for a long time at what he held. Finally, he looked at the last sheet. He said nothing but frowned as he gazed into her eyes.

"Birth certificate for my great-grandfather. He owned land there," Lynn said, touching the paper. "I didn't remember these ..." She pointed to the papers Matt held. "... until you started talking about Sam. His death, his ..." Her voice trailed off. "It reminded me; that's all."

Suddenly retreating into her own world, she began to pace around the perimeter of the room, running her hand along the wall. After circling the room twice, as if it were some tribal ritual, she went to its center. Shoulders slumped and eyes downcast, she talked to the floor instead of Matt.

"He died here." The silence hung like a heavy curtain waiting for the breeze of life to move it again. When she looked at Matt, there were no tears on her cheeks.

"Our bed was here, and he was in it. He died because there was nothing else they could do. No wonder drugs left to try. No new experimental treatments available. Nothing. All our savings, all our assets gone, dissolved to make him well, and nothing worked. Yet, all that time, our wonderful, trustworthy, 'I feel your pain' government was spending who knows how many millions of dollars developing magic, new treatments that might have saved his life, if they'd been known about."

"Do you honestly believe those people have worked any miracles? Look at the fatalities, the deformities, the oddities—" Matt started.

"Yes, I do," Lynn interrupted, suddenly very much alive. "Some of those people were given a new lease on life. They were given youth. Others were given abilities. Even others got years they never would've had otherwise. Look at me; I even got a new life!" Her laugh sounded bitter.

"A new life?" Matt said solemnly and then frowned. "But, at what cost? They took away all you knew. Messed with your head, your soul. They—"

"Look," she interrupted. "I'll tell you a secret. I didn't go out to California just to interview that congressman, to find incriminating evidence about this whole project. I had all I ever needed to blow the man sky high before I went out there. Congressman Jordan is a dirty politician, and politicians, like shoes caked with mud, leave a trail of dirt. It wasn't too hard to find his dirt." Matt's brows rose.

"I could've finished his career, if that had been what I'd wanted to do. No, I went because I'd learned enough about what was going on to have some hope that he might be able to help. Help *me*." A deep sadness filled her eyes.

"But he wouldn't. Not even when I implied I could expose him with my story, use it to ruin all of them—he just laughed and said I had no clue as to who I was up against. Said he would never worry about me ever blowing a story up on him. I knew he had the means to give me what I wanted, but he refused."

Lynn strolled to the wall and leaned her forehead against it. Suddenly, she slammed her fist against it, causing the window to rattle. Then turning to Matt, she said in a quiet but firm voice, "I vowed I would get him back someday. I'd make him pay. I left the office that afternoon convinced I would win his war and prove him wrong." She laughed, but there was no glee. "But they got me, got me good. Now, if I live, what choices do I have?"

"If you live?" Matt said. "Of course you'll live. I'll live. We'll all live and be just fine."

"Oh really?" Her sarcasm sliced the still air. "Go ahead; believe what you will. Me, I choose to see the truth."

"The truth?"

"Why I was saved, brought back to life. Unfortunately, you were just in the wrong place at the wrong time. But, lucky you, you'll regain your life, your career. Go on as if none of this ever happened. Even if Barry's plan doesn't work and that place stays in business, you'll be just fine. Me, well, that's another story." She pushed from the window and started pacing.

"I'm sorry," Matt said softly as he matched her gait and tried to take her hand in his. "I'm sorry about all of it, about Sam, about what's happened to you. But you will be okay. I know it." However, her words chilled him, filled him with a bad premonition.

Vehemently, she pushed his hand away. "I told you before; don't be sorry."

"Why? You obviously care, a lot."

She turned to him. Her lips trembled, but her body was rigid. Then, she sighed as if accepting defeat. "There's nothing more to say. Sam lived, he married me, betrayed me, and then he died."

"Betrayed?" Matt mouthed the word, but it had no sound. She nodded.

"Yes, betrayed. Is that such a shock to you? His betrayal took away everything I had. I don't know if I can ever forgive him for that." Her voice brimmed with bitterness.

"He was such a charmer, so perfect, so endearing; everybody loved Sam, but few ever saw the truth. I never had a clue. I trusted him, believed what he said. I had no reason to doubt his word. It wasn't until he got sick that I learned the truth. You want to know the irony of it all? The people robbing me of me are the very ones who could've saved Sam." She laughed bitterly. "Isn't that just a kicker? Screwed twice in life. They say, things happen in threes. Wonder what the third will be?"

Matt grasped her shoulders and gently pulled her to him. For a fleeting second, she allowed herself to lean against the solid wall of his chest. Just as quickly, she pushed him away.

"I don't need your pity. I'm a survivor. I'll get past this, move on, start again."

"Why do you do this to yourself? Why do you push people away? Is it ... are you ... afraid to love again?"

She spun viciously on her heels and glared at him. Her face was red, and she looked like an explosion waiting to happen. Instead, she whispered, "I can't! Never again. Don't you get it?" she screamed, suddenly. "He didn't betray me for another woman. No, it was a man. Men actually. Too many to count!"

Without warning, she pushed past him and ran for the door. Fingers gripping the knob, she turned and said softly but firmly, "Do yourself a favor; *run*, don't walk, away from me." She pulled the door open and slipped through as it closed quietly behind her. As she ran down the stairs, the sound of her feet hitting the boards punctuated the silence of the empty apartment.

The first picture Barry found in the folder showed a stretcher out on open pavement. Lights were pinpoints in the background, as was an airplane. The stretcher must have been on a tarmac at the airport. It looked like a body was on it, covered by a sheet. Barry started to pass it by, when something caught his eye. A shock of dark hair, a pale hand. He commented lightly, "Stretcher? Ambulance? I thought you had some celebrities here. Dignitaries. Something I could use."

Tim pushed the picture aside. "Forget that one." He flipped past several more scenes of an ambulance and people milling about. Then, he found Harry's prize photos. "These. See?" He tapped the picture of the congressman greeting the plane. "These are the ones we were talking about."

Barry studied each picture, sometimes nodding his head. He saw the congressman and the red-haired woman waiting by a private jet and then with their arms extended to shake hands with the secretary of defense and the vice president of the United States—all fairly normal-looking pictures. Yet according to his two guests, these pictures were taken in the past two days, and he'd heard nothing about the arrival of either man. Politics being what they were, no one like that arrived anywhere without some kind of press coverage, unless it was something so important, so secret, it was worth sacrificing a few photo ops and poll approval points.

"Yes," Barry said, finally looking at Harry and Tim. "I think I'm willing to buy these pictures from you." Barry flipped the last of Harry's pictures facedown and tapped the stack. "I can use these in an upcoming series I'm planning."

"Series?" Harry asked. "I never knew you dabbled in that kind of reporting. I thought society and weddings were your thing."

"They are! Can't you see ..." He flipped to the picture of the redheaded woman holding the congressman's arm. "There's potential here!" Barry forced a wink, praying Harry believed him.

"Yeah, potential for a lawsuit from the congressman's wife."

Barry shook his head playfully. "Harry, come on. No more danger here than if you sell to some tabloid."

"Yeah, but I'm not planning to sell for the entertainment side of it. I'm more concerned about the news value of these."

Barry pushed his chair back and stood. "Concerned about newsworthiness now?" He chuckled loudly. "Well, no matter. You can take it or not. After seeing these, I know why our editor didn't want them. But I do. I can use them in my work. It's your choice; take it or leave it." Sweat pooled under Barry's arms and ran down his neck. They must never know how urgently he needed those pictures.

Finally, Harry sighed. "Okay with you, Tim?" Tim nodded. "Barry, you drive a hard bargain." Harry extended his hand and shook Barry's. "But you've got a deal. How soon can we expect a check?"

"Right now." Barry hoped he didn't look too eager as he whipped out his checkbook.

"What? No company check? I thought you were going to use these for your series."

"Oh, I am. But I'm sure you don't want any delays in payment. I can get reimbursed." He scribbled the amount on the line and tore the paper from the book. Holding the check before Harry, he said, "Now, to cover myself, I need this signed." He produced a sheet of legalese imprinted with the newspaper's logo.

Harry's brows rose. "What's that?"

"Oh come on, Harry, you know the routine. It's your standard form guaranteeing that you won't sell them to another source; the paper now owns the rights, et cetera, and on and on."

"Covering all your bases, eh, Barry? But with your fees, guess we can afford it this time." Harry signed the page, passed it to Tim to sign, and then handed it back to Barry.

"Thanks, gentlemen," Barry said as he took the folder from Tim and patted it. "Good luck in your hunting."

The day had worn into evening, lasted through the night, and dissolved into the next morning. Sunlight streamed through smudged and grimy windows beside Barry's desk and wafted through the rising steam from his sixth cup of coffee since 4:00 a.m. The caffeine was about the only thing keeping him going, that and raw fear mixed with rising anger. Barry raised a stiff neck, stretched, and glanced out the window, surprised to realize he wasn't bone tired through and through.

He'd done it. Hours had melted into one another while he'd pounded on the computer, pulling up old files, tracing old notes. He'd even managed to retrieve the notes Lynn had stored in the various email accounts she'd set up. As pieces fell into place, even more than his greatest hopes allowed, he'd compiled not only a detailed outline of what he planned to do but had also written the first article, stored it electronically, buried under several layers of passwords and encryption, and had sent hard and electronic copies of his notes and documents to three different mailboxes, both snail and email.

With what he'd discovered in the past thirty-six hours along with the DVDs brought from the facility, Barry was sure he had all he needed to blow that operation wide open. He couldn't wait to get the news back to Lynn. They didn't need to worry much longer. In a few hours, he hoped, it would be going to press. Once on the front pages, he was sure Matt and Lynn's safety would be assured.

Glancing at the wall clock, Barry was surprised it was nearly 7:00 a.m. Darlene would be in any moment. He couldn't leave without talking to her first. Pulling his papers together and all his notes, he locked his desk and shuffled off in the direction of her glass-walled command center at the edge of the newsroom.

Despite the early hour, the newsroom throbbed with activity. Its frenzy grew each day in direct proportion to the sun's climb across the sky. Scores of people talked; some shouted, while others were absorbed in their notes, eyes squinting as they peered at flickering computer screens. Editors shouted orders at underlings, and Barry's boss was no exception. She ranted as she paced the floor.

"I find this totally beyond comprehension. I'm surprised that you, Barry Swindmore, could or even would involve yourself in this. It's totally out of your league. Readers expect to see your byline associated with weddings or some other society nonsense." Barry's face fell, but Darlene didn't seem to notice. "I can't go to press with this preposterous story! I'll lose my job, not to mention yours! Don't you even care about that?"

"Yes, I care. I care about society, something you think is nonsense. Because I care about their well-being, I have to print this story. Besides …" He patted the now-worn folder in his lap and then pointed to the outline spanning several sheets of paper on his boss's desk. "… you're not listening. I have the proof here. I tell you, we're talking Pulitzer."

"Pulitzer for creating a national firestorm? Even if it were true, which I fully doubt, all these miracle cures and such that the government has supposedly funded for years, doing all this testing and keeping it secret, who's going to believe you, you of all people, Barry Swindmore, 'Houston's Inside Ear to the Movers, Shakers, and Wedding Chapels'? You, and the *Chronicle* too, will become nothing more than a laughingstock. Besides …" She got very serious. "… Barry, even if every word you print is irrefutable, provable, and solid rock, you're just one man trying to take on the behemoth US Government. You're no match for them and their spin doctors."

Barry chuckled. "No doubt, this current administration has some of the best in the business of spin, but remember one David and one Goliath?"

Darlene smiled for the first time. "You're a tad bigger than David, I believe."

"And tell me, dearie, is bigger not better?"

"Okay. Okay, you win. I want confirmation of every presented fact, and any supposition or inference is to be stated as such and therefore clearly spelled out as not corroborated. Is that clear?" Barry nodded. "How soon will you be ready to roll?"

"First in the series is ready now. Copy is already in your inbox on the network. Next installment will be ready by tomorrow's deadline."

"That soon?"

"That soon." Barry grabbed his papers and the folder and started from her office. Darlene's words stopped him.

"This isn't like you, Barry, to be interested in such things. Care to tell me about it?"

Barry shook his head. "I can't. Confidential sources. They have to be protected at all costs."

"Well, I hope they are protected, because I think they could be in a world of trouble should the wrong people find out where they are right now."

Back at his desk, Barry felt a sudden sense of urgency. Grabbing his bag and stuffing it with everything he felt was important, he rechecked the locks on his files and desk. The click of his shoes as he shuffled quickly down the newly polished tiles of the hall was drowned in the ebb and flow of life encircled in the world of ink and newsprint.

Outside, the sun's warmth caressed his face. The day promised heat, humidity too. Evening would bring more of the same. He cranked the engine of his car, and looking behind him, he slowly backed from his space. From the corner of his right eye, he thought he saw the movement of another car and hit the brakes. Another glance around him and he shook his head. *Too little sleep, too much caffeine.* Straightening the wheel, he pushed the gas pedal down, and the car moved forward. Barry let out a long sigh.

As he turned from the parking lot and maneuvered across several cross streets until he found the feeder road that would push him into a southbound entrance to the Southwest Freeway, he realized Lynn and Matt had expected him back the previous evening. They must be worried sick. Maybe, just maybe, Lynn remembered how he used to forget time when he worked on a story.

Waiting at a stoplight to the merge entrance, he flipped on his cell phone and dialed his home number. It rang and rang, ten times, no answer. Answering machine didn't pick up either. Odd.

Green light. Barry slammed the pedal down, feeling a new urgency to get home. There must be a good reason Matt and Lynn didn't answer. Well, he had told them not to answer. But what if the worst had happened? God forbid, he would be even more determined to see the press shed the light of justice on those who perpetrated their demise.

Just before merging onto the freeway, Barry noticed a dark sedan glide smoothly into place behind him, nudging its way between him and the Toyota previously guarding his tail.

Can't be, Barry told himself as the car effortlessly followed him onto the freeway. He was just too tired, too keyed up. He'd had way too much cloak-and-dagger lately. He'd spent the past day and a half digging through supposed conspiracies and corruption. It had to be just his imagination.

He turned on the radio and caught the morning news broadcast. Nothing of interest, until, *"And finally, the president is on an extended leave, getting some much-needed rest and relaxation at the order of his personal physicians. It has not been revealed how long he intends to remain sequestered, but White House sources have assured all that he remains in command and control of the country. They insist the president merely needs some extended rest. After these messages, more news."*

Barry's pulse slammed against his ears. Extended rest! If they only knew! Barry glanced in the rearview and saw the dark car switch lanes and ease up behind him. Barry shook his head. *Can't be.*

Unexpectedly, that nutcase reporter the paper had hired and fired a few months back came to mind. Barry suddenly wished he'd paid more attention to the man's ramblings. He had constantly ranted about the widespread espionage of the government on its people. Big Brother in three persons, that's what he'd said. Barry had laughed him off, as had most everyone else.

"Oh, think it's funny, huh? Let me tell you, they know what you eat, when you sleep. They read your mail and check your garbage. They listen in on your conversations, even when you're not on the phone. Why, they've got these new technologies that can let them hear what you say through your windows. Why, they even monitor what you watch on TV. Emails are all screened. Nothing is safe!"

"Man, you're crazy!" Barry had shouted in the sorry reporter's face and stomped off. The following day, the reporter disappeared. No one knew just where he'd gone. All assumed he'd been fired. Now Barry wondered.

An opening between two tanker trucks appeared, and Barry sped up and swerved into the space. He no longer saw the dark car. With a sigh, he swiped at the sweat beading on his forehead. Cranking up the air conditioner, Barry let the breeze blow directly on his face. Still, he dripped sweat as if he worked in a lumberyard.

The truck to the right swung onto an exit, and on impulse, Barry veered behind it. As he sped down the ramp, he caught a glimpse of the dark car in his rearview, cutting in front of a car and aiming for the exit.

Barry's breath caught in his throat. He was definitely being followed. Why? Had some of those high-tech gadgets been pointed at his house? How dare they! He had rights. Some amendment protected him, he was sure. He opened the glove compartment and rummaged until he found his trusty bottle of Tums. After swallowing a couple without chewing, he let his breath out slowly and tried to relax, to think of what to do next.

If they indeed were following him, then they knew something. Barry faked a couple turns, trying to throw them off, but the car stayed on his tail. Finally, he ran a red light. Cars honked, and hands gestured at him, but he made it successfully through the intersection, effectively trapping the dark car.

Once home, Barry ran inside; he didn't take time to notice if anything was out of order or if anyone had been there. He didn't even stop to wonder where Matt and Lynn were. He headed straight for his closet.

"Thank gawd!" he said aloud when he found the DVDs just as he'd left them. After stuffing them in a small bag, he ran back to the front door and quickly to his car. Backing into the street, he pressed the gas pedal and sucked in a lungful of cool, air-conditioned air and smoothed the ruffle of hair on his head down. Exhaling slowly, he said aloud, "Got to act calm. Got to keep cool."

He turned the corner and noticed a large, windowless, white panel van parked by the curb. He was nearly to the next street when he saw a dark sedan turn the corner behind him.

"Oh my gawd!" The sweat returned, and his heart skipped several beats. They knew. But did they know what he'd done?

CHAPTER 18

Desperate to catch Lynn as she fled the apartment and her demons, Matt burst through the door, skipped down the steps, and jumped over a bank of privet bushes. Dashing across the side yard toward a grove of pines framing the complex, he shouted, "Lynn, please don't! Don't run from me." Panting, he stopped by her side and took her arm. "I'm not the enemy!"

Lynn stopped, chest heaving and breath short, and stared at him, wild-eyed, an animal in a fight-for-life panic.

"I know you aren't," she whispered as he pulled her to him. "I wanted you to be, because I couldn't bear the pain again. I had to make you the enemy, because if you weren't ... well ... I couldn't let it happen again. I—"

A sudden stirring, like wind rising abruptly before a thunderstorm, erupted. The woods came alive in a startling rush. Shadows solidified into tall figures. Dressed in black, they blended with the deepening night. Silent and quick, they surrounded Matt and Lynn before either could utter a small gasp. Handcuffs secured their arms, and hoods slipped over their heads, ensuring they could neither see nor yell for help.

Dragged across the grass, kicking and squirming, Matt realized that was it. They had been found. The dreaded "bad guys" had them in their grasp.

The dragging stopped. Matt felt himself pushed against an unforgiving metal surface. Doors slammed, and something hit him hard. The black world about him was silent.

Later—how much later, Matt wasn't sure—he was awakened. The hood was gone, and bright light filled his vision. He was in a hospital bed. Leather straps held his arms and legs immobile. In a bed beside his, he spied Lynn. The same straps held her captive. Her eyes, wide and dark, brimmed with fear. He tried to smile at her, but she looked away from him.

Across the vast, open room, a door swung inward, and Congressman Jordan and Ms. Cherie Pittstorm strolled in as if arriving fashionably late for a party.

"Good evening," Cherie said warmly. She extended her hand to Lynn and then retracted it quickly. "It's so good to see you, *again*. Goodness, how I've missed you. Really, I have."

Lynn pushed down into the mattress trying to get as much distance as she could from the woman. Sweat ran down her cheek and shone in the bright light.

"What's the matter?" Cherie continued. "Aren't you glad to see your boss? Afraid you might get a little lecture for skipping out on work?" She clucked and pointed her finger at Lynn. "No need to be afraid if you're doing what you're supposed to do. But get your finger stuck in the cookie jar and you're sure to get caught. Looks to me like you got your entire body stuck, in the past, and that's what made it so easy for us to find you."

Cherie turned to the congressman. "I told you we'd find her there. Too many old memories in that apartment, memories that just wouldn't stay repressed. She just had to go back and see if she could find anything that might help her finish her story, blow the whistle, and spill the beans, or is it the milk? I forget which it is, but she's going to save the world, or is it yourself, dear?"

Cherie scratched her forefinger under Lynn's chin. "That's it, isn't it? You're not out to save the world, but yourself." She turned to the congressman. "Thom, you were right, partly. She did want a little of our miracle potion for herself. She needed to get rid of a pesky little HIV infection. Well, I think we can do it, can't we? Clear up her insides, that is. Put them to good use."

Matt tried to catch Lynn's eye. She refused to look at him.

The congressman nodded, but he didn't speak. He pointed with his chin toward the door.

"Okay. I know you're in a hurry." Cherie winked at the man. "Like my little alcove, huh?" She turned to the white-jacketed men who had entered the room.

"Don't waste any time. Get them ready." To a dark-suited man who followed the doctor, she said, "Potter, this time, keep a constant eye on them. In a little while, you won't need to bother, because they won't be able to run, or do much of anything else, for that matter. But until then, you'd better not let them get past you and your bunch of dim-witted clowns you call security agents!"

Cherie turned back to the congressman. "As for us, we'll have a leisurely visit in my office while our two friends enjoy our gracious hospitality." She winked and took his elbow. "Come along now."

Barry's adrenaline rush was on high. He pushed the gas pedal as far as it would go and didn't signal as he swerved suddenly to his left and onto the next street. What he didn't expect to find was another dark sedan, blocking the road.

Barry slammed the car in reverse and not looking behind him, popped the pedal to the floor. Tires squealing, he jerked the wheel and careened in a half circle. Some immovable object stopped him abruptly, and glass exploded and showered as metal crunched.

Slowly, he glanced behind him. Another dark sedan, like the first, had pulled in behind him and blocked the other end of the street. Barry had rammed into it, pushing in the front door to the passenger's side.

Sticking his finger in his mouth, Barry gnawed at his nail. Sweat ran down his chin. Maybe he wasn't so good at this cloak-and-dagger conspiracy stuff. Two men in dark suits emerged from the front car and three more from the one behind him. By the time they got to Barry's side of the car, his hands were in the air and shaking.

"Please don't shoot!" Barry shouted as they opened his door. There were no guns in sight, anywhere.

"Are they awake yet?" Cherie paced before the two prone bodies in hospital beds side by side. A thin white sheet was all that covered them. Neither moved, only the telltale rise and fall of their chests gave any hint of life sustained. Cherie stopped pacing and puffed hungrily on a cigarette. One of the white-coated men beside her frowned.

"Not here. Not now. See the oxygen tanks? Want to start a fire? Or better yet, blow the place up?"

Cherie blew smoke in his face and laughed. "Come on, Charles. Do you always have to be so melodramatic? I know what I'm doing. There's no oxygen running in here."

"Not now, there isn't," Charles Benson answered slowly, "but soon, there will be. That is, if you intend to continue with your plan. It will be necessary to keep the organs viable until they can be removed and preserved."

Cherie nodded slowly. "Okay, I see your point. It is a little premature." She ground her cigarette out in a paper cup half full of cold coffee. The door opened, and another man in a white jacket entered.

"What do you have for me, Phillippe?"

"Blood work is in. All results are negative."

"Negative, you say?" Cherie seemed unable to believe her ears.

"That's right. They're free and clean. No diseases, no infections, nothing objectionable. You've got yourself a group of harvestable organs."

"What about the president? Did you get what you needed for him?"

Phillippe nodded. "We took two pints of blood, more than

enough for him, maybe a little too much for her." Phillippe glared at Lynn. "The president's receiving the first doses now. But I think all will be well. He's already responding dramatically. I believe he's out of danger as we speak, and that all you planned for him will be successful."

Cherie glanced at the man in a dark suit standing opposite her and clapped her hands together.

"It's really going to work. Not only have we proven we can extend life, alter it to our means, we can even make a tidy profit on our rejects, by cleaning them up and selling the parts." She giggled wickedly. "We push forward now. No more worry about these two." She sighed and shook her head. "What a trip they've been. Why, to get away from us once is a feat, but twice? Well, no one does that and survives."

Cherie rubbed her hand across Thom Jordan's back. "The secretary of defense is waiting for our call. All we have to do is say yes, and we can put it all to bed, tonight."

"And the president?"

"What about him?" Cherie's smile faded slightly. "There's no reason to be concerned with him now. You heard he's out of danger. And his first test, signing into law that legislation, well, it'll be proven within the week. It's all roses for us, now. Isn't that what you wanted?"

Thom Jordan's smile wasn't as bright as Cherie's. "What's the matter, Thom? Not saying much tonight? Scalpel got your tongue?" Cherie's grating laughter escalated.

"Nothing's the matter; I just have some things on my mind."

"Other than me?" Her voice softened to a purr. "What could possibly be more important?" Her hands were under his collar, probing and tickling, toying with him. "I don't get you, Thom. All these years, we've been planning and sacrificing and doing all we could to get to this point. We've sold it to the highest bidder, and who would've ever thought our own country would outbid some of those Middle-Eastern oil conglomerates?" She pointed at the two bodies before her. "Why we're even going to make a nice, tidy profit on the side. Money will never be a problem again."

"Just spending it will," Thom muttered.

Cherie looked genuinely surprised at his comment. "When I kicked the sand off my feet after leaving Foley, Alabama, I vowed I would never be poor again, that I would have all I wanted and would do with it whatever I pleased. Now that I'm within grasp of my goal, I'm certainly not going to change my plans over some lame attempt on your part to guilt me into doing something different."

Thom narrowed his eyes as he glared at her. With a small shake of his head, he pushed her away and strode to the side of one of the beds. Abruptly, he turned to one of the doctors standing nearby. "Let's get this over with."

Charles Benson nodded and stepped to the head of Matt's bed. He slipped an oxygen mask over Matt's nose and mouth and adjusted the flow rate. Next, he went to Lynn's bed and did the same.

"Wait!" Cherie interrupted. "Don't we want to wake them first? We can't end it all while they're asleep, unaware and pain free." Her wicked laugh grew louder. "Don't these two deserve to know how their bodies will further benefit those most deserving?"

Thom shook his head as he looked at her. "Sometimes I can't believe you're real. You're such a sadist, a real class act," he added with a sarcastic tone.

Cherie grinned her Cheshire-Cat grin. "Of course, I'm so glad you agree!" She pulled a cigarette from her case and lit it. Inhaling deeply, she said, "Oh man, this is good."

Matt yawned and stretched. Slowly, arms and legs feeling heavier than he could ever imagine, he pushed himself upright. His body didn't want to cooperate. It strained and fought valiantly to keep him from victory, yet Matt persisted and managed to sit up. He glanced about him. The cabin seemed empty. There was no fire under the mantle, nothing cooking on the stove. Darkness permeated the room, light neither filtered through the windows, nor shone from anywhere except for a flickering lantern centered on the kitchen table.

A slight movement in the shadows, and Matt's heart leaped, accelerated by fear and then surprise.

"Ah, I see you're coming 'round now. That's good. But you don't have much time, not much at all. You've got to do something quick before …"

"Before what?" Matt thought he shouted, but it seemed he whispered, because the farmer put his hand behind his ear.

"Sorry, son, I'm having trouble hearing you. Your voice is so soft tonight. I can hardly make out your words."

Matt stared at him, desperately trying to keep his image from wavering. What was wrong?

"What is it I need to do?" he finally managed to ask.

"Save yourself. Save her. It's up to you." The farmer slowly stood. He seemed bent, tired, and suddenly old. His life appeared to be accelerating toward an end. Matt felt a sudden cold in his gut. Ice seemed to stream through his veins.

"How do I save us? How can I do it?"

The farmer's voice was faint and fading. "Fight them. Don't ever stop. Fight them to the end."

In the corridor outside the brightly lit room where Matt and Lynn slept on their deathbeds, a herd of dark-clothed figures slipped silently into the hallway. Like oil seeping through the ground and flowing thickly but silently around every obstacle met, men in soft-soled shoes emerged from most every door and corner of the hall. Quickly, and quietly, the black-clad group positioned themselves by the entrance to the main lab and waited for their signal.

Outside the building, nearly three times as many waited. Security agents, formerly under Potter's direction, had been detained, taken away, and otherwise eliminated from the picture. The facility was now in the complete control of the FBI, and Sculler and Maderm were responsible for the change in command.

The assault team's leader, waiting by the door, turned to the one man most valuable in helping them gain their position, Potter. The team leader gripped Potter's shoulder briefly and mouthed the word, "Thanks." Then, he glanced back at his group, held up three fingers and then two. When he reached one, the group moved as one and stormed through the doors.

Potter backed away and watched, his role complete. He only hoped these people remembered his help when all the smoke cleared and the punishment was meted out. After all, he'd only followed orders. He had been employed by Uncle Sam, and he was always obedient. Sighing, he strolled quietly toward an exit. The long-anticipated retirement on the beaches of North Carolina, idly sitting in the sand, sipping lemonade—well, it had all but faded.

The farmer's face disappeared. The chill deepened, and Matt shivered. But there was something warm there too. The cold hadn't completely filled him. Warmth crept over his body, like slow-moving lava, and his skin began to sting. He shook his head. His arms and legs were alive again, vibrant, full of energy. He opened his eyes.

A mask covered his nose and mouth, and he heard the hiss of forced air. He was still bound by the leather straps, but he could move his head. Turning as far as he could, he caught a glimpse of another bed beside his, a body on it covered by a sheet. Suddenly, it felt like there was a cold spike in his heart. Lynn! She wasn't moving.

Frantic, Matt pushed against the binds holding him. He moaned as he fought the restraint, too weak to budge its unbending force. A flash—a vision of the farmer, words telling him to hurry—that he must fight flickered in his mind. He couldn't let them win.

Matt kicked, and the bed's wheels rolled slightly. He kicked again, and it jerked again. He kept wiggling, fighting for life. There was movement from behind. He heard footsteps.

"Ah, I see he's coming to. Maybe you should crank up the oxygen a little more. I want him totally aware of everything." The female voice was smooth, confident.

The white-jacketed man glared at the woman. "I will when you put that cigarette out!"

"Oh, all right." The woman tossed the butt of her cigarette into the trash can by the desk.

"Can we hurry this up? What about the girl? What are her signs?" It was a male voice.

"Oh, Thom," the woman chided, "be patient. Charles knows what he's doing. Don't you, Charles?"

Charles Benson, that Cherie woman, Thom Jordan—who else was there he couldn't see? Matt squirmed until he managed to get his head so that he could see his enemy. Dr. Benson smiled down at him.

"Just a little prick here." The doctor grinned as he flashed a long hypodermic needle so that the artificial light glimmered on the golden liquid in the syringe. He lowered the needle until it pricked through the skin on Matt's arm. Suddenly, the doors burst open, and the room flooded with dark figures.

Frantic scuffling and shoving broke out, and somewhere in it all, Matt's mask was torn from his face. Screams erupted, and the bustle grew frantic. Crashes filled the air as glass broke and objects were thrown. His bed was bumped and pushed so much that he grew disoriented.

Suddenly, there was a new round of screaming and pushing. Someone shouted, "The waste basket! It's on fire. There's oxygen in use here. Get it out, now!"

One of the black-clad figures broke loose from the melee and ran to Matt. Frantically, he worked to free him from his bonds.

"The girl," Matt tried to ask, but his voice was hoarse, and the man seemed to have trouble hearing him. "The girl, where is she?"

As he shrugged, the room turned into a blinding, bright white. Like when one exhaled and then filled one's lungs to bursting, the room seemed to expand and then contract as all the air was sucked out in a giant explosion. The walls caved, and the ceiling tumbled down. Fire filled every vacant space, and the last thing Matt remembered was smoke clouding his vision and the sensation of choking, desperate for air as the flames robbed the space of the last of its oxygen.

CHAPTER 19

The sun was still two hours away from rising, but Katie Grayson was up. She paced the kitchen floor, waiting for the coffee to finish its eternal dripping. Jerry sat at the kitchen table, head propped on his hands, and eyes closed. The FBI agent assigned to them by Sculler sat across from him, and the big man fidgeted constantly as if some Texas ants were in his pants biting the fire out of him.

"I just don't understand," Katie said as she pulled three mugs from the cabinet. Her hands shook, but the steel-plated armor guarding her soul kept her emotions in check. She spoke first to the agent and then to Jerry. "What do you think they did with them? Will they be all right?"

The agent looked down at his feet before answering. "I can't lie to you, ma'am. Things could look better, but …" He tried to smile. "… we do have our best working on it. We'll get to the bottom. Maderm and Sculler will be sure of that."

"But we haven't heard from them. We don't even know what they planned. Only said something was breaking, and they would have news for us soon. So, where are they?"

The agent shrugged. "We're just to sit tight and wait for their word."

"Can't do that." Katie poured the first cup of coffee. "I'm awakened in the middle of the night and told something's happened but I can't be told yet just what, and I'm just supposed to sit tight?"

"Come on, girl." Jerry gripped Katie's wrist and pulled her toward him. "We're all freaking here, and there's just not much more we can do but wait."

Katie squirmed from Jerry's grip and returned to the coffeemaker. She poured two more cups and set them on the table. "Sugar? Cream?" Both men shook their heads.

While the two men seemed content to sip their coffee in a leisurely way, Katie couldn't sit still. A relentless energy pounded inside, releasing its venom as she paced. Back and forth, she walked; her two companions remained silent. Finally, when she could stand it no longer, she grabbed the TV remote and pointed it at the set in the den. CNN Headline News filled the room.

"Allegations concerning a large-scale cover-up and conspiracy have been made against the United States Government regarding medical research and testing. A report in today's Houston Chronicle *states that Congressman Thom Jordan of California, Secretary of Defense Christopher Steven, and other, as-yet-unnamed government officials have conspired to produce and test on human subjects, against their will, a new series of compounds, which reportedly can prevent aging, heal cancer-ravaged tissue, and in some, generate new living tissue. While these compounds have reportedly accomplished all of the above, in some, it is believed serious side effects resulted, some of which were terminal."*

As the reporter spoke, a grainy picture of the congressman and a red-haired woman greeting the secretary of defense as he descended from a private jet at Houston's George Bush Intercontinental Airport flashed on the screen.

"Confidential sources claim to have irrefutable proof of this conspiracy and indicate plans to further prove government coercion and involvement in a scheme that has been in development for over sixty

332

years. As more details become available, we will keep you informed. Now on to other news ... uh ..."

The reporter stopped midsentence and glanced at a sheet of paper that had been thrust before her eyes. *"This breaking news just in ..."* She coughed and cleared her throat before continuing.

"At approximately 11:00 p.m. central daylight time, there was a large explosion in the pine woods of southeast Texas, north of Houston. While the exact cause of the explosion is unknown at this time, sources say it occurred in an unoccupied building situated on unused government property approximately twenty miles northeast of Conroe. It is not known if there were any casualties. However, sources confirm a large area surrounding the facility has been evacuated. Rumors of a biological contagion being released by the explosion have spread rapidly throughout the region. We'll keep you informed as details come in. Stay tuned for more after these messages."

Jerry and the FBI agent had silently joined Katie, watching, absorbing the news, mouths open. The FBI agent slapped his hand across his chest. "Looks like they've opened the box, Pandora's box, and they don't even have a clue as to how many bees are hidden in that cave."

When Matt awoke, metal rails of a hospital bed surrounded him. Shaking his head, he glanced at the bandages on his arm and leg and felt the one on his forehead. The room was so familiar; had he been there before?

Katie Grayson ran into the room, followed by Jerry and Chad.

"Oh. honey!" Katie fell on her son. "Does it hurt much? You were so lucky. You really didn't get burned much at all. But all those others ..." She shook her head. "You were so lucky to have survived."

"Survived?" Matt whispered. "Was I the only one?" Vague flashes of memory surfaced. Orange flames, pine woods, running, fighting for his life. "You know, I had the weirdest dream," Matt said. "I was in a plane crash, and we found this little town. The people there were still in the forties. And there wasn't a doctor until I went to town and found one and … Wow, was it weird!"

Katie frowned, as did Jerry and Chad. "Why do you think that's so weird?" she asked.

A chill ran down Matt's back. "You didn't answer. Was I the only one?"

"Only one what?" Jerry asked gruffly.

"Survivor?"

Jerry glanced at Katie and Katie at Chad. No one seemed to want to say anything.

"It was rough, Matt. You had a rough time of it. They barely got to you in time. You were going under when they found you. And then there was the explosion. Some didn't make it."

"But her, where is she?" The panic alarm was ringing, and Matt tried to crawl from the bed. Katie and Chad held him down.

"Come on. Answer me! I'm tired of all this. I want to know. Did she make it?"

A small smile erupted on Katie's face. "Yes, she did."

"So, where is she?"

The smile faded. "I don't know. They got her out before you. She was out of the building before the explosion. All we know is she wasn't harmed by it."

"It wasn't a dream," Matt said quietly, more to himself than to the group before him.

Katie took his hand in hers and squeezed it tightly. "Oh, son, I wish it were a dream, but it isn't. It did happen. But you can be proud. You and your … uh … friend, well, you were responsible for bringing to light the mess going on at that place. You began its end."

Chad grabbed the remote and turned up the volume on the TV. The local news was just beginning. The anchor started the lead story.

"Today, a little over a week after the fiery explosion that demolished a portion of the now-infamous government-sponsored research lab in

the pine woods near Conroe, Texas, Congressman Thom Jordan, one of the facility's directors and grandson of one of the founders, was indicted by a federal grand jury on five charges of fraud and conspiracy. In addition, Defense Secretary Christopher Steven was also indicted on two counts of fraud and conspiracy. As details surface, we have been led to believe further charges are forthcoming. An employee of the facility and one of its directors, Cherie Pittstorm, was indicted earlier this week on two counts, one of aiding and abetting both Congressman Jordan and Defense Secretary Steven and another of conspiring to defraud the United States Government. An independent counsel has been named to further investigate the government's role in this facility. Political analysts and observers are in rare agreement that only the tip of the iceberg has been discovered in this seemingly deep and far-reaching conspiracy.

"In further developments from the aftermath and cleanup of the massive explosion, which consumed nearly all of the main research facility, all bodies and individuals linked with the facility have been accounted for, except for one. A search is still in progress for one Phillippe Degenaveux. He is believed to have been at the site of the initial explosion and therefore, presumed dead, but the coroner's office has yet to identify any remains belonging to him.

"In other news, the president, back in the Oval Office after an extended period of rest and recuperation from some minor health problems, jumped back into action today as he signed into law the hotly contested Congressional Bill 456. White House observers were shocked by his action, stating they were certain he was against the appropriations measure, which in part contained massive spending directives for new health-care initiatives. Aides and friends of the president are baffled by his turn, and there has even been speculation that possibly he returned to the office too soon. However, White House physicians and the president's personal physician have assured the public that the president has never been in better health than at the present time. More after these messages."

Chad bent over and pulled up a stack of newspapers. He tossed them onto Matt's lap.

"I've been saving these for you while you were snoozing in that bed there. Boy!" He chuckled. "Seems you've developed a real liking of Hermann Hospital. Second time this year you've spent a week sleeping away like a baby, missing all the great news of the century."

Matt glanced at the papers. Headlines broke a story he never would have believed had he and Lynn not lived it. His picture, along with hers, was plastered on the front page of one of the daily issues. Other issues held headlines that chilled him deeply. Barry had done as promised. His series was the talk of the nation and the world.

"Lucky for you, those FBI agents, Sculler and Maderm, managed to connect with your friend there." Chad pointed to the paper and a picture of Barry Swindmore. "They caught him just before some people from that facility could manage to nab him. Barry figured out what must've happened to you two. He's the one who told them to get back to the facility and get you out of there!"

Matt stared at his brother. "Sculler and Maderm, do I know them?"

Chad chuckled. "I think we need to do a little catching up!"

Indeed, Matt had not dreamed it all. The facility was very real. Human testing had been conducted under the thickest of cloaks. And while the secret testing had been brought to light, it seemed the public was more concerned about the potential of the miracle drugs rather than the sins of those who'd developed them.

Maybe it was the irony of it all. While so wrong, it held such promise. They had cured some forms of cancer, given people new leases on life. Some had regained a youth long lost. And others, well, others had been given gifts no one in this life was prepared to receive.

The farmer's face came to mind. Matt could see him smiling, happy, and radiant. The warmth filled Matt, and his spirit seemed to soar. As he considered it, he could see Lynn's face, smiling, happy too, hugging the old man. Weird, Matt shook his head.

"Daydreaming, were you?" Jerry squinted as he leaned over Matt. "Looked like you were out of here for a bit."

"Maybe I was."

"Well, don't go too far. You're a hot item right now. Not only does every director in Hollywood want you working for them, they want your story too! I've got three proposals waiting. They want you to produce, and star in, if you want, films about you and your story. Feel up to it?"

Matt looked at the faces before him. His family, his agent, everyone who mattered the most was there, everyone, except for one.

"There're some things I've got to take care of first," he said as he pulled the covers up to his chin and shut his eyes, praying for yet one more miracle.

The night swirled about him, shifting and drifting, cloaking him in its secrecy. Warm vapors rose from the earth, carrying on them the earthy scent of a ground baked by the sun until fresh and warm, ready to cool in the evening breezes. The moon, almost full, watched, peeking through gently swaying treetops. Even though the Man in the Moon's face was turned on its side, he smiled.

Perched on top of his mom's front porch steps, Matt felt the complete desolation and isolation of loneliness. Glancing again at the moon, he sighed.

Exhaustion slumped his shoulders. The information, the circumstances, the events, the nightmare that was all too real, all fought for space, demanding reason inside the limited amount of his body designated for his cranium. Suddenly restless, he jumped down the final three steps to the brick walk.

Home from the hospital, ostensibly healed, ready to return to the demands of his work in Los Angeles, Matt knew he had every reason to be ecstatic. He'd survived, truly, and in the process gained even greater recognition and demand for his work. But, the consuming emptiness inside wouldn't be sated by the world's accolades.

Matt rambled aimlessly across the uneven bricks, not sure what he planned. He had no energy left, yet he was unable to sit still. The others had long ago given up, both on him and on the day. Chad was in his room sleeping; his mom was in hers. He wanted to be in his, but he couldn't let go of the tension cramping his muscles.

As he strolled away from the house and the night deepened and shadows grew larger, he felt as if he carried the burdens of the world on his shoulders. Despite his knowledge of all that had happened, he didn't want to admit but deep down knew that he had played a part in the ending of the charade, the farce of the facility. People, most of whom he'd never know, now owed him a debt of gratitude he didn't want. Nothing could ever compensate for the lost years, the time robbed from them. Yet, some had benefited. Some had gotten extra years as a result of the misguided work.

Hands in his pockets, he continued to walk further from the house, but the emptiness followed. He couldn't escape it. He knew there was only one thing that could fill that cold, aching spot in his heart. *No, can't think like that*. It would never work out. *She won't have anything to do with me.* The silent arguments continued. *Lynn can never love me,* he concluded, making his heart constrict, and he gasped for breath, the sensation was so real.

He should never have let her go. He'd stood there and watched her walk away, so in love with her that he was willing to do whatever she asked.

"Matt, this all started because I tested positive for HIV." She had refused to look at him. "I can't escape it, not for the rest of my life. You know that. If I love you, then I can't be with you. I can't condemn you to the life I have because of my own selfish desires."

Tears had trickled down her cheeks, and her pain was as tangible and hard as concrete. It would take a chisel of more horsepower than he possessed to break through her walls.

"Lynn …" He'd gripped her hands tightly. "… don't say no, to you or to me. We can overcome this. We can have a future." He laughed sadly. "Look at what we've survived together. Surely, this is nothing by comparison."

Her face had softened, and a little warmth crept into her eyes when she smiled. But the sadness remained. "Oh, how I wish things were different. How I wish I could change them. I was so sure I'd found the answer when I went to California to meet the congressman. I truly thought I'd found the story of the century and a cure as well. It was the cure I really sought. But the facility is gone now, the research along with it. I guess I missed out." She'd shrugged. "It was a good try, but I didn't quite make it. Sometimes, that's just how the cards fall." She had straightened then and extended her hand to him.

"You saved my life. For that, I'll always be grateful. Now please, let me save yours." She'd hugged him briefly, turned, and run to her waiting car.

As Matt remembered their parting, tears ran down his cheeks. He wanted to kick himself, or worse, hurt himself. How could he have ever let her walk out of his life like that? How could he stand by and let the best thing that had ever happened to him stroll away as if she were nothing?

Matt found himself by the edge of the woods that ran on both sides of the long, curving drive that led to the house from the main road. The only sounds were those of cicadas, crickets, frogs, and a few other assorted species of the animal kingdom, who joined in one humming chorus. He'd always loved their song; as a child, they had assured him summer was still strong and school was only a dark spot in the distant future. On many hot, sultry nights, those same night sounds had soothed him to sleep. They'd kept his mind away from the monsters of sleep and on the simple realities of life. How he wished they could bring soothing comfort that night.

Lynn drove as fast as she could get the old Escort to go. Barry, in the seat beside her, gripped the armrest with one hand, his seat belt with the other. Lynn wove through the light traffic on the Harris Toll Road expertly, as if she'd done it all her life.

"I can't believe it, Barry," she glanced at him as she moved into the center lane. "It's just unreal. Something I'd hoped desperately for and thought I'd never get, not especially after all that happened. Now, it's true."

"Yes, honey, it's true. You're alive and well, and it looks like you'll be in that state for quite a while, unless ..." He puffed on his cigarette and then crushed it in the ashtray as a fit of coughing racked him. "... unless you keep driving like you're running from hell."

"Maybe I am running from hell. Sure feels like I've been there."

"Well, dearie, you're not there now. And it can't come get you. You got that cure you needed and wanted so badly."

"And more." Lynn beamed as she considered whom she was going to see. "Just think, Barry, I'm really going to meet him! Promise you'll be gentle. Be considerate. Remember, I'm breaking my own rule by letting you get this story. Never let personal issues mingle with work."

"But you were personally involved. Your work pushed you into it. I'll be considerate." He laid his hand gently on her knee. "You're my friend." He seemed to choke on the word, and Lynn thought she caught a glimmer of a tear in his eye. "I do only my best for my friends. You'll be pleased with the story, I'm sure."

"Best? How can anything top your series? You brought down a sizable chunk of the United States Government. Opened the eyes of a nation and most of the world and then survived the ensuing storms that erupted. Isn't a Pulitzer enough? How much more do you need?"

Barry didn't answer. A slow car loomed in front, and Lynn jerked to the right lane. She stomped on the accelerator, and the car seemed to slow before it caught itself and moved forward.

"I hate this car. It's got to be the slowest one on the road. To make it up the on-ramp, I have to turn off the air conditioner or the thing just sits there. I feel like I have to wind my rubber band to get it to go!"

"Well, why didn't you get something else? That fancy boyfriend of yours, couldn't he afford something better? Problem is you just don't treat him right. Now, what he needs is someone who will give him the treatment he deserves." Barry's eyes twinkled.

Lynn glared at her friend. "First of all, he's not my boyfriend.

Never has been, never will be! So, why is it you refuse to believe me when I say, I said good-bye? He's out of my life."

"Sizzh!" Barry lightly touched Lynn's arm with his forefinger and then jerked it abruptly back as if he'd burned it on her skin. "Hot, aren't we? Didn't mean to land on any nerves, dearie, but some things are obvious, even to one so love impaired as me."

For a moment, Lynn looked as if she might slap him. Words bubbled on her lips, but none untangled her tongue. Barry erased his grin and said quietly, "He doesn't know, does he?"

She shook her head. "I didn't find out until yesterday. I haven't seen him in almost two months. I told you, he's gone. I read he's back in LA getting ready to start another movie. He's out of my life, and I'm glad! That's right, glad. All he did was cause me trouble, and I don't need trouble. I can get enough of that on my own, thank you very much!"

Barry chuckled and crossed his arms over his chest. He clucked like a momma hen. "Lordy, girl, if you aren't in love, I don't know who is. Just do me a favor, when you plan the wedding, don't have any of that outrageous Pepto-Bismol pink all the girls are going for these days. It's enough to turn everybody's stomach sour before they ever reach the reception and eat some tainted fish eggs."

"Barry!" Lynn shouted. She jerked the wheel, sorely tempted to ram Barry's side of the car into one of the concrete walls lining the freeway. "There's no wedding, because there's no boyfriend! Now, will you please drop the whole thing?"

Barry leaned back in his seat and glared at her from the corner of his eye. "Well, dearie, if there ever is one, I must direct it for you. You know, weddings are my specialty."

"I know," Lynn whispered.

An hour later, they found the rutted road leading to the old farmer's house. It wasn't as hard to find as Lynn had feared. She was surprised she remembered so much of the lay of the land, considering the circumstances of her visits to the place. But, conversations with Sculler and Maderm had forced her to remember the way. In hours spent before them, she'd answered every possible question, remembered every detail of every minute of her horror. To their credit, she owed her life to them, for they had arranged the assault that had freed her and Matt from that horrid facility. But the agony of their questioning afterward had caused her to question her gratitude for their deed. Still, it was their urging that had caused her to get another blood test. And it was their information that had proved what she'd begun to suspect.

At the cabin, Lynn cut the engine and suddenly found it hard to move. As she sat staring at the little white house, its significance washed over her. Her life was rooted there. It had literally ended and begun there. If it were not for the farmer and his care, she would not be alive at that point and place in time.

The door opened, and the old man, grinning broadly, rushed out to greet them. He swooped Lynn into his arms and hugged her tightly as if he'd never let her go. When he did push her back, tears ran down his face, as well as Lynn's.

"I can't believe it. I wanted it to be true but never in my wildest dreams." He pulled her to him and hugged her even harder.

"Oh, but you can't wish it any more than I have!" Lynn squeezed him back as Barry watched and dabbed at his eyes.

"Lordy," Barry muttered, "I thought weddings were the only thing to do me in." He dabbed again and then blew his nose loudly. "Don't you think we'd better get going with this?"

Nodding but saying nothing, Lynn dropped her arms and grasped the farmer's hand as he led the way inside the old house. As usual, the place was filled with a tempting aroma.

"Oh, just a little stew like Martha used to make." He stopped and clutched his heart. "Oh, how I miss her." His chin wavered. "Since the facility was ... well, you know, our treatments have stopped. She didn't last a day. And I don't know how much time I have left." He'd aged considerably since she'd last seen him, frighteningly so.

"There's nothing they can do?"

He shook his head slowly. "All the serum was destroyed in the explosion. And the formulas? Well, who knows where they are? Some say they were destroyed. Others say they don't know. But who can trust those politicians? They're all liars!"

"But we've got to do something! We'll find those formulas. I'll find someone to reformulate them. I've just found you. I can't let you go now! I'll—"

Her great-grandfather grasped her hand. "I've lived a full life, two times over. It's time for it to end. Do you realize had it not been for those people and their little experiment, we'd never have known each other? My time would've ended long before yours began. Think about it. There's your miracle. We got to meet and know each other. There's only one thing I regret."

"What's that?"

"I just wish Martha could be here for this. She so longed for grandchildren, and when our son was killed in that fire ..."

"My father's father?"

The farmer nodded. "Well, we gave up hope, knew there would never be any more offspring. It was an end to our lineage."

"But it's not, is it? Dad was taken in by an orphanage, and I'm here!"

"Yes, you are. You are the sole survivor, the only one to continue the family line."

Barry cleared his throat. "Not quite the sole survivor." Lynn jerked toward Barry and frowned. He narrowed his eyes and glared at her. "Don't tell me you're not telling him!"

"What is it?" The farmer glanced quickly from Lynn to Barry.

Lynn swallowed and said softly, "No, it appears I'm not the only one. Some records I was shown claim I'm related to the president of the United States. They claim he was taken to a different orphanage and that he and my father were never told about each other. But I never really believed them. Now with all that's happened, I may never be able to find out, and that's okay. I found you, and that's more than enough for me. And despite all the bad of that place ..." Lynn looked into the eyes of the old farmer as a tear slipped down her cheek, and she smiled. "... it seems the treatment did one thing good. I got my cure."

The farmer's grin was wide. "That so?" He hugged her tightly. Chin against her head, he said softly, "Well, looks like more than one good thing came out of all this."

Lynn backed away and stared into his eyes. "Maybe a lot of good will come, but it will take time. Someday, someone will find those formulas and recreate the work. We can only pray next time around that someone won't go and get greedy."

"But it will be a while," the farmer replied. "For now, you've got your life back, and I've had more than I deserved of mine. We should be thankful. God has blessed us. We should never refuse what He gives."

Lynn stared at her great-grandfather, the man whose life she'd nearly missed, but by the irony of her mishap had found. Her time on this earth with him would be short, but the precious hours they did have were worth more than the price she'd paid to gain them.

"What do you mean, 'refuse what He gives'?"

"Just that. When He gives you a gift, don't dare throw it back at Him. And He's given you one of His greatest, laid him at your feet, and you walked away."

Lynn's jaw dropped as she stared at him. "What? How did you—"

He grinned, and his tooth glimmered. "There're lots I know. It was His gift to me. They started giving me those treatments, those compounds from the facility. Remember, I told you how I could see things, hear them too, even things that were happening far away? It wasn't a dream. It was as real as us sitting here now. I soon learned I could send my thoughts to people. And I could know when those people needed me. It's how I came to be there for you ... and Matt." His voice softened on the last word.

Lynn couldn't seem to make her tongue work. She stared at the old farmer, amazed by his words.

"Go to him now," he whispered. "He needs you. He's dying inside, and you alone have the ability to give him life. His pain is deep and growing deeper." He took her hands in his, and his warmth crept through her body and lodged in her soul.

"How could you? How do you—"

"Know? It's like I said. It was His gift to me. He used them ..." The farmer nodded toward the outside. "... to give it to me. I'm just taking advantage of what's been given." The farmer glanced past Lynn at Barry.

"We'll have to finish this another time. She has somewhere she needs to be right now."

Barry's face split into a giant grin. Nodding rapidly, he gathered his things. Quietly he said, "Yes, sir," and gripped Lynn's elbow. "Come on, dearie. I believe we have to get your suitcase packed and you off to the airport!"

Hair longer, a mustache covering a previously clean-shaven face, dark glasses over his eyes, Phillippe glanced over his shoulder. Announcements from loudspeakers covering the entire concourse rattled on nonstop, first in English and then Spanish. *Why not French?* he wondered. He shrugged and continued scanning the rows of lockers, looking for his number. Finding it, he quickly inserted the key and pulled the manila envelope from the small interior. After pulling a smaller envelope from the larger one and stuffing it into his breast pocket, he rammed the larger envelope into his small carry-on bag and zipped it shut.

Fingers clamped tightly about the handle of his bag, he looked over his shoulder and hurried toward the departure gate for his flight, Houston to Sao Paulo, nonstop. He'd never been there before; he'd never been anywhere before as a very wealthy man. This was the first trip of many, he hoped. *The papers.* He patted his pocket.

His new fortune was compressed and compiled into an envelope he could fold and stuff into his inner pocket. He already had a contract for the development of the first of Dereck's formulas. Poor Dereck. Pity actually, the man had met with such an early demise. He had been so bright, so insightful, and so decent. But then again, if Dereck hadn't, he wouldn't be contemplating a very lucrative future. Everyone else who could possibly lay claim to what he now possessed was either dead or behind bars. And before they could get from behind those shackles and out to freedom, he'd be long into business. Copyrights and patents, it would all be his, and he wouldn't sell his soul to the United States Government. No, Brazilian businessmen were his benefactors now. They were ready and more than willing to underwrite his research and production of the miracle drug of the century.

Phillippe grinned as his flight was called. He gave the attendant his boarding pass and slipped into his first-class seat. A martini in hand and music in his ears, he leaned against the headrest and smiled. What more could he ask for? He had it all. And soon, select others in the world would benefit from his good fortune. Life was good, very good indeed.

The day had been long, hot, and miserable. The prolonged Los Angeles heat wave made the air stifling and still. He longed for the mugginess of Houston, for the sweat of a hard day's labor, for the fulfillment of accomplishment.

He paced the floor, script in hand, unseen. Each time he looked at the words, they blurred and melted into one dark blob on the white page. "Blast it all!" he shouted and threw the papers on his desk.

Matt ripped the shirt from his back and tossed it across the room. Sweat glistened on his chest despite the air-conditioning. His pacing intensified, and he was suddenly tempted to call Jerry and tell him to forget it. He just couldn't do it. The script held too many reminders of the hell he'd suffered. Tears slipped from the corners of his eyes. It was too soon. Maybe he should do another project first. Someone pounded on his door.

Feeling like he walked in slow motion, he went to the door and reluctantly pulled it open. The words, "Not now, Jerry," were on his lips when he saw her face, and her eyes found his. Like a spasm, he sucked in sharply and hesitated, unsure whether to open the door wider or slam it in her face.

Lynn stared at his bare chest, hard and lean, rising above the belt of his jeans. His hair was rumpled and his eyes red. He'd been crying. The lines in his brow showed the agony he suffered. She hated herself for it.

She moved toward him and slowly reached for his hand. He looked into her eyes and said, "Why, Lynn? You killed me once. Why again?"

Tears filled her eyes. She wanted so very much to erase the hurt, the pain. But so much had happened.

"Matt, things are different now." He stared at her; his arms were crossed, and he said nothing. She whispered, "All the hell I went through, something good came of it. Those treatments, they cured me."

His eyes locked on hers. For minutes, though it seemed like hours, he stared at her. Then slowly as if some force outside his body controlled him, he unfolded his arms and opened them to her.

For several moments, she was frozen, unable to move. Her eyes returned his stare. Then suddenly, she sucked in a lungful of the hot, claustrophobic air. She fell against his chest, and he pulled her into him and held her for a long time.

His life, his energy flowed into her soul. It roused her from her lethargy. It filled her with new life, a new reason to live.

"I love you, Matt," she whispered against the skin of his hard chest. "I love you so very much."

There was no hesitation. His lips found hers and hungrily, as if she would vaporize any second, he devoured her with kisses, hot and wet all over her face and neck. As he kissed her, his love flowed into her soul until she overflowed with the joy of it all. Her knees weakened, and he gripped her and held her so hard, she melted into his side as if they were one. New hope bubbled up. New life was laid before them. It was all they needed. It was full. It was theirs.